"Female, stop running. If you please myself and my friends, perhaps we'll let you live."

Sasha stopped moving and threw her shoulders back. "I'd rather die."

The Kalith pushed his long hair back from his face, his smile turning nasty. "That won't be as fun for us, but if you insist . . ."

Larem didn't want to kill his own kind, but he wouldn't let them hurt Sasha, not when she was his to protect. So far they hadn't noticed him; he wasn't sure about Sasha.

He paused long enough to jerk the tie out of his hair, letting it hang free down around his shoulders. Raising his sword, he started forward, calling out a traditional greeting among Kalith warriors in their own language. "My brothers, how fare thee?"

The leader jerked his attention away from Sasha long enough to answer, "My brother, we are about to fare very well."

Then his eyes flared wide as he took in the human attire Larem wore, and his smile turned feral. "You speak our language, but you carry the stench of Paladins."

Sasha finally recognized him. "Larem?"

Turn the page for red-hot reviews of Alexis Morgan's seductive novels. . . .

"Good stuff!"

—*Romantic Times*

DARKNESS UNKNOWN

"A fabulous read. . . . Passionate, hot, and very sexy."

—*Fallen Angel Reviews*

"Fresh and exciting with the same depth of character and emotional punch we've come to expect from Ms. Morgan."

—*Fresh Fiction*

REDEEMED IN DARKNESS

"Captivating, compelling, and totally hot!"

—Alyssa Day, *USA Today* bestselling author of *Atlantis Unmasked*

IN DARKNESS REBORN

"Utterly compelling. . . . Great sexual tension and action. Really terrific and totally unique."

—Katherine Stone, *New York Times* bestselling author of
Caroline's Journal

These titles are also available as eBooks

Bound by Darkness

A Paladin Novel

ALEXIS MORGAN

Pocket Star Books

New York   London   Toronto   Sydney

Pocket Star Books
A Division of Simon & Schuster, Inc.
1230 Avenue of the Americas
New York, NY 10020

This book is a work of fiction. Names, characters, places, and incidents either are products of the author's imagination or are used fictitiously. Any resemblance to actual events or locales or persons, living or dead, is entirely coincidental.

First Pocket Star Books paperback edition May 2011

POCKET STAR BOOKS and colophon are registered trademarks of Simon & Schuster, Inc.

For information about special discounts for bulk purchases, please contact Simon & Schuster Special Sales at 1-866-506-1949 or business@simonandschuster.com.

The Simon & Schuster Speakers Bureau can bring authors to your live event. For more information or to book an event contact the Simon & Schuster Speakers Bureau at 1-866-248-3049 or visit our website at www.simonspeakers.com.

Cover design by Craig White

Manufactured in the United States of America

10 9 8 7 6 5 4 3 2 1

ISBN 978-1-4767-8666-7
ISBN 978-1-4391-7607-8 (ebook)

To Susan Mallery—just a note to say how much I value your support and your friendship—not to mention all the laughter. You're proof that one of the best things about this business is all the wonderful people we meet along the way.

Acknowledgments

Danielle Poiesz, I want to take this opportunity to say how much I appreciate all the hard work you put in from start to finish to help my books shine. It means a lot to know you're always there. Thanks for all that you do!

Bound by Darkness

Chapter 1

Slamming his fist into the wall wasn't the smartest thing Larem had ever done, but it was that or punch his roommate. Since the current situation wasn't Lonzo's fault, he'd aimed his temper at something that wouldn't bruise—or hit back—although right now a good down-and-dirty fight held some appeal. Pain was slow to register, but his blood stood out in stark relief against the wall's white paint.

"Damn it, Larem, was that really necessary? I hope you didn't break anything; it's your night to do the dishes." Lonzo's comment held an equal mix of worry and disgust. "We both know Devlin has no choice in the matter. He's only asking that you and Barak lie low for a while. Besides, it's only temporary."

Larem flexed his hand gingerly. Nothing broken. Nothing solved. He was still caught between two worlds, neither of which wanted to lay claim to him.

"Yeah, right. Why not make it easier on everyone concerned and tell the Regents to make one big cage and stuff all your pet Kalith into it?" Larem said bitterly.

Swallowing hard against the acrid taste of his rage, he slowly turned to his worried friend. "Or better yet, shove us back across the barrier. With any luck, the Sworn Guardians will solve the problem for you with just a few swings of a sword."

Lonzo had his own temper and shoved Larem hard, sending him bouncing back against the wall. "Don't be such a dumbass. None of us would let that happen."

Larem got right back up in his friend's face. "Correction, Lonzo. *Some* of the Seattle Paladins wouldn't want that to happen, but you're paid to follow orders. If the Regents decide they want us gone, what can you do to stop them? If you refuse to rid the world of a few inconvenient Kalith, they can always find others who will."

He looked down the hall where more Paladins were congregated. "And they wouldn't have to go far to find them."

A deep voice joined the discussion. "You're wrong, Larem. That's not happening. Not now, not tomorrow, not ever. We owe you and the others too much."

Larem wanted to believe Devlin Bane. He really did, but he'd been betrayed too many times by his own kind to easily accept that his former enemies would behave any differently. Gods above, he missed his old life so damned much. As a Blademate to a Sworn Guardian, he'd known his place in their world and served his people with honor.

Here, he accepted a paycheck from the Paladins

for teaching weapons practice a few hours a month. He hated living on their charity, but he was still learning his way in this new life. Eventually, he'd be able to strike out on his own and be free to make his own choices. Some days he seriously thought about crossing back over into Kalithia and taking his chances that his death sentence would be rescinded. So far he'd resisted the urge.

Another Paladin came out of the conference room and headed straight for Larem. "This new policy is crap, and you know it."

Hunter Fitzsimon glared at Devlin, his green eyes blazing with pure rage. "I have more reason than most to hate what comes boiling across the barrier at us, but Larem is different."

Devlin rolled his huge shoulders, no doubt trying to shrug off some tension. "Listen up, all of you. You'll get no arguments from me on that score. However, until this new rep from the Regents is actually here, we just need to be careful. Arguing by e-mail won't change anything, but I can and will make our case in person."

"Yeah, right, and if he doesn't buy what you're selling? What then?" Hunter turned his attention to Larem. "Pack up your things. You're coming home with me and Tate. The apartment over the garage is yours as long as you need it."

Devlin looked like he wanted to argue, but then the big man shut his mouth and shrugged. "He's right, Larem. I can't guarantee this new guy will listen to me. If you'd feel safer moving up north with Hunter, I wouldn't blame you. Go camp out in Hunter's apartment, at least until the dust settles and we know more what we're dealing with."

For the first time since Devlin had called the morning meeting to order, Larem didn't feel quite so alone. As tempting as it was to take off with Hunter, the thought of hiding out didn't sit well with him. A warrior both by training and by nature, he would not run.

"I'll wait to see what happens. Besides, I'm not the only one affected by this order." Larem nodded down the hallway to where Barak q'Young stood talking to his sister, who had two Kalith children at home. "We can't all go into hiding."

Devlin sighed, clearly tired of dealing with all the bureaucratic bullshit. "This guy is supposed to show up by the end of the week. I suggest we go about business as usual until then."

Like anything had been "usual" for Larem in a long, long time. "Are we done? If so, I'm out of here."

Without waiting for an answer, he headed for the gym, intent on working off some anger banging blades with someone, anyone. A few seconds later both Hunter and Lonzo caught up with him. He'd rather be left alone for a few minutes but couldn't fault them for their show of support. The least he could do was show his appreciation by bruising them up some.

The three warriors walked into the gym and headed straight for the rack of practice weapons. Larem reached for one of the Kalith-style curved blades that the armorer had recently added to the collection. After a few warm-up swings, he tossed his shirt in the corner and faced off against his two friends.

"All right, gentlemen, who wants to bleed first?"

Hunter's wolfish grin was a mirror reflection of Larem's own. With a quick salute, the battle was on.

Watching Chaz Willis squirm was a rare pleasure. Right now the two of them were staring out of a tenth-floor office window at the sidewalk below. Thanks to her fiery red hair, it was easy to pick Sasha out of the crowd even from that height.

Her father glanced at George, his mouth a straight slash of anger. "Look, I know Sasha takes her orders from the entire Board of Regents, but I really hate this. No matter how much I argue, she won't listen to reason."

George sipped the glass of expensive scotch Chaz had poured for him, savoring the twin burns of the liquor and his friend's frustration. "I understand where you're coming from, but you really need to lay off the girl before you drive a permanent wedge between the two of you. She's well qualified for the job and deserves a chance to prove herself."

Chaz topped off his own glass and took a large swig. "Shut up, George. She's my daughter. That gives me the right to interfere when I think it's in her best interest."

"And she's my goddaughter," George snapped. "Don't screw this up for her because you're not ready to cut the apron strings. She's all grown up—it's time you realized that."

Chaz glared at George over the rim of his glass. "I don't doubt my daughter's abilities. But as both her father and a Regent, I have some misgivings about what kind of situation we're sending her into. We both know

Kincade made a mess of things in Seattle, and it's not finished yet."

George strolled over to perch on the side of Chaz's desk. "You're thinking he wasn't working alone."

Chaz finally turned away from the window. "I'm thinking we don't know. I don't want Sasha caught up in any fallout. By the way, I'm still pissed you helped her rally enough support to get this assignment in the first place. You should've stayed out of it."

"Chaz, you and I both know that Sasha deserves this chance. Besides, we need someone out there who we can trust to do the job right. Would you rather the Board pick someone else, someone we can't control?"

For the first time all morning, Chaz laughed. "If you think you can control Sasha, especially from almost two thousand miles away, you've sorely overestimated your influence on her."

George clapped him on the shoulder. "Come on, Chaz, how much trouble can she get into? We both know Devlin Bane and the rest of the Paladins have no use for number crunchers. At best, they'll tolerate her. At the worst, they'll ignore her. They certainly won't trust her. Meanwhile, we've managed to buy ourselves some time to deal with Kincade himself. We have to find out who else was involved in his shenanigans before we assign a permanent Regent to that sector."

"That's just the problem—Sasha doesn't see her assignment to Seattle as a stopgap measure. She has every intention of being appointed as the new Regent for that whole area. We'll just have to find a way to monitor her actions carefully."

Actually, George suspected Sasha would report in only when she absolutely had to and, even then, tell them only what she wanted to share. To maintain control over the situation, it would be better to have another pair of boots on the ground.

"Maybe we should have another man on-site. You know, to keep an eye on her."

Chaz immediately perked up. "Good idea. She'll kick our asses if she finds out, but I'd sure feel better about the situation. Any suggestions who we can trust to keep a low profile?"

After running down his mental list of possible candidates for the job, George made a quick decision. The man he had in mind had served as a reliable spy in the past. There was no reason to think he wouldn't this time.

"Yeah, I do. We've even used him before in similar situations."

"Good. Call him."

George hit a number on his speed dial. When the guy on the other end picked up, George kept it simple.

"Pack your bags. You just got transferred to Seattle. I want someone I trust to keep me informed about what's going on out there and to do what's necessary to keep things from going to hell. There's a bonus in it if you get there by the end of the week."

A minute later George hung up, satisfied he'd done the right thing. Certainly Chaz looked happier. Now, only time would tell if he'd made things worse or protected his agenda.

• • •

Sasha's plane had flown disturbingly close to Mount Rainier on the way over the Cascades, but the view of the mountain from her hotel room was stunning. The helpful pilot had also pointed out St. Helens and Mount Adams, two of the other volcanoes in the region, as he guided the plane into its final approach to Seattle. A chill slithered over her skin at the memory, but she resisted the urge to close the drapes. She had to get used to the sight eventually, and the sooner the better.

Granted the three peaks were beautiful, but she knew their truth. Underneath all that magnificent splendor beat the cold hearts of killers. At times unstable, always unpredictable, and when the mood hit, totally lethal. Even if the mountains didn't do the killing themselves, they also harbored the Others, crazed murderers from another world. Sasha couldn't just enjoy the volcanoes' rugged beauty, not when she knew about the trained warriors who lived and died under those scenic slopes, all to keep people like her safe.

The Paladins—a society shrouded in secrecy. Even working for the Regents, she'd caught only an occasional glimpse of the St. Louis contingent. Her father had done his best to protect her from the world the Paladins lived in. Even with her limited experience, she knew why.

They were warriors in the finest sense of the word— alpha males in all their glory, the kind of men who attracted women wherever they went. But not her. Not again. She knew better. It'd been another secret she'd kept from her father and the Regents; if they'd found out, they might have terminated her employment immediately. Despite the passage of time, the memories remained sharp and clear; the pain still ached like an old sports injury that acted up whenever it rained.

But enough of that. It was time. Ignoring the flutter of butterflies in her stomach, she picked up her briefcase and left her room. Her first meeting with her new charges was scheduled in less than an hour.

Devlin Bane, a legend in their world, hadn't been happy when she'd refused his request to meet with him one-on-one ahead of time. He'd raised some valid points in their brief flurry of e-mails, but she didn't want anything to color her first impressions of the Paladins stationed in the Seattle area. Besides, it was pretty much a sure thing that they'd close ranks to shut her out. Fine. They had good reason not to trust the Regents anymore. She expected to have to work long and hard to break through their firmly ingrained "us versus them" mentality.

If she could reestablish a positive working relationship, though, she'd guide them back into compliance with the regulations established by the Regents for the good of all. The Paladins were the best at what they did, but somehow this bunch had gone way off track—to the point of harboring the enemy among their ranks.

Her father and some of his associates were all for shipping the ringleaders out, scattering them over the globe. She'd managed to convince the Board as a whole that to do so would only spread the contagion.

No, containment was the appropriate goal and her first in a long list. As the elevator whisked her down to the ground floor, a surge of pure adrenaline hit her veins. The battle for control was about to begin.

It was time to report to the conference room. Larem had reluctantly agreed to attend the meeting as the sole Kalith representative in the crowd. Barak and Lusahn had offered to come, too, but Devlin had advised against it. At least he'd agreed that one of them should be there to hear what the representative had to say. Larem had no idea why the Paladin leader had picked him and hadn't bothered to ask.

Larem joined the long line of Paladins making their way toward the meeting place. A fair number simply ignored him, tolerating his presence only because they'd been ordered to. Inside the room, he paused to locate his friends, who had promised to save him a place. Lonzo and Hunter stood along the back wall near one of the exits. Lonzo was on duty and needed to be the first one out the door if the barrier crashed.

"Hey, roomie, thought maybe you'd changed your mind." Lonzo scooted to the side to make space for Larem between himself and Hunter.

D.J. joined them in the back, his eyes flitting around the room. "Rumor has it the new administrator has been ducking Devlin. What's up with that?"

Lonzo shrugged. "Maybe he's afraid of the big man."

Hunter laughed, his ruined voice holding little humor. "If so, maybe the guy is smarter than we gave him credit for. Think if one Regent rep went missing, they'd get the message and leave us the hell alone?"

Larem ignored the banter, focusing instead on a sudden stir at the front of the room. Devlin had walked in, but for once he wasn't the one leading the parade. Whoever had entered just ahead of him was too short to be seen over the assembled Paladins and guards.

Interesting.

Few in the crowd had even noticed that the party was about to begin. Devlin looked back to bark something at Trahern, who had followed him into the room. The other Paladin nodded and immediately stuck two fingers in his mouth and blew hard. The shrill whistle brought all conversation to a screeching halt.

Devlin walked up to the podium and glared around the room, his eyes locking up with Larem's briefly. He gave a slight nod before moving on, maybe expressing his approval that Larem had dressed in jeans and a flannel shirt to better blend in with his companions. He'd also tied his hair back with a leather thong, although Larem wasn't the only male in the room sporting hair down past his shoulders. Devlin himself wore his dark hair long although it lacked the sprinkling of gray that gave the Kalith people their distinctive look.

"Okay, everybody, listen up. I'd like to introduce our new administrator, who's here on behalf of the Board of Regents."

Before he could complete the introduction, the crowd turned restless as several Paladins shouted out comments and questions. Larem didn't bother to join the chorus of angry voices, figuring it wouldn't accomplish anything. Still, there was part of him that was glad the Paladins weren't going to make it easy for the Regents' representative to impose his will over them.

Devlin obviously had a different take on the situation. When the rumbling continued, he shouted, "Will you guys shut the fuck up!"

Then he flushed red as he turned to face his unpopular companion. "Sorry about that."

Lonzo looked like he'd swallowed a worm. "Did Dev just apologize to a Regent?"

"Yeah, that's just wrong." D.J. rose up on his toes to see better. "Well, I'll be damned."

"Yeah, you will," Hunter muttered, "but can you see the guy?"

D.J. shook his head, as if to clear it, before answering, "He's a she."

That had all of them stretching their necks, hoping to see over the crush of oversized men that filled the room. Finally, the new administrator made it easier on everybody by climbing up on a chair. As the woman waited for her unwilling audience to fall silent, she did her own fair share of staring back at them.

Larem's heart lurched in his chest. Not only was he a she, but she was striking. Or at least she would be if she didn't wear her flaming red hair yanked back from her face in that unruly wad at the nape of her neck. He couldn't see what color her eyes were from across the room, but they looked dark and intelligent. Her clothing was plain yet showed off her compact feminine curves rather nicely.

If she was nervous facing a boisterous crowd of angry men, it didn't show. He respected that about her, but then he'd served with a female Sworn Guardian long enough to know that courage wasn't determined by gen-

der. The woman's gaze swept past Larem without pausing, which would ease Devlin's concerns but left Larem
feeling oddly disappointed.

When she cleared her throat and prepared to speak,
he crossed his arms over his chest and leaned against the
wall. When she was done, he'd report back to Barak and
Lusahn before deciding what to do next. His first choice
was to stay right where he was because he had com-
mitments he didn't want to renege on. Too many were
depending on him and his particular skill set. If forced,
he'd hide out at Hunter's place for a while, but that
reeked of cowardice. No, if he and this woman were to
be enemies, it suited his nature to face her directly.

"Gentlemen, my name is Sasha Willis." Her voice
had an appealing huskiness to it as her words rang out
over the room, carrying to the far corners with a surprising amount of confidence. Larem wasn't the only one
who straightened up to get a better look at her. There
was a lot of power crammed into that petite package.

"My last name may sound familiar as my father is a
member of the Board of Regents. I have been serving
in Ordnance for the past five years, reporting directly to
the Board."

Once again, she panned the room, as if assessing
each man individually before continuing. "You have absolutely no reason to trust me at this point, and I certainly don't blame you for feeling that way. Too many
times the organization has failed you. But I'd like to
change that. Rest assured that I have the utmost respect
for the Paladins and the amazing job you all do."

She drew a deep breath. "For starters, I plan to meet

with the Handlers to reestablish a set schedule for all types of testing, including scans."

Once again, murmurs of discontent started building. She ignored them and waited for silence to settle over the room before speaking again.

"I am well aware that Colonel Kincade used scans as a punitive measure. I've already issued orders to ensure that practice will cease immediately. Diagnostic procedures are to be done on a regular schedule only, unless the Handlers feel a particular case warrants more frequent monitoring."

Larem bet that his eyes weren't the only ones that immediately sought out Trahern. It was common knowledge that his test results had been getting steadily closer to the edge for years. They all knew that the only reason the Paladin still lived and breathed was because Brenna and Laurel had been too stubborn to give up on the man the last time he'd died. By all reports, it had been a close call. Too close.

"In that same vein, I'm happy to announce that I will be authorizing additional staff and funding to enable Dr. Young to continue her studies in that area. She and I will be discussing the matter in greater detail in the near future."

Trahern looked happier, but not by much. Devlin had left the administrator's side to stand next to his longtime friend in a show of support. From the look the Willis woman gave him, she hadn't missed the gesture or mistaken its meaning.

"I will be studying all of your files, hoping to familiarize myself with everyone who is stationed here in Seattle, starting with the Paladins. As time allows, I'll move on to the guards and other support personnel. I understand that we also have special guests living and working here in Seattle. I will be dealing with them, too."

Okay, so that definitely sounded like a threat to him. At least she hadn't come right out and demanded that the local Kalith population be rounded up for immediate disposal. That didn't mean she wouldn't at some point. He doubted his friends would appreciate the dark turn of his thoughts, but then they had nothing to fear from the Regents. Paladins were too short in supply for their masters to risk alienating them completely.

The meeting was evidently winding down as Sasha Willis continued. "I know you all have questions, ones I hope to answer in time. For now, I want to extend my personal gratitude for the work you've done, and continue to do, here in Seattle. Thank you for your attention, gentlemen."

Then she hopped down off the chair and made a beeline for the door. Once again, Devlin headed for the podium. His men fell silent, waiting to hear what their leader had to say.

"Like the lady said. We have questions and she has no answers—yet. I'm asking that you give her a chance."

"What fucking choice do we have?"

The comment came from somewhere in the middle of the pack, but Larem didn't recognize the voice. Devlin must have, though, because he shot the guy a sharp look.

"The long and the short of it is, none at all, but let's not assume the worst until we have to. I'll say it again:

give the lady a chance. She can't be any worse than Kincade. Who knows, she might even surprise us. Now, get your asses back to work."

The grumbling this time sounded more like the usual kind. Lonzo made his escape, heading for the tunnels. D.J. muttered something about having an e-mail to check into and then plowed through the crowd with his usual disregard for those in his way.

Larem had almost reached the door when the warning blast of the Klaxons went off. He ducked back out of the way, clearing the path for the Paladins behind him as they all rushed to answer the call of duty. Part of him envied them their clear purpose in life, but at the same time he hated the necessity for it. How many of his own people would die before the barrier was restored? How many of his Paladin friends would bleed?

He watched as Hunter and D.J. followed Lonzo into the elevator that plunged down to the tunnels below the city, their game faces on.

"Larem!"

Devlin came charging up, his favorite sword clutched in his hand. Larem instinctively retreated a few steps before common sense took over and reminded him that they were friends, or at least not enemies.

"What do you need, Devlin?"

"Find Sasha Willis and make sure she made it out safely before all hell broke loose."

Both men looked around, but if she was in the area, Larem didn't see her. That came as no great surprise. The milling crowd of Paladins pretty much all topped six feet, making spotting one small human woman almost impossible.

"I'll find her."

Not that he wanted to. But for Devlin's sake, he'd make sure the woman stayed out of the way of those who had work to do. Pencil pushers, as D.J. called those in administration, played no role in the daily grind of a Paladin's life. If the Willis woman managed to get herself in the path of the fighting, she'd learn the hard way why she had no business trying to tell the Paladins how to do their jobs.

Larem ducked back into the conference room in case the representative had sought refuge there, only to find it completely empty. Where could she have disappeared to so quickly?

Her office was located a few blocks away in the admin building, while this one housed the Paladins themselves. It also contained some of the research facilities, including the geology department where Barak and his mate both worked. If he didn't find Sasha Willis soon, he'd ask his friends to join the search.

The closest exit was down the hallway, past Devlin's and some of the others' offices. He headed that direction first.

Sure enough, he spotted her hovering outside Devlin's door. She looked up as Larem drew near. He wasn't sure what to do. After all, he was only charged with ensuring she hadn't been caught in the crush of bodies rushing down to the tunnels.

Mission accomplished. Job done. He could get back to his own business with a clear conscience, at least after he reported to Barak what had been said in the meeting. He kept his eyes straight ahead, intending to walk right by the woman without making any contact. Unfortunately, she had other plans.

"Excuse me, but did you happen to see where Devlin Bane went?"

Larem slowed his steps just long enough to answer, "He headed down to the tunnels when the alarm went off."

She cocked her head to the side, as if puzzled by his answer, but maybe it was his Kalith accent that surprised her. Humans often mistook it for German or eastern European. With luck, she would as well.

Finally, she slowly nodded, as if he'd confirmed her suspicions. "I'd ask when he'll be back, but I know that depends on how long the barrier stays down and how many Others are waiting to charge across."

What could he say to that? He settled for saying nothing. Before he could walk away, though, she stopped him again.

"Sorry, but I'm kind of turned around. Can you point me toward the exit? I'll head back to my office until Bane returns."

"The door to the alley is back this way."

He waited while she jotted Devlin a quick note. As she stuck it on the small corkboard the Paladin leader kept on his door, Cullen walked into sight, offering Larem the perfect opportunity to make his escape. After all, Devlin had thought it best if all the Kalith kept a low profile for a while. How could he do that and act as escort for the woman they were all supposed to avoid?

"Hey, Cullen, I'm late for an appointment. Could you show Miss Willis how to get back to her office?"

Without waiting for his friend to respond, Larem walked away. Maybe he should feel guilty for forcing Cullen to take over, but Sasha Willis had already picked up on his accent. If she recognized him for what he was, who knew where that would lead?

He doubted anyone connected with the Board of Regents would appreciate Kalith warriors wandering around unescorted. In fact, no one would be surprised if orders didn't come down to do a lot more than restrict their access to Paladin facilities.

Just before the turn at the end of the hall, Larem risked one last look back. Cullen was showing Miss Willis something on his computer screen, giving Larem the perfect opportunity to study the woman without her knowing it.

She was listening intently to Cullen and nodding occasionally. Cullen, one of the resident computer geniuses, looked impressed when she said something and pointed toward the screen.

But it wasn't just the woman's intelligence that held Larem's attention. While almost all Kalith had dark hair and pale gray eyes, Sasha Willis was the opposite. Her hair was a deep red, the warm color of embers burning brightly, and her eyes were dark as night.

A couple of curls had escaped from her attempt to subdue them. His hands itched to pull those pins from her hair and set it all free. Such fiery beauty shouldn't be restrained. He bet she hated the halo of curls that would surround her face, softening the strong angles of her high cheekbones and full mouth. How would she taste? Tart? Sweet?

He had no business wondering about such things, and just his luck, he'd been caught staring. Rather than run, he nodded in her direction and then calmly walked away. Perhaps she'd think he'd only been assuring himself that she was receiving the help she needed. Rather than worry about it anymore, he headed for the geology lab to consult with Barak and Lacey.

Chapter 2

Sasha did her best to follow Cullen's detailed explanation about the network he and D.J. had designed for the Paladins. So far, she'd understood most of what he was saying, at least until she'd sensed someone staring at the two of them. Straightening up, she took a slow, casual look around.

It didn't take long to spot who was watching them—the guy who'd initially helped her was still lurking nearby. The question was why he felt compelled to hang around, especially when he'd jumped on the first opportunity to hand her off to someone else.

Interesting man, though. He moved with such quiet dignity and spoke English with an odd cadence, as if it wasn't his native language. No surprise there. Paladins lived and worked all over the world. He might have been transferred into the area from almost anywhere.

As he nodded and then turned away, she forced her attention back to the computer screen. Who was he?

She could ask Cullen but found herself oddly reluctant to do so. Besides, all the local Paladin personnel files were waiting on her desk back in the admin building. She could always shuffle through them to find out his name later.

The only thing that bothered her was why she found him so oddly compelling after such a brief encounter. Sure he was handsome, but all the Paladins she'd met so far had that inborn charisma so characteristic of alpha males. Most likely this particular guy stood out from the crowd only because she'd encountered him one-on-one, rather than as part of that angry mob she'd faced earlier.

She realized that Cullen had stopped talking several seconds ago. "Sorry. I guess I'm still trying to take all this in."

He shot a quick look down the hall where the mystery man had gone. "Want me to show you the way out now, Ms. Willis?"

"I'd appreciate it."

Cullen logged off his computer and stood up. "It's down this way. The door leads out into an alley where we keep a guard posted all the time. Since you're new, I'll walk you out to make sure there's no problem."

"That's very kind of you."

They walked in companionable silence. She noticed another hall branching off to the left just before they reached the door. "What's down that way?"

"Just some labs," Cullen said, shrugging as he opened the door to the alley.

As she followed him outside, she wondered why his reaction had seemed a little too casual, as if he were trying to deflect any interest in those labs. Maybe she was reading too much into it, but she strongly suspected that he was relieved when she didn't ask any more questions.

That was all right—for now. Eventually, though, she'd learn far more about the entire organization than any of them were going to be comfortable with.

Larem watched as Lacey Sebastian studied the array of monitors and seismographs that ran the length of her lab. Lines of tension bracketed her mouth as she made notes on her clipboard.

"How bad is it?" he asked.

She checked the numbers one more time before answering, "Bad enough. Although based on these readings, the barrier should stabilize in the next few seconds."

Barak was holding on to the edge of the counter, his knuckles white, his face gray and stony. All Kalith had some affinity for the barrier, but he felt it the strongest. Lacey watched her mate with sympathy as they waited.

Finally, the dials did one last jump before settling down to normal levels.

Barak's shoulders sagged as he released his death grip on the counter. "It's back up and holding strong."

All three of them breathed a deep sigh of relief knowing the fighting far below in the tunnels would end shortly. Lacey recorded the last of her data before setting her clipboard aside. Then she poured a cup of tea and set it down in front of Larem along with one of her famous chocolate chip cookies. Done with her hostess duties, she pulled up a stool and sat down between him and Barak.

"So, this new administrator, what did you think of him?"

He considered how best to respond. "First of all, her name is Sasha Willis."

He paused to let that little surprise sink in before continuing. "She showed great courage by confronting all the Paladins at once. Her first action was to authorize more funding and personnel to assist Dr. Young with her studies. She also said the scans would only be used as a diagnostic tool. That seemed to relieve some of the Paladins, especially Trahern."

Barak q'Young nodded. "His readings have been a matter of concern for some time. I was in Missouri when they almost ended Trahern's life permanently. It was a tough call, one that no one wanted to make. However, thanks to Brenna's faith in her mate and Laurel's willingness to give him every possible chance, they saved him."

Barak sipped his tea. "But that's no guarantee that they'll be able to help him if he were to die again."

Larem cringed. As a healer himself, even if only an amateur when compared to the talented and dedicated Dr. Laurel Young, he shuddered at the thought of having to put down a Paladin warrior who had burned up all his chances. Few people would have the courage to make that kind of decision even if it was necessary and the kindest thing to do.

As if sensing Larem's distress, Lacey laid her hand on his shoulder briefly. She had better reasons than most to understand the situation, because her brother Penn was a Paladin. No one knew how many times a Paladin could survive the cycle of living and dying without losing the last hold on his humanity. Devlin Bane had been beating the odds for years, but it was highly doubtful his friend Trahern would be so lucky.

"Maybe with the extra support, Laurel will be able to find some answers." Lacey rubbed her temples, as if she'd suddenly developed a headache.

Should he try to help her? His newly discovered ability to heal was a poorly kept secret, even if no one talked about it much. Larem set his tea aside and angled his stool around to face Lacey.

"Shut your eyes for a few seconds."

She didn't question his order. Larem gently spread his fingertips along her forehead and temples, chanting under his breath. Then he closed his own eyes and drew upon the pool of healing light stored deep inside his mind and soul. A small stream of warmth flowed along the hidden pathways written in his flesh and bones. Almost immediately Lacey sighed, letting go of her tension and pain.

He added another small burst for good measure. "How does that feel?"

"Fabulous! Nothing I'd tried touched my headache, but now it's completely gone." Lacey's face lit up with a broad smile. "You, sir, may hang out in my lab anytime. I'll even make sure to keep a steady supply of cookies and your favorite tea around as bribes."

"Do I have any say in this?" Barak asked.

"No!" Larem answered, laughing when Lacey said it at the same time.

"That is what I thought."

Barak didn't look at all worried, though. He had no reason to be, because the Kalith warrior and the human woman loved each other deeply. Larem wasn't the only one who was a little jealous of the happiness the two had found together.

For some reason, the image of Sasha Willis popped into his mind. Granted, he hadn't spent much time in the company of human women other than the mates of his friends. While he liked them all, they were strictly out of bounds for him. So were the few he'd met outside the organization, because of the need to hide his true identity. It was safer for all concerned if he kept everyone at arm's length.

So what was there about Sasha that tempted him to cross that line, especially after such a short meeting? Part of the answer was obvious—he was drawn to her exotic red hair and simple beauty. But there was also something about her that reminded him of Lacey, Laurel, and even Brenna, Trahern's woman. All of them were strong, independent females, and he suspected Sasha was much the same.

Not that he had any business to be thinking of her except to wonder what effect her presence would have on his life here in Seattle.

Barak interrupted his thoughts. "Did the new administrator say anything else we should know about?"

"She plans to review all the files on the Paladins, then the guards will come next, followed by other support personnel. She didn't mention us by name but said she would be dealing with the 'special guests' that were living among the Paladins."

Barak winced. "Interesting. You'd have to wonder what exactly she meant by that. How did the Paladins react?"

"Pretty much as you'd expect. Her remarks about the scans caused a stir, but she refused to take questions, saying she wanted time to review the situation here in Seattle first."

Barak looked impressed. "That may have been the smartest approach. No one would take it well if she came in announcing a bunch of changes without first learning the lay of the land. It had to come as a relief to all the Paladins not to have to deal with having another scan done just because someone was in a bad mood."

Larem had been part of the group who had brought down the former administrator in the Seattle area, Colonel Kincade. The bastard had abused his power to torment those who served the Regents, all for his own greedy purposes. No wonder the local Paladins had such distrust of anyone outside their own tightly knit circle.

Barak passed Larem another cookie. "Hunter mentioned he invited you to stay at his place for a while. Are you going to accept?"

"No, not yet. I prefer to face a problem, not run from it. If this Willis woman is going to come after us, I want to be here to defend my new life."

Barak glanced over at Lacey. "I told you he wouldn't leave."

Lacey smiled in approval. "I'm glad, Larem. There's strength in numbers."

He met his friends' worried looks head-on. "I agree. We all have a lot to lose if the Regents decide that our presence is detrimental to the organization. I'd rather we stand our ground than hide like cowards."

Lacey walked over to her mate. "No one could possibly think Kalith are cowards. Not when all of you have proved your worth over and over again."

He hoped she was right, but he had a bad feeling about the whole situation. Even if Sasha Willis had good intentions, that didn't mean those above her in the organization would support any of her decisions. That made it all the more important that he find a way to exist in this world without depending on the Paladins for anything.

Barak was frowning big-time. "How sure are you that she didn't immediately recognize you as Kalith?"

Where was Barak going with this? "I think she would've said something if she had. Why?"

His friend stared at his mate briefly until she nodded. He drew a deep breath before speaking. "Cullen and Lusahn stopped by earlier. We were thinking that if the opportunity presented itself, one of us should try to get to know her, maybe offer to show the Regents' new representative around a bit. The only question was how to do that without raising suspicions."

Suddenly, Larem really wished he hadn't mentioned his brief encounter with her after the meeting.

Barak kept right on talking, his words coming in a rush as if he couldn't spit them out fast enough. "Of course, we'd assumed the new representative would be a man, but the fact that she's female could actually make it easier for you to gain her confidence. You might gain better insight into how she plans to handle our situation, with the added benefit of her getting to know you as a person before she realizes you are the enemy."

"Why me?" he asked, even though he knew. He still wanted to hear Barak say it out loud.

His friend's eyes shifted back to Lacey. "You are the only one of us who doesn't have a mate. If she discovers your identity, you could easily move into the apartment over Hunter's garage until the dust settles."

In other words, Larem was expendable. He couldn't believe what he was hearing. "What about Devlin's specific orders that we stay out of sight?"

Lacey joined in. "I'm guessing Miss Willis would have her own reasons for wanting to keep any such relationship under the radar, especially since she thinks you're one of the Seattle contingent. She's here to oversee the Paladins and wouldn't want to give the appearance of playing favorites."

She reached out to take Larem's hand in hers. "We know this is asking a lot of you, Larem. But Cullen and Lusahn have finally got Shiri and Bavi feeling secure in their new lives in this world. The last thing they want to risk is having to uproot them again."

Not to mention that Cullen himself had to remain near the barrier; the need for that proximity was hard-wired into his Paladin nature. Lacey, too, had strong ties to Seattle. Because of her brother, she'd focused her life's work as a geologist on making the world safer for all the Paladins. It wasn't likely she'd be able to continue those same studies outside of the Regents' organization. Barak wasn't just her mate but also her research partner.

By process of elimination, that left Larem. His powerful sense of honor warred with his loyalty to his friends over the idea of deliberately misleading a woman he'd barely met. It wasn't a decision he could make on the spur of the moment.

He set his cup back down on the counter, barely refraining from heaving it against the wall in frustration.

"Thank you for the tea and cookies, Lacey. You've both given me much to think about. I'll let you know what I decide."

Then he turned his back on his friends and walked out.

Half an hour later, Larem reached his destination. As soon as he stepped inside, he was hit by a cacophony of barks, yips, and growls. The musky smell of damp concrete and medicine clogged his head, but he breathed it in without regret. Here, no one knew his DNA wasn't human or would've cared if they did.

All that mattered was that he had a good touch with frightened animals and cared enough to show up when he said he would. The pay was lousy—mostly tentative licks accompanied by a few wags of a tail—but that was enough. He reached for his lab jacket, filled his pockets with some treats, and headed in to see which patients the vet had lined up for him to work with today.

As soon as he stepped into the clinic, Dr. Isaac looked up and smiled. "Larem, my boy, come on in. Your buddy has been watching for you, not that he'd ever admit it."

The old vet nodded toward a pen at the far end of the room where a wary pair of brown eyes watched them both with a great deal of suspicion. Larem didn't blame the dog for his caution; he had good reason to mistrust humans in general. Of course, there was no way to tell the animal that Larem wasn't human, and he wasn't sure it would matter in the least. Trust once lost was slow to return.

Since Larem had some experience with that himself, he didn't take it personally. Still, he thought he was finally making some real progress with the dog.

He approached the cage slowly, letting the mixed breed catch his scent before speaking. "Hey there, fellow. How are you feeling today?"

Not that he expected an answer, but he was mastering the trick of communicating soothing energy with his voice. The dog stubbornly resisted any friendly overtures. But with each approach, it was taking Larem less time to slip past his defenses.

He knelt down and held out a couple of treats, once again letting the patient set the pace. "Let me know when you'd like these, and then we'll go for a walk."

For the first time, the dog's ears perked up. He might not trust humans in general, but he did seem to enjoy the time he spent outside in the run. The last time Larem had coaxed him into accepting a leash, he'd taken the dog for a long walk as a reward.

Judging by the slow tail thumping going on, it was time to try it again. That pleased him every bit as much as it did the dog.

"Son, I don't know where you got your magical touch with skittish animals, but it's been a real godsend around here. I wouldn't have given that fellow any chance of ever making his peace with people, not after the way he'd been abused. He still doesn't like the rest of us much, but at least he's willing to take a chance on you. That's something. By the way, that's the name we've been using for him—Chance."

Larem didn't know what to say to that, but the vet's

validation of his worth meant a lot to him. It had been a long time since he'd felt appreciated for more than just his strong sword arm.

"We'll be back in a while. Once he's had a good run, I'll try to convince him to let you give his injuries a quick check."

"Sounds good." The vet turned his attention back to the small dog he'd been examining when Larem walked in.

Larem tried out the dog's new name. "All right, Chance, let's get you out of there for a while."

Chance lurched to his feet, favoring his right back leg. The bones were healing up fine, but it was clear that it still hurt. Larem opened the cage door and set more treats down within easy reach. Eventually, he hoped the dog would accept the offerings directly from his hand, but there was no need to rush things.

The two pieces of freeze-dried liver quickly disappeared, and then the dog walked right up to Larem and rubbed against his legs. Larem reached down to pat Chance on the head and got his fingers snapped at for his efforts. Still, the attempt had been only halfhearted, a reminder that they weren't yet BFF.

He smiled at the dog. "All right, then, I'll watch my step. Let's go."

Outside in the run, he let Chance off his leash and sat down on a bench to watch the dog explore his surroundings. That in itself was a huge improvement. The first time Larem had lured Chance outdoors to one of the runs, the dog had huddled in one corner and growled anytime Larem made a move in his direction.

Larem took it as a compliment that right now Chance was totally ignoring him, meaning the dog sensed Larem posed no threat. After sniffing his way around the pen, Chance slowly walked toward Larem. He stopped a few feet away, his head cocked to one side as he considered his next action. Finally, having made his decision, Chance closed that last bit of distance and rested his head on Larem's knee.

This time when Larem raised his hand to pet Chance's head, the dog sighed softly and accepted the offer of friendship. Larem lifted his face to the sun, offering himself up as a conduit of its healing warmth. Slowly, the bright, healing light poured through him to soothe the dog's pain and encourage his leg bones to knit. After a minute or two, Larem eased back on the flow.

His gift was still too new for him to know how much was enough without overwhelming an animal's ability to cope with the accelerated healing, especially in Chance's weakened condition. Most of the time Larem settled for easing pain and soothing traumatized spirits. Convincing an injured animal to accept care was half the battle.

He still wasn't sure what it was about this particular dog that was so special. It certainly wasn't his appearance, although the dog looked a whole lot better now than when he'd first arrived at the shelter. That first day, the dog had been all bones and dried blood. He'd already put on considerable weight but needed to gain a few more pounds. Standing about thirty inches high at the shoulder with an intelligent face, Chance bore a striking resemblance to a white wolf.

When Larem had asked Dr. Isaac what breed Chance was, the old vet just laughed. "All I can say is that his ancestors weren't very particular who they mated with. From his build and size, I suspect he's got some Great Pyrenees in him and maybe some shepherd, but there's no telling for sure. He's his own man and a loner by nature, I would say."

Now that Larem thought about it, that assessment might just account for why he and Chance had hit it off. Both of them had been hurt by those who mattered to them the most and were struggling to find some peace in their lives.

"How about we take that walk now?"

Chance agreed, whining softly as Larem snapped the lead back on his collar. Larem often walked the streets of Seattle, trying to outdistance the restlessness that plagued him more and more lately. At least with Chance trotting along at his side, he didn't feel quite so alone.

Sasha was about half a second from going stir-crazy. What the heck had happened here in Seattle? She'd spent the past few days reviewing the budget and meeting with various department heads, and so far, it was unanimous: no one was happy. Everyone had their hands out wanting more money, more staff, and more supplies. God, if she granted even half the requests, the Regents would fire her for incompetence.

However, even at first glance it was obvious that some of the complaints were legitimate. Right off the bat, she'd ordered all departments to inventory their supplies, figuring there was no way to tell what was needed until she knew what they had.

But it was definitely worrisome that she'd heard the same complaints from all corners. Promises had been made but not kept. Less important items had been stockpiled while orders for others, especially those crucial to the well-being of the Paladins, had been either delayed or out-and-out denied. From what she could tell, jealousy and competition had been encouraged between the various factions. No wonder the resulting work atmosphere had become so toxic.

It was as if someone had set out to torment the entire Seattle contingent, making it all but impossible for the group to function. Only the dedication and loyalty of the support personnel, not to mention the Paladins themselves, had kept the organization performing at all and the city from being overrun with crazies.

Throwing a temper tantrum would do little to alleviate the situation, no matter how appealing the thought might be. The real problem was that she had no idea if this had all been part of Kincade's determined efforts to screw with the Paladins or just a series of unrelated events that had come together to make a total mess of things. Clearly the entire sector had suffered from the lack of a responsible Regent overseeing the day-to-day management.

Right now, she didn't have time to investigate the history of individual problems in any depth, not if she wanted to get things back on track as quickly as possible. Once she made some progress in restoring basic services, then she'd start digging.

At least the Regents had authorized a certain amount of discretionary funds for her to draw upon as she saw fit. Although substantial, it wouldn't even come close to covering all the gaps.

She walked over to the window, needing a few minutes to collect her thoughts. "Prioritize, Sasha, prioritize."

Yeah, right. Great idea, but every department head she'd spoken to had pointed out how crucial the missing items were. The real difficulty was in determining which requests were more urgent than others, and who could be counted on for sound advice on the subject.

All things considered, Devlin Bane was the obvious choice. After all, he knew firsthand what directly impacted his men's ability to fight and survive the devastating injuries they were subject to. She would've talked to him before now, but so far he'd avoided setting a time and date for their first one-on-one meeting.

Granted, she couldn't blame him for the instability of the barrier, but her gut feeling was that he was determined to duck her as long as possible. Okay, she got that he had no reason to love the Regents interfering in his business, but the situation wouldn't improve if he didn't even give her a chance.

She didn't want to come down too hard on him, though, not if she could avoid it. After weighing and discarding several possible approaches, she'd finally decided it would be best if she invited him and Dr. Young to her suite for drinks, safe from the prying eyes that followed her every move here at the office.

Rather than extend the invitation by e-mail or by

phone, she'd deliver the invitation in person. Maybe she was being a bit paranoid, but everyone knew there were several world-class hackers among the Paladins. With the current atmosphere of mistrust, she wouldn't really blame them for illegally monitoring her e-mails and phone calls. There'd been no sign of that happening, but she sure wouldn't put it past them.

She'd grab some lunch along the way and then go knock on Devlin Bane's door. The Paladin might not appreciate her showing up unannounced, but he'd get over it once she made it clear that she needed his input on how to further improve things for his men.

So far, she'd barely spoken to Devlin, but he and Jarvis, his Missouri counterpart, both had reputations of fighting long and hard for those who served under them. If anyone knew what the Paladins needed, he was the man. The fact that Bane's wife, Dr. Young, was one of the more forward-thinking physicians among the Paladins' Handlers was a definite bonus. If Sasha couldn't trust their judgment when it came to the Paladins, they were all screwed.

She grabbed her jacket and headed for the door.

Chapter 3

*L*arem leaned against the wall, honing his boot knife and listening to the ongoing discussion. So far no one had said anything of much use. Finally, Devlin held up his hand, signaling it was time for everyone to shut up and pay attention.

"Okay, here's how I see it. I've been ducking Ms. Willis, but eventually I'll have to meet with her. By all reports, she's spent her time doing exactly what she said she'd do: reviewing personnel files, meeting with department heads, and scheduling more of the same. It's too soon to tell where all this is going—"

Before he could finish that thought, his phone rang. Grabbing the receiver, he barked, "Bane here, what's up?"

He listened briefly before responding, "Thanks, I owe you one."

"Speak of the devil. Damn it, just what I needed." Devlin slammed the phone down and looked around at the men gathered in his office. "Sorry to break up the party, but we have seconds at best to clear out before Sasha Willis gets here. That was the guard calling to say that he just let her in through the alley door."

Devlin immediately shoved a stack of paperwork out of sight into a file drawer. Then he glared at everyone, making it clear they weren't moving fast enough.

"Damn it, make yourselves scarce. I'd just as soon she not see all of you here. Don't want anyone to get the impression we're plotting against the establishment."

Although they had been. Devlin had called them together to discuss emergency plans in case the Regents decided to come down hard on anything, especially on the subject of the Kalith living among the Seattle Paladins. Trahern led the parade out the door, followed by Cullen and Lonzo, leaving Barak and Larem bringing up the rear.

By the time Sasha Willis was due to appear, the Paladins were all back at their desks and looking busy. Larem, on the other hand, had some time to kill before heading to the shelter. He followed Barak across the office.

Barak picked up on his situation. "If you need a place to hide, you can join Lacey and me in the lab."

Larem shook his head. "That's all right. Cullen set me up with a desk where I can hang out until I need to leave for the shelter."

"Okay, but the offer is always good." Barak quickly disappeared, going the opposite direction from the lab, probably taking the long way around to avoid passing Sasha Willis in the hall.

Larem poured himself a cup of tea before settling

in at his desk with one of the medical texts that Sworn Guardian Berk had been slipping across the barrier from Kalithia to him. Hunter had brought him the latest stack when he'd driven down to Seattle for the first meeting with their new administrator.

Normally, Larem found the writings of other Kalith who shared his rare healing abilities fascinating, but right now, he could hardly force his eyes to stay focused on the page. Instead, his attention kept wandering toward the other side of the office.

He would've been torn over the idea of cultivating the administrator's friendship under false pretenses no matter what, but he was especially so with Sasha Willis. He hadn't seen her again since that first day and so avoided making a decision one way or the other. He suspected his time had about run out unless he took the coward's way out and hid. But the others were depending on him, so given the opportunity, he'd have to act.

Damn it, why did she have to show up while he was still there? More importantly, why hadn't he left while he had the chance? The answer was simple: he wanted to see her again, to see if his memory of her held up to the reality.

That she'd want to meet with the head Paladin wasn't a surprise, but it was clear that Devlin hadn't been expecting her. Glancing around the office, Larem realized he wasn't the only one staring down the hallway. Several of the Paladins, even those whose desks weren't in this particular area, were hanging around and pretending to be busy.

As soon as the woman came into sight, all pretense of getting any work done ended. Larem had to give her credit. Once again, having all those male eyes focused solely on her didn't faze her in the least. She calmly headed straight for Devlin's office door and knocked. While she waited for him to answer, she did a little staring of her own.

Her gaze swept across the room. Her mouth briefly softened into a smile when she spotted Cullen, one of the few who'd actually spoken to the woman. When the Paladin jerked his head in a sharp nod of acknowledgment, she smiled more broadly before her eyes continued scanning the men.

When she spotted Larem, there was a brief flare of recognition, and he could've sworn he felt a brief surge of warmth from all the way across the room. Once again, he was struck by her beauty. The deep green of her blouse set off not only the red in her hair but also her creamy complexion. Was her skin as soft as it looked?

After a second, her expression settled into a puzzled frown. Had he stared too long, or had she suddenly figured out who—or rather what—he was?

Either way, it wasn't his problem. He deliberately broke off the silent exchange and forced his focus back to the book he was reading. Far better that he spend his time satisfying his curiosity about his gift of healing than worrying about the opinions of one human female, even if she was a beautiful one.

And if he tried hard enough, he might just convince himself that was true.

"Don't just stand out there pounding on the door. Come in."

At Devlin's bellow, Sasha tore her attention away from the men scattered about the office and back to the one she'd come to see. Even so, she found herself reluctant to look away from that guy seated in the back corner. He was one of the two men who'd helped her find her way out of the building on that first day.

Now that she was working her way through the Paladin files, she readily recognized Cullen. From what she'd read, his nickname of "The Professor" certainly fit with the first impression she'd had of him. He'd been quietly helpful when he'd shown her the exit, making sure to introduce her to the guard stationed out in the alley.

But it was the other man who aroused her curiosity. There was just something different about him. Even from a distance, he stood out from the crowd. She didn't know why, but he did. Eventually she'd run across his file and perhaps find some answers.

Rather than get caught staring, she opened Devlin's door and poked her head in. He glanced up from the pile of papers spread out on his desk and tried to look surprised to see her. Cute.

She hadn't missed seeing the guard hitting a number on speed dial as soon as he let her into the building, although she didn't fault him for making the call. It was his job to monitor who came and went. Her only concern was what Devlin had been up to when the guard called to warn him of her approach.

Now wasn't the time for inquisitions, so she'd let it pass—this once.

"Ms. Willis, come in and have a seat." He rose to his

feet. "Can I get you a cup of coffee or tea? Or maybe a bottle of water?"

"Water sounds good. I've already had way too much caffeine today."

While he got two bottles out of the small fridge in the corner, she sat down, choosing the chair that offered a clear view of the door. Odd that it seemed important, but it did. Safer somehow, although she didn't sense any kind of threat coming from Devlin himself.

He handed her the water and then returned to his own side of the desk. After popping the top on his own bottle, he asked, "So what brings you to our neck of the woods?"

"I wanted to discuss something with you, but not over the phone." She took a long drink of water, giving him time to consider the unspoken message behind her comment.

His dark eyebrows shot up in surprise. "You think someone has bugged your line?"

"Not exactly," she said, frowning. "But I don't know that they haven't either. What I need to talk to you about is a bit sensitive, so I didn't want to take any risks. Besides, it was a good excuse to get out of the office and away from the stacks of financial reports on my desk for a while."

Devlin grinned. "God knows, I understand that. Despite all the hours I spend on the computer, I'm drowning in paperwork. So what's up?"

She'd pondered various approaches on the way over without really coming up with anything that felt right. Judging from what she knew about Devlin, she decided to be blunt.

"I've been meeting with department heads for the past few days. It won't come as a shock that I keep hearing different verses of the same song over and over again. The bottom line is that things have been badly mismanaged for some time. I plan to fix that, but I can't do it alone."

She paused, waiting to see if Devlin wanted to join in the chorus of discontent. It didn't surprise her when he kept his thoughts to himself and waited for her to continue, maybe to see if she'd hang herself.

"So here's my thought on the subject. It's going to take time to sort through all the accounts before I can effectively deal with all the finger pointing that's going on. However, I will tell you the same thing I've told all the other department heads: I fully intend to get to the bottom of the problem."

Thinking back to an earlier confrontation, she sighed. "As I told two angry supervisors this morning, I'll eventually figure out why one department got a lifetime supply of paper clips and the other can't get any. But honest to God, neither of them grasped that, while I understand their frustration, their problem is small potatoes when compared to the big picture."

"Seriously? Paper clips?" Devlin's mouth twitched as he reached into his desk drawer and pulled out a couple of boxes. "Here, maybe these will help."

He might be teasing, but she took them anyway. "Thanks, that's one fire out. Now, if only everything else was as easy."

"Glad to be of help."

Devlin leaned back in his chair and propped his feet

on the desk, definitely looking more at ease than when she'd first arrived. Time to get down to the business at hand.

"Spit it out, Ms. Willis. The worst I can say is no."

Not that he had the right to refuse any reasonable request, but reasonable was in the eye of the beholder. Feeling she was about to step over a precipice, she took a deep breath and went for it. "Okay, here it is. My focus has to be on whatever makes it possible for the Paladins to function."

Leaning forward, she continued, "You have a reputation of putting your men first, a policy I agree with. Don't get me wrong. I'll be reviewing your budget and expenditures to make sure they're in accordance with the guidelines established by the Regents."

She made direct eye contact, telling him without words that she meant it. "I figure it's in your best interest to work with me. So, insofar as I'm trusting anyone around here, I'm going to trust you because your men will suffer if we don't get things under control. To that end, I'd like to invite you and Dr. Young to join me at my hotel suite for drinks."

His bright green eyes saw too much. "I'm guessing the occasion won't be purely social, that what we discuss will be off the record and in private."

"Let's just say I have some concerns about the security measures in place. Shall we say tomorrow night at seven? If that conflicts with Dr. Young's schedule or if the barrier decides to act up, please let me know and we'll reschedule."

As she stood up, Devlin did the same. To her surprise, he held out his hand. "Thank you for coming, Ms. Willis. I'll check with Laurel and let you know one way or another."

"Sounds great." Then she gave him a pointed look. "Before I go, do you need time to call ahead to warn anyone else I'm on the loose?"

Then she smiled and walked out without waiting for his response.

Still restless, Sasha had no interest in immediately returning to her office. She'd meant to ask Devlin about a tour of the place but decided to see what she could learn if she wandered around by herself for a little while.

As she walked through the cluster of desks outside Devlin's office, she could feel the weight of all those suspicious eyes following her every move. No doubt someone was already warning Devlin that she hadn't headed straight back to her office.

She didn't take it personally, but neither would she let their suspicious natures impede her progress. She glanced down a narrow hallway and noticed a bank of monitors mounted on the wall, just at her eye level. It didn't take long to realize that what she was seeing was various views of the famous Seattle Underground.

Although she'd read that the Paladin headquarters were built into the hillside adjacent to the sunken sidewalks and buildings, she hadn't expected to be able to watch sightseers wandering by on a tour.

What would those people think if they were to learn that the subterranean world they believed long deserted was actually occupied by a secret group of warriors?

Probably that they'd stumbled into a science fiction movie set.

The thought made her smile. The movies had nothing on the reality of the Paladins' world. When the last tourist was out of sight, she moved on, although still not ready to get back to her office and that stack of work.

A short distance later, she realized she could hear the faint sound of voices. She paused to listen. They were coming from down the hall on the right. The sign on the door indicated that it was part of the geology department, probably one of those labs that Cullen had mentioned the other day. Curiosity had her heading for the lab door. Rather than barge in uninvited, she knocked and waited to see who answered.

Larem stopped talking at the same instant Barak turned to face the door. For Lacey's benefit, Larem explained, "Someone's out in the hall. By the sound of the footsteps, it's most likely a woman."

Lacey looked at both males in disgust. "I hate it when you two go all spooky Kalith on me."

She set down her clipboard just as the mystery woman rapped on the lab door. "No one around here ever knocks."

Larem rose to his feet, his internal alarms going off—he knew exactly who it was. "Lacey, it's probably Sasha Willis, although I thought she would've left the building by now."

"What could she want? I heard she's talking to the department heads, not lowly employees." Lacey started for the door. "Not that it matters. I'll go let her in."

Larem quickly blocked her way. "Let me handle this. Maybe she's gotten lost. I'll act as if I were just leaving and guide her back toward the exit."

Barak stopped him. "So you're going ahead with our plan?"

"That depends on whether she's learned that I'm Kalith. If not, I'll see what I can do. One thing, though, if she sees the two of us together, she's more likely to figure it out."

"You're probably right," Lacey agreed. "But if she insists on seeing my lab, let her in. We have orders to cooperate within reason."

Larem braced himself and opened the door only far enough to look out. Just as he suspected, it was Sasha Willis. When she recognized him, she took a step backward and then another, which irritated him no end. He'd made no threatening moves. Why was she acting as if he had?

"Ms. Willis, are you lost?"

Without waiting for her to answer, he closed the door behind him and headed off in the direction of the exit. "If you'll follow me, I can show you the way out."

She looked past him at the door briefly before falling in step beside him. He automatically adjusted his strides to make it easier for her to keep pace with him. Fortunately the geology lab was only a short distance from the exit. At the end of the hall, he stopped.

"The door to the outside is in that direction," he said, pointing to the left. "Devlin Bane's office is back the other way."

"I know. I was just doing some exploring and heard voices."

Looking up at Larem, she finally smiled. "However, this is the second time you've offered to come to my rescue, Mr.—um, I'm sorry, I guess we haven't actually been introduced. I've been trying to put faces with names, but I haven't figured everyone out yet. After all, there's only one of me and a whole lot of you guys."

So he'd been right. She'd assumed he was a Paladin. "My name is Larem q'Jones."

He deliberately softened the beginning of his last name, hoping she wouldn't pick up on the prefix that would label him as Kalith. He wasn't ashamed of his heritage, but neither would he flaunt it right now.

Rather than continue the conversation, he stepped past her to lead the way the last little distance to the exit. He pushed the heavy door open and stood back to let her walk out ahead of him as he debated whether to pursue the unexpected opportunity to spend more time in her company. For the sake of Bavi and Shiri, Lusahn's children, he'd make the effort and see where it led him.

That he'd like to get to know her for his own selfish reasons was beside the point.

His decision was further solidified as soon as he spotted the guard on duty. Duke had made it abundantly clear that he had little use for any of the Kalith. The man turned at the sound of the door opening and frowned when he spotted Larem standing with the new administrator.

If Larem relinquished his escort duties now, leaving Sasha Willis on her own, Duke wouldn't hesitate to give her an earful about the Kalith in general and him in particular. That was the last thing Larem needed, especially under the circumstances.

He was reasonably sure Duke wouldn't say anything right in front of him. All of the guards had a healthy respect for Larem's ability to wield a sword. If the man shot his mouth off now, he had to know he'd pay for it the next time they faced each other in weapons practice.

She interrupted his thoughts. "Thank you, Mr. Jones."

"Please, call me Larem, and actually I was about to leave when you knocked on the door. I have to be somewhere soon anyway."

As they passed Duke's position, he sensed the hatred coming off the guard in waves. The man probably felt justified in feeling the way he did, but Larem had never done anything to warrant such hostility. Luckily, it appeared that his companion was unaware of the situation.

Or maybe not. When the two of them had turned the corner, she looked back and frowned. "Weird. That's the same guard who was on duty when I arrived, but he seemed much friendlier then."

What could Larem say to that? The answer was simple. On the way in, she hadn't been in the company of the enemy. If Duke and the others like him thought the new administrator was soft on the issue of the Kalith, they wouldn't take it well. Their previous boss, Colonel Kincade, had done his best to instill a great deal of animosity between the guards and both the Paladins and their Kalith allies.

Sasha continued speaking. "He wouldn't be the only one who wasn't happy to have me underfoot around here. I know my presence makes a lot of the people un-comfortable."

Larem glanced back at Duke, resisting the urge to smirk. "Maybe he's just having a bad day."

And Larem's presence had surely made it worse.

"Maybe." She sounded doubtful. "I don't know how anyone could be having a bad day when the weather is so beautiful."

She smiled up at the sky as they walked along. "I'd heard that Seattle was always gray and gloomy, but it's been sunny every day since I arrived. I'm hoping I can squeeze in some of the tourist things while I'm here. What would you recommend, Larem?"

Larem smiled to himself. When was the last time he'd had the opportunity to spend even a few minutes enjoying the company of a beautiful woman, simply soaking up the warmth of a late summer afternoon? Especially a woman who wasn't the mate of one of his friends? Never in this world and only rarely in his own.

He considered her question. "I enjoy the water more than the mountains myself. Recently some friends and I went whale watching on the Sound up north of here. Orcas can be amazingly playful."

He and Hunter had spent the day out on one of the excursion boats with Hunter's mate, Tate Justice, and three of Tate's elderly neighbors. It had been an incred-ible experience for all of them.

"That sounds wonderful," Sasha said, smiling. "I'll definitely keep that in mind. I also want to go to the zoo. All through college, I used to volunteer in the nurs-ery of the St. Louis Zoo. When things settle down a bit, I might look into doing something like that again."

As they strolled along the sidewalk, it occurred to him that they might actually have a few things in common, starting with a shared love of the sun and working with needy animals. And even if she didn't know it, like her, he was mistrusted or even hated by a good portion of the people he came into contact with on a daily basis. Not that he could tell her that without revealing his true origins.

That small connection had him really hating the idea of using her, even to protect the Kalith children. Not to mention how much worse it would be when she figured out that she'd been spending time with an Other. No doubt that friendliness in her dark eyes would quickly be replaced by revulsion.

The words slipped out of his mouth before he chickened out altogether. "Do you have time for a cup of coffee?"

She checked her watch. "Sure, why not?"

Even fearing it was a mistake of major proportions, he couldn't bring himself to regret the invitation. After all, one latte didn't translate into a long-term commitment; he was just testing the waters. They headed into one of the coffee shops that dotted the Seattle landscape. After placing their orders, they found a table next to the window.

Sasha sighed as she sat down. "This was a great idea. It's been a long day already, and I still have a lot left on my to-do list. Thanks for suggesting we stop."

"You're welcome." He wrapped his hands around his venti coffee and absorbed its warmth.

She sipped her vanilla steamer. "Eventually I'll settle into a routine, but there's a lot for me to figure out. And it's not just the job. You know what it's like when you move to a new city. Everything is so different."

She had no idea *how* different it had been for him, but now wasn't the time for that particular conversation. "True. I've only been here a few months myself, but there is a lot I like about this area."

Sasha tilted her head to one side as if to study him. "I've been trying to place your accent, but I can't."

How best to answer that one? He settled for a version of the truth. "I've served near the barrier in several different locations over the years. How about you? I hear you moved here from St. Louis, but is it where you're from?"

"Nice dodge there, mister," she said with a smile. "I won't press for details. I know how Paladins like to keep their secrets."

As did Kalith warriors, but he didn't correct her assumption. "It comes with the territory."

"And understandably so. But to answer your question, my father has served as a Regent in the Midwest most of my life. I grew up and went to school in the St. Louis area, so this is my first big move."

Her dark eyes looked a bit sad as she toyed with a paper napkin. Could she be as lonely as he was even though surrounded by a crush of people? Almost of its own volition his hand settled over hers, taking as much comfort from the brief touch as it was meant to give.

"You've got a lot to deal with right now, but soon things won't seem so strange. At least that's been true for me."

Her eyes met his, her smile a bit shy. "You're a nice man, Larem Jones. At least now I feel like I have one friend here."

He slowly withdrew his hand, knowing he had no business trying to be her friend, much less touching her. When she found out that he was Kalith, she'd probably scrub that hand raw to remove any trace of his. But right now all he could think about was how soft her skin was and how kissable her mouth looked.

It was definitely time to put some distance between himself and temptation. "I should be going or I'll be late."

She nodded and stood up. "Yeah, me, too."

They walked out the door together. He stopped at the next corner. "This is where I leave you."

Her smile warmed his day. "Thank you again for the coffee break. I definitely needed it. Next time will be my treat."

He just knew he was going to regret this, but for the sake of Lusahn's kids, he had to try. "Actually, I come by here most days about this time. You know, if you happen to be in the area."

"I'd like that. I can't tomorrow, but the day after would work for me."

"Then it's a date." *Not really.*

She held out her hand for him to shake. His hand dwarfed her much more delicate one, but there was unexpected strength in her grasp. He should let go, but she didn't seem to be in a hurry to break their small connection either. The heat of the sun had nothing on the intense awareness he was feeling at the moment. It was all he could do to maintain even a small distance between them, when what he really wanted was to find out what would happen if they did more than shake hands.

When she finally tugged on her hand, he smiled and let go. "Enjoy the rest of your day, Miss Willis."

"I thought we'd gotten beyond the formal stage, Larem."

"Sasha, then. I'll see you in a couple of days." Then he bowed his head slightly before walking away.

Chapter 4

*D*uke's day had truly sucked big-time. He hated patrolling the alley outside the Paladins' headquarters. It was hard enough to be polite to every Paladin who strolled by, but it really burned his ass to put up with those damned Kaliths acting as if they owned the place.

Things had been changing over the past few months and not for the better. Colonel Kincade had had his faults, but at least he'd known the guards were the real heroes around the place. The Paladins fought like madmen, but they could afford to be reckless with their lives. They weren't playing for keeps, because even if the fuckers were killed they didn't stay that way. Freaks.

The guards, though, were pure human stock, guaranteed to bleed and die if their wounds were bad enough. That was why the Paladins usually bore the brunt of the fighting, but not always. Sometimes the barrier went down too often or stayed that way too long for the Paladins to handle it all on their own. That was when the guards were thrown into the battle as sword-fodder.

Duke punched out, picked up his gear, and left the building. Home next or a quick stop at the local watering hole for a cold one? No contest.

It didn't take him long to reach the bar where the guards hung out. He spotted a few of his buddies at a big table on the far side of the room. He signaled the waitress to bring him a microbrew and a burger before weaving his way through the clutter of tables and chairs.

"Hey, Duke, come park your ass over here," one of them yelled.

He tossed his bag in the corner and pulled up a chair. He knew most of the guys at the table, but the one on his immediate right wasn't familiar.

He stuck out his hand. "Hi, I'm Duke. You must be new."

"I must be," the guy said after giving Duke's hand a firm shake. "My name's Rusty. I just transferred in from California."

"What brought you up here? From what I've heard, the California office is a pretty cushy assignment."

The guy shrugged, his gaze sliding past Duke as if to see who might be listening before answering. "Seems lately all the action is up here."

What the hell was that supposed to mean? "I don't understand."

Once again, Rusty seemed to hesitate. "I heard rumors about the stuff the Paladins have been pulling up here. Like hanging out with the enemy, arresting the local administrator—you know, stuff. That last one was a shocker for sure. I'd always heard good things about Colonel Kincade."

He quit talking long enough to stop a passing waitress. He held out a twenty-dollar bill. "Miss, would you bring me and my friend each another beer."

"Hey, you don't have to do that," Duke protested.

"You can buy the next round." Rusty munched on a handful of pretzels. "So what did you think of him?"

"Who?" Duke asked, although he could guess.

"Kincade."

Duke wasn't exactly thrilled with the direction of this conversation. Still, there was no reason not to answer. "The man always gave the guards a fair shake, but he had problems with the Paladins and their pet Others. A couple of months back, they arrested him and shipped his ass back east for the Regents to deal with. No idea what they had on him. Some folks think they faked the charges because he didn't put up with their crap."

Duke was one of those folks, but he kept that to himself.

Rusty sneered. "Yeah, I'd heard that, too. I could hardly believe it when I saw a pair of those Others wandering through headquarters all alone. Maybe Kincade had the right of it."

"Yeah, maybe."

Rusty took a long pull off his beer. "I hear Kincade's replacement is a woman. Is that true?"

Duke nodded. "Sasha Willis. She seemed nice enough at first."

Rusty's eyes lit up with interest. "Something happen to change your mind?"

Okay, maybe Duke should shut up now before he said something he shouldn't. "Nothing. She's been real friendly. I just get twitchy when people start poking their noses in our business."

That much was true, but it was watching her act so friendly to that bastard Larem that had Duke seeing red. Time to change the subject.

"So tell me, Rusty, are you a baseball fan?"

Sasha stared at the door, waiting for a knock that seemed destined never to come. Not that her guests were late, but a lot rested on the success of this meeting. She had so many questions and suspected that if anyone had the answers, it would be Devlin Bane and Dr. Laurel Young.

There was one major problem with the plan. Earlier in the day, she'd discovered some substantial irregularities in the Paladin financial records. Someone had authorized salaries for three additional Paladins, only these particular individuals were apparently phantoms. Their names didn't appear on any duty rosters, nor had she been able to find any personal information on them.

She clenched her hands until they hurt. Without a doubt they weren't phantoms at all. No, they had crossed from another world, one that bred crazed killers. Everyone knew the Seattle Paladins were sheltering the bastards, but it had come as a shock that they were using Regent funds.

The whole idea made her furious. How many Paladins had died because of them? Eventually she'd have to confront Devlin with the evidence, but unfortunately, right now she needed his support, as well as that of his wife. Devlin Bane was crucial to maintaining stability in the region. She couldn't risk exposing the problem—not yet anyway.

The Regents thought the Seattle crowd was unruly *now*. She could only imagine how bad it would be if she toppled their leader and brought him up on charges of treason and theft. Not that he'd spend a single minute in a civilian jail or courtroom. The only option when it came to a Paladin who was out of control was a lethal injection. The thought made her physically ill.

The long-awaited knock finally came. She drew a calming breath and pasted a smile on her face, hoping it looked more sincere than it felt. Nervous now that the moment was upon her, she wiped her sweaty palms on her slacks and opened the door.

"Devlin, Laurel, please come in."

As they entered the room, Laurel made no effort to be discreet as she checked out Sasha's suite. "Nice place."

"Thanks. It's still a hotel room, though. I'm looking forward to finding a place of my own."

Sasha led the way toward the living area. "I haven't had a chance to look yet, but I hope to squeeze in some time this weekend."

"So you're planning on staying in Seattle for a while?" Devlin asked the question as he settled into the corner of the sofa. "I'd gotten the impression you were the scouting expedition and that the Board of Regents would assign someone permanently after you reported back."

Okay, so he had contacts back in the Midwest that she hadn't known about. The Regents' plans for the area were supposed to be a secret.

"I'm hoping they'll consider assigning me permanently. After all, by the time I've finished my assessment, I will know the inner workings of this sector better than any current member of the Regents would. Any other person would have to start over at square one."

"Makes sense to me, especially if you find you like it here," Laurel said, frowning. "You know, maybe I could help with your apartment hunt. I own a condo here in town that's just been cleaned and painted top to bottom. We'd planned to put it up for sale, but I'm in no hurry, especially with the market as poor as it is. It's even mostly furnished."

Sasha considered the offer. That would so simplify her life. "If you're sure, I'd love to see the place."

Laurel pulled a key ring from her purse and laid it on the coffee table. "When you get a chance, check it out and let me know what you think. We can work out rent and stuff if you like it."

"Thanks, I appreciate it."

Another knock at the door signaled it was time to play hostess. "I had the hotel prepare some hors d'oeuvres for us and bring up some of my new favorite wine from a local vineyard."

On her way to the door, Sasha glanced at Devlin. "Unless you'd prefer I sent down for some beer?"

Laurel laughed. "Oh, does she have your number, mister!"

"Very funny, Laurel." Devlin looked mildly insulted. "Seriously, wine will be just fine."

For the next half hour, the three of them made small talk. Laurel and Devlin gave Sasha recommendations about restaurants and told her the sights worth seeing around town. Sasha told them about her first visit to the famous Pike Place Market.

"You know, until they started slinging salmon over the counter, I didn't believe they really *threw* fish around. I was just glad I wasn't in the line of fire." Sasha laughed at the memory and mentioned other shops she'd checked out.

She looked at Devlin. "One of your men was nice enough to suggest whale watching while I'm here."

The Paladin looked puzzled. "Who was that? I don't recall any of them mentioning they'd gone. Not that I'd mind if they did. They all deserve more time off than they get."

"Larem Jones. I ran into him after I left your office the other day. Since he was headed in the same general direction, we stopped for coffee."

She poured herself another half glass of wine, but that didn't keep her from noticing the concerned looks exchanged between her guests.

"Oops, did I let the cat out of the bag? If he was AWOL for a day, please don't let my big mouth cause him problems," Sasha said.

"No, that's fine. Larem's relatively new to the area. I'm glad he's been enjoying some of the sights on his days off." Devlin tossed back the last of his wine and set the glass down on the table with a shade too much force.

Interesting. The time she'd spent in Larem's company had definitely been one of the highlights in her stay so far. But rather than press the matter—or admit that she and Larem had met again since then to wander along the waterfront and to visit the aquarium—it was time to get back to business.

"Look, I know you've both had a long day, so I'll get to the point. I won't lie to you about my purpose in being here. Yes, I want to make things better for the Paladins in any way I can. I assure you that I have the utmost respect for both their service and their sacrifices."

She paused to let that sink in before she dropped the hammer. "But quite frankly, the Board of Regents has some serious concerns over the events that have transpired here in Seattle the past couple of years."

Devlin leaned forward, resting his elbows on his knees, all pretense at casual conversation gone. "Which events would those be? The one where a Regent went rogue back in Missouri and killed Judge Nichols, all right under the Board's nose? Or when Colonel Kincade, one of their favorite lapdogs, was trafficking in stolen goods and illegal immigration?"

Laurel jumped in. "Not to mention that he went out of his way to make life a living hell for the Paladins here. I know you've promised additional funding, but what if it's too little, too late? Without naming names, I can personally testify that Kincade's brutality caused permanent damage to some of my patients."

Sasha watched as the doctor struggled for control.

Although Kincade had hidden his tracks well for a long time, she had no doubt that Dr. Young was telling the truth.

Laurel entwined her fingers with Devlin's and stared at their joined hands. "I'm sorry, Sasha. I know Kincade's actions were not your fault. However, no one on the Board of Regents would listen when I repeatedly reported what was going on. The additional funding is wonderful, but it's a little difficult to be grateful for what should've been forthcoming all along. I also resent the Board sitting in judgment on decisions that were made under very difficult circumstances."

How horrific were the scenes playing out in Laurel's mind to fill her dark eyes with such utter grief? Now wasn't the time to ask.

"Look, all I can tell you is that the Regents will be taking a more active approach to governing the whole organization worldwide. Like it or not, they realize that they've contributed to the situation by giving individual administrators like Kincade far too much autonomy. They feel—and I agree—that we must step back and assess what is working now and what has worked in the past. Once we have a clearer picture of the situation, then we can all move forward together."

Devlin looked thoroughly disgusted. "Sasha, do you have any idea how many times I've heard that same bullshit over the years? Yes, there have to be some rules in place, but I have a hard time with a bunch of paper pushers and number crunchers sitting in a boardroom making decisions without consulting those who actually get their hands bloody day after day."

"But without rules . . ." Sasha started to protest but stopped. "Okay, I get what you're saying and even agree, to a certain extent. One reason I volunteered to come is that I want to hear your side of the discussion. I'd like to think that ultimately we share the same goals.

"It's imperative that I learn everything I can from the ground up, without restriction or interference. I've been involved in similar situations before this, although not on the same scale, and I can tell you one thing that doesn't work is anything less than total transparency from both parties."

Devlin clearly wasn't buying it, not completely anyway. "So where does that leave us? What do you want from me?"

Sasha considered her words carefully. "I have some discretionary budget I can use any way I see fit. Part of that is already earmarked for Laurel's department, but I'd like your take on how the remaining money can best be put to good use. I want it to have a direct, positive impact on the quality of life for the Paladins.

"To that end, I'd like a report from you by the end of next week with any suggestions you might have. It would help if you could prioritize them, but we can discuss that in more detail once I've had a chance to review the report."

There. She'd laid her cards on the table. It was up to them to play theirs next.

Devlin slowly leaned back, still holding his wife's hand as if it helped keep him grounded.

"I'll work on the report, but not alone."

Sasha nodded. "I was hoping that you and Laurel would put your heads together on it."

"And we will, but I'll want to bring a few of my men in on it, too."

Not exactly what she had wanted to hear, but neither did she want to shoot him down right out of the gate. "Who do you have in mind?"

Devlin's mouth quirked up in a small smile. "Does it matter?"

They both knew she hadn't had time to get to know the locals well enough to judge who would have useful input and who wouldn't. Even so, she needed to maintain some control over the situation.

"No, I suppose not. I'd appreciate it if you limited it to no more than five of your men, ones who can keep a secret. I don't want the other department heads demanding their 'fair share' of the budget. Depending on your suggestions, they may end up getting some of the pie, but only if it has the impact we want."

Devlin looked decidedly happier. "Okay, then it's a deal. For what it's worth, the guys I have in mind are Blake Trahern, Cullen Finley, D.J. Clayborne, and Lonzo Jones."

He repeated the names more slowly when Sasha reached for a pad and paper.

"They're all good men and know how to keep their mouths shut. When your whole life has been one big secret, you learn early how to fly under the radar. They also hang out in my office a lot, so no one will think anything of it if they're in there more than usual."

"Perfect."

She studied the names, noting Lonzo's last name

was the same as Larem's. Were they brothers? And why wasn't Larem on Devlin's list? Hmm.

"I want to thank both of you for coming tonight. We've made a solid start on fixing what's been broken for way too long. I'm hoping these changes will help us all get back on track."

She really did. Men's lives depended on it. Too many had died already because of bad management and simple carelessness.

"I will be seeing a lot of both of you as we move forward. As you've probably already guessed, I believe in hands-on management. I'm well aware that will ruffle some feathers, but I'm convinced the problem has been the lack of direct contact between those who control the purse strings and those who do the bleeding."

Devlin shook his head. "Look, I know you mean well, but there are areas that are off-limits to civilians, and for good reason."

Time to make her position clear. If she blinked now, she'd lose all chance of maintaining control. "I'm sorry, but you don't have the authority to restrict my movements, Devlin. I can—and will—go wherever I need to. The Board of Regents has granted me full access."

Then she offered what she hoped was a conciliatory smile. "Just tell me where I need to be careful."

"You may have the right to see anything and everything, Ms. Willis, but I'm the one responsible for the safety of all who enter Paladin headquarters. I will not allow you to wander the tunnels unescorted. And before you think we're trying to hide something, Lacey Sebastian works for the organization as a geologist and is under the same restrictions."

"I see." And she did. "I promise to use common sense, but I can't let you dictate how I do my job."

Neither of her guests looked convinced, but they couldn't say they hadn't been warned. "Again, all I'm asking is that you give me a chance. And if you have a problem with something I've done or said, I'd appreciate your coming straight to me with it. My door will always be open."

"I hope you mean that." Devlin stood and helped Laurel up off the sofa.

Sasha followed them to the door. "See you soon."

Once they were gone, Sasha got ready for bed. A few minutes later, she crawled between the sheets and turned out the bedside light.

God, it had been a long day—too long. She had no doubt that tomorrow would be just like it, but right now she was too tired to think that far ahead.

Instead, her mind filled with the image of Larem Jones smiling as he walked away from her. She really hoped she hadn't gotten him in trouble with Devlin. Maybe she should warn him. No, bad idea. Her working relationship with Devlin was too fragile to risk getting between him and one of his men.

As she drifted off to sleep, her last thought was that she'd just have to find some other excuse to see Larem Jones again.

Larem stared at the flyer on the shelter bulletin board and cursed. It had been two days since he'd last seen Sasha after spending an afternoon with her down at the piers. Forty-eight hours of spinning his wheels and getting nowhere on his assigned mission of further befriending her. Torn between wanting to spend more time with her for his own selfish reasons and his guilt over the whole idea of spying on her, he'd considered and rejected several ideas.

He pulled the paper down off the board to study it further. There was going to be an outdoor concert at the zoo to raise money for various animal-related causes. It was exactly the kind of event that would appeal to Sasha, not to mention himself. Dr. Isaac even had tickets for sale right there on the premises—so it couldn't be simpler. *Just buy the tickets and make the call.*

But were the gods smiling upon him or out to drive him crazy? Only one way to find out. He reached for his phone and started dialing.

Larem waited at the edge of the rose garden by the zoo entrance, trying to find Sasha in the milling crowd. The early evening air was heavy with the perfume of the flowers. He slowly filled his lungs, enjoying the calming combination of their scent and incredible beauty. As always, it seemed as if everything in this world was more intense, more vivid, than back home in Kalithia. His world had its own beauty, but it was definitely different.

"Hi, Larem. I hope you weren't waiting long."

He opened his eyes and smiled down at Sasha. "Not at all. We have plenty of time before the concert. I thought you might enjoy a stroll here in the rose garden before we go inside."

"I'd love that."

As they walked along, neither of them said much, but the silence felt comfortable rather than awkward. After a bit, she stopped to admire a particularly spectacular blossom. He had no idea what it was called, but it was the color of fire—a burnished gold center deepening to a dark red along the edges of the petals.

It reminded him of Sasha's hair, set off to perfection by the dark purple shirt she wore with a long white skirt that swirled around her ankles as she walked. Once again she'd twisted her hair up on top of her head. He pictured himself kissing the elegant curve of her neck just before he removed the wooden sticks to set her hair free.

He'd dearly love to see it down loose around her shoulders—or better yet, spread out on his pillow as he kissed that sprinkling of freckles on her nose. Something of what he was thinking must have shown in his expression, because when Sasha glanced in his direction, she blushed and immediately hurried on toward the next bed of roses.

But she did take his hand and tug him along in her wake. That small gesture vanquished the knot of nerves in his chest. For the moment, it was enough to pretend they were just an ordinary couple out to enjoy an evening of music and each other's company.

The concert was winding down, the musicians putting one last burst of high energy into their encore. Sasha couldn't remember the last time she'd enjoyed a night out more. Larem had produced a blanket from his pack for them to sit on. After they'd staked out their spot, he'd gotten each of them a lemonade and a piece of strawberry shortcake.

Watching him savor the sinful berries heaped high with whipped cream had been an amazingly sensual experience. It was almost as if he were tasting the decadent dessert for the first time.

She barely knew the man, but there was just something about him that stirred emotions in her that had lain dormant for a long, long time. First college and then her heavy work schedule had left little time for a social life. Or at least that had been her excuse. The truth was, when she'd met David Booker, she'd fallen fast and hard for him. Although she'd known the risks of getting involved with a Paladin, she'd hadn't been able to help herself. And when he'd died, it had almost destroyed her.

Yet here she was, risking the same kind of pain all over again. At twenty-eight, she should be old enough to know better, but obviously not. The more time she spent in Larem's company, the more reckless she felt. How would it feel to kiss that stern mouth? What kind of lover would he be? Maybe she should just toss the dice and see where the night led them.

Despite its being late summer, there was a chill in the air as the sun went down. Larem noticed when she shivered and leaned toward her. "Are you cold?"

"A bit. I'm not used to the way the temperature drops here at night."

He hesitated, then wrapped his arm around her shoulders and pulled her in close, sharing the warmth of his body.

"Is that better?" His voice was a deep rumble near her ear, sending a whole different kind of shiver through her.

Oh, mama, yes!

But she kept that comment to herself and just nodded. Too bad the concert was about to end. She could've happily spent hours sitting right there, enjoying the night with Larem.

When the song ended, the crowd surged to their feet, applauding loudly. She reluctantly joined them, immediately missing Larem's touch.

He folded up the blanket and stowed it back in his pack. "The zoo is open for another hour. Want to wander around a bit before we call it a night?"

"Sure."

It seemed only natural for him to take her hand, especially with the jostle of the people surrounding them. In just a few seconds, the crowd thinned out, leaving the two of them wandering down a path with only a handful of others nearby.

"Did you like the music?"

Larem nodded. "Very much. We should do this again sometime. I think they do a whole series of concerts here."

"I'd like that." *A lot*.

When a smaller path branched off to the left, Larem took it. The sign said it led toward the animals of the African savanna. As dark as it was, they'd not likely be able to see much, but at the moment she didn't care. She was really hoping Larem was more interested in finding them a bit of privacy than seeing what the zebras were up to.

Sure enough, when they were alone, he dropped his bag on the ground and turned to face her in the faint glow of a distant lamppost. His big hands gently came to rest on her shoulders. She responded by sliding her palms up the hard planes of his chest. His pale eyes stared down into hers for the longest time.

"I hope you don't mind, but I've been wanting to do this all evening."

Before she knew what he was going to do, he tugged the chopsticks out of the knot on top of her head. The heat in his smile climbed several degrees as he finger-combed her hair, sending the unruly waves spilling down around her shoulders.

"I knew it would feel like silk. You should wear it down all the time."

"It gets in the way when I work."

His accent thickened considerably when he murmured, "Then wear it this way just for me."

Then he kissed her—finally. His lips settled over hers, gently at first but then with considerably more fire. He tasted hot and male and potent. Grabbing on to the soft cotton of his shirt, Sasha held on with all the strength she could muster. The feel of his hands as they touched and tempted warmed her from the inside out. The man sure knew how to heat up a cool Seattle night.

She liked that about him. Before she could tell him so, he lifted her off the ground and carried her backward several steps.

"Uh, Larem?"

"The bench," he murmured.

Then he sat down and settled her across his lap. Oh,

yeah, he was just full of good ideas. She kissed him hard and deep, the tip of her tongue inviting his to play.

Sasha didn't know about Larem, but she was about to go up in flames as his fingertips brushed across the curve of her breasts. She arched into his touch, asking for more. He didn't hesitate, cupping her breast in his palm with a gentle squeeze and coaxing her nipple into a hard peak with his finger and thumb. Immediately a need for so much more pooled deep inside her, making her wish they were somewhere more private.

Then his hand settled on her ankle before stroking upward, slipping under the hem of her skirt. He hesitated just below her knee.

"Sasha?"

Her name became both a caress and a question on his lips. Her breath caught in her chest as she read the intent in his eyes. She should stop him. It was too much. Too fast. Too soon. But she couldn't find the words or the will to hold back. Instead, she buried her face against his neck, drawing in the scent of his skin.

Larem took that as a yes. Smiling against her hair, he pressed a soft kiss on her forehead as his hand resumed its journey. She sighed and closed her eyes as he took his time to learn the soft curve of her knee.

"Kiss me," he demanded as he stroked the top of her smooth thigh.

Her lips found his, opening for him like roses in the bright light of the sun. Oh, yeah, this moment was so perfect, her response to his touch beyond anything he'd hoped for. He eased his hand between her legs, going slowly to give her a chance to protest. She didn't, not even when he sought out the center of her heat.

One stroke had her moaning, two had her arching up, her legs squeezing tight against his wrist and locking his hand in place. He continued the gentle assault, stroking and pressing, wanting nothing more than to lay Sasha down and make love to her.

For now, he'd settle for having her come apart in his arms. He eased past her flimsy panties, stroking deeper, faster, harder.

"Larem! Please, I can't—"

He wanted to give this to her. "Yes, you can. I've got you. Just let go."

Then she shuddered, her head falling against his shoulder as the storm broke within her. He held her close as they rode it out together. When he finally remembered how to breathe, he tugged her skirt back down, struggling to find the words to describe what the moment had meant to him.

But then he heard the sound of approaching footsteps. They ended abruptly with an embarrassed, "Whoops! Excuse us!"

They both froze until the intruders retreated. Sasha suspected she was blushing big-time, but then Larem laughed quietly and pressed one more kiss on the top of her head.

"Whoops, indeed," he said with a chuckle.

She reluctantly joined in the laughter. What had she been thinking, to let things get so far out of control? Not that she could bring herself to really regret it.

"I don't know about you, but I haven't gotten caught making out like that since I was a teenager."

"It's been a while for me, too," he agreed. "But they're still good memories."

Then he set her back on her feet and stood up. After picking up his pack, he said, "I guess we should be moving on."

He kissed her again before they headed back toward the main path. She laced her fingers with his as they made their way to the exit, where she called for a cab. As they waited, Larem's cell phone rang. His expression went from happy to grim in the space of a heartbeat as he listened to the person on the other end of the line.

"Don't worry about me. Just go."

He listened another few seconds, holding the phone in a white-knuckled grip. "No, I'm sure. And, Lonzo, watch your back. I don't want to break in a new roommate. I've barely got you trained." He hung up and loosed a deep breath.

"What's wrong?" she asked. A knot of pure fear settled in her chest.

"That was Lonzo. He's been called out again. The barrier near St. Helens is still down. They're sending in a second wave to support the guys who've been fighting since noon. It sounds pretty bad."

He stared up at the sky the whole time he was talking, the vein on the side of his neck visibly pulsing. Clearly knowing his friend was headed into combat was hitting Larem hard.

"Are you being sent in, too?" she asked, mentally crossing her fingers that he wasn't.

He simply shook his head, offering no explanation. She didn't miss the fact that he was flexing his sword hand as he stood there. Obviously he wished he were being ordered into the fray.

Suddenly images of David's memorial came rushing back to Sasha, only this time it was Larem's picture being displayed, surrounded by flowers. Even if it didn't happen tonight, it would someday. A crippling pain lanced her heart. There was no way she could endure that again.

What had she been thinking, getting involved with another Paladin?

Luckily, her cab pulled up, forestalling the need to say anything more. The ride back to her hotel was blessedly short. Larem's thoughts were obviously elsewhere, which left her alone with her own. Despite how much she'd enjoyed the evening—especially the part after the concert—Lonzo's phone call had been a splash of ice-cold water, forcing her to face the risk she was taking.

Larem slid out of the backseat and offered his hand to help her out. After he paid the cabdriver, she led the way over to the shadows at the side of the entrance.

She couldn't even begin to smile. "Larem, listen, I have something to say. I hope you'll understand that it's nothing personal."

But it was. It had everything to do with what he was and what he did for a living. He knew it, too.

"I had a wonderful time tonight. I can't remember the last time I enjoyed myself more, but . . ." She paused, finding it nearly impossible to talk around the lump in her throat. David was her secret, and she didn't know Larem well enough to share. She settled for the easy lie.

"But as the new administrator, I have too much on my plate right now to get involved with anyone, especially a Paladin who technically works for me. I'm truly sorry, but I hope you can understand."

His reaction struck her as odd. Rather than getting angry, he actually laughed, although it had nothing to do with humor. She wasn't sure how to respond.

"What's so funny?"

Once again, he ran a strand of her hair through his fingers. "No, it's not funny. I believe the correct word is 'ironic,' but I do understand all too well. Good-bye, Sasha."

He brushed his lips across hers one last time and walked away, disappearing into the night.

Chapter 5

Sasha had spent the days since her date with Larem wading through paperwork until she thought her eyes would bleed. Anything was better than second-guessing her decision not to see him again. Still, trying to clean up the mess left by her predecessor hadn't helped her mood at all, leaving her wanting to take a baseball bat to the man. Kincade, not Larem.

She had to give him credit, though. The bastard had done a bang-up job hiding his tracks. Finally, she'd borrowed D. J. Clayborne's services from Devlin to work on the computer files. She'd left him back in her office to do his magic on Kincade's personal computer. Hopefully, he'd have better luck.

But right now, she had a date with adventure.

The last time she'd spoken to Devlin, he'd reluctantly agreed to give her a brief tour of the tunnels under the Paladin headquarters. She was excited about the prospect of finally seeing the barrier for herself.

Then, in his last e-mail, Devlin told her that he'd been called away because Mount St. Helens was once again causing problems. Luckily, he'd arranged for Lonzo Jones to meet her at the elevator at two thirty that afternoon.

She'd almost canceled, not sure she wanted to spend time with Larem's roommate, but decided that was silly. The man could hardly hold it against her that her last date with his friend hadn't ended well. That is, if Larem had even told Lonzo about it.

Either way, she was about to find out. The shortest route to their meeting place led her past Devlin's office and the cluster of desks that surrounded it. The entire area was empty and silent. The hallway leading to the elevator was equally deserted.

"Lonzo, I hope you didn't forget about me. I was really looking forward to this," she whispered to herself, looking at her watch.

Maybe he was simply running late. Just in case, she needed to call her assistant to clear her calendar for the remainder of the day. When she tried her cell, though, she had no reception, probably because she was right over the barrier.

She did an abrupt about-face and went back to use one of the landlines. For good measure, she'd leave Devlin a message, too, thanking him again for arranging the tour. If Lonzo came while she was gone, surely he'd wait a few minutes.

He watched the big boss disappear back down the hall, hating the way the bitch strolled through the place like she owned it. It was bad enough the Regents had sided with the Paladins against the one man who'd ever backed the guards over those prima donnas. But instead of someone to kick ass and take names, they'd sent that *woman*, all because her daddy was a Regent. Did she really think she was capable of handling all the shit that went on around here?

Well, maybe a little scare was in order. The barrier readings down below had been stable for several days. Perhaps getting trapped below ground would be enough to send her running home to papa. It was worth a shot.

It sounded like the Paladin assigned to escort her had been delayed for some reason, too. With luck, the guy wouldn't show up until she was already in the elevator and on her way down to the tunnels. After scribbling a few words on a sticky note, he stuck it on the elevator door and took off down the hall.

Sasha spotted a note on the elevator and sighed. She'd missed Lonzo by a matter of minutes. Hopefully he hadn't bailed on her.

She peeled the note off the door and read it. Good, only the meeting place had changed. She keyed in her security code on the touchpad to summon the elevator up from below. It didn't take long.

After one last look up and down the hall, she stepped inside. The doors whooshed shut and the elevator dropped, making her feel as if the floor had fallen out beneath her feet. Her stomach churned as she held on to the handrail with a death grip. The pounding of her heart was the only sound as she plummeted toward the barrier.

Seconds later, the elevator hit the ground with a jarring thump. She swallowed hard as the doors slid open. Outside, the air smelled of damp rock as she poked her head out to look around. The elevator was tucked in behind a stone outcropping, severely limiting her view. Other than a distant buzz that sounded like the hum of high-power wires, the heavy silence made her wonder exactly where her escort was waiting for her.

"Lonzo?" No answer. She tried again, louder this time, but still with no success.

What the heck was going on? Darn it, she'd been really excited about the chance to see the barrier first-hand after all these years of hearing people struggle to describe it. She read Lonzo's note again. It clearly said he'd be waiting by the barrier for her, but she couldn't see it from where she stood. She moved tentatively forward, reluctant to wander very far from the elevator.

Surely it wouldn't hurt to take a quick peek around the corner to look for Lonzo before she returned upstairs. She crept forward, straining to hear even the slightest hint that anyone else was in the tunnels. The motion-activated lights flickered on as she moved forward, illuminating the tunnel for some distance in each direction. The place was empty as far as she could see.

Her intention to stage an immediate retreat was put on hold as soon as she saw the dazzling, solid sheet of energy. Words couldn't describe the swirling colors that changed and shifted and then changed again. It might be deadly to the touch, but why had no one ever told her the barrier was beyond beautiful?

She had to get back but hated to look away for fear she'd miss a wisp of color that might never be seen again. It wasn't lost on her that she stood mere inches away from another world, one unlike anything she could possibly imagine. All she knew for certain was that it bred cold-blooded killers who destroyed lives, leaving more than just their intended victims bleeding and hurt.

She closed her eyes to block out the mesmerizing murmur of power and beauty, wishing she could slam the door on her memories as easily. But some things—and some people—deserved to be remembered despite the pain that never faded. David's dark chocolate eyes and broad smile were burned into her brain, their image as bright now as when she first met him. Eight years wasn't all that long, but it seemed like forever since she'd last touched his face or tasted his kiss.

He was her first love. He'd sworn her to secrecy before confessing he was a Paladin. Two days after he'd proposed to her, he'd died, first from a sword wielded by an Other, and then a second time from a syringe full of poison administered by his Handler.

She shivered, but not entirely because of the chill in the subterranean tunnels. Time to get back topside. She'd check in with Devlin later to reschedule the tour and demand an explanation from Lonzo about why he'd ditched her. She headed for the elevator, but the steady buzz from the barrier increased in volume.

Looking back, she frowned. What the heck? The barrier was no longer opaque. The colors were still bright, but she could see shadows moving through the translucent curtain. Okay, this was bad. Maybe really, really bad. One of the two most common signs that the barrier was about to go down was that it thinned out, revealing hints of the world that lay beyond.

The other sign was sudden streaks of sickly colors replacing the vibrant, healthy ones. Sure enough, gangrenous yellows and greens started to appear at the top near the ceiling of the tunnel and spread rapidly across the entire expanse.

She took off running for the elevator. She had to get it open—now. Her fingers shook as she keyed in the code. No response. Why hadn't she at least thought to hold the elevator on the lower level for the few minutes she'd been looking around?

Devlin had been right—this was no place for a civilian to be wandering alone. As she waited for the elevator to return, she hoped she lived long enough for him to say he'd told her so.

His spur-of-the-moment plan appeared to be working. He quickly keyed in the high-level security code that would recall the elevator and keep it topside. His clearance didn't warrant that kind of authority, but it helped to have friends in high places.

He grinned as he felt the small blast of air that signaled the approach of the elevator. Then he wiped his fingerprints off the keypad and headed down the hall, this time to leave the building. It wouldn't do to be seen lurking in the area once Sasha Willis managed to find her way back up topside.

"Come in and sit down." Devlin led the way into his office and dropped into his own chair. "I just got back from an all-nighter down at St. Helens, but I need to talk to you."

"What about?" Larem asked, although he could probably guess.

"Last Friday Laurel and I had drinks with Sasha Willis. Imagine my surprise when your name came up in conversation."

"You already knew we'd met. I couldn't very well ignore her."

"Damn it, Larem, I thought you had more sense. What the hell were you thinking? The last thing I wanted to hear out of Sasha Willis's mouth was that the two of you have been hanging out."

From past experience, Larem knew the best course of action was to let Devlin rant until he ran out of temper or breath, whichever came first. Trying to reason with the man before that happened would be a wasted effort. It didn't take long.

"Well? Care to explain?"

Larem shifted in his chair, trying to come up with an answer that was close to the truth but wouldn't set Devlin off again. He sure couldn't admit that he'd first sought her out because the Kalith and their closest allies didn't exactly trust Devlin's ability to ensure their safety. Worse yet, he'd also spent time with her because he wanted to.

If Devlin was upset about him and Sasha sharing a cup of coffee, the man would go ballistic if he found out they'd actually gone out more than once, especially if he knew about their last date.

But it was over. To avoid running into her again, Larem had made a trip up north to visit Hunter and his mate for a few days. Upon his return, Lonzo had warned him that Devlin was hot on his trail.

"Last Tuesday, Ms. Willis was nosing around in the building after leaving your office and ended up by the geology lab. I was the one who answered the door because she'd already met me but hadn't yet figured out that I am Kalith. I assumed that could change quickly if she saw Barak and me at the same time. Rather than risk inviting her in to meet him and Lacey, I chose to escort her out of the building. We parted a few blocks later after having a cup of coffee."

Devlin ran his fingers through his hair in obvious frustration. "Fine. I get why you intercepted her at the door, but the exit to the alley is right down the hall from where you were. The smart thing to do would've been to tell her to go straight and then turn left. Why didn't you?"

Telling Devlin that it was because he wanted more time in her company would not be an acceptable answer. "I pretended to be on my way out so that she wouldn't feel as if she were interrupting anything in the lab. However, Duke was on duty and saw me. Since he hates me, and I figured he'd waste no time in telling her who and what I was, I stayed with her so he'd keep his mouth shut. Once we were safely past him, I left Ms. Willis as soon as I could without being rude."

Larem leaned back in his chair and watched as Devlin processed the information. Finally, the big man slowly nodded. "So you lingered over coffee just to be polite, knowing each minute she spends with you makes it more difficult for you to blend into the crowd around here?"

Okay, so much for fooling Devlin. "The last thing I want—or either of us needs—is for her to get too curious about me, which is why I left town for a while. She hasn't seen me in days, so hopefully her attention is focused elsewhere by now."

"Yeah, well, it is. Unfortunately, it's on me. She's got me jumping through so many fucking hoops, I can't—"

A knock at the door kept Devlin from finishing that thought. "Come in!"

Lonzo poked his head in. "Hey, boss, sorry to interrupt, but I think we've got a problem."

Devlin's eyes narrowed. "Aren't you supposed to be giving Sasha Willis the grand tour?"

"Yeah, well, I was, but I had a flat tire and just now got here. I tried her number and then yours. When neither of you answered, I called D.J. to stall her, but he's over in the admin building working on Kincade's stuff."

He stopped to take a breath. "The rest of the crew just got back with you, so I ran the last few blocks to get here. There's no sign of the woman anywhere. Even worse, the elevator is on lockdown. It won't accept my access code. Honest, boss, I wasn't more than ten minutes late."

Larem had a bad, bad feeling about where all this was headed. He rose to his feet, ready to . . . what?

Charge to her rescue? Yeah, like that was going to happen. Besides, there was no actual proof Sasha was in trouble.

Still, he knew for a fact that she'd been exploring different areas in the building lately, because the guys had been talking about all the odd places she'd been seen. Would she even hesitate to go exploring if her assigned guide didn't show up?

Devlin looked even more worried. "I'm the only one around here who has the authority to shut the elevators down completely, and I sure as hell didn't do it."

Then he checked his cell and cursed; the battery was dead. He dug out his charger and plugged it in to listen to his messages. "Son of a bitch! I don't know where that woman is now, but she was definitely here a few minutes ago."

The words were no sooner out of his mouth than the Klaxons started blasting. Devlin immediately grabbed the sword he'd yet to put away after his long night of fighting.

He glared at Larem again. "Keep your fingers crossed that she's either back in her office or already on her way up from the tunnels, because if she's not . . ." Devlin shook his head, not wanting to follow that thought to its obvious conclusion. "I've got to go."

Larem stayed where he was, frozen by the spectre of what would happen to Sasha if the Others got their hands on her. The light-sickness made them little better than animals, out of their heads and raging out of control. If Devlin and his men didn't get to Sasha first, Larem could only hope that she died quickly.

He stared at the weapons displayed on Devlin's wall and at one sword in particular. Then he was on his feet and reaching for the Kalith blade. The Paladin leader had no doubt captured it from an Other who'd had the great misfortune to cross Devlin's path.

Devlin had never ordered Larem to stay out of the tunnels, but then he hadn't really needed to. The last thing Larem wanted was to face his own people in battle. This was different, though. Who knew what kind of hell Devlin and his men were walking into? They could be wading through puddles of blood with no time to spare to hunt for Sasha. Maybe they'd be able to shove her back into the elevator and send her up to safety, but maybe not.

Larem headed for the elevator at a dead run, doing his best to steer clear of the Paladins and guards still pouring in. With battle fever running high, not all of them would immediately recognize Larem as an ally. There were also those among the guards who hated anyone with Kalith blood even more than the Paladins did and might use the situation to rid their world of one more enemy.

The elevator was still in use, warriors milling around and waiting for their chance to wade into the fray far below. No sign of Sasha.

D.J. came running up, stuttering to a full stop when he spotted Larem. "Are you fucking nuts or suicidal? What the hell are you doing here?"

"Devlin thinks Sasha Willis might be trapped down below. Someone has to hunt for her while you guys fight."

The Paladin looked sick. "Son of a bitch! Just what we need."

D.J. studied the massing warriors. "Come with me."

The two of them ran back the way they'd come, not stopping until they reached another elevator at the far end of the building. "This one will bring you out on the right level, but not immediately by the barrier."

D.J. keyed in his code and then repeated it to Larem. "Use it to haul your ass back topside as soon as you find her. Be careful if you get near the fight. If things are as bad down there as they were last night at the mountain, it'll be hard to tell friend from crazy. Wouldn't want you to get skewered because some paper-pushing twit can't stay where she belongs. Your buddy Hunter would kick my ass off a cliff if I let that happen."

Then the Paladin was gone, leaving Larem to his own mission. As the elevator carried him down into the darkness, he prayed he got to Sasha in time.

"Oh, God," Sasha whispered, peeking around the corner at the barrier.

As the seconds ticked by, its energy continued to weaken, leaving no doubt that the Others were poised to pour across en masse as soon as the barrier crashed. She retreated to the dubious safety near the elevator, which still hadn't returned. After keying in her code, she pressed her ear to the cool metal, hoping to hear it coming.

Nothing.

Then the scream of the alarms echoed through the tunnels, calling the Paladins to defend their world. That the cavalry was on its way was the good news. The bad news was that no civilian's security code worked on the elevators when there was fighting going on, not even hers. She'd have to wait for the first load of Paladins to disembark before she could ride the elevator back up to safety.

But only if it got to her before those . . . those animals did. Had the barrier failed completely? She inched her way to the edge of the outcropping. Mustering her courage, Sasha peeked around the corner only long enough to confirm her worst nightmares stood but a few feet away. The center of the barrier was ripping apart, leaving enough room for the Others to pour through.

Except for their clothing, they looked human, at least at first. But on closer inspection, that pasty gray skin and those freaky pale eyes set them apart. Some hollered at the top of their lungs as they charged across, the guttural sounds pure gibberish to her ear. But there was no mistaking the hatred in their voices. They gradually spread out, curved blades clenched in their fists, looking for a fight.

So far, none had turned in her direction, but it was only a matter of time before some of them came looking for the fastest way to the surface. She slipped off her high heels and gripped one in each hand, knowing they would provide little protection against anyone armed with a sword. But if she pegged someone in the head, it might distract a pursuer long enough to give her time to get away.

She had no idea where she'd end up, but standing

there by the elevator was sure suicide. As soon as one of the Others came any closer, she'd be trapped. Hoping the blare of the alarms would hide the sound of her footsteps, she started moving away from the barrier, first slowly and then faster and faster.

Where were the Paladins and the guards? Surely they should've been there by now, but then maybe it was her fear that made it feel as if she'd been trapped down there for hours already.

She slowed as she reached an intersecting tunnel. Which way to go? Right or left? Did it really matter when she didn't know where she was to begin with? Okay, right it was. The motion lights immediately flickered on to guide her. Clever technology, but they also served as a beacon to anyone who wanted to follow her trail.

Stopping to catch her breath, she waited for the lights to go back off, leaving her shrouded in darkness. As her pulse slowed, she could gradually hear more than the sound of her own heart pounding. Footsteps. Lots of them. Screams echoed down the passage and the clash of metal against metal. Obviously the troops had arrived. She prayed for the safety of the men she'd gotten to know. Larem's face flashed in her mind.

The shuffle of footsteps was louder this time, but with all the noise it was hard to know how close they were or whether any Others had gotten past the Paladins. All she knew for sure was that the footsteps were headed her way. The darkness wouldn't protect her for long. As soon as any of them drew close enough to trigger the lights, she'd be exposed.

No sooner did that thought cross her mind than the lights behind her flared. A band of four male Others shielded their eyes from the glare, but that didn't keep them from seeing her. The one in front bellowed something as they all charged forward. She didn't need to speak their language to understand what they had planned for her.

She screamed, threw her shoes as hard as she could, and took off running. As she ran for the corner ahead, the lights from that direction came on, too. Trapped! She had no idea who was coming toward her, but she knew full well that to stop where she was would be certain death.

She charged forward, hoping against hope that Devlin had gotten her message and sent someone to look for her. *Please, God, please. Please let it be someone I know.*

Her steps faltered as a curved blade appeared from around the corner. It was an unwritten rule that no Paladin carried a blade of that shape. She was running straight into a trap. With nowhere to go and no hope of survival, she stopped where she was and began to pray.

Chapter 6

*T*he battle at the barrier was in full swing. Larem chanted the prayers for the dead and dying under his breath as he made his way through the tunnels. How many of the Kalith were men he'd known when they were sane, when he still served their people as one of Lusahn q'Arc's Blademates? Not that it mattered. Neither he nor they were the same people they used to be.

Larem flexed his fingers on the pommel of his borrowed weapon, his mind flashing back to a time when he would've joined the battle to protect his own kind. Now he had friends among the Paladins, and his people considered him a traitor. As always, he was a man caught between two worlds, neither of which much wanted him.

At least for the moment, he had a definite purpose. He backed away from the battle, needing to find another way around. Before he'd gone two steps, he saw D.J. in the middle of the fight, wielding his double-headed ax with deadly purpose.

What D.J. didn't see was the Other coming up behind him with his sword swinging right at the Paladin's neck. Before Larem could shout out a warning, Trahern burst free of the melee long enough to remove the threat with one blow from his broadsword. Larem prayed for the soul of the dead warrior and walked away.

A narrow branch of tunnel cut back in the direction he needed to go. The profound relief he'd felt that D.J. had been spared disturbed him on a gut level. The dead Other had been someone's son, brother, friend. Now he was nothing but a pile of bloody meat to be disposed of and forgotten. Larem understood the Paladins' reluctance to view their enemy as anything but rabid animals, but as a healer, he ached for all those who suffered a sickness for which there was no cure.

The never-ending cycle of death made him furious, and seeing it firsthand left him freezing cold inside. He trudged on, concentrating on the task at hand and doing his best to block out the screams of agony that bounced through the tunnels and echoed in his soul.

Larem quickly learned to keep his focus on the floor and away from the sudden bursts of light that nearly blinded his sensitive Kalith eyes. When he reached a long stretch of clear passage, he broke into a run, slowing only when he reached the other end. Cocking his head to the side, he listened hard.

Heartbeats just ahead. Four had the staccato beat of Kaliths lost in the frenzy, but one was purely human. Either it was Sasha being hunted by his kind or else the four Others had managed to corner a Paladin alone. Either way, Larem had to intervene.

Bracing himself for battle, he rounded the last corner and came face-to-face with his worst nightmare come true. Four Kalith males were fanning out, closely stalking Sasha. They were enjoying the hunt, laughing maniacally as she retreated.

The one in the lead spoke to her, his English rough but his meaning all too clear. "Female, stop running. We don't want you to be too tired to be of use to us." He looked toward his companions. "If you please myself and my friends, perhaps we'll let you live."

Sasha stopped moving and threw her shoulders back. "I'd rather die."

The Kalith pushed his long hair back from his face, his smile turning nasty. "That won't be as fun for us, but if you insist . . ."

Larem didn't want to kill his own kind, but he wouldn't let them hurt Sasha, not when she was his to protect. So far they hadn't noticed him; he wasn't sure about Sasha.

He paused long enough to jerk the tie out of his hair, letting it hang free down around his shoulders. Raising his sword, he started forward, calling out a traditional greeting among Kalith warriors in their own language. "My brothers, how fare thee?"

The leader jerked his attention away from Sasha long enough to answer, "My brother, we are about to fare very well."

Then his eyes flared wide as he took in the human attire Larem wore, and his smile turned feral. "You speak our language, but you carry the stench of Paladins."

Sasha finally recognized him. "Larem? Thank God you're here."

He ignored her as the three Others sniffed the air, growling low in their chests. One of them reached out toward Sasha, laughing when she shrank against the wall to avoid his touch.

This was going to end badly. Larem knew that and so did they. Still, for the sake of the oath he'd sworn to serve his people, he had to try. "My brothers—"

"We are not your brothers, not if you live in the light, traitor!" The leader sidled closer to Sasha, his sword sliding back and forth in a promise of the fight to come. He switched to heavily accented English. "Tell us how to escape these tunnels and maybe we'll let the woman live."

Larem lowered his blade slightly, hoping to reduce the growing tension. "I am no traitor, but I will not let you harm the woman. She has done nothing to you."

"She is human. That is enough."

Time to try another tactic. "The light in this world has strengthened my gift of healing. Let me help you become the honorable warriors you were before the sickness took you."

For a second, the Other hesitated, but then his eyes narrowed in suspicion. "You lie! The healers of light and their skills are lost to the darkening. You want to steal our prize and bed the woman yourself. Why else would you be prowling these tunnels?"

"I am Blademate to Lusahn q'Arc and sworn to protect those who cannot defend themselves, human or Kalith." Larem brought his sword back up in full challenge. "Retreat now or die."

The spokesman for the Others looked back to his three friends. "Silence this fool while I enjoy the woman. Once he has bled out, we will all have her— often."

The closest Other charged forward with violence in his eyes. Larem's scream mixed with Sasha's as he answered the Kalith's attack, cursing the gods for forcing him to kill those of his homeland. His opponent was an experienced swordsman but nowhere near the caliber of a Blademate. Larem left him bleeding on the ground and took the fight to the next one.

The leader was now holding Sasha by her hair, drawing in deep breaths of her scent. She kicked at him, but her bare foot did little damage. She had more success clawing at his face, even drawing blood. He immediately shoved her against the wall and pinned her there with the full press of his body against hers. Larem shouted out a warning in Kalith, telling the bastard in great detail what Larem would do to him if he took his assault on Sasha any further.

The other two took advantage of the distraction and charged him. It would be nothing less than a miracle if Larem managed to eliminate both bumbling crazies quickly enough to prevent the remaining one from hurting Sasha. With a quick spin, he slashed one across the neck. The male dropped to his knees, his sword clattering to the ground as he tried to stop the blood gushing from his throat.

Two down, two to go. There was no sign of sanity left in either of them. The kindest thing Larem could do was to end their lives quickly and cleanly. Stepping around the two bodies at his feet, he held out his free hand and dared them to join in the deadly dance.

"Come on, Others," he said, sneering as he called them by that hated name. "I grow bored with this. Give me the woman or give me your blood. I don't care which."

Sasha gasped in horror or outrage, but he was more intent on drawing the two killers toward him than protecting her delicate sensibilities. "At least your friends had the honor to die in combat. Know that if you run, you will be cut down like so many weeds by Paladins."

To show his disdain, he turned his back to walk away, although each step that put more distance between him and Sasha was torture. The ruse worked to draw the third fighter out again. Larem took two more steps forward before stepping to the side, rightly guessing the Other's charge would carry him past Larem's position. Now he was between the two remaining Kalith, which would prevent them from ganging up on Sasha.

After bringing his headlong rush to a stop, the Other circled back to challenge Larem. The light disease was in full force now, making the Other's movements jerky and out of control. The sick feeling in Larem's veins was the same one he felt when they put down an animal at the shelter that was too far gone to save. It was much too simple to slip past the warrior's guard and end his life.

By now, Larem drew little comfort from chanting the prayers for the dead, but he went through the motions because his duty and his honor demanded it. Weary to the soul, he wanted nothing more than to end this slaughter.

"Your turn."

This time, the final Other didn't hesitate. He pressed

a sloppy kiss on Sasha's mouth while he hugged her close with his free hand. "I'll be back to finish what we've started."

She immediately wiped her lips with the back of her hand and spit on the ground. "Never, you bastard!"

Larem admired her courage, but if she provoked the male, he might just kill her before Larem could stop him.

"Sasha, back away and shut up!" he barked, barely lifting his sword in time to block his enemy's blade.

The Others had saved their best swordsman for last. Despite the illness burning brightly in the male's eyes, he retained enough of his natural-born ability to put up a good fight. Larem was better, but only just. Sweat dripped down his face, stinging his eyes as the battle dragged on. The longer it lasted, the greater the chance his opponent would get in a lucky blow.

He couldn't let that happen, no matter how much he admired the fighter's skill with the blade. Had he been someone's Blademate as well?

No time for such thoughts.

Finally, Larem feigned a misstep. His opponent fell for the ruse, leaving himself wide open for attack as he lunged forward, swinging his blade with all the strength he had. Instead of killing Larem, he found himself impaled on Larem's borrowed sword, the curved blade cutting deep and wide through his chest.

The Other slowly sank to his knees, sanity briefly returning to his gaze as he looked up at Larem in confusion.

"My brother?" he whispered, the light in his eyes fading quickly.

Larem dropped to the ground and gathered the dying Kalith into his arms. Perhaps he could save at least this one. Chanting under his breath, he pulled out his medicine knife and held it up toward the ceiling as he asked the gods to share their healing strength.

As he prepared to plunge the ceremonial knife down into the Other's heart, the warrior shuddered and breathed his last. Larem cursed and flung the knife down the tunnel. Once again, his magic had failed him, and his people. He held the body close for a few seconds longer as he whispered the death prayers for each of the fallen Kalith.

He grieved for their loss, even knowing that their lives had really ended when the sickness first whispered in their minds. If they hadn't died by his sword, they would've faced the same brutal end at the hands of the Paladins.

At least with him there, someone mourned their passing.

"Larem? Are you all right?" Sasha asked.

He ignored her question because the answer was obvious. Hell no, he wasn't all right; he wasn't sure he ever would be. Her recklessness had cost these four their lives and Larem another large chunk of his soul.

He shoved the body off his lap and pushed himself to his feet. There was nothing more to be said. The Paladins would dispose of the bodies; he didn't know how and didn't care. No matter what they did, it was an abomination. Only the knowledge that they were caught up in the same horrible cycle of death and disease as the Others kept him from charging off to join the battle he could still hear raging back at the barrier. The only question was whose side he'd take, knowing it wouldn't really matter as long as he died fighting.

But his duty wasn't done. He'd vowed to get Sasha to safety. That much he could do.

"Are you hurt?" He held his hand out to brush her hair away from her face, but jerked it back when she flinched at his touch.

Fine. Her response pissed him off royally, to quote his roommate, even if he understood why she felt that way. The sooner he got her topside the better. "Come."

Sasha shrank away from him. "You're one of them, aren't you?"

He ignored how much her reaction hurt. He'd always known she'd hate him when she finally saw him for what he really was. "Right now what I am is your way out of here."

She retreated another step. "But where are we going? The elevators are back that way."

He snagged her arm before she gave in to panic and glared down at her. "So is the fighting, Sasha. Too many from both worlds are already bleeding, so you'll understand if I'd rather not kill any more of my people. Now, follow me or not. It's your choice."

He let go of her, hating the fear in her eyes when she looked at him and hating himself for his part in putting it there. Then he walked away, stopping long enough to retrieve his blade before moving on. Surely she'd show the good sense to stay with him. If not, he'd force the issue, but he hoped she'd at least trust him enough to get her to safety.

•   •   •

Sasha stared at the four broken bodies fallen on the ground. So much blood. Its bitter copper scent filled her head and overloaded her senses. Her stomach churned, foul acid burning the back of her throat. God, would this nightmare never end? It had been hours since she'd last eaten, so it was nothing but dry heaves as she leaned against the wall and retched.

Please, let it stop. She needed to follow Larem even if he was one of them—Kalith, Other, the name didn't matter. If she lost sight of him, her life might very well end right there in the bloody passageway. She tried to straighten up between heaves, but that only made the pain worse. After stumbling forward a few steps, she had to stop and close her eyes to ward off the dizziness.

As she did, she felt someone beside her and panicked. "No, please no! Get away!"

"Sasha, calm down. It's me."

She sagged in relief at the sound of Larem's deep voice. Despite everything, he hadn't abandoned her.

"Hold still and don't fight me."

His accent was deeper than usual, but his voice was far more gentle than it had been only seconds before. His hand, cool and soothing, rested lightly on her forehead, and his arm slid around her waist, supporting her weight.

He murmured something. The words were unclear, perhaps in his native tongue, but their effect was miraculous. The nausea disappeared almost immediately, as did the cramping. When he removed his hand, she looked up into his pale gray eyes.

"Better?"

She nodded. "Much."

The chill came flooding back into his gaze as he stepped away and retrieved his sword. "Now, let's get out of here."

She glanced back toward the other end of the passage, careful to avoid looking at the bodies along the way, and then followed Larem around the corner. He was moving fast enough that she almost had to run to keep up with him.

She had so many questions for him—now that her brain was starting to function again—but she suspected she wouldn't like his answers. Like, why had he let her think he was human? She'd known there were Kalith living among the Paladins, but no one had even hinted that they had the run of the place. Was he even supposed to be down here?

Now wasn't the time to worry about it, not when her life depended on him. Her eyes strayed to the bloody blade he'd wielded with such skill and terrible grace. Would she ever get over the horror of seeing four lives ended right in front of her? Or the knowledge that she'd come so close to being—*no, don't go there*. What might have happened didn't matter right now.

Larem came to an abrupt halt. "Quiet now. We don't want to draw attention to ourselves. Wait until I make sure the way is clear."

Sasha froze, her ears ringing with her ragged breath and pounding heart. Gradually, other sounds began to make sense. Horrible sense. Swords banging and clanging. Screams of pain and whimpers of agony. Larem progressed a few feet, holding his sword out to the side as if expecting to be attacked.

Finally, he motioned her forward. "Don't look."

But of course she did.

The ground was littered with bodies. She watched as a line of Paladins formed up. They slowly pushed forward, forcing the ragged band of Others to retreat back across the barrier. Men in guard uniforms were busy dragging the dead and wounded Paladins back out of the way, leaving the Others where they'd fallen.

Larem drew back beside her. "Sasha, snap out of it! We've got to get the hell out of here. Those guards might not hurt you, but they'll come after me given half a chance. I do not want to die because of your stupidity."

Okay, enough was enough. "It wasn't my stupidity. Lonzo left me a note telling me to meet him down here."

"Like hell he did. He had car trouble and didn't get back until just before the barrier failed."

"But—"

"That's enough!"

Larem all but dragged her along until finally he stopped outside an elevator. As soon as she saw the number pad next to it, her heart sank.

"Larem, my code won't work. We're trapped down here until Devlin sounds the all clear." Her voice went up an octave as she spoke; the thought of spending another minute trapped in this hell was unbearable.

Larem was already punching numbers into the security system. "This one will work."

Sure enough, she heard the low rumble that signaled

the elevator was on its way. She leaned against the wall, relieved beyond words. As fried as she was feeling, she still wondered why an Other would've been trusted with a high-level security code.

The more she thought about it, the more obvious the answer. It wasn't his code at all. Someone had broken protocols by giving it to him, most likely one of the Paladins. Under the circumstances, she wasn't about to complain.

She stepped to the back corner of the elevator and considered how best to handle the situation. "Thank whoever gave you the code. Tell him there will be no repercussions for the security breach."

Her good intentions seemed to only make Larem madder. "That's awfully generous of you, considering he broke your precious rules to save your life."

"I didn't mean it like that. I understand why he gave the number to a . . ." She stopped. She would do better to keep her mouth shut.

But it was too late. "A what, Sasha? An alien? An Other? An animal? How about a monster?"

Each question was an arrow-sharp accusation. "I'm sorry, Larem. I was trying to do the right thing."

He turned toward her, his eyes burning with fury. "The right thing would've been to stay the hell out of places you don't belong. Because of you, my friend delayed his arrival below in order to share that number *and* the location of this elevator with me. As it is, there aren't enough Paladins to hold back the invasion. How many were placed at extra risk because he was late to the fight or because they were concerned for your safety and not totally focused on the battle?"

Dear God, she hadn't thought about that. Even though it wasn't her fault, she'd inadvertently put others at risk. "Regardless of what you think, I didn't go down there uninvited. I'm telling you, Lonzo left me a note."

He stalked toward her, dropping his bloody sword to the floor as he cornered her. "Then let's see it."

She held out her empty hands. "It's gone. I must have dropped it. God, Larem, none of this was supposed to happen. All I can say is that I'm sorry."

"Yeah, well, that doesn't mean I have to forgive you. Because of you, I betrayed my vow to protect my people. Those Kalith died at my hand, and I have to find some way to live with that. As you now realize, I am Kalith, just as they were."

He was standing so close that she could feel the tension thrumming through his body. This was no time to notice how long his eyelashes were or how they framed his intense eyes. The memory of what they shared that night at the zoo flashed through her mind.

Her hand lifted to touch his cheek. "But you're not like them."

He shook his head. "No, I'm not, but only because they were sick with the need for light. That's the only difference."

At her touch, he tangled his fingers in her hair, tilting her face up toward his. "But one thing you would do well to remember, Sasha Willis—I might not be human, but I am a man. You enjoyed my kiss once. Think you will enjoy it this time, knowing what I am?"

Then his arms snapped around her and his angry

mouth crushed down on hers. When she gasped in shock, his tongue swept past her lips. She'd never tasted pure fury before, but she had no doubt that's what was flavoring Larem's kiss. She should push back, should fight to wrest control from him, but rather than feeling threatened, she felt safe. Rather than this being a claiming, Larem's kiss was a cleansing, washing away some of the fear and horror of the past half hour. A small voice in the back of her mind told her this was crazy, that she should be revolted by the prospect of kissing this . . . what?

Before she could figure out the answer to that question, Larem ripped his mouth away from hers and lurched back to the other side of the elevator. He was breathing hard. His mouth that had felt so soft and forgiving against hers was now a straight slash of anger.

To add insult to injury, he scrubbed at his lips with the back of his hand as if to wipe away her taste. The soft ping of the elevator finally reaching its destination echoed in the heavy silence between them.

As the two of them stalked out, she stopped to say, "This didn't happen."

He smirked down at her. "Do you really think Devlin Bane won't find out that you were down there? Or that you almost managed to get not just yourself, but me, killed?"

"Not that." She jerked her hand between the two of them. "I mean this—us. *This* didn't happen and it won't again."

"Why? Afraid what it will do to your precious plans if it gets out that you've been sullied by an Other?"

Okay, that did it. "Forget it. I'm out of here."

She marched away, her shoulders squared, her heart aching. Darn that man anyway! How did all this go spinning so far out of control? No matter how hateful Larem had been, he'd still risked his life to save hers.

Her father might think all Others were a subhuman life-form, but she now knew better. Clearly Larem was a man of honor, one who was suffering because of what that honor had just demanded of him. All because of her.

Okay, so she'd try one last time. But when she looked back, he was already walking away.

"Larem? About what you did—thank you."

For a second she thought he might have slowed down, but he never glanced back. It was surprising how much that hurt. She ignored the renewed pain and moved on down the hall herself.

After everything that had happened, it was tempting to call it quits for the day. But she couldn't—wouldn't. No, she'd return to her office until she knew the situation was under control. If things were bad enough, as the Regents' representative she might need to put in a call for assistance from another sector, either in the form of supplies or even for reinforcements until the Seattle Paladins were back at full strength.

A certain Kalith warrior wasn't the only one who understood the meaning of duty.

Larem walked laps around the halls of the Paladin headquarters. How many times had he passed by Devlin's office? Did it matter? No. It did occur to him that the circular route was symbolic of what his life had become—an endless struggle to get nowhere.

And wasn't he just the perfect example of a pity party? That was another useful expression he'd learned from his roommate. He closed his eyes, praying that Lonzo was not among the dead. Granted, as a Paladin, he wouldn't stay that way for long, but there was no guarantee he'd awaken the same man he'd been.

Larem managed a small smile while he thought about Lonzo Jones. The two of them had been thrown together by forces beyond their control. Larem had been dragged into this world because Lusahn q'Arc, the Sworn Guardian he'd served, had chosen a human lover—a Paladin at that—over any worthy male of their world. Not for the first time Larem wondered how different things would've been if he had gathered up the courage to speak for her himself, before her life had become entangled with Cullen Finley's.

Instead, both she and Larem had been condemned to be executed as traitors. Lonzo had been part of the rescue party led by Cullen and Lusahn's brother Barak. But as the group had fought its way back across the barrier, Lonzo had been badly injured, and Larem had saved the Paladin's life. In payment of that debt, Lonzo had offered Larem a home and the use of his family name on the forged paperwork that made it possible for him to function in this world. Larem didn't know which of them was more surprised by the fact they'd become fast friends.

What would his roomie think of Larem's earlier stupidity? Not the part where he fought to save Sasha from those four Others—Lonzo would respect that. No, the part when he'd given in to the urge to kiss her again, not that Lonzo knew about the first time.

What had Larem been thinking? When he'd found her, she'd been only seconds from being raped and killed. Then what had he done? He cornered the woman in the elevator and forced himself on her. Shame made his skin run hot and then cold.

Although, as he thought back, at first she seemed startled, but within the space of a heartbeat or two, her mouth had softened, her tongue tangling with his. What had he hoped to accomplish by such foolishness? He'd be damned lucky if she didn't issue orders to toss his carcass back across the barrier—or through it. Being fried would be just punishment for his twin sins of betraying his people and taking advantage of a woman in such a fragile state.

As he started yet another lap, the all clear finally sounded. For the first time in hours, the band of pressure across his chest relaxed enough for him to draw a full breath. He circled back to the elevators and waited. Once he knew how the Paladins had fared, he'd report in to Devlin and then go home.

He found a spot tucked out of the way of the emergency med techs waiting for the first batch of wounded to arrive. Only after the living were treated and stable would Laurel Young and the other Handlers start caring for the dead, hoping to ease their journey back to the living.

Larem might be able to help with that. His magic had certainly worked to bring Hunter Fitzsimon back from the dead. Somehow, though, he doubted Laurel or her boss would stand by and let Larem stab any of their patients through the heart on the off chance his magic would work again. Even so, his hand strayed to his Kalith knife and held on tight as the elevator doors slid open, bringing the scent of fresh blood.

Devlin walked out all but carrying a young Paladin who was new to Seattle. After surrendering his burden to the capable hands of the waiting techs, he patted the kid on the shoulder and murmured something that had the young recruit smiling through his pain.

Leave it to Devlin to know just the right thing to say. Then for a few seconds, the look of confidence on Devlin's face slipped and his own exhaustion and pain showed through. Larem pushed his way past the growing crowd to the weary leader's side.

Devlin's eyes widened in surprise. "What do you want? You shouldn't be anywhere near here right now."

Larem latched on to Devlin's thick arm and held on tight. "Stand still," he ordered.

He quickly chanted one of the new spells he'd learned, pulling energy from the electric lights overhead. For a second their glow actually dimmed as he felt the healing power pour through him and into the Paladin.

"What the hell was that?" Devlin whispered as he jerked his arm free of Larem's grasp.

For the first time in hours, Larem smiled. "That was me giving you enough energy to chew out my ass. What was I thinking?"

Devlin rested the point of his sword on the floor and

leaned on the pommel for support. "And I want to do that why?"

Before Larem could reply, a voice in the back of the crowd yelled, "One of the Others escaped! Kill him!"

Devlin brought his sword back up into fighting position as they all looked around for the enemy. A guard unfamiliar to Larem stood pointing right at him from across the crowd. Then there was a bloodcurdling scream as a sword came slashing through the air straight at Larem. He blocked one blow with his own blade while Devlin wrestled the guard to the floor with the help of Trahern, who had just stepped off the elevator. The whole time, the guy kept screaming.

Larem backed away, hoping the guard would calm down if he got out of the line of sight. Instead of calming down, though, the guard continued to thrash, almost succeeding in bucking off his captors. "He's getting away! He's getting away! Kill him before he kills us!"

"Son of a bitch! Will somebody please tranq this guy?" Devlin bellowed.

One of the medics quickly filled a syringe and jabbed it into the guard's arm. Larem had no idea what drug it was, but it was fast acting. The guard's eyes rolled up in his head and his body went slack.

Devlin and Trahern stood aside to let the medics take over. When it seemed order had been restored, Devlin turned back to Larem. As soon as he did, he blinked twice and snagged the arm of one of the medics, pointing in Larem's direction.

What were they looking at? Then he felt the warm drip, drip, drip along his leg. He glanced down to see the right side of his jeans was already soaked with blood—his blood. How had he missed noticing that the guard had actually landed a blow?

But now that he knew, the pain started, followed by waves of dizziness. He dimly heard someone shouting his name as the floor came rushing up to meet him. When the darkness threatened to overwhelm him, he fought against it, knowing it was a losing battle.

Devlin was cursing, but Larem was pretty sure that it was Trahern who'd drawn his sword and stood over him. Protecting him? Really? It was too much to assimilate, his thoughts too slippery to hold on to. Finally, it was just easier to embrace oblivion and let the world fade away.

Chapter 7

The numbers all blurred together and nothing added up. Sasha rubbed her eyes, hoping that it would help her make sense out of the data. But no, it was all still gibberish. There had to be a pattern lost somewhere in all those columns of numbers, and she was determined to find it. Just not now.

Yesterday had been a total disaster. Despite Lonzo's note, she'd acted so stupidly, venturing down into the tunnels. And if in fact he hadn't written the note, who had? And why? At this point, would anyone even believe her that the note actually existed?

No matter what, she definitely owed apologies to more than just Larem. Considering everything, she was surprised that Devlin hadn't yet called to rip into her over what had happened.

No sooner had the thought crossed her mind than her phone rang. Ignoring it would be the coward's way out, so she reached for the receiver and braced herself for the worst. But instead of a mighty roar, she was relieved to hear a different man's voice—her father's.

She punched the button to put him on speakerphone. "Hey, Dad, how are you?"

His familiar voice filled her office. "I'm fine. I'm more worried about how you're doing."

Guilt had her wincing. "Why? What have you heard?"

She regretted the words as soon as they slipped out.

"Nothing, but it sounds as if maybe I should have. What's going on out there, Sasha?" His tone made it clear he'd tolerate no evasions.

She settled for a half-truth. "The barrier has been unstable in the region for a few days. You know how it is. That always makes things tense for everyone involved."

Especially for her this time, not that she was going to tell her father about that. If he found out, the Regents would likely order her to catch the first plane back to St. Louis, and she'd spend the rest of her career counting paper clips to make sure everyone got their fair share.

Luckily, her father knew exactly how bad things could get whenever the barrier decided to yo-yo for days at a time. "How many casualties?"

"I'm waiting on the final report." Or actually, any report at all, something she'd have to check into as soon as she got off the phone.

"If it keeps up, inform the Board in case we need to send in some temporary reinforcements."

She really hoped it didn't come to that. They both knew that if they pulled Paladins to help one area, that left someone else shorthanded. "I'll let Devlin know when I talk to him."

"Good idea."

As he spoke, she could hear him tapping his pen on his desk, a sure sign he had something on his mind, most likely something she wouldn't like. It wasn't long in coming.

"So otherwise, how are you doing, Sasha? Got anything to report yet on the mess Kincade left behind?"

She so didn't need the great inquisition every time they talked. "Are you asking as a Regent or as my father?"

To her relief, he actually laughed. "Okay, maybe a little of both. How about I take off my Regent hat and settle for just being your dad?"

"Well, in that case, I'm doing fine. There's a lot to learn, not to mention a whole new cast of characters for me to get to know. The good news is that I think I may have a lead on a place to live. I'll know more by the end of the week."

Not that her father would be happy to hear that little tidbit. He'd made it perfectly clear that once she had done a full review of the current state of affairs in the Seattle region, she was to come straight home. That last part wasn't going to happen, not if she could help it.

There was a long pause followed by a heavy sigh. When he spoke again, resignation mixed with a dash of humor in his voice.

"Time out for a nag from your parental unit: make sure the place has a security system and is in a good neighborhood."

She smiled and shook her head. "I will, Dad. Besides, it was Dr. Young who offered to rent me her condo. I figured I could trust her judgment, considering how well respected she is within the organization."

That was true, at least in certain quarters. There were also those who thought her efforts to drag Paladins back from the edge of insanity were too radical to be trusted. However, Sasha was determined to funnel every last dime she could into helping Laurel pursue her studies.

Even if she managed to save only one Paladin, it would be worth it. No one deserved to suffer the way David had.

Despite his warrior nature, he'd been nothing but gentle with her. They'd had so much fun together; the man had sure known how to have a good time. She'd been naive enough to think their time together would be measured in decades, not months.

Sasha suddenly realized her father had started talking again.

"I didn't quite catch that," she admitted.

"It was nothing important. You're obviously distracted, so I should let you go." He sounded hurt.

"Sorry, Dad, I've got a meeting coming up, and I'm still getting ready for it." She laughed softly as she added, "The one thing I learned from you is to always be better prepared than everyone else at the table."

He sounded a little happier when he responded. "Too late to butter up the old man, Sasha. I know you've got a big job on your hands cleaning up Kincade's mistakes. Let me know if I can help. I'd certainly be glad to vet your reports before you send them to the Board and make suggestions if you'd like me to."

"Thanks, Dad. I appreciate the offer." Although she wouldn't take him up on it. She needed the Regents to see her as an individual, not merely an extension of her father.

"Okay, then. Don't be so long between phone calls, young lady. I worry. So does your Uncle George, although he won't admit it."

"I promise to give him a call. Take care, Dad."

After hanging up, Sasha rubbed her temples, trying to ease her headache. She kept trying to tell herself that she'd put the events of yesterday behind her but knew it for the lie it was—she'd been jumpy and tense all day.

And not just because she kept expecting Devlin Bane to show up in her doorway demanding answers or even her resignation. How bad had things been after the dust settled?

She shut down her computer. It was time to go find some answers. Rather than confront the Paladin in his office, she'd do an end run and check in with Laurel instead. Besides, the Handler was closer, since the medical labs were also located in the admin building just two floors down from Sasha's own office.

The two guards on duty snapped to attention when she stepped out of the elevator. As soon as they recognized her, they abruptly turned back to the security monitors in front of them. Neither one even so much as smiled, which struck her as odd. Up until today, they'd both been friendly enough. Obviously the fighting had cast a pall over everyone's mood.

She headed across the lobby to the medical labs where Laurel and the other Handlers worked. Given what Sasha knew about Paladin physiology, most of the warriors should've been treated and released by now, leaving only the most seriously injured—and the dead—as patients.

The doors to the lab swung open with a soft whoosh; the air was chilly and scented with chemicals and stale blood. Sasha paused just inside and shivered.

One look around had her considering a quick exit. The near side of the lab was crowded with stainless steel tables that served as patient beds. They were all full. On the far side, a single table stood alone, curtained off from view. She wasn't sure she really wanted to know who was sequestered over there or why.

One of the techs was busy taking vitals, but when he spotted her, he went over and tapped Laurel on the shoulder. The Handler immediately motioned for Sasha to join her, patting the chair beside her. Sasha tiptoed around the edge of the room, skirting the hodgepodge of tables and trying not to disturb any of the sleeping patients.

As Sasha sat down, Laurel yawned loudly enough that her jaw cracked and popped.

"Sorry about that. What brings you to our little piece of paradise?"

It wasn't hard to see the woman was operating on willpower and caffeine. "Laurel, when's the last time you had any sleep?"

The Handler managed a small smile. "Don't worry about me. I've caught a few winks here and there, and Dr. Neal is due to relieve me in a few minutes."

Laurel looked around the room. "Most of the guys are past the critical stage now and resting easy. There's just one that I'm still worried about. The usual onslaught of wounds is bad enough, especially when the barrier is going up and down."

Laurel paused, her eyes straying back toward the curtained area. "But his injuries shouldn't have happened at all."

"Was it some kind of accident?"

Laurel held her clipboard tightly. "No, it was deliberate, and that makes me absolutely furious. He didn't deserve this."

Before Sasha could ask who was lying on that shrouded table, Devlin Bane stepped out from behind the curtain. His gaze zeroed in on her, and he made a beeline straight across the room.

"Laurel, his IV is running out," he said, his eyes boring a hole straight through Sasha. "Before you go, though, can Sasha and I borrow your office for a few minutes?"

Laurel stood up. "Sure, but if you can't keep your voice down to a dull roar, take the discussion somewhere else. My patients need their rest. Especially him."

Who *was* it behind that curtain?

"We'll use the scan room. It's soundproof."

Without waiting to see if Sasha followed him, he cut back across the room toward a door in the far corner. Laurel rolled her eyes and then patted Sasha on the shoulder.

"Don't worry, he's not nearly as scary as he likes to think he is." Her broad grin invited Sasha to share the fun of yanking her husband's chain a bit. "On the other hand, he is loud. You might want these for your ears. I find they help."

Sasha smiled and reluctantly accepted the pair of cotton balls. "Guess I'll go see what's on his mind."

Laurel walked with her. "Just remember he gets like this when his buddies are hurting."

The Paladin on the nearest table joined the conversation. "Yeah, he's one big teddy bear. I can't tell you how much it meant to me when he threatened to kick my ass up and down the hall if I didn't get better damned quick." He feigned wiping a tear from his eye. "I get all choked up just thinking about it."

Laurel stopped long enough to fluff the Paladin's pillow for him. "Yeah, I know, Lonzo. It's embarrassing when the big guy gets all mushy."

Her patient laughed and then winced. "Ouch. That sucks. I always forget how much a gut wound hurts when I laugh."

Then his expression turned serious as he gestured toward the nearby curtain. "How's he doing? Any change?"

"He's no worse, so that's good. I'll keep you posted."

"Thanks, Doc." Lonzo settled back against his pillow and closed his eyes with a sigh. "When he wakes up, tell him this isn't going to get him out of working."

Sasha smiled at the typical guy way of showing concern. The man must have been badly hurt if his injury was worse than Lonzo's. She wished she could think of something to say that would express her appreciation for his sacrifice, as well as his friend's. She also wanted to ask him about the note, but now wasn't the time. Instead, she braced herself and hurried over to where Devlin stood waiting.

She stepped into the scan room, feeling more than a little claustrophobic when he shut the door. Devlin was a big man, broad-shouldered and well over six feet. She found herself mentally comparing him to Larem, who was nearly as tall but built along much leaner lines. She bet Devlin fought with brute strength, whereas Larem's style was graceful but deadly.

Devlin motioned for her to sit down on the patient bed while he took the desk chair. It creaked in protest when he leaned back and crossed his arms over his chest.

"You want to tell me what the hell happened yesterday?" His green eyes burned through her, as if he could read the truth even before she spoke.

She gave it to him, short and sweet. "I assumed a note I found was from Lonzo, but evidently it wasn't. To make matters worse, I lost it down in the tunnels, so I can't even prove the thing actually existed. Saying I'm sorry for what happened after that won't fix a damn thing, but I am. But that doesn't change the fact that things went to hell, and not just for me."

"No shit." Devlin leaned forward, resting his elbows on his knees. "But I need details so I can do damage control."

She could see the same signs of near exhaustion etched on his face as those that marked his wife's. Somehow that made him seem more approachable.

She'd been staring at her hands, then she looked up. "God, Devlin, in all these years no one ever told me the barrier was so unbelievably beautiful. All those impossible colors, the power of it humming all around you, drawing you in."

There was a bit of sympathy in Devlin's world-weary eyes even though his voice had turned cold. "Beautiful, yeah, but also damn deadly. You can get lost in all that wonder and forget that if the barrier doesn't fry you, the bastards waiting on the other side will slice and dice you and then dance in your blood."

His angry words lashed out at her, but she could hardly blame him when he'd lived so many years watching that happen.

She gave him a quick summary of the day's events. As she finished, tears burned down her cheeks, but she ignored them. "Thank goodness Larem found me. He tried to talk those Others into letting me go. They wouldn't listen, so then they fought."

She closed her eyes as if that could block out the memory. "God, I've never seen anything like it."

She wouldn't have been down there at all if she hadn't insisted on seeing the tunnels for herself. That truth hung heavy between them.

She forced the rest of the story out, lancing the wound in her mind. "Until yesterday, I hadn't realized Larem was . . . is one of the Kalith you've been sheltering. He hadn't told me, either, but I guess I can't blame him for that."

"No, you can't. But now you know they're not that different from us, Sasha. Hell, we Paladins even share some of their gene pool."

That fact had rocked their world when it had come

out a few years earlier. She replied, "I knew about the common DNA, but all I've ever heard about the people from Kalithia is that they were out of their heads, monsters out to kill anybody and anything that crosses their path. Larem's certainly not like that."

Devlin nodded. "There's a huge difference between the Kalith warriors and those crazy bastards we call Others. Larem, Barak, and Lusahn are all three highly trained warriors. I'd trust any of them at my back anytime. I don't know if that's what you want to hear, but it's the truth."

"I believe that, Devlin." She finally wiped at the tears still streaming down her face. "It hurt Larem so much to kill his own kind—and he did it because of me. I'm not sure he'll ever forgive me for putting him in that position, even though it was unintentional. Heck, I'm not sure I'll ever forgive myself."

Devlin tossed her a box of tissues. "He'll get over it. Just give him time. Besides, once he found out you were down there, there would've been no stopping him.

"Back in Kalithia they have Sworn Guardians, an elite militia made up of highly trained warriors. Both Barak and his sister Lusahn were Guardians, and Larem served as one of Lusahn's Blademates. Their job was to protect their people, and they take that calling very seriously."

"How did Larem end up living here?" She was certain he wouldn't have walked away from his duty to his people lightly.

"That's his story to tell, not mine."

Okay, so they both had secrets about Larem to protect. She went on, "I haven't talked to him since."

But she hadn't stopped thinking about him or that kiss.

"Needless to say, I was pretty much a wreck after what happened. Now that I've had a chance to calm down, I'd like to thank him. Do you know how I can get in touch with him?"

For the first time, Devlin didn't meet her gaze directly. "That might have to wait awhile."

She froze, unable to move, as all the jagged pieces started to fall into place. Lonzo's worry about his friend. The curtained-off area. Devlin's questions.

"Devlin, what happened to Larem after I left?"

He drew a deep breath and let it out slowly. "He came looking for me in the triage area outside the elevator, where we bring all the wounded and the dead. He wanted to fill me in on things, but his timing wasn't the best. We lost a couple of guards yesterday, which is always extra hard on everyone. Paladins mostly come back from fatal wounds, but for guards, dead is dead.

"One of their buddies took the news badly, and when he saw Larem standing there, he lost it. We subdued the guy and shoved a tranq in his arm, but not before he severed Larem's femoral artery. We almost didn't get him to Laurel in time."

Sasha couldn't catch her breath, couldn't think, couldn't scream no matter how badly she wanted to.

"Oh no you don't, woman!" Devlin rolled to his feet and shoved her head down between her knees. "Come on, Sasha, don't faint on me!"

He reached back to hit a button on the console behind him. "Laurel, get me a wet rag and smelling salts or some such shit."

Seconds later, the door banged open and Devlin's wife charged in. "Darn it, Devlin, I don't have time for this. What did you do to her? You can't yell at Sasha like you do your men."

Poor Devlin. Sasha managed to draw in enough air to defend him. "He didn't yell."

"Then what's wrong?" Laurel pressed a cool cloth against the back of Sasha's neck.

"He told me about Larem."

By then, Sasha had straightened up enough to see the look exchanged between Laurel and Devlin. What were they thinking?

"Just tell me he's going to be okay."

Laurel answered, "It's been touch and go, but he's stable now. We have him sequestered because it bothers some of the Paladins when they regain consciousness and sense a Kalith nearby."

Then she sat down beside Sasha. "Their blood is different enough from ours that we didn't want to transfuse him with either human or Paladin blood. Barak donated a pint for him, but it wasn't enough. We had to make do with plasma and IV fluids, and then let nature take its course. Luckily, Larem has some of the same ability to heal as the Paladins do."

"Can I see him?"

Again the looks flew between Laurel and Devlin. He arched a brow and she frowned. Finally, Laurel slowly nodded.

"Okay, but here's the deal. If he's awake, I'll ask him

if he wants to see you, and whatever he says goes. If he's asleep, you can take a quick peek, but then you're out of there. Right now, Larem needs rest more than he needs company."

She softened that last remark with a small smile, but it still hurt more than it should have. There was no way Sasha would do anything that would adversely affect Larem's recuperation. Still, she couldn't fault the Handler for her caution. It was her job to protect her patients, no matter which side of the barrier they'd been born on.

Trying to appear calmer than she felt, Sasha nodded. "Whatever is best for Larem."

While she waited, she turned back to Devlin and brought up another subject. "I'm guessing you haven't had much time to work on your list of suggestions for me. With your men still on the mend, you're short-handed right now, so screw the report. It can wait."

Devlin gave her a weary smile. "Thanks, I appreciate the attitude. Shouldn't be more than a day or two before we're back up to full strength—as long as the barrier decides to behave."

Then the Paladin patted her on the back. "This thing with Larem was not your fault. When I find the bastard who was playing games with you, I'll skewer him myself."

She appreciated the sentiment, but it sure felt as if she was partly to blame. "Larem wouldn't have been there if it wasn't for me."

"Yeah, but the guard who attacked him has a reputation of hating our Kalith friends. If the guy was bent on revenge, he could've just as easily attacked Larem some other time."

"Maybe, but—"

Before Sasha could say more Laurel stuck her head back into the room. "Come on. He's asleep."

"I'll be right there." Sasha started for the door, then stopped to look back at Devlin. "Thanks for everything you and your men do for us all, Devlin. I figure that doesn't get said nearly enough."

He actually grinned. "Or at all."

"Then I'll add that to my list of things that should be changed around here. If there's anything you need, don't hesitate to ask."

As she walked away, Devlin stretched out on the cot in the scan room, probably to stay close to his men. She closed the door softly and headed straight toward the curtain that separated Larem from the rest of the wounded.

"I think Devlin is conking out in the scan room," she whispered to Laurel.

"I figured he might. He hates to go far when there are this many of his men down. Mine isn't the only lab that's full right now."

Laurel motioned for Sasha to follow her. "It's better that you don't stay long. And speaking as a doctor, you should take it easy for a day or two yourself. Physically you might be fine, but emotionally is a whole different matter. Try to get away from the office this weekend and do something relaxing. If you need to talk, give me a call."

"Thanks, Laurel." She gestured toward the wounded

men resting across the room. "All things considered, I don't have much to complain about."

"You sound just like Devlin. He bleeds for his men even when he isn't one of the wounded himself. Go check on your friend. I've got a few things to finish up before my boss relieves me."

If Sasha wasn't mistaken, that was approval she saw in Laurel's eyes. "I promise to keep the visit short."

Now that the moment was upon her, she found herself reluctant to step beyond the curtain that sheltered Larem from the rest of the world. Talk about cowardly. Shaking her head in disgust, she moved the thin fabric out of her way.

Once again the tears started. His complexion, always pale, now had a bluish undertone that couldn't be good. She cataloged his condition, noting that they had him hooked up to drains and IVs, and machines to monitor his recovery. Gone was the intensely vital warrior who had fought for her life. And in his place, there was this . . . this bruised and battered man who looked all too fragile. Was it really less than twenty-four hours ago?

She gently brushed a soft lock of his long hair back from his forehead. Coal black shot through with silver was such an odd color to frame such a young face. She doubted he was more than a year or two older than she was.

Her father would probably freak out big-time if she were to admit that she found a Kalith handsome. Heck, it wasn't all that long ago that she would've laughed at the idea herself.

But not now.

She whispered a small prayer for his quick recovery. It was time to leave, although she did so reluctantly. Somebody should stay close by in case Larem needed anything, but she'd promised to keep her visit short. Maybe Laurel would allow her to return tomorrow if she kept her word and left quickly.

"Sleep tight, Larem. Get well fast." She gave the sleeping man's hand a gentle squeeze before bolting for the exit. The last thing she needed was for him to wake up and find her crying.

Chapter 8

*L*arem hoped she was gone. He wasn't sure how much longer he could fake being asleep. Not with Sasha's hand on his, her soft voice whispering near his ear. At first he'd thought it was a dream, just another in a long line that he'd had since first meeting her. But no, he was hurting too much for this to be anything other than reality.

He slowly inhaled and immediately recognized the blood and chemical stench of Laurel Young's medical lab. For a few seconds he was confused about how he came to be stretched out on one of her stainless steel tables before it all came trickling back. Talking to Devlin about what had happened down in the tunnels. Someone swinging a sword—a guard maybe. Trahern protecting Larem from further attack.

Then periods of total oblivion mixed with the occasional vague awareness of pain. Voices—some familiar, some not. He hated knowing he'd been at the mercy of strangers. Granted, he trusted Laurel Young, but he didn't know how her coworkers felt about having a wounded Kalith for a patient.

The whole idea left him feeling vulnerable. With that in mind, he moved his arm enough to realize he wasn't chained down as the Paladins usually were. Good. Not that he could muster much of a defense if he was attacked.

He heard footsteps. Someone was coming, but not Sasha. He quickly closed his eyes just in case. A draft of cool air washed over him as his visitor pulled the curtain back.

"You can open your eyes now, Larem. She left."

Relieved that it was Laurel Young, he did as she said. He had questions for her but found it hurt too much to talk. He managed a hoarse whisper. "Water?"

"Sure thing." Evidently his request pleased her, because she was smiling when she held a straw to his lips. "Take little sips."

The chill of the water slid down his throat, soothing away the dry pain. The effort it took to swallow pretty much sapped what little energy he had. He closed his eyes briefly and tried again. "Status?"

Laurel set the glass aside and checked his breathing and pulse with her usual efficiency. Her fingers felt strong and impersonal against his skin, unlike the warmth of Sasha's brief touch. The comparison bothered him. He shouldn't be thinking about Sasha at all. Not after the events of . . . when?

"How long?"

Laurel finished her cursory examination and looped

her stethoscope around her neck. "Since yesterday afternoon. We had to surgically repair your femoral artery. At least your Kalith healing ability has finally kicked in, so you're well on your way to making a full recovery."

She adjusted the flow of the plastic bag of fluids that hung on a pole at the head of his table. "We gave you a unit of Barak's blood to make up for the puddle you left behind on the floor. I'll check your blood count later, but it's been climbing steadily."

No wonder he felt as if he'd been run over and left for dead. "Anyone else?"

Laurel bit her lower lip before answering. "Well, you know how the Paladins like a good party. Once one of them gets to come hang out with me, they all want to come. Lonzo is still here. Which reminds me, he said to tell you this wouldn't get you out of doing chores. If you want to argue the point, I'll wheel him over to see you as soon as he feels up to it."

"It's my week to do the laundry." But then fear for his friend sent a shard of new pain ripping through Larem's chest. "Is he badly hurt?"

"He was. He's better, just like every other Paladin who managed to get himself cut up the past couple of days." She reached to offer Larem water again.

"We also lost a couple of the guards. Sorry, I don't mean to be such a downer."

She held the straw to his lips. "I'm going off duty for a few hours as soon as I'm done here with you, but my boss will be around to check on you while I'm gone. If you need anything, press the button there on the side rail. If Dr. Neal is busy, my technician Kenny will come running."

Larem took a long drink. "Thanks."

The Handler seemed reluctant to leave. She insisted on fluffing his pillow and then adjusted the light overhead. What was she trying not to say?

"Laurel, spit it out, even if you think I won't like it. I can't put up much of a fight right now even if it does make me mad. Later maybe, though." He held up a shaky fist to demonstrate.

She stopped fiddling with the dials on the monitors and turned to face him. "Okay, hard-ass. Here it is."

Laurel bent down to whisper in his ear, reminding him that the curtain only gave the illusion of privacy. They weren't alone, and any Paladins who were awake could hear every word if they weren't careful. Laurel knew that better than most, so he'd have to trust her judgment on the matter.

"Sasha Willis stopped by to see me and ended up telling Devlin everything about what happened between the two of you yesterday. That's how she found out you'd been hurt. I don't mean to be telling tales out of school, but she took it hard."

Sasha told Devlin everything? Somehow Larem doubted that. She'd never want anyone to find out she'd knowingly let a Kalith touch her—or that she'd liked it.

"That's okay." What else could he say?

"The thing is, I think she'll be back. You know, to check on your progress." There was a great deal of curiosity in Laurel's dark eyes, but she was too tactful to press for details.

"Thanks for the warning."

"If you don't want to see her, I can tell her that I've restricted visitations until you're fully recovered."

Oh, he wanted to see Sasha all right. Too much, in fact. But considering he'd been attacked by a guard, feelings were already running high against him right now. The last thing she needed was to be seen favoring the enemy.

"She's just feeling obligated because of what happened." And he didn't need her gratitude, *especially* because of what had happened.

Laurel's eyes narrowed in obvious doubt. "We'll see how you feel about it tomorrow. We don't get a lot of visitors anyway, so I can honestly say that we're not really set up for it. I need my patients to get all the rest they can while they're here."

Laurel stood back up and laid the back of her hand on his forehead. "No fever. You're definitely on the mend. I'm glad, Larem. Very glad. Now get some sleep. You'll need all the energy you can get to duke it out with Lonzo over the whole laundry thing."

"Tell him to bring it on."

"I'll do that. Right now, though, a feather could knock both of you over. It wouldn't be much of a contest, so I won't be starting a betting pool anytime soon."

"Don't blame you." He was a healer himself and recognized when someone else was running on empty. "I'll be fine, Laurel. Go get some rest."

"Nag."

"Somebody should."

He managed to hold on to consciousness until her

footsteps faded into the distance, leaving behind only the soft chorus of beeping machines to lull him to sleep. And if the last thought he had was of Sasha, well, no one had to know.

Contrary to Dr. Young's advice, Sasha was back in the office bright and early Saturday morning. She'd already lost too many hours over the past couple of days to take the whole weekend off as well. At least she had the place to herself for the moment.

Where to start? E-mail first and then she'd follow up with D.J. to see if he'd made any progress. Later, maybe she'd take a short break and go back downstairs to the lab and check on the status of Laurel's patients, one in particular.

As she logged in to her account, she sipped her white chocolate latte with cinnamon and whip, postponing having to wade through the unending barrage of e-mails. Back home, her local barista had laughingly called the combination a "Sasha special." Hopefully she'd be living in Seattle long enough to become a regular at the coffee shop here, too. That would be nice.

A knock on the door startled her out of her reverie. "Come in!" she called.

D. J. Clayborne stuck his head inside the door. "Hi. I thought I'd let you know I'm back working on the bastard's records this morning. Didn't want to freak you out if you heard me banging around next door."

"I appreciate the warning, D.J." She picked up her coffee. "Can I see what you're working on? I promise not to hover."

"Sure thing. Give me a few minutes to get started first."

The Paladin took off for Kincade's old office at just short of a run, which seemed to be his only speed. Even when he was sitting at the computer, he was always in motion—foot tapping, his hand pounding the desk with a rhythm only he could hear, anything to burn off some of his endless supply of energy.

A few minutes later, she heard D.J. start cursing a blue streak. She hurried into the adjacent office to find him staring at the computer screen with the strangest look on his face.

"D.J., what's wrong?"

When he didn't immediately answer, she moved closer, careful not to startle him. "What's up?"

D.J. finally looked up and blinked. Then he shook his head as if to clear it and shrugged. "Sorry, Sasha, it's nothing to do with you. Just a strange e-mail. I've gotten a couple lately I haven't been able to figure out. I suspect it's a Paladin friend yanking my chain."

His smile turned wicked as he rubbed his hands together. "Once I manage to track them back to him, there will be hell to pay. I'll fry more than just his damn hard drive."

Then he looked chagrined. "Oops, probably shouldn't have said that in front of you. Don't suppose you could forget you heard anything?"

All she could do was laugh at the incorrigible hacker. "Heard what? I'm just standing here enjoying my coffee and watching you working hard to decipher Kincade's files."

D.J.'s eyes twinkled with good humor as his fingers flew over the keyboard. "Yes, ma'am, that's exactly what I'm doing. I expect to make some solid progress, too, because I'm all about staying on task. Just ask Devlin."

D.J. went from playful to predator, leaning forward to study the screen. "Gotcha, you bastard."

He pulled out his cell phone. "Cullen, get your worthless ass over to the admin building now. I'm in Kincade's old office, and I'm going to need your help with this."

Cullen was the other computer whiz among the local Paladins. Rumor had it that between him and D.J., there wasn't a server in the world that would be safe if they decided to go on the prowl.

Sasha moved closer. "Did you find something interesting?"

"What?" He actually looked surprised to see she was still there. "Yep, I've found Kincade's offshore bank accounts. Cullen's actually better with tracking that kind of thing than I am, although not by much. We might just be able to strip those accounts and get back some of our own. But if I'm reading this right, Kincade had some playmates."

D.J. studied the screen again. "We'll also see where these transfers lead us. It's too early to start pointing fingers, but a couple originated in the Regents' server in . . ."

He paused as if trying to choose his words carefully. Sasha waited for a second and then prodded him. "Originated where?"

He swallowed hard and answered. "Admin in St. Louis. But, hey, that could be misleading. Kincade was damn good at hiding his tracks, so this might be a false trail."

A shiver of dread washed over her, as if someone had just tromped on her grave. The last thing they all needed was for this mess to lead back to another Regent, not to mention there were only a handful stationed in the St. Louis sector. Fewer still when she eliminated the two she trusted implicitly—her father and her Uncle George. She wasn't about to start pointing fingers at any of their close associates without having hard evidence to back up the accusation.

But neither was she here to protect the guilty. "D.J., we need to nail these guys whoever they are. If you do get any of the money back or the names of Kincade's accomplices, the steak dinner's on me. Your choice of restaurants. Cullen, too."

"It's a deal."

He went on keyboarding, muttering under his breath as he did so.

Time to get back to her own work. Once she made some headway, she'd take a brief break and check in with Laurel. By now, most of the Paladins should be up and about. According to the morning reports, the barrier had finally stabilized long enough for everyone to have a peaceful night.

Well, except for her. Her dreams had been full of nightmarish images of Others chasing her through the darkness, blood dripping from their swords, their pale eyes flaring with the need to kill. The strange part was that she hadn't just been running from them but toward someone else. She'd awakened with her heart pounding right before turning that final corner to safety. Rather than be relieved the nightmare had ended, she'd been disappointed because she hadn't gotten even a glimpse of who had been waiting for her.

Although she could guess.

As soon as she sat back down at her desk, her cell phone rang. She almost let it go to voice mail now that she'd finally gotten into a productive rhythm. Unfortunately her conscience wouldn't let her ignore it for long. As the representative for the Regents, she needed to be available twenty-four/seven. Lives could depend on it.

A glance at the caller ID eliminated that possibility, not when her godfather was calling. Hopefully he and her father wouldn't make a habit of checking up on her every day or two. She gave up and answered.

"Hi, Uncle George, what's up?"

Evidently her lack of enthusiasm showed in her voice. George laughed and said, "Gee, why don't you try to contain your excitement, Sasha? You wouldn't want me to think you're happy to hear from me or anything."

She winced. "Okay, my bad. I'm trying to wade through an unbelievable number of e-mails, most of which say nothing and accomplish even less."

"Welcome to the world of upper management, my dear. I take it you're in the office and not out enjoying the day."

"I originally planned to stop by the office for just a

few minutes but decided to put in a couple of hours to clear a few things off my desk."

"Well, at least try to get out in the sun for a while. That is, if it ever actually shines in Seattle. Any truth to the rumor that people there don't tan, they rust?"

She grinned. "You know, I think that's a rumor the people out here started to discourage others from moving here. It's been sunny and warm since I arrived."

"Okay, if you say so. But speaking as your favorite honorary uncle, I'm hoping you don't like it too much."

Without waiting for her to respond, he went on. "At least I see the barrier has stabilized, so that's good."

"Yeah, it is. I was going to stop by the labs on my way out to see how the wounded are doing." She paused. "We lost two guards, so that's been tough on everyone."

"Rumor has it that another problem almost got solved." George's voice turned chilly. "Too bad that didn't work out."

Sasha's brow furrowed. "What problem was that?"

"I understand that one of the guards almost eliminated one of Seattle's pet Others. I suppose they've even wasted our limited resources patching up the bastard. Far better for all concerned if they'd let him bleed out and die. Good riddance all around."

She couldn't believe her ears. How could anyone even begin to think Larem's death would be beneficial? George's disappointment was beyond disgusting.

As tempting as it was to rip into him for his callous attitude, she had to learn how he'd found out about the attack so quickly. She sure hadn't said anything and seriously doubted that either Devlin or Laurel would've reported the incident. The last thing any of the locals wanted to do was draw attention to the Kalith living among them.

"Wow, the grapevine must be in full swing. How did you hear about that so quickly? I just learned about it myself late yesterday." She kept her voice neutral, aiming for mildly curious rather than outraged.

It didn't work.

"It must have been in one of the reports that came in this morning—maybe from the medical team." George rustled a bunch of papers in the background. "I can't seem to put my finger on it at the moment."

Yeah, right. She knew him better than that. The man had a mind like a filing cabinet with every bit of information sorted, categorized, and easily retrievable. He obviously had no intention of telling her how he'd found out. Fine, but at least she now knew there was a spy here who reported back to Uncle George and most likely her father, too.

She'd drop the matter for now. George wouldn't tell her anything he didn't want her to know, and there was no use in antagonizing him. Even so, she was furious. She'd like to think she'd feel the same way no matter who'd been attacked, but that would be a lie.

Did her father agree with her godfather's sentiment? Would he feel different if he knew that Larem had fought long and hard to save her life? She couldn't share that information with George, though, without admitting she'd managed to get herself trapped in the tunnels. If the spy hadn't told him, neither would she. Odd, though, that the guy had reported the incident involving Larem but obviously hadn't mentioned her part in it.

Better to change subjects. "Well, I'd better go if I want to get out of here anytime soon. By the way, did Dad tell you I might have found a condo to rent?"

"Well, my feelings on that subject are on a par with your father's, but we both know you'll make your own decisions. Even so, it seems like a lot of effort when you have no idea how long you'll actually have to be there."

Yeah, she did know how they felt. She really didn't want to be reminded that her assignment might only be temporary, but at least she'd diverted his focus from the attack on Larem.

"Take care and don't spend the whole day in the office reading reports either. Go play golf or something."

"Don't worry, I won't be here much longer." George was back to shuffling the papers again. "Don't forget to keep me posted on your progress in deciphering Kincade's accounts."

"Take care and don't spend the whole day in the office reading reports either. Go play golf or something."

"Don't worry, I won't be here much longer." George was back to shuffling the papers again. "Remember to keep me posted on your progress in deciphering Kincade's files."

"There's nothing to report." Yet. Nothing concrete, anyway. No use in stirring up a hornets' nest until she knew more.

After they exchanged good-byes, she hung up. The

conversation had left her unsettled. Rather than delve back into her e-mail, she decided to see if Cullen Finley and D.J. had made any strides.

Sasha shut down her laptop and packed it up to take with her. After turning off the lights, she headed down the hall.

She paused to listen to the rumble of two male voices, laughing when D.J. suddenly whooped loudly and shouted, "Why you sneaky SOB!" Cullen's response was quieter but clearly just as excited.

Both of them looked up as soon as she stepped through the door. Cullen smiled at her. "Hey, Sasha, look what we found!"

They made room so she had a clear view of the computer screen. "Kincade wasn't just ripping off the Kalith by letting them buy their way into our world. The greedy SOB was also stealing directly from the Regents."

Cullen pointed at a line of numbers. "Not only that but D.J. was right about Kincade making deposits into accounts that lead straight back to St. Louis. Now we know for sure he wasn't alone in this. If we can follow the money trail, we might just find out who else is involved."

"Think you can do that?"

D.J. acted insulted. "Hey, you're not dealing with amateurs here. As long as you're sure you want us to see where this leads us, given enough time, we'll nail them."

She believed him. "Keep me posted. For now, I'd like to keep this between the three of us. Well, make that four since I figure I'm second on your list of people to call, right after Devlin."

"We will." Cullen's eyes had a teasing glint in them. "And who knows, we might even call you first."

"Yeah, right, like that's going to happen," she said, laughing. "I'm out of here. Lock the office when you leave."

Before she reached the door, two cell phones rang, neither of them hers. Both Paladins answered at the same time.

"On our way!"

Her pulse sped up as both men shed their good humor, revealing the deadly warriors beneath the façade. Cullen quickly shut down the computer.

"What happened?" she asked.

"Lacey called Devlin from the geology lab to warn him that she's seeing fluctuations in the energy levels down near St. Helens. We're heading there to beef up the coverage just in case."

She shuddered, the memory of the battle she'd witnessed all too clear in her mind. "Do you need a ride back to your headquarters? My car is parked in the garage next door."

Cullen stood up. "Thanks for the offer, but I've got my car here, too."

"We'll be back." D.J. picked up a duffel she hadn't noticed earlier. It clunked when he slung the strap over his shoulder. No doubt his portable weapons stash.

She had a powerful urge to hug the two men. It would probably only embarrass them, and she really didn't know either of them well enough to presume.

She settled for saying, "Be careful out there, guys."

"We always are," D.J. said, winking at her on his way out the door.

Somehow she doubted the truth of that statement, but she didn't call him on it. Instead, she headed downstairs to Laurel's lab. She caught herself pausing to check her hair in the gleaming stainless steel door. God, how dumb was that? She was here to check on the status of the injured, not to make an impression on anyone.

But, even so, her hands shook as she pushed open the door.

"Checkmate."

Larem tried not to smirk at his roommate's defeat, but it was hard. Lonzo leaned forward to study the board, obviously still trying to figure how Larem had managed to corner his king.

"Listen, you alien jerk, you must have cheated. Did you move the pieces around when I wasn't looking?" Lonzo started resetting the board. "This time I'll keep my eyes on you the whole time. Try anything again, and I'll get someone to sneak in my sword past the guards."

Larem sipped his glass of ice water. "Is it my fault you left your queen vulnerable? Perhaps you should ask Cullen for some tips, or even D.J."

Normally Lonzo would've taken offense at the suggestion that anyone—especially D.J.—could show him up in chess. However, right now his roommate was too busy staring at something across the room to respond.

"Lonzo? Is something wrong?"

"Not really. Sasha Willis just walked in, and it looks like our favorite Handler is not so happy to see her. What's up with that?"

Larem wasn't about to tell Lonzo that Laurel knew he was reluctant to see Sasha again. His roommate already knew that Larem had broken protocol by going down into the tunnels to save her. It was what happened afterward that he had no intentions of confessing.

Time to redirect Lonzo's attention. Tapping the game board with his finger, Larem asked, "Are we going to play or not?"

"Yeah, we are." Lonzo moved his pawn and then looked past Larem again. "Or maybe not."

Someone was coming toward them—Dr. Young, not Sasha. Larem knew it without even looking. "Can we finish this game later?"

"If I'm still here." Lonzo grinned at him. "Laurel is threatening to kick me out this afternoon. Said she wants the space for someone who really needs it."

Larem countered Lonzo's move, mostly to postpone dealing with the problem over by the door. "Guess that means you'll have to do the laundry this week. She already said I should stay here until tomorrow."

Lonzo shoved another pawn off its square. "Fat chance. The dirty clothes can wait until you get home."

Laurel stepped around the table so that she was facing Larem. "Sorry to interrupt the game, guys. Lonzo, I need to check you over before I sign off on your discharge. I might need the bed space."

The Paladin went cold. "Son of a bitch, what happened this time?"

"Nothing so far. Lacey sent out a notice that the energy levels are fluctuating again south of here." Laurel looked grim. "I want to make sure I'm ready. You know, just in case."

Lonzo swept the chess pieces back into a beat-up box, added the board, and then jammed the lid back on. "Sorry, Larem."

"Not a problem."

When Lonzo was gone, Larem turned his attention to Dr. Young, still all too aware of the woman who was hovering just out of sight behind him. "Doc, make sure Lonzo knows you're not releasing him to join the fight. He was still wincing in pain and rubbing his side when he thought I wouldn't notice."

Laurel's eyes narrowed as she watched Lonzo make his way back to his bed. "That sneaky jerk! And he's been complaining nonstop about me keeping him so long. I should've known better than to trust him. You two might get to finish that chess game after all."

Then she dropped her voice. "Sasha Willis wants to make sure you're on the mend. Okay if I send her over?"

"Sure." He wanted to know how she was doing, too.

Before walking away, Laurel motioned for the other woman to come forward, pulling the curtain partly closed. "This is the first time Larem's been up for any length of time. I don't want him to overdo."

"I won't stay long. I promise."

Sasha stood in front of him. As she stared into his eyes, her hand fluttered down to gently rest on his arm. "I thought I'd stop by to see if you needed anything."

He savored the small contact and slowly moved to cover her hand with his own, afraid she'd step back out of reach. Yes, there was something he needed. Before Sasha came into his life, it had been a long, long time since anyone had actually held him, touched him, kissed him.

Two days ago he'd been out of control and out of his mind. What had he been thinking when he'd latched on to this woman and poured everything he had into that kiss? More importantly, though, what had *she* been thinking when she kissed him back?

Not that it mattered, not if he'd become a target for the guards. The last one who'd gone rogue had tried to kill Laurel. It had taken the unlikely alliance of Barak q'Young and Devlin Bane to save her. Larem wouldn't put Sasha in the same kind of danger. He had to drive a wedge between them and make a clean break of things.

He gave her the only answer he could. "I have everything I need."

She actually looked disappointed as she peeked out at the remaining Paladin patients.

Finally, she looked back at him. "Laurel says everyone is on the mend, including you. You definitely look better than when I stopped by yesterday."

"She'd mentioned that you'd been in to check on the wounded."

Although he bet he was the only one she'd actually touched, even cried over. His skin tingled with the remembered feeling of her gentle fingers against his when she'd thought he was asleep.

Sasha stepped back and shoved her hands in the pockets of her jacket. "Yes, well, it's my job to make sure everyone was all right—the guards, the Paladins, and the—"

"Other?" he offered when she hesitated. He knew

she didn't see him that way, but he couldn't let them get any closer.

"Darn it, Larem, don't put words in my mouth. You're not one of them. You forget, I've seen the difference up close and personal."

Despite the anger blazing in Sasha's eyes, she'd dropped her voice to a whisper. He did the same.

"You can tell yourself that if you want. Does it make it easier for you to stomach the fact that you let yourself be kissed by one? Touched by one? Remember that night at the zoo?"

"I haven't forgotten a single moment of our time together."

Neither had he, but that changed nothing. He eased his feet down onto the floor, determined to finish this conversation standing up.

Still conscious of the fact they weren't exactly alone, he leaned in close and whispered near her ear, "Sorry if it bothers you so much, Sasha, but it's nothing less than the truth. Kalith, Other—the words don't matter because they don't change what I am. Maybe it makes me sick to think that I kissed a human. Ever think of that?"

She jerked back as if his words had been a physical blow. "No, I can't say that I did. Sorry I've burdened you with my human cooties. I didn't realize you aliens found us so repugnant."

He watched in grim silence as she stalked away, her back rigid, anger obvious in each step she took. She picked up the computer case and purse she'd left by the exit and slammed her way through the swinging door. He wanted to charge after her, to admit he hadn't meant what he'd said, but he wouldn't. For her sake, it was the right thing to do.

At least his wounded leg held up until she was out of sight before it gave out on him. He grabbed on to the side of the bed, barely managing to save himself the indignity of hitting the floor. After a few seconds, the room quit spinning enough that he could crawl back up on the cold steel without asking for help.

He stretched out and concentrated on taking long, slow breaths, seeking to center himself, to block out the world and the jagged edges of pain shooting through him. A few seconds later, Laurel appeared at his side with a syringe in her hand.

"This will help you rest."

She made no move, allowing him to make the final decision; taking human drugs was iffy because of his Kalith physiology. This time, though, he'd risk it. A little oblivion sounded damned good right then. He held out his arm so she could inject it through his IV.

"Thanks, Laurel. Maybe it will help."

It wouldn't, not really. But for the next couple of hours he wouldn't have to care.

Chapter 9

*C*haz Willis stared at his reflection in the window, on the whole pleased with what he saw. He prided himself on how far he'd come from his humble roots. It had been an uphill battle to shake the dirt of poverty off his shoes, but he'd done it and never looked back.

Of course, few people had any idea how much power he actually wielded, because the world of the Regents and Paladins was a secret one. He liked that. It meant that there were fewer rules he had to play by, which only made the game that much more fun. After all, the government couldn't regulate what couldn't be openly acknowledged as existing in the first place. Only a handful of highly placed men in each country that housed Paladins knew of their existence—and for good reason.

The clock on the wall tolled the hour, reminding him that his fellow Regents were due to arrive soon. Footsteps approached, their sound muted by the thick

Persian rug on the floor. Chaz turned around to acknowledge the Paladin's presence.

"Excuse me, sir, but I thought you'd like to know I've finished sweeping the house. Everything's clear. If you don't need me for anything else, I'll get out of your way."

"Thanks for coming on short notice, Jake. I'll walk you out." Chaz headed toward the foyer with one of the few men they all trusted to make sure no one had bugged their homes. After all, if the Regents who gathered together couldn't speak freely, then what was the point?

When they reached the front door he said, "Tell Jarvis I appreciate him letting me borrow your services again."

"Not a problem."

With the few minutes Chaz had left before the others arrived, he studied the agenda for the night's meeting. Most was routine, but his fellow Regents were starting to press hard for details about Kincade's escapades and their far-reaching effects on the Seattle sector and beyond.

Unfortunately, Sasha had remained remarkably close-mouthed about her findings so far. After all, she was her father's daughter. She wouldn't tell them a damn thing until she was good and ready. He couldn't fault her for that, even if it was inconvenient for him and his plans.

Luckily, he had his own source busy gathering intelligence out there. Rusty had reported the fighting up and down the I-5 corridor had been incredibly bloody and vicious, although it had finally settled down some. Additionally, a guard had damn near killed one of the pet Kalith. Too bad he'd failed.

A car pulled into his driveway, the first of his guests arriving right on time. Tonight's agenda also included discussion about what to do about Colonel Kincade himself. It really was a damn shame Devlin Bane had let the bastard live. Yes, the Paladin had shown admirable restraint and all that, but he'd left it up to the Regents to decide the traitor's fate.

Unfortunately Kincade knew where a lot of skeletons were buried. Who knew what would happen if he started naming names? They all stood to suffer if that happened. God knows who would be tainted when Kincade was finished. Maybe it would be better for everyone if the bastard were to die in custody. It had happened before.

The doorbell chimed softly. Time to put his game face on.

Duke pounded the heavy bag, his hands aching from the punishment, but he kept going. In his head, he wasn't hitting heavy canvas patched with duct tape at all. No, he was beating the enemy to a bloody pulp.

He stopped the swinging bag with his hands, needing a moment to let his lungs catch up. Thanks to the past few days of fighting, he was tired and sore, but he'd been unable to unwind enough to sleep.

With good reason, too. Every time he closed his eyes, he heard the dying screams of his two friends. There would be no coming back for them, not like the Paladins. God, even after years of fighting beside them, he still couldn't get used to seeing them dead one day and back up walking around the next. It was creepy. Unnatural.

He used to think they were okay, even considered them heroes. But that ended the day Devlin Bane let his prick start making his decisions for him. When that soft-hearted Handler he'd married told him to let that first Kalith live, things had gone to hell and stayed that way.

Duke unleashed his pent-up rage on the bag, pretending it was that bastard Larem. It didn't help.

Another day at the most and Larem would be back on his feet. Duke hadn't been the only one who'd hoped the Kalith's wound would be fatal. But no, just like the Paladins, his ability to heal had kicked in and dragged him back from oblivion. What a fucking damn shame.

One of his fellow guards had tried to do the right thing by ridding the world of the pale-eyed killer and failed. Maybe the next attempt would succeed. With another punch, he imagined the sweet slide of a metal blade through Larem's gut. A bullet would work, too, but where was the fun in that? He wanted that Kalith to die slowly and screaming for mercy, just like the guards had down in the tunnels. And Larem would only be the first.

Right jab, left. Right jab, left.

As he counted down the last of his routine, he thought about the other rumor he'd heard. Something about Sasha Willis. He didn't want to believe it and wasn't sure he did. But, God knows, there was certainly precedent for it.

Yesterday she had stopped by to visit Laurel Young's lab and check on those injured in the fighting. That much was all right. Hell, he'd even applaud her efforts to bolster the morale. It had been too damn long since any of the upper management paid much attention to the grunts in the trenches.

That wasn't the disturbing part. She'd had a long talk with Devlin Bane behind closed doors. Again, okay. But then she'd made a beeline to the curtained-off area where they'd stashed the wounded Kalith. What was up with that? Surely with a Regent for a father she knew better than to mistake the guy for anything but craziness waiting to happen.

But then Lacey Sebastian was shacked up with Barak despite her own brother being a Paladin. Cullen Finley was living with a Kalith woman and her two brats. It was like some kind of disease.

Last two reps—right, left, repeat. Finished. Maybe now he was tired enough to sleep. Picking up his gear, he headed for the showers.

Odd. There was something stuck in the door of his locker—a folded-up piece of paper. He listened hard to see if he was alone. On the way in, he'd passed that new guy, Rusty, but no one else. For sure, the paper hadn't been there earlier.

It creeped him out big-time. What if he'd been cursing the Kalith's name out loud without realizing it? If someone, anyone, had heard him, it could be disastrous. He needed this job no matter how bad things had gotten lately.

If this was some kind of prank, he'd beat the culprit to a bloody pulp. That's what it had to be. Right? Only one way to find out: read the note.

The message was written in block letters: YOU ARE NOT ALONE IN HOW YOU FEEL. WE'LL BE IN TOUCH SOON.

What the hell? Duke spun around, looking for any sign that someone had been watching him. His skin crawled at the possibility. He was still alone in the locker room, but all of a sudden the thought of using the facility's shower lost its appeal. He'd wait until he got home to clean up, then order in a pizza and watch whatever game was on television.

Tomorrow would be soon enough to think about the message and what it might mean. Either way, maybe it was time to look for a new job. Trouble was, he wasn't qualified to do anything but security work, and no one else paid like the Regents did. If he hung in there for just a few more years, he'd walk away with a generous retirement package. That was the carrot at the end of the stick that convinced most of the guards to find some way to cope with all the weirdness connected with their job.

But days like these past few made him seriously wonder if the money was actually worth it. Right now, he'd have to say probably not. With that happy thought, he walked out into the Seattle night.

Sasha paced the length of her hotel room. She'd only wanted to know that Larem was on the mend. That's all. Under the circumstances, she'd felt she owed him that much.

Instead, he'd acted like the biggest jackass ever. What was wrong with him? Sure, he was hurting and justifiably upset about being stabbed by a guard. Did that mean he had to take it out on her? She had no intentions of being a handy target for his anger ever again.

Nope, next time their paths crossed—*if* they crossed—she'd freeze him out.

Yeah, she knew just how that would play out. His pale eyes would look so sad as she brushed past him with only the barest of nods. He'd turn to stare longingly after her, wishing he hadn't acted like such a jerk. She could just see it.

Like that was going to happen. She flopped down on the couch and hugged a pillow. Working up a nice case of righteous indignation was fun and all, but it didn't change the facts. Regardless of Larem's bad behavior, she'd been the one in the wrong. Her actions had put the man—no, the Kalith—in mortal danger not just once but twice.

He knew it, and so did she.

Worrying about him was bad enough, but she also hadn't heard how things were going for the Paladins Devlin had sent south to Mount St. Helens and Mount Adams. Maybe her father had been right to maintain a careful distance from the men who fought and died for the Regents. Knowing they were fighting for their lives was bad enough in the abstract, but knowing them personally took it to a whole new level.

She reached for her laptop, and shot Devlin a quick request for an update. She wrote another message to Lacey Sebastian, hoping the geologist would have good news for her.

Now all she could do was wait. Luckily, she was saved by a knock at the door. She wasn't expecting company, and a quick peek through the peephole wasn't any help. She opened the door only as far as the chain allowed.

"Hi, can I help you?"

The woman looked a bit chagrined. "Okay, I'm betting Laurel didn't get around to calling you. She was supposed to let you know I'd be stopping by. I'm Brenna Nichols. You might have known my father, Judge Nichols."

That was a name Sasha recognized for sure. "Yes, of course. I knew him from my father's poker nights. His death rocked the whole organization."

Brenna's smile drooped a bit. "So I eventually found out."

Sasha could've kicked herself. Judge Nichols had been one of her father's good friends, but he had chosen to keep Brenna ignorant of his secret connection to the Paladins.

Sasha closed the door long enough to unfasten the chain. "Come on in. Can I get you something to drink? Water? Pop? Or I could make coffee."

"Water sounds good. I try to avoid caffeine when Blake's on duty." Brenna sank down in the closest chair with a sigh. "I don't know about you, but I have a hard time relaxing when the guys are on call."

Sasha pulled two bottled waters from the mini fridge and handed one to Brenna. "Yeah, I know what you mean. Back in St. Louis, I didn't actually come into contact with many of the Paladins and never visited their headquarters, so the actual fighting was definitely more abstract."

"Be grateful. Their headquarters down in those caves can be a pretty scary place. Been there, done that, don't want to go back."

Sasha had heard the stories and grinned. "You do have a certain reputation back in Missouri."

"Oh, really?"

Sasha smiled. "Yeah, the general opinion is that no one should ever risk getting between you and Trahern—and he wasn't the one they said people should be afraid of."

Brenna grinned, looking pretty proud of herself. "Blake's worth fighting for."

Sasha thought back to her brief time with David and had to agree with Brenna's assessment. Could Sasha have saved him if she'd been there at his side? She'd never know, but it hurt to think it might have been possible.

She realized that Brenna was watching her. "Sorry, I didn't mean to space out on you."

"No problem, but if I had to guess, I'd say maybe you've had some firsthand experience yourself."

But she also seemed to realize that it wasn't a topic Sasha was ready to talk about, because Brenna immediately changed the subject. Sort of. "I thought you might need to talk about what happened with Larem down in the tunnels."

Sasha winced and sat down on the sofa. "I'd really hoped the whole incident would stay a secret, but that was probably naive. I guess everyone thinks it's my fault he ended up getting hurt so badly."

"Oh, no. No one blames you for that." Brenna moved forward on her chair. "And I didn't hear about it through the rumor mill. Laurel told me because she thought you might like to have another woman to talk to, and she couldn't leave the lab."

That was a relief, though Sasha knew it would get

out eventually. "That was nice of her. I'm not used to being able to talk about my job."

Brenna nodded. "It wasn't until recently that Laurel had any women friends who she could really be honest with for that very reason. Slowly, though, we're building up a nice support group. Besides her and me, there's Lacey, Lusahn, and now Tate Justice. Thank goodness for e-mail. Since all of our men have a tendency to want to smother us, we occasionally rebel and go out on the town together."

Of course, they were all drawn together by their love for the men in their lives. Sasha's situation was different. Then Larem's handsome face flashed through her mind. She shook it away. He had nothing to do with this. It would be nice if they would include her in some of their girls' nights out, and she said so.

Brenna finished the last of her water. "The more the merrier, especially when it makes the guys nervous about what we're actually up to. I did have another reason for dropping in on you. Laurel asked me to take you by to see her condo."

Sasha didn't hesitate. It was the perfect excuse to get out for a while. "That would be great. Let me get my purse."

An hour later, they let themselves out of Laurel's condo and locked the dead bolt. Sasha wanted to boogie right there on the sidewalk. The place was perfect. Absolutely perfect. It was big enough if she ever decided to get a roommate, but cozy enough that she wouldn't rattle around inside it by herself.

"I'll give Laurel a call later and work out the details. I had my stuff put in one of those storage pods, so I can have it shipped out here with just a phone call."

Brenna led the way back to her car. "That was smart of you. I know Laurel will be glad you want to rent the place."

As the two women headed back to the hotel, they passed a man walking along the other side of the street. Something about him caught Sasha's eye. In fact, if she didn't know that Larem was still a patient in Laurel's lab, she would've sworn it was him. She twisted in her seat to look back one last time, but he'd already turned the corner.

Brenna glanced over. "Someone you know?"

"I thought so for a minute, but I guess not."

The last thing she wanted to do was admit that she was imagining the Kalith warrior stalking the streets of Seattle. Time to change the subject.

"So tell me, how is your research into the history of the Paladins coming?"

Larem's leg was killing him as he limped his way down the street and cursed the gods' sense of humor. Couldn't they have made it so that his erratic gift as a healer would at least work better on himself? Yes, his body was repairing itself far faster than a human's would, but it still hurt like hell.

Earlier, he'd waited until Laurel was ripping into Lonzo for lying, to sneak out of the lab. His poor roommate should've known better than to try to put something over on the Handler. Laurel had too much experience with Paladins to let him get by with his ruse.

On the other hand, she had no reason to think Larem would be in any great hurry to vacate the place, especially after his near collapse right after Sasha left. Because of his Kalith metabolism, the pain medication she'd given him hadn't lasted nearly long enough. Once it had worn off, all he could think about was getting the hell out of the lab and back to his duties at the shelter.

The animals he worked with always soothed his restless spirit. All they needed to make them happy was a gentle touch and acceptance. His hand twitched as he remembered how good it had felt to have Sasha squeeze his hand when she thought he was asleep. Maybe that's why he and the dogs got along. They had that much in common.

He walked through the back door of the clinic, doing his best to shrug off the pain and frustration of the past few days. His furry friends had enough problems of their own without having to pick up on his tension. As soon as he started across the room, several heads turned his way. Most weren't human, but one was. Dr. Isaac smiled and headed straight for him.

He clapped Larem on the shoulder. "Hey, I was getting pretty concerned about you. Usually if you're going to miss a shift, you call."

"I'm sorry to have worried you, Doctor." Larem opened his locker and slipped on his lab coat. "I hope my absence didn't cause any problems."

The vet was frowning when Larem turned back toward him. "You're limping. What happened? Are you all right?"

"I injured my leg. It just needed a few stitches." Major surgery, actually, but confessing that would only worry the man. "It happened right before my shift yesterday. I'm sore, but otherwise fine."

"That's good." Then Dr. Isaac jerked his head toward the cages on the far side of the room. "Better check in with Chance over there first thing. He's been staring at the door nonstop. I'd even go so far as to say that he's been missing you. If you can convince him to forgive your transgressions, I'd like to check him over."

Knowing the dog, Larem planned on making a cautious approach. "He'll no doubt make me pay for keeping him waiting."

Yeah, he'd have to make up for lost ground with the temperamental dog. At least that would give Larem something else to focus on other than Sasha's dark eyes and halo of fiery hair.

"Hey, Chance, I'm back."

A quick snarl made it perfectly clear how the dog felt about that. He'd been lying down but immediately lurched to his feet as Larem approached his cage, a growl rumbling deep in his chest. At least he wasn't repeatedly charging against the door of the cage the way he had in the beginning.

Larem dragged a low bench over to the cage and gingerly lowered himself to sit. The position was far from comfortable for his leg, but it beat sitting on the floor. He closed his eyes and turned his focus inward, seeking the warmth and light. His supplies were low, but he was able to pull additional energy from the sunlight streaming in from a skylight.

When he'd amassed enough to share, he turned his gaze on the dog, keeping his attitude neutral. Slowly, he let the healing warmth trickle toward the animal, concentrating on the damaged leg to ease any residual pain. The growling slowed and then disappeared. The trickle became a stream until finally Chance lay back down, his big head resting on his front paws, and his body relaxed.

The two wounded souls sat in peaceful companionship for quite some time. When Larem thought the dog would accept his approach, he stood up and reached for one of the leashes hanging on a peg on the wall. Chance's ears quirked forward as he followed Larem's every movement with interest.

He remained calm when Larem attached the leash and led the way over to the examination table. "Chance, behave yourself, and I'll take you for a long walk."

The dog immediately sat down as if understanding the terms of the deal. Dr. Isaac kept his movements slow and deliberate as he came toward Chance.

"Good boy, this won't take long, I promise."

Larem had been prepared to intervene if the dog decided to act up. But Chance remained still while Dr. Isaac ran expert hands over his fur, only whining a little when the vet pressed and poked his bad leg. Then to everyone's surprise, Chance accepted a couple of treats directly from the doctor's hand as soon as the exam was over.

"He's doing great, Larem. I swear you work magic with my patients. Go ahead, you two. Take your walk, but don't overdo it. It's a nice day and someone should get to soak up some of that sunshine out there."

"We'll be back in a while."

"Take your time. And Larem," Dr. Isaac said, his faded blue eyes twinkling, "one of these days, maybe you'll trust me enough to explain how that secret mojo of yours actually works. In case you're wondering, I do know how to keep a secret."

Then he walked into his office and shut the door, leaving Larem staring after him, both stunned and speechless. At least Dr. Isaac hadn't sounded angry. Would he ever figure these humans out? Probably not.

Finally, Chance whined and tugged on the leash. Larem smiled as he patted the dog on the head. "All right, my friend. Let's take that walk."

Chapter 10

$\mathcal{B}$ack in her hotel room, Sasha couldn't get the image of the man she'd seen on the street out of her head. She wasn't sure why, but she was convinced it had been Larem. Laurel hadn't said anything about him when Sasha had called her about the condo, but then again, she was the man's doctor. Maybe that whole patient confidentiality thing applied.

The good news was that the barrier had finally stabilized, so the Paladins could stand down. Devlin had e-mailed Sasha to say he'd set up a rotating schedule to give everyone a little extra time off. She just hoped the barrier cooperated long enough to give them a chance to catch up on their rest.

Still, neither Devlin nor his wife said a word about Larem. If it had been him, where was he going? He'd been heading in the same direction he'd gone after they'd stopped for coffee.

Maybe she should take a short walk herself. Work

could wait. While the sun was still up, she'd get out and enjoy the fresh air. She pocketed her keys and enough cash for a latte. Outside, the day had grown a little cooler. She could come to really love living here in Seattle. Although she was aware of her father's doubts the Regents would appoint her to the job permanently, that didn't mean she shouldn't do her best to prove him wrong.

Of course, any more "incidents" would crush any chance she had. On some level she didn't regret what had happened despite how horrific it had been. Instead, it only solidified her determination to make things better for the Paladins and their guards. How many of the existing Regents had firsthand experience in what it was like for such brave men?

Very few, she would guess, and that needed to change. Sometimes she thought the Regents were almost petrified. Anything new, any change in how things were done, and they responded by digging in their heels. They hated that Devlin had married a Handler, but five minutes in the couple's company and Sasha had known for certain it was a love match.

Yes, she understood the Regents' concern about the Seattle Paladins allowing Kalith to live in their midst, but again they didn't know any. Granted, she'd only met one, but if Larem was typical of his kind, then she couldn't see how the world was worse off because of his presence.

Now if she could only keep him out of her thoughts for a while. Hoping coffee would help, she hung a right and headed for the nearest coffee shop. Thanks to a short line, she was heading back out the door sipping her favorite combo in just a few minutes.

What next? Certainly, she wouldn't go hunting for the elusive Kalith male who had already made it clear that he wanted nothing to do with her. Maybe Larem was right to feel that way, considering what he had gone through because of her. And there was still the question of who had tricked her into going down into the tunnels alone and why.

The sun had gone behind the clouds, darkening her mood. She did her best to shake off the shadows. Far better that she savor her drink and the sunshine as she walked back to her hotel. No doubt that would be the *smart* thing to do.

Before she reached the end of the block, though, an enormous white dog came barreling around the corner dragging its owner along by its leash. She had no idea what breeds had donated their DNA to produce this particular dog, but the results were definitely intimidating.

Most of the people around her scattered to get out of the dog's way, understandably leery of an animal with teeth that would give the average alligator a run for its money. Not to mention the fact that he probably tipped the scales pretty close to where Sasha herself weighed in.

She'd been so intrigued by the dog, she hadn't yet noticed the owner. The dog came to an abrupt stop right in front of her. When she looked up, she couldn't believe her eyes, and her heart lurched in her chest. Larem. Despite their earlier encounter, she badly wanted to touch him, if only to make sure he was all right.

"Larem? Aren't you supposed to be resting?"

His reaction to seeing her was interesting. If she had to guess, she would've said he looked embarrassed or maybe guilty. "I had things to do."

She held her fingers out to the dog to sniff. "I can see that."

"Be careful, Sasha. Chance isn't particularly fond of people."

But in direct contradiction to Larem's warning, Chance gave Sasha's fingers a quick lick and then plopped his backside down on the sidewalk, clearly in no hurry to get away from her. Moving cautiously, Sasha reached out to scratch the dog's chin, laughing when he groaned and leaned into her hand.

His easy acceptance made her smile. "See, you're not so tough, are you, big guy?"

Then speaking to his two-legged companion, she added, "Would you like me to watch him while you get a cup of coffee?"

It was clear that Larem was hesitant, but finally he handed her the leash. "I'll be right out."

"Take your time. We're doing fine."

Larem really hadn't wanted coffee, but it gave him an excuse to get away from Sasha for a couple of minutes. For sure, he shouldn't have left her alone with Chance. The dog was too unpredictable even if he had been on his best behavior since they had left the clinic.

While waiting for his order, Larem kept a wary eye on the pair outside on the sidewalk. The sunshine brought out the gold highlights in Sasha's hair as she talked to the dog. Chance had his head cocked to the side, looking as if he understood every word she said. With his tail doing a slow sweep back and forth on the sidewalk, Chance was happily soaking up every bit of attention she was offering.

Larem should be pleased the dog was capable of bonding with a human after all he'd suffered at his former owner's hand. But in fact, what he was really feeling was jealous. He should be ashamed of resenting the badly abused animal's ability to charm Sasha, but he wished like hell he was the one she couldn't keep her hands off of.

But he also recognized lonely when he saw it. After all, he lived with it on a daily basis himself. He appreciated the friendship so freely given by Hunter and Lonzo, but that didn't mean he really fit into their world. Sasha had much the same problem. No matter how good her intentions, those she most wanted to help viewed her as an outsider. Trust and friendship might be slow in coming.

"Sir, your coffee."

"Thank you." His respite was over.

After dropping a couple of dollars in the tip jar, he headed for the door. As soon as he walked outside, Chance stood, his wagging tail picking up speed.

"He's a nice dog." Sasha handed the leash back to Larem. "Would you mind if I walked with you?"

Yes, he would, but not for the reasons she might think. But he'd always preferred to face his problems head-on, and she was definitely a problem for him.

"We're not going far. Chance needs exercise, but I

don't want him to overdo it." Not to mention Larem's own leg wasn't back to full strength.

"I noticed he favors one leg. What happened?"

"His former owner used him in dog fights for money."

Sasha gasped. "That's awful! The bastard should be gutted for that!"

Larem agreed with her bloodthirsty reaction. "The police and Animal Control got a tip and were able to break up the ring. Unfortunately, some of the dogs were too far gone to save. Chance was almost one of them. The vet was able to repair the damage, but the dog's lack of trust for anyone on two legs made it difficult to treat him after the anesthesia wore off."

"He obviously trusts you." She hurried her steps long enough to be able to pet the dog's head. "I can't imagine mistreating an animal like that."

"It's taken a lot of hard-fought battles for me to get him this far. You've gotten closer to him in the past fifteen minutes than I did in weeks."

"But you laid the groundwork."

Even so, Sasha seemed pleased by his assessment as they continued down the street. At the end of the block, she stopped. "I'd better go. The past few days have put me behind on a few things. But D.J. and Cullen have managed to make progress on Colonel Kincade's files. He sure left things in total chaos."

No surprise there. "That man was a monster."

One who had played games with lives on both sides of the barrier. His involvement in the theft of the blue stones from Kalithia had led directly to the series of events that destroyed Larem's old life and forced him into this one. Instead of serving his world as an honored warrior, here he was walking a dog. He drew great satisfaction from being able to soothe the wounded spirits of Dr. Isaac's patients. But life in this world wasn't the same and never would be.

"I won't argue that. Unfortunately, Kincade managed to hide his activities so well that no one even suspected what he was up to."

Larem disagreed. "The Paladins certainly knew, but either no one wanted to hear what they had to say on the matter or someone was covering for him."

"Why do you say that?" Sasha came to an abrupt halt. "Do you know something specific or are you just guessing? My father and the other Regents would've done something if they'd known."

All right, either she was gullible or too innocent to see the darkness in others. He suspected it was the latter.

"Sasha, the man got away with robbing my world for *years.* He had to have left a trail, especially when it's obvious that he wasn't working alone. There was the guard who tried to kill Laurel, and that Regent in Missouri who shot Trahern. Not to mention whoever killed that very same Regent before Jarvis and the Paladins were able to interrogate him."

Sasha's pale skin took on an ashen hue. He reached out to steady her, but she jerked back out of his reach. "You're not privy to the inner workings of the Regents."

"No, I'm not." He stepped closer, deliberately crowding her. "But I have personal experience in dealing with what happens when someone decides the rules don't apply to him. If it weren't for Kincade's unbridled greed, I wouldn't be stuck here with you."

Sasha's eyes briefly widened in obvious shock, then narrowed in anger. "Well, I'm sorry for burdening you with my presence."

Chance whined, clearly confused by the sudden change in the atmosphere. He looked from Larem and then back to Sasha. Larem hadn't meant his comment to be an attack on her, but he didn't regret the blunt truth he'd spoken.

"You're not the Regents, Sasha." But she was their representative, and they both knew it.

"No, but I hope to be one, and I respect the work they've done and what they stand for."

He flexed his hands, trying to control his temper. "Don't ask me to cheer them on when their successes are written in the blood of my people."

She stepped closer, getting right in his face. "If your people would stay where they belong, there'd be no need for the Regents at all. And what about the Paladins? You seem to have no problem with them."

"No, I don't. They are honorable warriors."

In fact his problem at the moment was how much he wanted to wrap this woman in his arms to protect her from everything dark and ugly in this world. She was both strong enough and resilient enough to handle anything that might be thrown at her, but he hated to see her idealism get battered and bruised.

He busied his hands petting Chance's soft fur. "I'm sorry, Sasha. I didn't mean to pick another fight."

It was obvious her own temper was running hot, too,

but finally she sighed and retreated a step. "Yes, well, like I said, I have work to do."

He stayed where he was, watching her walk away and wondering how things had spun out of control so quickly. It didn't help that Chance tried to follow her, fighting to break free of the firm grip Larem had on his leash.

"Down, boy." He tugged Chance back by his side. "We have to let her go."

Finally, Chance whined and gave up, his head down and his tail drooping. Larem knew exactly how the big dog felt—it was as if the sun had dimmed and its warmth faded. Both males stood and watched Sasha until she disappeared around the corner. Frustrated and weary, they made their way back to the shelter.

God, Sasha so didn't want to be having this meeting right now, but neither did she have a good reason to postpone it any longer. Devlin would've come to her, she supposed, but she'd decided that he might appreciate her meeting him on his own turf. It would be interesting to see how this played out. Right now, she'd be grateful if they just got through the next hour without any bloodshed.

Okay, that was an exaggeration, but she'd had a crappy weekend, thanks in part to the fight she'd had with one Larem Jones and his buddy Chance. She wasn't mad at the dog, but she certainly had to question his taste in humans. No, make that his taste in humanoids. Chance probably didn't care about the distinction, but right now it was an important one to her.

If she were being honest about it, she forgot about that distinction herself whenever she and Larem were together, at least right up until he shoved the truth in her face again. Like yesterday when they'd been having such a nice time and then their conversation totally derailed.

Well, now she got it. He hated everything that was important to her. Maybe she shouldn't be so defensive about the Regents, but Larem shouldn't lump them all in with criminals like Kincade.

Granted, he had made a couple of good points. Obviously Kincade hadn't been functioning in a total vacuum. Someone else had to have known he'd been up to something, and the memories of the rogue Regent operating in Missouri and his subsequent murder didn't do much to reassure her.

But right now she had more immediate problems to deal with. She slowed as she reached the alley, smiling at the guard on duty, who was unfamiliar to her. His hand strayed to his weapon, leaving it there even when she flashed her identification badge. After a quick glance at it, he jerked his head toward the door before turning his attention back to the street.

She thought he even muttered something rude under his breath as she passed by, but she wasn't sure enough to call him on it. There was definitely something off about his reaction though. Certainly it was a far chillier welcome than the guards had given her when she first arrived in Seattle. She added it to her mental list of problems to be dealt with as time allowed.

She punched in her authorization code on the keypad and yanked the door open. As she started down the hallway, a familiar figure stepped out of the hall on the right. He turned to walk in the same direction she was heading. Great. Larem was the last person she wanted to see right now.

She dropped back, hoping to avoid any contact. Her ruse didn't work; the man stopped to look back at her. Except it wasn't Larem after all. Given that there was only one other male Kalith who might be roaming these halls, he had to be Barak q'Young.

He waited for her to catch up with him. "You must be Sasha."

"I am, and you must be Barak." She smiled, mostly from relief.

Barak glanced at the briefcase she held in a tight grip. He gave her an odd look before asking, "Are you heading toward Devlin's office? If so, I'm walking in that direction myself."

When she nodded, he fell into step beside her. "So how are you finding life here in Seattle? How does it compare to your home in Missouri?"

At least one of them was capable of carrying on a conversation. "It's really lovely here, and definitely different from Missouri. Not better, just different. You visited with Devlin, didn't you? So you've at least seen some of the area."

He nodded. "My trip was quite brief, but I did get to see part of the Ozarks. Very different from the mountains here. What I remember the most was the heat."

She laughed. "Yes, it does get pretty steamy in the summer. Thank goodness for air-conditioning."

"Indeed." He slowed to a stop. "Well, here we are. It was a pleasure to finally meet you. Perhaps you'd like to join Lacey Sebastian and me for dinner one evening."

"I'd like that," she said, finding that she really meant it. "Just let me know when."

He continued on, cutting through the cluster of desks to where Blake Trahern was talking with Cullen Finley. Both men nodded in her direction as she made her way over to where Devlin was leaning in his doorway obviously waiting for her.

"Am I late?"

"Nope, right on time. Come on in." He straightened up and led the way into his office. "Coffee?"

"Nothing, thanks."

She pulled her chair around to the side of Devlin's desk, hating to have the huge expanse of scarred wood between them while they talked. Somehow sharing the corner of his desk seemed friendlier than sitting on opposite sides.

"Have you had a chance to go over the list I e-mailed you?" Devlin said as he sat, his chair creaking in protest. "Just so you know, I did ask some of the guys for their input."

There was a twinkle in his eyes that made her wonder how much editing he'd had to do before sending along their suggestions.

Knowing D.J., she bet there'd been some doozies. "I take it that a few of the ideas were more interesting than appropriate. Care to share?"

Devlin laughed. "'Interesting' is a tactful way to put

it. But, yeah, a couple were quite creative and possibly illegal in some states."

While he spoke, she set her laptop on the edge of the desk and booted it up. "Okay, now you've got my imagination running wild. Tell me your favorite, and I promise not to repeat it, or even ask who came up with it."

The Paladin leader shoved his long hair back out of his way as he gave the matter some thought. "Beer on tap in the barracks down in the tunnels almost made the list."

She grinned at him. "While I can understand the appeal, the thought of unlimited alcohol mixed with swords sounds like a disaster waiting to happen."

"Yeah, that's why I had to say no." Clearly he regretted that being the case. "But otherwise, I tried to make sure that anything that made the final cut would offer the greatest bang for the buck and have the most impact on the Paladins themselves."

"Overall, you did a great job coming up with some pretty creative ideas. We can't afford to do all of them, at least not immediately, but I'd still like to send all of the suggestions back to the Board. I think they'd benefit from hearing what's really needed from the actual boots on the ground."

"Sure, go ahead." But Devlin seemed skeptical.

"What's wrong?"

"Look, Sasha, I know you mean well, but I have asked for almost everything on that list at one time or another, and I've always been shot down. There's never enough money or personnel or some other lame-ass excuse."

Just that quickly his good mood was gone, along with her own. She was getting tired of having to defend the Regents and everything they did for the Paladins. Rather than try that tactic again, she steered the conversation back to the list.

"I can't speak for decisions made in the past, but here's what I can do now." She turned the screen so he could see it. "Of your top five items, I thought these two should be given the most priority."

She highlighted the ones she meant. "If you agree, first thing tomorrow I'll submit the request to purchase more physical therapy equipment for the gym and to hire three more trained medics to work in the labs. I like the idea of recruiting candidates with military backgrounds. It only makes sense."

He nodded. "That was one of Laurel's suggestions, but the guys agreed. With more medics doing triage and treating the more superficial stuff, the Handlers can get started on the serious wounds and the dead faster."

Sasha couldn't help but shudder at the images that came flooding back. The blood, the screams, the dead and dying.

Devlin cocked his head to the side and stared at her for several seconds. "Flashback?"

"Yeah, it's getting better, but every so often it takes me by surprise." She mustered up a small smile. "If you want to yell at me some more for what happened, go ahead. You won't be saying anything I haven't already told myself."

"Actually, don't take this wrong, but all things considered I'm almost glad it happened."

Although she wouldn't have wished it on her worst enemy, she'd had the same thought herself.

Devlin continued, "I know it was tough on you, and you probably still feel guilty about what happened to Larem. But now you have a lot better understanding of what it's like for us down in the trenches. It will make you a better Regent than most."

Okay, that surprised her. How did he know that was her dream? She sat back and crossed her arms over her chest. "I never said I wanted to be appointed as this area's Regent."

"You didn't have to paste your ambitions on the nearest billboard, Sasha. If all you were here to do was assess the situation, you would've shown up, reviewed a few files, and then headed back to St. Louis. Besides, if your stay was going to be temporary, you wouldn't be moving into Laurel's condo. Not to mention the way you keep poking your nose into places where it doesn't belong."

Okay, she was tired of hearing that last part, too. "Other than the tunnels, as administrator I should have free access to all facilities. How else am I supposed to know what's going on?"

He held up his hands in surrender. "I don't mean to piss you off, but I've seen my share of do-gooders come through here over the years. I'm smart enough to take whatever you're willing to give me to make things better for my men. That doesn't mean I'm naive enough to think that this new enlightened attitude will last. It never does."

She fought to control her temper. "Once again, I can't change what was or wasn't done in the past. I've already said I'll order the equipment and hire the medics. That still leaves some money in the budget. We can talk about other options later if you'd rather."

Devlin pinched the bridge of his nose. "I think we got off track here. I really do appreciate what you're doing. I even believe you'd like to see some changes in how things are done. I'm just saying don't be surprised if these funds suddenly dry up when you try to use them."

He obviously believed every word he said. A sense of dread settled in the pit of her stomach. What if he was right? Would the Board backtrack on their promise when she sent through the authorizations to utilize the funds? She'd already processed the request for additional funding for Laurel's studies. If approval didn't come through in the next couple of days, Sasha would start pushing.

"Let's go over the rest of the list. I'll do what I can."

He nodded. "That's all anyone can do. At least you're trying, which is more than Kincade did in all the years he was here."

As praise went, it wasn't much. But then she was here to do a job, not to win any popularity contests.

"Okay, how about item number three?"

Chaz looked around for something to kick. According to Rusty's latest report, his daughter had come within a hair's breadth of getting herself killed. What the hell had she been thinking? Civilians weren't allowed in the tunnels for good reason.

He'd talked to her since the attack, so she'd obviously survived the experience. But why hadn't she reported the incident? He was her father, damn it! This was exactly the kind of thing that made him wish she'd chosen another career path. One that wouldn't get her killed by crazies.

To make matters worse, she'd been saved not by the Paladins but by one of their fucking pet Others. The last thing Chaz wanted was for Sasha to come into contact with those freaks. God knows, the Paladins were unstable in their own right, but no one knew for certain what caused the Kalith to turn into Others. The bastard could've turned on her as easily as not.

The thought of a phone call telling him his little girl had been butchered was the stuff of nightmares. He had half a mind to hop the next flight to Seattle and drag Sasha right back to St. Louis where she belonged. The only thing stopping him was the knowledge that he might not succeed and that she'd never forgive him for even trying.

He also wanted to know where Rusty had been when all this was going down. George had made it clear to the guard that his primary duty was to make sure Sasha was safe. Yes, he had to pull enough shifts to make his transfer to Seattle seem legit, but screw that if it meant he couldn't manage the job he was really sent there to do.

At least for now Sasha was safe and had hopefully learned her lesson. He'd only seen the aftermath of the battles Paladins fought and that was horrible enough. He'd had nightmares for days after seeing a dead Paladin come back to life. Talk about a freak show!

Maybe seeing the carnage Others caused would be enough to ensure that she would figure out a way to rid Seattle of its Kalith residents. The Board of Regents had considered issuing direct orders to dispose of them, but he'd reluctantly argued against that idea. If they ever managed to piss off the Paladins enough that they walked away from the job, the whole world would be screwed, not to mention overrun with Others out for blood.

He picked up the authorization requests Sasha had submitted and skimmed them. After stopping to read them more carefully, he considered the implications and had to smile. His daughter sure was hell bent on making her presence known, and not just in Seattle. Once her proposed expenditures were approved, the Regents would be hearing from every Paladin installation in the world wanting some of the same, most likely starting with the ones right here in Missouri.

Maybe it was time to roll the dice and see what happened. He reached for his pen and scrawled his name on the requests.

Chapter 11

$\mathcal{D}$uke glared at the e-mail on his laptop. The sender's address was unfamiliar, the kind he normally deleted without opening. But the subject line on this one was clearly meant for him.

He read it out loud: "Duke, the bastards must die."

The body of the e-mail said more of the same, but again there was no signature to identify the sender. Okay, he was down with the idea if this guy was talking about killing those fucking Others who'd managed to worm their way into living on this side of the barrier. The adults should've been gutted the minute they crossed over and the two kids shoved back into their own world. Neither of those things was going to happen, not with a bunch of the Paladins ready to go down fighting to protect them.

So, yeah, he was ready to sign on to any feasible plan for getting things back to the way they were before that creepy Barak crossed paths with Devlin Bane. The e-mail said to simply send a blank reply if he wanted to know more. He'd do it in a heartbeat if he knew for sure it wasn't a trap.

"Who the hell are you?" he asked, wishing he could expect an answer.

His hand hovered over the mouse, his left forefinger itching to click the button. If he chickened out, he'd have to go on watching his friends fight and die, and for what? Not a damned thing if the Regents and the Paladins started treating the enemy with more respect than they did the guards.

He knew for a fact that part of the Seattle budget had been diverted to pay the three adult Kalith's salaries. Barak was paid to work with his woman. No doubt about how he earned his money. Hell, Duke would've applied for that job himself, but Lacey Sebastian had never given him a second glance.

The other two were "instructors." Sure, they could teach everyone how to counter the style of fighting the Others used. But in return, the Kalith now knew everything about the human weapons and how they were used.

The question he had was whether the Kalith could duplicate the technology used to produce firearms or stun guns. Who knew what kind of intelligence Barak and Larem had been sent across the barrier to gather?

As Duke considered his options, he wiped his sweaty palms on his pants. On the one hand, he could ignore the e-mail and go on just as he had been: reporting for duty, doing his job, and eating antacids by the handful. Or, he could click the button and see what happened.

He clicked the mouse before he could convince himself otherwise.

It wasn't until he was well into his six-pack two hours later that he remembered to check his mail. Sure enough, his mysterious contact had responded. Before opening the e-mail, Duke snagged another beer.

Okay, it was now or never. He opened the e-mail and scanned its contents.

"Well, I'll be damned."

He couldn't sit still, so he walked a couple of laps around the room before sitting back down at the computer to read the message again:

Friend, from now on we won't use names or at least real ones. This Sunday, take the ferry across to Whidbey Island and drive down to the state park on the south end. Be there at noon and carry a newspaper opened to the sports page so we can recognize each other. I can't tell you how many of us to expect and wouldn't if I could. You have one last chance to back out of the deal by replying with "cancel my subscription" typed in the subject line. Otherwise, you're in this for the long haul. The fight for our world begins now!

The words burned themselves into Duke's brain. After deleting the e-mail, he purged the trash file and then emptied the recycle bin, hoping to destroy all records of the correspondence except a hard copy. Sunday was his day off. Had the mysterious sender known that? It was pretty damned spooky how much the guy seemed to know.

Duke would know more come this weekend. Until then, tomorrow was another workday, and it was time for bed. But as he lay staring up at the ceiling in the darkness, he had to wonder whether he'd just signed his own death warrant.

The money had been approved. Sasha danced around her office whooping it up, grinning from ear to ear and toasting her reflection in the window. Her little celebration didn't last long though. It was no fun when she was the only one tapping her toes.

She dialed Laurel's number but decided against leaving a message when it went to voice mail. She also struck out when she tried Devlin. That was okay. In an hour she was due at Lacey Sebastian's house for a Saturday night barbecue. It would be a whole lot more fun to tell Devlin and Laurel in person.

The geologist had called with the invitation right after Sasha had finished up her meeting with Devlin. Lacey had warned Sasha that there was likely to be a mob, but that was okay. It would be nice to get to know the locals in a more informal setting.

Her father had made it a policy not to socialize much with the hired help, as he called anyone other than the Regents themselves. His theory was that maintaining an emotional distance made it easier to make the hard decisions. Maybe that worked for him, but not for her. The choices the Regents made had a direct impact on everyone in the organization. She wanted people to feel that she was approachable and open to their suggestions.

She ducked into the ladies' room to see how she looked. This time of year the weather could change in a matter of minutes, so she'd picked black jeans with a dark gold tank top and matching black jacket. Right now the sun was shining, but clouds were gathering out over the Sound.

Lacey had said they'd move the party inside if necessary. Since she didn't seem bothered by that possibility, Sasha wouldn't worry either. After retrieving the dessert she'd bought as her contribution for the evening, she flagged down a cab and gave the driver Lacey's address.

It wasn't hard to find the right house on the block. The driveway was overflowing with cars, with a few even parked on the lawn. She'd heard the Paladins had drawn straws; those with short ones remained on duty so the rest could party. Sasha paid the fare and climbed out of the cab feeling a bit intimidated by the number of people who'd shown up.

Even from the street she could hear the murmur of voices coming from the backyard—most of them male. She braced herself and headed for the front door. Someone must have been watching for arrivals, because the door swung open before she had a chance to ring the bell.

Her smile faded a bit when she saw who it was. "Larem, I didn't know you'd be here."

Although she should have. It only made sense that Barak and Lacey would invite all the Kalith in the area. Larem didn't look any happier to see her.

"Go on through the kitchen. Lacey is expecting a few more people, so I offered to man the door until they all arrive."

There wasn't much she could say to that, but she wasn't about to let his presence ruin the party for her.

Luckily, Laurel spotted Sasha as soon as she stepped out on the deck. The Handler made a beeline for her.

Sasha smiled at the doctor. "I'm so glad to see a familiar face, Laurel, especially because I've got good news!"

After Sasha told her about the funding, the two of them stood together, looking down on the backyard from the deck. There were only a few women mixed in the crowd. Sasha recognized Brenna standing with Trahern. The woman she was talking to had to be Lusahn q'Arc, her pale eyes and dark hair with silver streaks clearly marking her as Kalith.

But it was the men milling around the yard who drew Sasha's attention. Despite having met a fair number of them already, she found seeing them all together was overwhelming. Paladins varied in coloring and build, but each was a prime specimen in his own right. Maybe it was something about the way they moved with such power and confidence. Her companion picked up on the direction Sasha's thoughts had taken.

Laurel leaned her elbows on the railing beside her. "If it weren't for the whole secrecy thing, I've always thought if we could get these guys to pose for a calendar, we could all retire rich."

"You might have something there. I'd volunteer to organize it in a heartbeat. We could even use part of the money to fund some special projects here." She shot Laurel a teasing look. "Think Devlin would pose shirtless? I'm betting D.J. would for sure."

The words were no sooner out of her mouth than she realized they were no longer alone. Please tell her that Larem hadn't heard that last part. One glance at his face told the story. He'd heard all right and wasn't happy about it.

"Here. I thought you two might be thirsty." He shoved a soft drink at each of them and then stalked away.

Laurel grimaced. "Whoops. Something tells me Larem disapproves of the whole calendar idea."

Then she winked at Sasha. "Or maybe he hated the idea of you wanting to see D.J. and Devlin half naked."

"Yeah, right. And here I was going to ask him and Barak to pose for June and July."

Sasha took a long sip of her cola and watched Larem make his way across the yard to stand with a couple. The guy looked vaguely familiar, but not the woman. "Who are they?"

"Hunter Fitzsimon and his fiancée, Tate. They live about seventy miles north of here where he keeps an eye on another stretch of the barrier."

"I thought I recognized him. He's originally from Missouri, right? That's probably where I've seen him. I'd forgotten he'd been transferred out here."

Larem looked much more relaxed now that he was with them. "Is he good friends with Larem?"

Laurel nodded. "Yeah. Larem was part of the crew that brought down Kincade. He and Hunter struck up a friendship right after Hunter moved up north. Everyone was a bit surprised considering what happened to Hunter back in Missouri, but they've been good for each other."

The Handler was obviously referring to when

Hunter had been tortured to death by Others. Sasha didn't know all the details, but she'd heard enough to make her skin crawl. It was easy to understand why the friendship between Larem and Hunter would have come as a surprise.

Laurel popped the top on her drink. "But I shouldn't be standing here gossiping. Want to go mingle?"

"Sounds good." Sasha followed her down the steps to the patio. "Can you introduce me to Lacey? We've talked on the phone but haven't actually met."

"Sure thing. She's over there with her brother Penn and Barak."

Larem kept his eyes focused on Hunter and Tate, but he was all too aware of Sasha's movements as she drifted from group to group. Right now she was laughing at something D.J. had said. The jerk! He should—

Hunter's gravelly voice interrupted his thoughts. "Is something wrong, Larem?"

"No, why?" he asked, aiming for calm and failing miserably.

His friend smiled and pointed at Larem's hands. One was curled into a tight fist while the other clutched his drink hard enough to dent the sides of the can. "You're looking a bit tense there. Who's pissed you off this time?"

"It's nothing. I'm fine."

"Sorry, but I'm not buying that." Tate angled her head to look past him. "Who's the redhead?"

Hunter answered for him. "That's Sasha Willis, the new administrator assigned here. Rumor has it she's hoping to be promoted to Regent status and stay permanently."

Great, and here Larem had been hoping she'd go back to where she came from any day now. Of course, she probably wanted the same for him.

"The one who got herself trapped down in the tunnels?" Tate looked to Larem for confirmation. "The one you rescued?"

And killed his own people in the process, but he kept that to himself as he nodded. "That's her." Then he steered the conversation in a safer direction. "So how is your book coming along?"

Tate blushed. "It's almost done. I'm doing the final polish before I start querying agents to see if they'd like to represent me."

"It's really good, too!" Hunter bragged. "Although I'm still trying to decide if I was the inspiration for the lawman or the gunslinger in the story."

He looked down at his fiancée. "The sheriff doesn't get the woman, but then the gunslinger gets shot."

Tate looked outraged as she punched Hunter. "Hunter Fitzsimon, you promised you wouldn't read it until I was completely finished!"

"Yeah, well, I lied," Hunter said, rubbing his arm. "I wanted to know what it was about those two guys that made your eyes go all dreamy. Besides, you let Mabel read it."

Mabel was one of Tate's neighbors and a close friend. Larem was fond of the elderly woman and her two sisters. He asked, "So what did Mabel say about the book?"

Hunter snickered. "She said it needed more hot sex, but otherwise she liked it."

Tate's face turned rosy. "That's enough, Hunter. Let's talk about something else."

Larem smiled at the exchange. It sounded exactly like something Mabel would've said. She might be old, but she was definitely feisty. He also enjoyed seeing Hunter so happy. It hadn't been that long ago that he had raged out of control and tried to kill Larem with his bare hands just for being Kalith. The Paladin might still have his demons, but their hold on him had faded considerably since Tate had entered his life.

A man could face almost anything with the right woman by his side. Larem automatically sought out the corner of the yard where Lusahn q'Arc stood beside Cullen Finley, his arm draped across her shoulders. For once, the sight of her looking so happy with her human lover didn't send a shaft of pain twisting deep inside Larem's chest. In fact, he was glad for her. She'd created a nice family for herself with the Paladin and the two Kalith orphans she'd adopted.

At that moment, she happened to look in his direction. He smiled at her and nodded. Yes, she'd made decisions that had ripped his life apart. But looking back, he knew she'd done the best she could under difficult circumstances. The next time he caught her alone, he'd tell her that he was pleased that she'd moved on and built a new life in this world.

Which meant it was time for him to do the same.

Before he could pursue that thought or wonder why he'd been keeping track of Sasha's movements ever since she'd arrived, Lacey announced that dinner was ready. Everyone converged on the tables of food in one big rush, with the usual good-natured pushing and shoving among a few of the Paladins.

A couple of the idiots bounced into Sasha, sending her stumbling backward. Larem stepped out of line and caught her by the arm just in time to keep her from hitting the ground.

"Whoops, sorry, pretty lady," the closest Paladin said as he shoved his friend back out of the way, almost hitting her again. "Jerk, see what you made me do?"

Larem planted himself in front of Sasha and glared at the two fools. "Must you act like children?"

"Hey, I said I was sorry." The young Paladin took a step forward, his buddy moving up beside him. "Mind your own damned business."

"She is my business, so back off." Larem ignored Sasha's gasp of surprise— or maybe it was outrage—at his outlandish claim. Before he could deal with her, he had to do something about the two punks.

"And if we don't want to back off, *Other*, what are you going to do about it?"

Larem sensed more Paladins approaching, but they were allies, not enemies. Lonzo stood to his right, Hunter to his left. Lacey would not soon forgive him for turning her barbecue into a brawl, but it wasn't in his nature to run from a fight. If anyone gave ground, it wasn't going to be him. His two friends would happily provide backup, but he wouldn't need their help with these two.

Devlin Bane shouldered his way through the crowd. "What the hell is going on here?"

Larem kept his eyes focused on his opponents. "These two children almost knocked Ms. Willis down—twice. I was about to teach them some manners."

"Listen, you freaky-eyed alien, I'll—"

Before the youngster could finish, Devlin had him by the throat. "Not one more word, Craig. You hear me? Not one more word."

When the kid managed to nod, Devlin shoved him backward. "I don't know what started this and don't care, but it stops now."

Devlin shot a quick glance in Larem's direction. "You free Monday afternoon?"

"I am."

"Good." He reached over to brush a fleck of dust off the young Paladin's shoulder. "Monday at one, you and your buddy here will report to the gym for some quality practice time with Larem. Just to keep things interesting, if there's anything left of you when your lesson's over, you can each log some additional training with me."

Trahern had joined the group. "Not fair, Dev. How come you and Larem get to have all the fun?"

Devlin's smile was a scary thing indeed. "Fine, we'll take turns."

Lonzo and Hunter both chimed in. "Sounds like a good time. It's been a while since we've seen Larem in action. Who knows, maybe Barak will join us."

By now the two young Paladins were wide-eyed and pale. "But, sir, he's just a . . ."

Devlin got right back in his face. "Just how damned stupid are you, Craig? Larem is a close friend of half the men here—a friend they trust to have their backs. Do you have any idea how rare that kind of friendship is? Shut your mouth and leave now, both of you, while you still can. And on your way out, stop and apologize to Lacey and Barak for screwing up their party. Got that?"

"Yes, sir," they both managed to stammer.

"Good, now get out of my sight."

Devlin waited until they were gone before he walked away, shaking his head in disgust. Larem bit back the urge to tell the Paladin that he could handle his own problems, but he was all too aware of Sasha listening to every word of the heated exchange.

If she'd thought the Kalith were universally accepted by the people stationed in Seattle, she now knew the truth. But for every punk like Craig, there were two like Lonzo and Hunter, men who'd fought and bled beside him.

Gradually, the other guests turned their attention back to the food. Larem braced himself to face Sasha, expecting to see nothing but anger reflected in those big eyes of hers.

"Sasha, I—"

But she cut him off. "Don't sweat it. Jerks are jerks wherever they are. Luckily, those two are still young, so maybe there's hope for them. I am sorry, though, that they were so rude to you."

Okay, so he hadn't seen that one coming. "Are you all right?"

"I'm fine, although suddenly I'm starving." She looked past him toward the people working their way along the buffet. "I think we'd better get in line before the food is all gone."

Not sure if he was supposed to stick right with her or not, he hung back long enough to let a couple of other people go ahead of him. If Sasha missed him, she gave no indication. Pretending that it didn't bother him, he picked up a plate and started piling on the salads.

When his plate was full to overflowing, he grabbed a plastic fork and looked around for a place to sit. Hunter had evidently been watching for him, because he stood up and waved Larem over. Relieved to have a place where he knew he'd be welcome, Larem threaded his way through the throng toward his friend.

To his surprise, Hunter and Tate weren't alone at their end of the long table. Lonzo and D.J. sat flanking Sasha, leaving the only open spot directly across from her. There was no way to avoid sitting there without drawing even more attention to himself.

D.J. took a swig of his beer and set it aside. "Hey, Larem, I've got a question for you."

Larem braced himself. When it came to D.J., there was no telling what he'd ask. More than once he'd heard one of the other Paladins say that sometimes there was a complete disconnect between D.J.'s mouth and his brain.

"Go ahead and ask, but no promises that I'll answer."

Hunter laughed. "Perfect response, Larem."

Lonzo leaned forward to look around Sasha at D.J. "And remember there are ladies present."

The man in question gave them all a disgusted look. "Get off my back, Lonzo. I know how to behave in public. I just want to know if he dances."

What could Larem say to that? "Not with you. No offense, you're good looking, at least by human standards, but I don't make a habit of partnering with men."

When D.J. choked on his beer, Hunter pounded on his back. That didn't keep him and Lonzo from cracking up at the look on D.J.'s face.

"That is not what I meant, jerk."

Larem grinned at the flustered Paladin. "Then why don't you explain what you *did* mean?"

"After we clean up the food, Lacey said we could crank up the music and use the deck and patio for dancing. It occurred to me that I've never seen you or Barak dance. I just wondered if you both have two left feet or if Kalith just don't dance."

Larem's grasp of the nuances of English was far better than it used to be, but occasionally an expression threw him. It took him a moment to decide that "two left feet" meant clumsy.

"We can dance just fine."

"I was afraid of that." D.J. nudged Sasha. "The guys outnumber the women here tonight by about six to one. If Barak and Larem were out of the running, it would even the odds a bit."

With a perfectly straight face, Sasha shook her head. "Sorry to disappoint you, D.J., but it's me who doesn't dance."

The Paladin immediately wilted, his disappointment obvious and complete. "Oh, well, we'll just watch then."

Larem suspected Sasha was teasing the Paladin, but he didn't know for sure until she looked across the table and winked at him. Tate saw it and snickered. Finally, D.J. realized that he'd been had.

"Okay, lady, just for that, I claim the first dance."

"All right, but I have to warn you that I like to lead."

Lonzo, not to be outdone, said, "That's okay with me as long as I get the second dance."

Tate turned to Hunter with an expectant look. "Well?"

He groaned. "One dance. You know how much I hate it."

"Four." Tate crossed her arms over her chest, clearly determined to win this negotiation.

"Two."

She smirked. "Three plus two slow dances. Even you can manage to slow-dance."

"Fine." He tugged her closer for a quick kiss. "But you owe me."

"Deal."

Larem observed the interchange with mixed feelings. It was hard to see their obvious love for each other and not want some of that for himself.

Once again, he found himself watching Sasha talk to D.J. and Lonzo. There was no way he was going to sit on the sidelines and watch her dance with a series of Paladins. He'd seen people dancing on television. It couldn't be *that* hard, especially when the music slowed down. Most of the time, the couples swayed together, their movements looking a lot like foreplay.

A few minutes later, Lacey began passing out trash bags and the group made quick work of the mess. Food was packed up and the coolers restocked with pop and beer. The sun had gone down, so the only light came from the twinkling lights that Lacey and Barak had strung in the low branches of the trees and along the deck.

When the music started, D.J. grabbed Sasha by the hand and dashed for the makeshift dance floor. Hunter let Tate drag him along in their wake. He grumbled each step of the way, but Larem could tell he was really bluffing. As soon as they reached the patio, Hunter spun Tate and led her through a rather amazing display of dance steps.

For a man who swore he hated dancing, he looked pretty proficient at it. Devlin and Laurel were the next couple to join in, followed by Trahern and Brenna. Pretty soon all the mated pairs were dancing while the other males looked on in envy. But after the first song, all the women abandoned their partners and chose new ones.

Lonzo, not to be outdone by D.J., was showing off to a salsa number with Sasha, her pretty face flushed and happy as she did her best to follow his lead. Whoever was manning the stereo switched over to a slower pace after the salsa ended to give everyone the chance to catch their breath.

Larem had been waiting for that exact moment to make his move. He held out his hand to Sasha, giving her the final decision.

Sasha didn't hesitate, letting Larem pull her close as the gentle rhythms surrounded them. They fit together better than she would've thought considering the difference in their heights. Cocooned in the darkness of the crowded patio, she gave in to temptation and laid her head against Larem's chest. A heartbeat later, he nestled his head against the top of hers, his breath softly tickling her cheek.

Dancing with Lonzo and D.J. had been fun, but this was different. Ever since that instant when Larem had grabbed her in the elevator, she'd wanted to feel his arms around her again. It was insane, and she knew it.

That didn't make it any less true.

Unfortunately, songs never lasted more than a few minutes. As the final strains died away, she forced herself to step back. Larem resisted letting her go only briefly, but it was long enough to let her know that she wasn't the only one with regrets.

She held on to his hand, tugging him down so she could be heard over the heavy metal that started blasting from the closest speakers. "I'd like a cold drink before I get whisked away again."

He nodded and plowed a path through the crowd, towing her along behind him. When they broke through to freedom, he finally let go of her hand. It was for the best, but for the first time she felt the chill of the evening air.

"What would you like?"

Larem had leaned down close to her ear to ask. She turned toward him, toward that mouth that she very much wanted to taste again. For a second she thought he'd read her thoughts because he swayed toward her a fraction of an inch before abruptly standing back.

She blinked, wondering if she'd only imagined that small connection, but then she sensed another presence. They weren't alone. Lonzo was standing right behind them, popping the top on a beer. She realized she'd never answered Larem, but accepted the pop he held out to her.

"Thank you."

She hoped he realized she meant for more than just the drink. It was hard not to be disappointed by the missed opportunity, but it was definitely for the best. She didn't know what to do about the attraction she felt for Larem. Rather than stand there next to temptation, she set her drink aside and went looking for D.J.

Chapter 12

*L*onzo nudged Larem with his elbow. "You gotta quit looking at her like that. She's cute and all, but Sasha's the boss, not to mention her old man is a Regent."

Larem was tempted to tell his roommate to fuck off and mind his own business, but Lonzo was right. Larem was playing with fire, and they both knew who'd end up getting burned if her father found out a Kalith warrior was itching to get naked with his daughter.

"There's nothing going on."

"Yeah, right." Lonzo nodded toward the dance floor where Sasha was dancing with D.J. "I doubt anyone but me and Hunter know for sure that you're seriously interested in her, but you need to be careful."

"I had one dance with her, and so did you." He glared in D.J.'s direction. "Go talk to him. He's on his second."

Lonzo snorted. "Yeah, he is, but she isn't cuddling with him like she did with you. I've got to tell you, bro, those were some serious moves you put on her out there."

"So I was lucky enough to get a song with a slow beat instead of whatever you want to call that racket." His words came out as more of a growl than intended.

Lonzo understood him well enough to know that when Larem's accent grew thicker, his temper was on the verge of exploding. That didn't mean he'd back off.

"I'm not trying to piss you off, man, but you need to tread carefully. You already made waves when you went all heroic and saved her life, not to mention how you got all territorial when you faced down those two punks earlier. Toss in holding her close like that on the dance floor, and you might as well paint a sign on her back marking her as yours."

Anger slid through Larem's veins. "I didn't hear her complaining."

"No, you were both too wrapped up in each other to notice anything else. But I wasn't the only one watching, and there was definitely some speculation about what was going on. Maybe you could deflect some of that if you'd go dance with someone else. Better yet, a couple of someone elses."

That was the last thing Larem wanted to do, but he had to admit Lonzo was right. "Fine, I'll go dance, but the first person who laughs gets his ass kicked, especially if it's you."

Lonzo grinned. "Fair enough. Meanwhile, I'm going to steal Sasha before someone else does."

He laughed when Larem glared at him. "I'm just looking out for your interests, roomie."

"Sure you are."

"I sure as hell am." Lonzo turned serious. "I don't poach."

The party slowly wound down. With everyone pitching in, the final cleanup didn't take long. One by one, the cars and trucks disappeared from sight. Larem was catching a lift to the apartment he shared with Lonzo, but he wanted to make sure Sasha had a way back to her hotel. Yeah, she was a big girl and could find her own ride, but he couldn't seem to stop himself.

Lonzo, always the mind reader, leaned close and murmured, "Want me to ask her if she needs a ride?"

Larem's first instinct was to say no, but he gave in to the temptation. "Yeah, go ahead."

He watched as his roommate stopped to talk to a couple of friends, taking an indirect route to where Sasha stood chatting with Lacey. Smart thinking. That would lessen the likelihood that anyone would think anything of his casual offer to give Sasha a ride.

To reinforce the idea that Lonzo was operating on his own, Larem left the house to stand outside by the truck. Either Sasha would be with Lonzo or she wouldn't; all he could do was wait to see.

A minute later, the front door opened again. Larem had been leaning against the fender of the truck but immediately straightened up as soon as Sasha stepped out into the night air. He ignored the surge of excitement at seeing her coming toward him. Both the Kalith and the Paladins had superior night vision, so he carefully schooled his features to express only mild interest in her approach.

He ached to explore those feminine curves again, to crush her body against his somewhere a hell of a lot more private than a crowded patio. He closed his eyes and imagined how it would feel to dance with her, only stretched out on a big bed, her satin skin sliding against his. Damn, he couldn't let himself think that way.

She walked directly toward him, Lonzo tagging along slightly behind her. Larem waited until they were little more than a car length away from where he stood to open the passenger door for her.

"Are you guys sure the hotel's not out of your way?"

"Don't sweat it," Lonzo said, jangling his keys as he walked around to the driver's side. "It's not very far from our apartment."

"Well, I appreciate it."

She paused to eye the high step up into Lonzo's truck with obvious misgivings. Larem glanced around and decided no one was watching. He quickly swept her up in his arms and lifted her up to the seat, startling a gasp from Sasha and a laugh from Lonzo.

"Next time warn me!" she said, sounding more flustered than furious.

She immediately scooted over toward the middle to make room for him. Even as tiny as she was, the cab felt crowded, but maybe that was because every sense Larem possessed was running hot with her next to him. Pressed together, shoulder to hip, hip to thigh, her warmth soaked through the thin layers of fabric that separated them, the sensation guaranteed to drive him crazy.

He shifted his position, angling his back toward

the door, hoping to give both of them a little breathing room. It didn't help, not with the scent of her perfume filling in the small space that he opened up between them. Right now, it felt as if both time and Lonzo's truck were crawling along, intent on straining Larem's self-control to the limit.

Finally, they were back downtown and pulling up in front of Sasha's hotel. As Lonzo drove under the overhang, his cell phone chimed. He checked the text message and cursed.

"Sorry, folks, but I've gotta rock-and-roll. Devlin's calling in the troops."

Larem climbed out of the truck and then lifted Sasha down to the ground. "Drop me here. I can get back home on my own."

"You sure?"

"No problem. I could use a long walk."

A really long walk, like right off one of the piers. Maybe the chilly water of Puget Sound would cool his almost painful awareness of the woman standing beside him.

"So, did he say what was going on?" Sasha asked Lonzo

"Nope, but if it was really bad, he would've called rather than texting. Oh, well, never a dull moment."

The Paladin smiled down at her. "Thanks for the dances, Sasha." Then he grinned at Larem. "Don't wait up, Lucy."

Larem laughed. "Be careful, Ricky."

"I will."

Larem shut the door and the two of them watched

Lonzo drive off. Sasha shivered as she stared after the truck, turning toward Larem only after the taillights disappeared down the street. "God, I don't know how they stay sane and do what they do."

Larem stripped off his jacket and hung it around her shoulders. "Come on, Sasha. D.J.? Sane?"

She giggled. "Okay, you got me there."

"But to answer your question, they are warriors, born and bred to serve their people. They can't imagine living any other life. If you took it away from them, they wouldn't know what to do with themselves. Perhaps join your military, although some would have a difficult time concealing their special abilities."

Sasha's dark eyes studied Larem, seeing far more than he was comfortable with. He didn't want to hear whatever she was thinking.

When she did speak, she surprised him. "Would you like to come up for a drink?"

Yes, he'd love to follow her up to her room, but to share far more than a beverage. "Sasha, I've already been warned that people think I'm interested in you. Do you really think that would be wise?"

"Probably not, but I'm inviting you anyway." She looked past him. "If you're worried about going upstairs with me, we could walk down to that cafe and just get coffee."

Larem hesitated for all of two seconds before rejecting that idea. Out in public, there was no telling who might see them, but for the two of them to be together up in her room definitely wasn't smart either. Far better that he start the long walk home—alone. He led her around the corner, out of the bright lights and into the shadows against the concrete wall.

"It might be smarter if I just go, Sasha."

"Fine." She held out his jacket. "But why? I'd like to think we could at least be friends."

Friends? Like hell.

"You want to know why? Because two seconds after we shut the door to your room, Sasha, I'm going to want a whole lot more than a drink with you. And afterward, you'll want me to fade back into these shadows, acting like nothing ever went on between us, but that's not going to happen. If you're ready for that possibility, then by all means let's go up to your room and see where the night takes us."

He cupped the side of her face with his hand, brushing the pad of his thumb across her lips. "If not, let me go now before this goes any further. Before I hurt any more."

She answered him with a kiss, her sweet mouth softening his frustration. He pulled her into his arms, the perfect fit of her body against his reminding him of the melody that had played while they danced. Perhaps she heard it, too, because suddenly they were swaying in a rhythm meant only for the two of them.

He leaned into her, loving the feel of her soft breasts pressed against his chest. Her hands latched on to his wrists and then made their way up his arms, finally coming to rest on his shoulders. Their tongues slipped and slid and tempted, hinting at what was to come next if they were to continue down this path together.

Gods, when was the last time a female held him,

wanted him, and made him feel needed like this? Maybe never.

He became lost in this moment, lost in this woman, and then almost lost his life when he heard a popping sound and something hit the wall above his head, sending chips of concrete raining down on them both. Grabbing Sasha, he pulled her to the ground behind a nearby parked car.

Sasha clung to his hand. "Larem! Was that a gunshot?"

"Yes. Stay down while I look around."

He crawled toward the back of the car to peer up over the trunk. Nothing at first, but then the sound of tires squealing as someone ripped down the street and around the corner out of sight. Something wet dripped down his cheek. Had he been hit? He touched his finger to the liquid and studied it in the faint light.

"Larem?"

He retreated to where Sasha waited and helped her up. "They're gone. Let's get you inside."

She huddled by his side, her rapid breathing a clear sign of how badly shaken she was. "Shouldn't we call the police?"

"There's nothing they'll be able to do."

"But someone shot at us!" Anger replaced the fear in her voice.

Larem led her back to where they'd been standing to point at a splash of dark color on the wall. "Yes, they did, but apparently with a paint ball."

He fingered a lock of her hair, feeling the sticky residue there. "We both have it on our clothes and hair.

Maybe it was just a teenage prank. I'll call the police if you'd like, but we have no description, no license plate, and no evidence other than a splash of paint."

"The little jerks! A little lower and they might have hit the back of your head."

"But they didn't."

Her concern for him was sweet, but it was time to get her off the street and in to safety. Maybe it really had been kids playing around, but he wouldn't discard the possibility that the attack had been something more—a warning of some kind. If it was, Devlin would kick his ass for dragging the local police into Paladin business.

"Let's get you inside before that paint dries in your hair."

He took one more look up and down the street, unable to shake the feeling that someone was out there watching their every move. Devlin was busy right now, so he'd have to e-mail this to the Paladin to see what he thought.

Inside, he was grateful that the staff on duty was too busy with other customers to take much notice as the two of them hurried across the lobby. Luck was with them, because the elevator opened as soon as he pressed the button. He'd see Sasha safely to her room and then go back out to do some prowling. He didn't mind making a target of himself, but he wasn't about to risk Sasha being harmed.

Not that he wanted to leave her. He was all too aware that the two of them were only a moment away from enough privacy to finish what they'd started out-

side on the sidewalk. Better make his stay short and
sweet before temptation beat out good sense.

Sasha was cold and seriously buzzed. It was a relief
that it had been a paint ball and not a bullet, but even
so, the adrenaline still pounded in her veins, combined
with the aftershock of kissing Larem. She wanted nothing more right now than to get lost in his embrace.

Was that crazy? Probably.

She'd had her share of boyfriends, but other than
with David, the heat had quickly faded, and the relation-
ships had fallen apart. None of them—not one—rocked
her world with a simple kiss the way Larem q'Jones did.

Maybe it was the attraction of forbidden fruit, but
she'd outgrown her taste for bad boys years ago when
David died. No, there was something about Larem's solemn demeanor and warrior heart that made her want
more every time they touched.

Should she still invite him in? She didn't know what
he was thinking, but for her the question hung in the air,
heavy and demanding. She slid the magnetic key in the
slot and watched the light change to green. The handle
turned easily as one by one, the excuses to linger disappeared.

That's when she remembered that she wasn't the
only one splattered with paint. Larem's dark clothing
didn't show it as much, but there was no missing the
dried splotches on the side of his face.

"You'd better come in and wash up."

His pale eyes narrowed as he considered her offer.
"If you're sure you don't mind. It would be better if I

didn't wander the streets with a blue face." Then he smiled. "Who knows, someone might mistake me for an alien or something."

She forced a laugh. "Yeah, can't have that happening."

Sasha pointed toward the bathroom. "There are clean towels and washcloths on the rack."

Larem stood back. "Ladies first."

Inside the bathroom, she studied her face in the mirror. Larem had shielded her from most of the paint, leaving only a few droplets clinging to her hair and sprinkled across her right cheek. She made quick work of washing the paint out of her hair in the sink and then scrubbed her face clean.

"Your turn," she said as she walked back out into the suite, toweling her hair dry.

She had to admit that it felt strangely intimate to hear Larem moving around in her bathroom. As if his presence meant more than a friend stopping in for a visit. When the water shut off, she hurried across the room to look out the window rather than get caught staring at the bathroom door when he came out.

She felt Larem's presence as if he caressed her with only the heat in his eyes. He stood outside the bathroom in that silent way of his. She turned to face him, tossing the damp towel aside.

"Is there something else you want?"

He took one step toward her before he stopped himself. "Don't play games, Sasha. We've had this discussion. Yes, there is something else I want, but not at the price of living in secrecy. I'm only starting to build a life here, and I can't risk the possible backlash. Besides, we both know you stand to lose everything you've been working for if you get involved openly with me."

He knew he was right, and so did she. That didn't make the ache any easier to bear. The Board would never appoint her Seattle's permanent Regent if she took Larem as her lover. All her hard work would be for nothing. If Devlin was to be believed, another Regent appointee might not do a damn thing to fix what was wrong. Then there was the fact her father would be devastated by her decision.

Larem's expression hardened. "Right, that's what I thought. Good night."

His words rang out like another gunshot, only this one struck her in the heart. He'd almost reached the door before she remembered how to move, how to run. She latched on to his arm to stop him. With his strength, Larem could've shaken off her hold with little effort. Instead, he froze, staring down at her in silence as they both waited to see what she was going to do.

Darned if she knew. While her mind listed all the reasons she should let him go, her heart kept screaming that she'd regret it for the rest of her life.

"Larem, please."

"Please what?" he demanded when she didn't go on.

Sasha drew a breath and rolled the dice. "Please *me* and let me please you."

The atmosphere in the suite thickened, much the way the air did right before a storm broke with a crack of lightning and a rumble of thunder. Then the rain would come, washing the world clean and making it new again. That was exactly how it would be when the two of them came together—explosive and powerful. She just knew it.

Larem's arm trembled under her touch, as if he were fighting some powerful battle within himself. "Tonight only, or tonight and beyond?"

Okay, she was a coward for wanting to hedge her bets. But how could she promise the future when right now she was blind to everything beyond this one moment? He deserved honesty from her at the very least.

"Tonight. I know it's not much, but it's all I can offer."

He was tempted; she could see the hunger in his eyes. Then he was shaking his head and stepping away. The gap that opened up between them was far wider than the few inches he'd moved.

"I'm sorry, but I can't do this, Sasha."

When his hand reached out toward her, he stared at it as if it belonged to someone else. His touch was gentle but hurt her with the knowledge that it wouldn't last more than a heartbeat. She was the one who broke it off.

"I'm sorry, too," she whispered and backed away, her eyes filling with unwanted tears. "You said it yourself. I can't jeopardize my mission here. The Paladins need what I can do for them."

Larem jerked as if she'd slapped him, and maybe she had. He'd already lost so much since the day his life had become entangled with the Paladins. When he moved, she thought he was headed out the door, but instead he started right for her. She backpedaled only to find herself trapped between the wall and one extremely pissed-off Kalith warrior.

A wiser woman might have been frightened to have all that strength and temper focused solely on her, but she wasn't. Thrilled was more like it. Hungry. Aching. Oh, yeah, she ached.

"Sasha Willis, for this one night you are mine. Before morning, I'll walk out that door and not look back." His voice was little more than a growl, his accent thick and rough. "But know this, if you let me go, you'll regret it forever, because sometimes the gods run out of patience with fools and take back the gifts they've offered."

She didn't ask what gift the gods had stolen from Larem, and she wasn't sure she wanted to know. Right then it was all she could do to simply breathe as Larem began his seduction. The man's hands were everywhere, showing her things about her body that she'd never known.

After peeling her shirt off over her head, he slowly slid down the zipper of her jeans as his mouth hovered over her lips. His hand flattened against the slight curve of her belly and then slowly, so very slowly, eased between the heavy denim of her jeans and the thin cotton of her panties. Finally, his lips brushed against hers in a smile as his wicked fingers slowly worked against her core. They'd gotten that far once before. This time, though, it was just the beginning.

His touch soothed and tormented at the same time. When she closed her eyes and moaned, his tongue plunged in and out of her mouth, a promise of what lay ahead when they made it to the bed. If they made it to the bed. She needed him to strip off all his clothes and let her at that warm skin and taut muscle.

"Are you ready for more?"

She pried her eyes open and smiled, trailing her fingers down his chest, down and down until they found and tested the promise lurking beneath his jeans. "Are you?"

He leaned his forehead against hers. "I have been ready since the first day when you swaggered into the meeting with Devlin Bane."

"I didn't swagger." But she flushed with pleasure that he'd remembered the moment so clearly. She remembered it too. "You stood in the back row between Hunter and Lonzo."

He nodded as he rocked against her hand. "We need to get rid of these clothes."

Slowly, he slid her jeans down to her ankles, taking her panties with them. She braced her hands on his powerful shoulders as she stepped out of them. While he removed his shirt, she unhooked the front clasp of her bra, loving it when he froze midmotion as she let it fall to the floor.

Then he went into hyperdrive, his clothes scattering to the wind. She'd always felt petite around him, but clearly his clothes had somehow disguised how much of him there was. All over. Definitely impressive, even a bit intimidating. Before she could develop a full-blown case of nerves, Larem lifted her into his arms, pressing her against his chest with such care.

He settled her in the center of the bed and then backed away. "I'll be right back . . . protection."

He was gone and then he was back, his powerful frame stretched out beside her, his gaze lingering as if she were the dessert table at a buffet. When his mouth once again found hers, she gave up and gave in.

Gods, he loved the spicy flavor of Sasha's mouth. He couldn't wait to taste all of her. His anger and frustration had changed into something much more powerful. This might be his only night in her bed, but he was going to do his best to brand it in her memory. Maybe some other lucky bastard would eventually become her lover, but no way would he give her what Larem had. By morning, there wouldn't be an inch of her body that wouldn't burn with the knowledge of what they shared.

With that in mind, he turned his attention to her breasts. Their rosy beauty had struck him dumb at first glance. Would they taste as sweet as they looked? A flick of his tongue answered that question. Yes, they did. He feasted on one and then the other, loving the way they pebbled up against his tongue. Sasha loved it, too, judging from the way she thrust her fingers into his hair and held him close.

"Larem, that's incredible."

She rolled toward him, lifting her leg high over his hip, opening herself up to his touch. He was more than happy to give in to her demands, gently caressing her slick folds before testing her readiness for more as he suckled her breast with the same pulsing rhythm.

Sasha reciprocated by grasping his shaft with a sliding squeeze that had his eyes rolling back in his head. If he'd intended this to be a claiming, it was clear that road ran both ways. When she started to guide him right where he most wanted to be, he pulled back, even though the effort almost broke him.

"Give me a second."

He sat up and reached for the packets he'd dropped on the bedside table and ripped one open. Clumsy with desperation, he took far too long to sheath himself, but the extra time gave him back some of the control he'd lost. Throughout the process, Sasha knelt behind him, pressing her body along the length of his back. Her hands stroked his chest as she nibbled and kissed her way along his shoulders and neck.

He captured one of her hands and placed a damp kiss on her palm. "Still want this?"

If she had hesitated at all, he would've walked away. Maybe. He'd like to think he could've found the strength somehow. Luckily he didn't have to put it to the test.

"I want everything you have to give, Larem."

She moved back and lay down, holding her arms out to him. He didn't need to be asked twice. Not that he was going to rush things. These moments, above all else, were meant to be savored.

Sasha's breath came in shallow pants as Larem insisted on taking his sweet time making love to her. Her skin flushed hot and cold as he turned his intense attention to this spot and that. Finally, when he had her whimpering with need, he made his move.

His long hair had come loose, flowing in a dark wave down past his shoulders. She loved the silky feel of it brushing against her skin. He positioned himself over her, spreading her legs wide as they prepared to join their bodies at long last. She smiled and reached between them to guide him home.

He pressed forward, slowly, his eyes staring into hers with burning desire. When his cock was seated deep within her body, they both let out the breath they'd been holding, startling a small laugh from Larem. That pleased her, sensing that he rarely found much to laugh about in his new life.

She rocked her hips upward just as he withdrew, only to thrust forward again. He rewarded her efforts with more of the same, picking up speed and strength with each surge, until she no longer knew anything except the slide of his skin against hers, his body in hers. Trying to anchor herself in the swirling vortex of pleasure, she dug her fingers into his hips and held on, loving the flex and play of his muscles.

Then she arched up off the bed, calling her lover's name as she reached the breaking point. In response, Larem growled something in his native language as their bodies crashed together in a final explosion of pulsing heat.

She cried out at the beauty of it all as Larem buried his face against her neck. Then abruptly, he withdrew from more than just her body.

As he disappeared into the bathroom, she had to wonder if the chill in the air had anything at all to do with the air-conditioning.

Chapter 13

$\mathcal{D}$uke sipped his third cup of coffee, needing the jolt of caffeine to stay awake. He'd been parked outside of Sasha Willis's hotel for over an hour now, and it looked as if he had a long night ahead of him.

He'd received more orders by e-mail, asking him to keep a closer eye on what the new administrator was up to so he could report to the others at their meeting to-morrow. He glanced at his watch. Make that today, since it was now after midnight.

Earlier, he'd followed her to a barbecue at Lacey Sebastian's place. Most of the local Paladins had shown up for the festivities along with their pet Others. No sur-prise there since one of the Sebastians—Lacey—was shacked up with one of those freaks.

The Willis woman had taken a cab to the party, so he'd expected her to call another one to take her back to the hotel. Instead, she'd walked out with Lonzo Jones and his Other roommate, Larem. Yeah, that crazy Kalith had even lifted her up into the truck cab. She hadn't looked happy about having him touch her—it spoke well of her.

Afterward, Duke had hung back to make sure there wasn't any more to it than the two guys saving her cab fare. But that wasn't how it played out. Once they reached the hotel, Larem had once again put his hands around her waist and set her back down on the pavement. This time she'd smiled and leaned on his shoulders, where they'd lingered a little too long.

Lonzo had taken off right after that, leaving the two of them standing outside the hotel. Rather than see Sasha heading inside, though, Larem had tugged her around the corner into a pool of shadows. Duke had actually spilled part of his coffee in his lap out of shock at what happened next.

Sasha had not only let the Other kiss her, but Duke wouldn't have been surprised if she'd let the Kalith fuck her right there up against the wall. How sick was that? He used his cell phone to snap a couple of pictures to forward to his contact.

How could yet another human woman allow herself to be used by one of those crazies? She had to know what he was. Furious, he'd driven by and taken a potshot at Larem with his paint gun, the only weapon he'd had with him. He'd aimed at the back of Larem's head, but he'd been off by a couple of inches. Still, it was fun watching the lovebirds go diving for the ground.

Knowing the Kalith's uncanny night vision, Duke had taken off right after to avoid being recognized. He'd driven to the rear of the hotel to park and then slipped

into a back corner of the lobby just in time to see Sasha
and Larem duck into an elevator.

After hanging around for fifteen minutes with no
sign of Larem, Duke had bought a cup of coffee and
headed back out into the night. He'd circled the block
until a parking spot opened up that would give him an
unobstructed view of the hotel's front entrance. Sure,
Larem could go slinking out the back, but that would be
the wrong direction if he was heading home.

Duke's orders had been to watch, and that was what
he was doing. Once he knew how long Larem spent in
Sasha's room, he'd go home and report in tomorrow.
Although he had little info about the group that had
contacted him, he knew enough to know that they'd be
outraged by this development. He set his coffee aside
and picked up his paint gun, staring down the sights at
the bright light pouring out of the hotel entrance.

Too bad it wasn't a real gun instead of a wannabe
weapon. He imagined the satisfaction of watching a
bullet hitting the center of Larem's chest, exploding in
a spray of red blood instead of blue paint. Yeah, that
would feel damn good. Maybe next time.

Then, as if his imagination had conjured up the
alien, Larem walked out of the hotel, stopping long
enough to zip his jacket before shoving his hands in his
pockets and walking off into the darkness. It was damn
well about time the freak left. Duke checked his watch.
The bastard had been inside for close to two hours.
Plenty of time to get it on with the Willis woman.

Duke turned the key in the ignition. If he hurried,
he'd have enough time to get a few hours' sleep before

heading to Whidbey Island in the morning. Maybe he'd come home from the meeting with a new set of orders to follow, ones that involved settling the problem of the Kalith permanently.

Larem skirted the dim light of the sidewalk, preferring to keep to the shadows. It definitely fit his mood better than the warm glow cast by the streetlights overhead. He could've flagged down a cab, but he figured he stood a better chance of outdistancing the demons nipping at his heels if he walked home.

What kind of fool leaves the warmth of a willing woman's bed to hike his ass home through the damp mist of a Seattle night? His kind, evidently. Even now, it was all he could do not to go back and beg Sasha to forgive him for taking off as soon as . . .

As what? As soon as he'd poured everything he had, everything he was, into her? He'd planned to show her how good it could be between them and ended up learning something far more important about himself: he was a fool. And not just an ordinary fool. No, he was the kind who managed to destroy his own honor and hurt the woman he cared about, all at the same time.

He'd promised himself to make it so good for Sasha that she'd never forget him. Fine. He'd accomplished that, because the sex had certainly been spectacular. What he hadn't counted on was the emotional connection that had been forged between them.

From the instant they got skin-to-skin, he'd been able to sense what pleased her and then what pleased her even more. How she liked to be touched and tasted,

how hard and fast she liked to be taken, and how she'd
clung to him as they'd both found sweet release.

But he'd also known how much she'd hurt when
he'd turned away from her, unable to face what he'd
done. Oh, she'd hidden it well, agreeing that it was best
he leave so they could both get some rest. She had reports to write, and Larem needed to prepare for that big
match Devlin had scheduled on Monday against those
young Paladins. Besides, Lonzo might return home and
worry about where his roommate was.

Yet none of their reasons would stand up to the light
of day, because they were nothing but cowardly excuses.
Larem held his face up to the falling mist. What other
lies could he tell himself? How this night hadn't mattered when they both knew it had?

The worst part was that the farther away he got from
Sasha, the more he wanted to turn around and go slinking back to her door. He had few illusions that she'd let
him in, but the least he could do was apologize.

A vehicle drove past him, going slow despite the
lack of traffic. For the first time since leaving the hotel,
Larem took notice of his surroundings. Had that car
driven by before? He hadn't really been paying attention, but something about it was familiar. Of course, he
wasn't particularly knowledgeable about such things.
Trucks were easy. Cars, too. But the one that had disappeared around the corner ahead was somewhere in between. What were they called? Letters, not a name. "S"
something.

He kept walking and waited for the right description
to come to mind. Oh, yes, an SUV. Black and shiny. If it

went by again, he'd memorize the license plate number. Either D.J. or Cullen could use those mysterious computer skills of theirs to find the owner. If someone was paying too much attention to Larem's movements, he needed to know who it was.

Rather than take the direct route to the apartment, he backtracked a block, circled up the hill, and went back down a couple of streets over. If the SUV passed him again, he could be pretty certain the driver was taking more than a casual interest in Larem's business.

He was about to give up and go on home when sure enough, the car rolled into view. He must have done something to alert the driver to his interest because the SUV stopped abruptly. After a second, the driver turned in to an alley. Larem took off running, hoping to get a look at the license plate, but the driver gunned the engine and drove out of sight before Larem got close enough.

Great. First that paintball shot and now this. What was going on? He'd talk to Lonzo about it first chance he got. Alone now, he took the most direct route to the apartment, glad to get out of the danger that lurked on the dark Seattle streets.

The ferry ride across to Whidbey Island did little to calm Duke's nerves. He was too busy second-guessing his decision to attend the secret meeting at the state park to relax. God, what had he gotten himself into?

He still didn't know if he was going to be greeted by kindred spirits who were sick of how things were going or if he'd be facing the business end of a Paladin's sword.

Up until last night he'd been on the fence about whether to make the long trek to the park or skip it altogether.

Then he'd seen what he'd seen. How could Sasha Willis have hooked up with an Other? The very idea made Duke sick, not to mention seriously pissed. Maybe he'd feel differently if she was unaware of what Larem was, but she knew full well what she'd invited into her bed.

His fury had carried him through the night and all the way onto the ferry. But once the boat left the dock, near panic set in. Halfway between the mainland and the island, he was safe from the repercussions of his decision. But once he drove off the ferry, there would be no turning back. Hell, there could even be someone watching him now. That idea had his head swiveling like a weather vane in high winds. As far as he could tell, no one was paying any overt attention to him, but it wasn't much comfort.

The captain blew the horn, warning the passengers it was time to return to their cars on the lower deck. He'd come this far; he'd go the rest of the way.

Duke followed the signs to the park, slowing at the entrance to decide which way to go. Finally, he chose a parking spot at random, picked up the newspaper he'd been instructed to bring, and started toward a cluster of picnic tables. Maybe the guy wouldn't show at all, and Duke could relax in the sun for a while before heading back.

No such luck, though. As soon as he perched on a table a familiar figure appeared at the edge of the woods. It was that Rusty guy he'd met at the bar. Somehow he wasn't surprised, but Duke stayed seated, letting the man come to him.

Rusty hovered a few feet away. "Glad you made it. You came alone."

"Yeah, as requested." He aimed for casual but wasn't sure he succeeded.

"Good." Rusty cocked his head to one side and stared at him. "I have to tell you, I wasn't sure you'd show."

"Well, I did." Duke glanced around. "Where's everybody else?"

The other man finally joined him at the table. "For now, there's just us. The fewer people you know are involved, the fewer you can betray."

Okay, that had Duke seeing red. "Listen, asshole, I didn't come all the way here to be insulted."

"It works both ways, Duke. Those who don't know you're involved can't offer up your name to buy a little forgiveness if they get caught either."

True enough. Maybe he'd listen some more. "So why am I here?"

"Because you're as sick as I am of seeing the organization going to hell. We both know Kincade was on our side. Yeah, he had his faults, but he always gave the guards a square deal. Now he's in custody and the Paladins and their pets are acting like they own the whole fucking place."

Fairness had Duke saying, "They do most of the fighting."

Rusty sneered. "Yeah, but what else are they good

for? If they didn't get to kill all the Others they want, who else would they be killing—us? You know they're all hardwired to swing those swords."

"So what do you want from me?"

"Nothing you don't already do. Keep an eye on things. When you see something that shouldn't be happening, let me know."

Rusty stared up at one of the towering firs that surrounded them. "I was sent here by one of the higher-ups who is concerned about the dark turn this sector has taken. If we can build a case against the Paladins, maybe we can force the Board of Regents to clean house and assign a new Regent, one who will get things back on track."

"They already sent Sasha Willis to do that job."

Duke threw that out to see how Rusty would react. Did anyone else know about her association with Larem?

"She won't be here long. Her daddy won't let her stay. The last thing a Regent would risk is having his daughter take up with a Paladin."

Duke sneered. "You mean like the judge's daughter shacking up with Trahern?"

"Exactly." Rusty cleared his throat and spat. "How she can stand living with that crazy bastard I'll never know."

Duke gazed at the clouds scuttling across the bright blue sky, wishing he knew for sure if he could trust Rusty. It would be different if he knew who was really pulling the strings, but he understood the need for secrecy.

His companion stood up. "We shouldn't hang out here too long. So unless you've got something to report right now, I'm out of here. Wait fifteen minutes and then leave, too. I'll keep in touch. You do the same."

Duke almost let him leave, but in the end the rage he'd been fighting since the night before forced its way out.

"Before you go, there is this one thing, Rusty."

Monday afternoon, Sasha had no legitimate reason to be lurking in the hallway outside the gym where the Paladins honed their already lethal skills with bladed weapons of all kinds. She'd never had a chance to see any of them in action. Well, not before the other day in the tunnels, but that memory was blessedly a blur to her now.

The gym was two stories high, with open windows at the back that allowed spectators to watch from above. At the moment, she had the hall to herself. Every so often, she peeked in to see if anyone had arrived. Okay, so not just anyone—Larem. She was still a mass of unresolved confusion over what they'd done Saturday night.

Oh, he'd fed her a good line about why he needed to leave. One minute they'd been in perfect accord and the next he was running for the hills. It couldn't have been something she'd said, because he'd never even given her a chance to speak.

The jerk. She had spent most of yesterday working up a good case for being mad at him. That anger was definitely part of what she was feeling right now, but that wasn't why she was hanging around. No, the blame for that could be laid right at the feet of an overwhelming curiosity about what was going to go down once all the players arrived.

Devlin had clearly sided with Larem in that near dustup between him and those young Paladins. Even Trahern had waded in on Larem's side. If she hadn't missed her guess, the older Paladins were really looking forward to watching those youngsters face off against a highly trained Kalith warrior. She'd seen Larem in action and actually pitied them if he decided to unleash on them.

The sound of voices drifted up from the floor below. She edged closer to the opening and looked down. Paladins were pouring in from all directions. Most headed toward the row of benches that lined the walls, shoving their equipment bags underneath and out of the way.

She recognized Craig and his two buddies standing over in the corner whispering among themselves and watching the door with understandable trepidation. Their big mouths had gotten them into trouble. It remained to be seen how much they learned from the experience.

A sudden hush fell over the gym as Devlin walked in with Trahern at his side. Barak q'Young was right behind them, along with Hunter Fitzsimon, Lonzo, Cullen, D.J., and Penn. Obviously, Larem's supporters were out in number.

Her heart did an odd little leap when the man himself appeared. His dark hair was down, and he wore what had to be traditional Kalith clothing: close-fitting black pants and tunic with soft boots. She ignored the little surge of heat that flooded her veins at the sight.

Larem paused in the doorway to take a long, slow look around, then his eyes suddenly turned upward in her direction. She'd thought she was tucked far enough out of sight that no one would notice her, but she'd obviously been mistaken. Larem stared right at her.

She froze, unsure whether to wave or to take off running. She settled for holding her ground. Finally, he tore his gaze from hers and focused on the men grouped around the gym. It didn't surprise her that the reaction to his presence was mixed outside his immediate circle of friends. Of course, with Devlin and Trahern on his side, the rest of the Paladin contingent couldn't say much.

Larem stripped off his shirt, tossed it on the bench, and then did a series of stretches. God, she had it bad. All she could do was think about how amazing those supple muscles and that sleek skin had felt as he'd surged over her, in her. She'd like to think he was showing off a bit because she was watching, but for all she knew, this was his normal warm-up routine.

Finally Devlin stuck two fingers between his lips and let loose a shrill whistle. Silence settled over the room. He looked around, nodding at a few of the men as he did.

"Okay, we've got a little something extra planned for today's practice. Larem q'Jones is here to give some special training to Craig and company."

Devlin took a minute to look around again. "It seems every so often I have to remind some of you that the Kalith warriors who live among us do so because they've earned that right with their courage, their loyalty, and their blood. I will not tolerate anyone treating them with anything less than the respect they deserve."

Trahern and the rest of Larem's friends spread out around the room, their stances relaxed. But even from up above she could tell there was nothing relaxed about the way they watched the others in the gym.

When Larem was ready, he picked up his sword. Was it the same one he'd carried in the tunnels the other day? The shape was similar, but she couldn't be sure. There was no way to miss how comfortable he looked with the weapon in his hand, as if it were an extension of his arm.

When he walked to the center of the floor, Barak came with him, his own sword in hand. The two Kalith warriors faced each other, smiling briefly before putting on their game faces.

Devlin spoke up again. "Barak and Larem have agreed to give us a demonstration of the Kalith style of fighting before they work with a few chosen Paladins."

He shot a dark look to the corner where Craig and his friends looked a bit sick. Devlin obviously took pleasure in their discomfort. In some ways, she felt bad for the kids and wondered at Devlin's reasons for insisting on humiliating them in front of their peers. Obviously he had a point to make.

At some invisible signal, Barak and Larem charged at each other, shouting their challenge in their native language. When their swords clashed together, she grabbed the edge of the windowsill and held on for dear life.

Their blades were a blur of motion, the two swordsmen moving with terrifying grace.

As the bout continued, the Paladins gradually gathered closer, no doubt as entranced by the amazing display as Sasha was herself. How could the human body move that way? Of course, they weren't really human, but any differences were negligible. She had firsthand knowledge on the subject.

Gradually, the two men slowed down and then separated. With another nod and wider smiles, the bout was over. Applause broke out as Devlin tossed Barak a towel. Lonzo held one out to Larem along with a bottle of water. He took a long drink before handing it back. A quick swipe with the towel and then he headed back out onto the gym floor.

This time Hunter joined him, sword in hand. Once again, the two men saluted each other before the weapons came up and the action started. Their styles were markedly different but equally lethal. Hunter favored one leg as the match wore on, but he didn't back off at all. When he lunged forward at the wrong time, though, Larem hooked the Paladin's sword and yanked it out of his hand, sending the blade clattering across the gym floor.

Hunter froze, staring down at the curve of Larem's sword poised just shy of his carotid artery. His smile was slow in coming but no less genuine for the delay.

He backed away, laughing and shaking his head. "Damn it, man, that's the third time I've fallen for that maneuver."

Larem switched his sword to his left hand and held

his right out to Hunter. "We'll keep working on it until you learn to block it."

The two men shook hands, and Hunter clapped Larem on the shoulder before retiring from the floor. "I keep telling myself one of these days I'll actually win one against you, but thanks for not embarrassing me completely."

"You're welcome, my friend."

Larem stayed where he was. He ran a finger along the edge of his sword, perhaps checking it for damage. As he lowered it back to his side, he looked to where Craig stood watching, holding his own sword in a tight-fisted grip. Larem motioned for the young Paladin to come forward.

Sasha could feel the tension ramping up in the gym as the two men faced each other. The situation had the potential for turning ugly fast. She crossed her fingers and hoped for the best.

Larem studied his new opponent. They were about the same height, but Craig carried more muscle than he did. Without having seen the young Paladin in action, he figured his fighting style would be similar to Trahern's—more strength than finesse—although he could be wrong.

"Shall we?"

There was a certain determined grimness in Craig's expression as he nodded and brought his sword up into fighting position. Larem had to give the kid credit for facing him without flinching.

With a quick flick of his blade, Larem signaled that

the dance was on. Within seconds he was impressed. Craig's technique was rough around the edges, but he definitely had the potential to be one of the best. He'd never be fast enough to master the style that Barak and Larem used, but that didn't mean he wouldn't be just as lethal.

Larem flashed back to when he used to train recruits back in his own world, loving the challenge of tailoring the lessons to best suit each individual. Craig was a quick learner, countering when Larem deliberately left him an opening. The second time, though, Larem hooked the kid's sword and came close to striking it out of his hand.

He danced back out of the way and held his hand up to signal a stop. Craig retreated, his attitude clearly suspicious when Larem moved to stand beside him.

"You'll get yourself killed if you make that mistake in battle. Watch me." Then he went through the correct maneuver in slow motion, repeating it several times.

"Now you."

Craig mimicked his technique, flinching only slightly when Larem took hold of the kid's thick wrist and corrected the angle just a bit. "Good. Go through that several times slowly so that you do it right. Rushing only reinforces bad habits."

At least the kid listened. After a few more repetitions, Larem faced off against him again. "Okay, bring it on."

This time the young Paladin grinned, clearly loving the challenge. They both went at it full tilt, laughing when one or the other managed to score. Larem finally called a halt when he could tell the younger man was tiring. There was no use in risking injury to either of them by continuing.

Maybe next time their paths crossed, the encounter would be a peaceful one. To his surprise, Craig held out his hand.

"I apologize for my behavior the other night, sir. I'd heard that you and Barak were handy with a sword, but you're flat-out amazing. I appreciate the lesson."

Larem accepted the peace offering. "Anytime. And I mean that. You have great potential. If you and your friends would like me to work with you, don't hesitate to call me."

"I will, sir." Craig looked past Larem. "I guess I'd better go let Devlin pound on me some."

"Go easy on him, Craig. No use embarrassing him in front of everybody."

Larem was fully aware that Devlin and Trahern had walked up behind him. His new friend tried unsuccessfully to hide a grin, a mistake he'd no doubt pay for with a few bruises. Luckily, his Paladin DNA meant he'd heal quickly.

Devlin gave them both a narrow-eyed look. "Craig, go guzzle some water and collect your buddy. I'll be ready for you in a couple of minutes."

Craig gave Devlin a sloppy salute. "Yes, sir."

But before walking away, he turned back to Larem. "If you meant what you said, I will be calling you."

Larem nodded. "I'll look forward to it."

When he was gone, Devlin smiled at Larem. "That was well played. Looks like you've gained a friend—and a student. You down with that?"

Devlin was well aware of Larem's conflicted feelings on the subject of helping the Paladins in a way that would be used against his own people. However, this was his world now, and he needed to feel useful.

"Yes, oddly enough, I am. Especially because with a little help, in a couple of months he'll rival you and Trahern on your best day." He wiped down his sword, checking for any nicks to be smoothed out.

Trahern looked skeptical and a little insulted. "Care to put some money on that?"

"Sure. Say ten dollars? In two months, he'll face one of you in a match and win."

"A measly ten bucks?" Trahern snorted. "That's what I thought. You don't think he can do it."

"Okay, make it a hundred." A bet Larem was sure he was going to win. "Unless you're afraid Brenna will kick your ass when you lose the grocery money."

Trahern didn't rise to the bait. "A hundred it is. Now if you'll excuse me, I'm going to show these kids how it's done."

And he would, too, Larem had no doubt. The man was a legend among the Paladins as a killing machine with his broadsword. He tried not to think about what that meant for those Kalith who sought the light of this world, out of their heads with sickness and screaming for blood.

It was what it was.

Larem toweled off some of the sweat before putting his shirt back on. The whole time he forced himself to keep his eyes focused on his immediate surroundings instead of straying back up to Sasha. What was she doing there? Watching, obviously, but the real question was why? Was she worried or merely curious?

After putting his sword back in its scabbard, he sought out Hunter in the crowd. He spotted his friend standing off to one side with Penn and Lonzo, watching Trahern and Devlin square off against Craig and several others. Larem paused long enough to study the trainees, assessing both their strengths and weaknesses. Not bad, not bad at all. Working with them would be satisfying.

He walked up to Hunter. "You want to come to our place and chill for a while? Maybe get some carryout?"

"Sure. I've got time to kill while Tate hits the mall with Brenna and Laurel. I'll get my things. And, by the way, you're buying after making me look bad in front of my peeps."

"Fine," Larem agreed. "But how is it my fault that you left yourself wide open to attack?"

"Good point, but give me a minute and I'll figure out some way to blame you." Hunter headed back over to the bench to pick up his workout bag.

While he waited, Larem at last gave in to the need to see Sasha again, even if only from a distance. As soon as he looked up, she stepped back from the window, her attention now focused on something—or someone—on her own level. Why had her expression abruptly changed from curious to puzzled, even worried?

He checked the other windows along the balcony to see what had caught her attention, but all he could see were a couple of shadowy figures at the far end. They were standing at the wrong angle for him to see them clearly. But then it didn't matter who they were, not if they were bothering Sasha.

"What's up, Larem?" Lonzo followed his line of sight. "Who is that up there?"

"Sasha's standing by the far right window, but I can't see who's on the other end. But whoever it is, Sasha's not looking happy about it." He drew his sword again. "I'll be right back."

Lonzo blocked his way briefly. "Don't do anything stupid, Larem. I'll snag Hunter and we'll be right behind you."

"Fine."

That didn't mean he'd hesitate one second to skewer anyone who threatened Sasha. Lonzo and Hunter could provide backup if he needed it, but guarding that woman—his woman—was his job.

He rounded the corner and ran past the first staircase to the second one even though it cost him a few extra seconds. This route would bring him up on Sasha's end of the hall rather than risking her being trapped on the far side of a potential enemy.

The soft soles of his Kalith boots made only the slightest noise as he took the steps two at a time. He slowed his pace as he neared the top, not wanting to frighten Sasha by charging in, sword drawn. The stairs brought him up to the second floor just around the corner from where he could hear Sasha's voice along with the deeper ones of three human males. He didn't recognize the first two, but the third one was that bastard Duke.

Larem brought his sword down to his side and

slightly behind him in case he'd totally misread the situation. He paused for a few seconds, hoping to determine what was going on. Clearly Sasha's temper was running high, but he had no way of knowing why.

He listened for footsteps coming up behind him. Lonzo appeared at the top of the steps armed with an automatic along with his sword. Hunter must have decided to come up the other staircase, flanking the enemy. Not for the first time, Larem thanked the gods for the privilege of having such fine warriors ready to fight beside him.

"Guards," he whispered and held up three fingers.

Maybe he should let Lonzo take the lead as they rounded the corner, figuring the guards would be less likely to immediately go on the offensive against him. But when he motioned for Lonzo to go first, the Paladin shook his head.

"It's your party."

All right, then. He started forward with his friend only a few steps behind. Sure enough, two of the guards had Sasha cornered, her back against the wall.

When she tried to shove Duke away, he caught her hands and pinned them over her head. He leaned in closer. "No need to get violent, Sasha. We just want a few of the fringe benefits you've been offering the Paladins—or at least their pets. Surely our needs should come before that alien scum."

Before Larem could rush to her rescue, Sasha jerked her leg up and kneed the bastard. Duke howled in pain and raised his hand to retaliate. The guard standing watch caught Duke's hand on the downward swing and signaled to his friends they were no longer alone. The three men immediately turned in Larem's direction. Their facial expressions changed from smirks to frowns, then looks of fury, but at least they put some distance between themselves and Sasha.

"What's going on here?" Larem demanded, aiming the question at Sasha. It was Duke who answered.

"We were just discussing some special requests we guards have for the new administrator." His laugh was ugly.

"I'm guessing from the way she handed you your balls on a platter that the answer is no."

"Let's just say we tabled the discussion." The guard puffed out his chest and spat on the floor. "By the way, that was some freak show you put on down there, *Other*. It's a shame your buddy Hunter is too crippled to kill you while he had the chance."

Before Larem could respond, Sasha stepped right between him and the trio of assholes. "That does it! You've attacked me and insulted my friends. You three are suspended without pay pending an official hearing."

Okay, so much for keeping the situation from escalating out of control. Sasha wouldn't cower, but he'd hoped she'd at least use some common sense and stay out of the way. Now wasn't the time to tell these three that she'd back Larem over them, even if it did warm that spot in his chest that had grown cold since he'd left her bed.

While she was talking, Hunter appeared behind them. He'd obviously heard Duke's comment about his injured leg. Knowing the Paladin, there would be hell to pay for that crack. The guard would be lucky if Hunter didn't carve him up and leave him standing there holding his guts in with his hands.

The irate Paladin stopped just short of where the guards stood. "Gee, Duke, I'm sorry you were so disappointed in my performance. Why don't we head back down to the gym right now so you can see if you do better against Larem than I did? Or maybe you'd rather face me?"

Duke's face went pale. He was in a no-win situation. If he refused the challenge, he'd look like a coward. If he accepted the challenge, he'd bleed. Duke knew it, his friends knew it, and so did Larem and the Paladins.

As entertaining as it was to watch the fool squirm, Larem's priority was to get Sasha out of the line of fire. When she started to speak again, he caught her hand in his and squeezed, hoping she'd take the hint. She did, but she clearly didn't like it.

"Tell you what, gentlemen," Larem said, keeping his tone reasonable. "If you apologize to the lady now you can at least walk away in one piece."

When they didn't immediately respond, he gave them one last chance. "The clock is ticking. In ten more seconds, either you're on your way home or we'll teach you some manners. Your choice."

Duke made his decision. "Fuck you, Other. I'm not apologizing to any bitch stupid enough to spread her legs for the likes of you."

Chapter 14

Sasha flinched as if the bastard had actually slapped her. She shot a look at Larem, a hurt question in her glance. Was she asking how the guard had found out or if Larem had been the one who'd talked?

All things considered, he didn't blame her for wondering; but damn, she should at least know him better than that. He pushed the pain deep down inside to deal with later. He had far more pressing matters at the moment.

Starting with the fact that Duke was dead. The guard might not realize it yet, but he was already drawing his last few breaths. In the next few seconds, he would be nothing but a bloodstain soaking into cheap carpet. His two friends, too, if they got in the way.

Larem grabbed Sasha by the arm and shoved her back toward Lonzo. "Get her out of here. She doesn't need to see this," he ordered, knowing he could depend on his roommate to make sure she was safe.

Hunter already had his gun aimed at the guard closest to him. His leg might not be back to full strength, but that wouldn't interfere with his aim. Two shots would eliminate any problems Duke's buddies might cause.

"Larem, here. You'll need this."

Lonzo had the good sense to wait until Larem nodded before sliding his sword pommel first across the floor. Larem knelt down to pick it up while keeping an eye on the guards. He risked a quick peek back to see how Lonzo managed the maneuver without letting go of Sasha: the Paladin held her back with one arm around her waist.

When she spotted him looking at her, she renewed her struggles to break free. "Lonzo, let go of me! What are you three up to now? I won't have it, whatever it is."

"Sasha, go with Lonzo, please."

He wanted nothing more than to be holding her, soothing her, apologizing for her name being linked with his. "Go. I'll let you rip into me all you want later, I promise."

Duke obviously wasn't done shooting off his mouth. "Just wait until your father finds out what's going on. Do you think he and the other Regents will be happy when they find out what you've done? Hell, most of them know the Paladins are barely a step up from those animals themselves. I've always thought our job description should be zookeepers instead of guards."

It was definitely time to end this. "Lonzo, get her the hell out of here."

Larem waited until his friend dragged Sasha around

the corner and out of sight. Despite the difference in her size and Lonzo's, she was putting up a good fight. If he wasn't mistaken, his friend would have a nice collection of bruises on his shins from where she'd tried to kick herself free. His woman had a strong warrior's spirit.

When the sounds faded, he picked up Lonzo's sword and held it out to Duke pommel first. The human looked around in growing panic, evidently only now realizing the trouble he'd stirred up may have turned lethal.

He stared at the blade Larem held out as if it were a snake. "What's that for?"

"That's so when I explain your death to Devlin Bane, I can tell him that I gave you a chance to defend yourself."

When Duke made no effort to accept the weapon, Larem knelt down and slid it across the floor anyway. A human stood little chance against a Kalith warrior at the best of times, but they both knew Duke stood no chance at all if he didn't at least pick up the sword.

God, what had he gotten himself into? "You wouldn't kill an unarmed man."

He could hear his two buddies backing away, clearly thinking he was wrong about that. Any second now they'd break and run for cover. He didn't blame them. He'd be leading the charge himself if he thought he had a chance of getting away. But even if his friends forgot that Larem still had another friend with him, the Paladin stood ready to remind them.

"Where do you two dumb fucks think you're going?"

Hunter Fitzsimon's words dripped with the brutal chill of death. "You started this, but we'll decide when it's finished."

God, Duke never meant for this to go so far. Yeah, he resented the Kaliths strolling around like they owned the place, playing sword games with the Paladins and showing them up. That didn't mean he wanted to challenge a swordsman of Larem's caliber to a fight to the death.

He bent down to pick up the sword, hating the way the blade shook in his hand. Even more, he hated the cold amusement in the freak's pale eyes when he saw the shimmer of quivering steel.

"I will convey your apologies to Ms. Willis." The Kalith bastard ran his finger along the curved edge of his sword. "I know you regret what you said to her, but unfortunately you won't be in a position to tell her yourself."

Duke flexed his fingers on the sword, trying to adjust his grip on the unfamiliar pommel. He prayed for his life, prayed for forgiveness, and prayed for a quick and merciful death. As pissed off as Larem was right now, he would likely drag this out until Duke choked on his own blood and begged the freak bastard for release.

Larem switched his sword to his left hand. "There, Duke, to even things up I'll fight with my weaker hand."

Hunter's laughter rang out. "Oooh, nice touch, Larem. I like it."

Duke glanced back at his two friends. Oh, yeah, he was all alone in this. Even if they'd been interested in offering him a helping hand, Fitzsimon stood ready to stop them dead in their tracks. Literally.

Okay, Duke could die fighting or he could just die. A weird sense of calm settled over him. "You'll bleed, too, Other."

"So be it."

In a flurry of sword strokes that took less time than it took Duke to blink twice, he'd lost his weapon and found himself pressed up against the wall with the tip of Larem's sword staring him in the eye. The crazy fucker stood there smiling as if it were an everyday occurrence to gut someone for the hell of it.

"Duke, it would appear we've reached a crossroads in our relationship." Larem reached out to pat Duke on the cheek, smiling when he flinched.

"Hunter, why don't you let those two go? We wouldn't want their last memory of Duke here to be . . . tragic, would we?"

"If you insist, although it will certainly spoil some of my fun."

Hunter motioned for them to pass. "But just so you know, I will catch up with both you boys later."

The Paladin's comment was accompanied by the sound of two pairs of feet pounding down the hall and fading away in the distance. Duke knew every step they took diminished his chances of survival. No matter how cold-blooded the Other and his buddy were, they'd be less likely to slaughter him in front of witnesses.

Larem leaned in close enough for Duke to feel his breath. A vein pulsed heavily in Larem's neck, as if he were battling some damn strong emotions.

"There, now we can talk in private, Duke, starting with why you were watching me and Ms. Willis Saturday night. That was you who took a shot at us with the paint-ball gun, wasn't it?"

Duke managed a quick nod. "I was told to. Watch her, that is."

Larem's nostrils flared, as if scenting the air for a lie. "By whom?"

"The e-mail was anonymous." That much was true. He wasn't about to drag Rusty's name into this.

Hunter moved into sight. "And you do whatever stupid thing some unknown person tells you to do? God, I would've thought even a guard would be smarter than that."

Okay, he might be about to die, but that kind of crack was exactly what had Duke pissed off at the whole organization. He glared at the Paladin staring at him from behind Larem's shoulder.

"Yeah, that's right, Fitzsimon. Act all superior if you want to, but we're the ones who actually die when his kind decide it's time to party on our side of the barrier. *We* don't get second chances."

The sword point pressed closer, making it difficult for Duke to swallow without getting cut. How could he breathe, much less think, with that pale, ice-cold gaze on him? He closed his eyes and waited, frantically praying for deliverance.

When nothing happened, he pried one eye open to find Larem looking back at Hunter, his sword down at his side. What was going on?

"Call Devlin and tell him we have a present for him."

When Hunter stepped away and pulled out his cell phone, Larem turned back to Duke. "This is your lucky day, Duke. You can't say you didn't get a second chance now, can you? The good news is that I don't kill cowards. The bad news is that you will be spending some quality time with Devlin Bane. You should know that he hates people sneaking around behind his back, and that's what you and your buddies have been doing. Isn't that right?"

Duke felt like one of those damn bobble-head dolls as he nodded. God, Devlin Bane was going to kick his ass from one end of Seattle to the other, but that was still better than facing Larem any longer.

"Even more, he hates men who bully women, but not as much as I do."

Then with a move too fast to track, the sword was back at Duke's throat, this time cutting into his skin deep enough to hurt like hell. Warm blood trickled down Duke's neck; he ignored it, not wanting to provoke Larem any further.

"Again, you owe Ms. Willis an apology, but I'll tell her for you. Because, Duke, if you ever—*ever*—go near her again, I will finish what we've started here today. You can pass the message along to your anonymous *friend* for me, too. Got that?"

Duke bobble-headed it again. The last thing he saw was Larem's fist flying straight for his jaw. It connected before he could duck, and then all he knew was darkness and pain.

Larem stood over the pathetic lump of humanity, feeling just as disgusted with himself as he was with Duke. The world would be far better off without such scum in it, but he couldn't bring himself to end the bastard's life. One reason was that Devlin would not be happy to learn there was some kind of conspiracy going on, only to find out that Larem had permanently silenced their only lead.

Another reason Duke still breathed was that Larem's own sense of honor didn't allow him to prey on the weak and helpless. And Duke certainly fit that description. Larem had to give the fool credit for at least picking up the sword and trying to defend himself.

But finally, Larem had spared Duke because of Sasha. She would not easily forgive him if he had avenged her honor by killing the obnoxious fool. Larem figured there was a fifty-fifty chance he'd come to regret showing mercy, but he'd deal with that when the time came.

Hunter hovered nearby. "You did the right thing, but I would've backed your play either way."

The gods had truly blessed Larem by guiding his footsteps to cross paths with the Paladin. Hunter and Lonzo had both offered him unconditional friendship, a gift he cherished.

"I know."

Kneeling down at Duke's side, he held his hand out over the cut that was still bleeding, although more sluggishly than before. Closing his eyes, he shut out the world and withdrew into the center of his mind and softly chanted the words of healing. The power surged as the magic chose to do its work on the first try.

Finally, the last few words faded into the silence as Larem stood back up. His friend reached out to steady him, well aware that the magic took its toll, especially when Larem was already tired to begin with.

He immediately sensed they were no longer alone. Lonzo had returned with reinforcements.

"Devlin."

A faint hint of a familiar perfume told him that Devlin hadn't come alone. "Sasha."

Sighing, he turned to face the pair. "He's all yours, Devlin. Hunter can fill you in on the details."

The Paladin leader studied the body slumped against the wall. "Hell, from what Lonzo told me, I expected to be burying the bastard."

Hunter and Lonzo laughed, but Sasha didn't look at all amused. In fact, she looked ready to explode. She stepped past Larem as if he weren't even there to stand over Duke's body.

When she spotted the blood, her face turned ashen. "For God's sake, Larem, what did you do? Someone call for a medical team."

"Belay that order." Devlin squatted down to check Duke's injuries. "He's not badly hurt. Nothing an ice pack and a couple of aspirin won't cure."

After using the hem of the man's own shirt to wipe away some of the blood, Devlin shot Larem a questioning look. He shrugged, not wanting to discuss his reasons for undoing some of the damage he'd caused the guard.

"Lonzo, you and Hunter drag Duke downstairs to first aid. Laurel can check him over when she gets here."

The two warriors strong-armed Duke up off the floor and wrapped his arms across their broad shoulders. They half-carried, half-dragged the unconscious guard down the hall and out of sight. They weren't being particularly careful with how they handled him, an unspoken show of support for Larem that he appreciated. When they were gone, Larem picked up Lonzo's sword and waited for the storm to break. It didn't take long.

Devlin spread his feet and crossed his arms over his chest. It seemed that they were about to get a demonstration of his famous hot temper. Fine, he could unleash his wrath on Larem if he wanted to, but he'd better watch his mouth around Sasha.

"Okay, which one of you two want to explain to me what the hell happened here?"

Sasha's mouth was a straight slash as she threw back her shoulders, ready to do battle. Obviously she'd thought she'd be the one demanding answers rather than giving them.

"Your questions can wait, Devlin. Right now, I want to hear what Larem thought he was accomplishing by attacking a guard. I had already told them they were suspended and, pending review, possibly fired."

This was definitely not the time to be laughing. However, it was pretty damn funny watching a mountain of a man face off against a wisp of a woman and come out on the losing end of a glaring contest.

Right now, Larem would put his money on Sasha, but it would be better for all concerned if he drew their attention back to himself. He addressed his remarks directly to Devlin, hoping it would help him suppress the powerful emotions threatening to resurface as he recalled the events that had led him to this point in time.

"After I finished my bouts down below, I happened to look up and spotted Sasha watching from that window on the far end. When she turned to look at someone standing near her, I noticed her expression go from curious to worried, which led me to think that she was in danger."

She just had to contradict him. "I was handling it. And I was angry, not scared. You overreacted."

"I would dispute that, but if you say you were just angry, fine. Human emotions are not always clear to us poor aliens. Hunter and Lonzo accompanied me to offer their support if needed."

Ignoring how she flinched at the reminder of his heritage, he picked up where he'd left off. "Three of the guards had her cornered and were insulting her. Then Duke pushed her too far, and Sasha kneed the bastard. He shoved her against the wall and was preparing to hit her when we arrived."

Devlin was nodding. "Sounds like you handled this about right, although I'm also guessing there's something you're not telling me."

Larem reluctantly continued. If he went much further with the explanation, Devlin would figure out there was more to Larem and Sasha's relationship than either of them wanted him to know. All Larem could do was tread carefully.

"Duke had been spying on Sasha for an anonymous party. Seems he's not happy with things around here."

It would be too much to ask that Devlin stop there. But no, the man was like one of those hounds Dr. Isaac had told Larem about, the kind that stuck to a trail no matter what.

"And if Duke was spying on you, Sasha, care to share what he might have seen?"

Then he shot a suspicious look in Larem's direction when he added, "Or who?"

"Stop right there, Devlin." Larem stepped between Sasha and the Paladin. "It's enough for you to know that Lonzo and I offered to give her a ride back after the barbecue Saturday night. When Lonzo got your call to report in, he dropped the two of us off outside her hotel. While we were standing on the sidewalk, Duke shot at us with a paint ball, although we didn't know it was him at the time. I'm also sure that he followed me as I walked home."

"And what time was that?"

Sasha's cheeks turned pink, answering Devlin's real question even as she tried to deflect it. "How is that pertinent? I'd suggest you concentrate on finding out what Duke was up to."

"Fine, we'll play it your way." Devlin poked his finger toward Larem. "You and I will talk later. For now, go home and lie low. I know where to find you if I need you."

Then he walked off, leaving Larem alone with Sasha, perhaps not the best of ideas. As tired as he was, the last thing he wanted right now was another confrontation, especially with her.

As soon as Devlin was out of sight, Sasha turned her attention to Larem. But before she could say a word, he held up a hand to forestall her.

"Sasha, can we not do this now? Hunter and Lonzo are waiting for me."

She was already shaking her head as she mimicked Devlin's earlier stance, arms crossed, feet firmly planted. "Tough. They can wait."

If she wanted to do this now, fine. He crossed to the window and yelled down, "Lonzo! Hunter! Go on without me. I'll catch up with you later."

Then he set down both swords and leaned his back against the wall, his arms crossed just like hers.

"So what do you want to talk about?" he asked, careful not to laugh when she stomped her foot in frustration.

She flung her hands out to the sides. "Darn it, Larem, don't be a fool. I know you better than that. What were you thinking, confronting three guards like that?"

After seeing him fight, did she really think he couldn't handle three humans by himself? He pushed away from the wall and glared at her. "I was never in any danger. On his best day, not one of those guards could outfight a Kalith warrior."

She rolled her eyes. "You think I don't know that? But what if they'd pulled a gun? No matter how fast you are with that sword, you can't outsmart a bullet."

That she was worried about his safety pleased him. "So then what's the problem? Those men were clearly out of line."

"It's enough that they'll be suspended and maybe even fired, but you had to resort to violence. Don't you think that was a bit extreme?"

No, he didn't. It was bad enough what they'd said about Hunter, but Duke's behavior toward Sasha was unforgivable. "Duke had to be punished for what he said about you, about us. I am a Blademate to a Sworn Guardian, Sasha. It is my life's purpose to protect those I care about. I would not be worthy of the title if I were to let scum like Duke insult the woman I—"

Whoa, going too far with that. "If I hadn't challenged him, Hunter or Lonzo would have. It was my duty and my honor to do so. Duke should count his blessings that he still breathes. And if you think Devlin or Trahern would've handled the situation any differently had their females been involved, you don't know them very well."

Sasha was so out of her depth right now. This man had already killed once to protect her and almost did so again. How was she supposed to deal with something like that? Part of her wanted nothing to do with a man capable of such violence, but she also felt grateful. That he was equally capable of amazing tenderness and passion only served to confuse her even more.

She made the only choice that made sense. "I can't do this."

"Then don't. We've already made that decision. If Duke hadn't stuck his nose in our business, we wouldn't even be having this conversation, especially if you'd stayed away from here in the first place. I don't remember anyone inviting you to join today's festivities."

Larem leaned in closer, crowding her physically now as well as emotionally. She could've told him not to bother. After spending her whole life surrounded by dominant men, she'd learned to stand her ground or be trampled in the process.

Drawing on all the authority she could muster, she let him have it. "I'm in charge around here, or hadn't you noticed? I have every right to observe anything that goes on, even if it's a bunch of boneheaded men playing games."

Larem laughed, but it had nothing to do with humor. "You may pay the bills, Sasha, but that's not the same as running the place. Devlin is the one whose word is law. Without his support, you would get nowhere with all the changes you seem so hot on making. And those games you refer to help ensure your Paladins have the necessary skills to survive."

His words slammed into her. "This conversation is going nowhere. You go hang out with your friends. I'll go do my job. It's been nice." She started to walk away but didn't get far.

"I'll show you nice."

One powerful arm lifted her up off her feet while Larem's free hand drew her leg up around his waist. Somehow, her other one needed no encouragement from him to follow suit. Her skirt rode high around her thighs, leaving only the thin silk of her panties between her and Larem's trousers. The full contact with his body burned straight through her, making her all too aware of the emptiness inside her. An emptiness that only this man could fill.

She tangled her fingers in the black and silver silk of his hair and planted her mouth on his, demanding entry and offering no quarter.

He carried her to the corner that offered at least partial privacy from the windows that opened over the silent gym below. She applauded Larem's clear thinking, because at the moment all of her own thoughts were focused on getting as close to him as possible.

Her back bumped up against the wall, momentarily jarring her out of her passion-induced fog. What were they doing? What a stupid thing to ask when the answer was so obvious. The real questions were why they'd ended up in each other's arms again and how far was she willing to let this go.

Larem felt her hesitation and his hand froze, hovering at the elastic band of her panties. Once again he was offering her a last chance of refusal. They both knew this had to stop. This shouldn't happen.

"Hurry!" she whispered, before she regained her sanity.

He set her back down on her feet, fumbled with the buttons on his fly, and then tore off her panties. Then she was right back against that same wall, with nowhere left to go but on the wild ride of hunger that drove them both.

When he slid into her, it was one of the most perfect moments in her life. And when she walked away from him a few minutes later, it was one of the worst.

Chapter 15

$\mathcal{T}$ hree weeks passed, each day dragging by slower than the one before. After Larem's last talk with Devlin, he'd avoided spending much time around headquarters. The leader was seriously pissed about Larem's involvement with Sasha in defiance of his previous order to stay away from her. Well, at least Devlin was finally getting what he wanted.

Duke's future with the organization was still up in the air. He was restricted to limited duty, and his activities were being closely monitored—not to mention his e-mails and phone calls. From all reports, he was abiding by the rules, but Larem suspected he was just waiting for the uproar to die down before trying something again.

Lonzo had promised to keep his ear to the ground for any rumors linking Sasha to Larem. So far, Duke and his two buddies were keeping their mouths shut on the subject. He was glad for her sake.

One good thing had come from that day, though. Craig had actually called, asking if Larem was still interested in giving him lessons. The young Paladin was on temporary assignment down near Mount St. Helens, but they were scheduled to start upon his return. Until then, Larem was back to trying to find some meaning in his life. Lonzo had gone on the same mission and was due back any day. While he'd been gone, Larem had spent the long nights walking the streets of Seattle between sessions of studying Kalith healing.

The only bright spots were the hours he spent in the undemanding company of his four-legged friends at the animal clinic. He'd had several successes healing both the physical and emotional wounds suffered by Dr. Isaac's patients, but he knew his greatest victory was Chance.

The big dog was now trusted to wander free around the clinic for hours at a time, returning to his pen only to sleep or when there was another dog in the clinic who might go on the attack. His enthusiastic greeting every time Larem walked in the door helped hold the loneliness at bay.

On this particular morning Larem knelt down on one knee in front of Chance and gave the dog a good ear scratch. "Ready for your walk, boy?"

His happy whine and thumping tail were answer enough.

"Silly question, Larem. That dog has been watching the door for the past half hour." The vet looked at Chance over the top of his glasses. "I hate to say it, but it's time we start looking for a home for him."

Larem's stomach plummeted. He'd known the moment would come when Chance would move on and that it was a good thing. The big fellow deserved a whole lot of happiness in his life. That didn't mean it would be easy to let him go.

"Have you had anyone interested?"

"One couple looked at him but then decided he was too big for their yard." Dr. Isaac reached over to pet Chance's head. "I know you'll miss him, but some lucky person is going to offer him a home. We'll make sure it's an extra good one."

"That's what we've been working toward." Which was true, but that didn't mean Larem was happy about it. "Come on, boy, let's get going before the rain starts."

Outside, he let Chance choose their route. They'd spent so much time exploring together that the dog knew the streets around the clinic as well as Larem did. He even seemed to sense that it was important to cruise by a certain coffee shop on each trip. Sometimes Larem stopped to buy a cup of tea or coffee; sometimes he didn't, but every time, the two males paused to look inside just in case Sasha happened to be there.

So far, they'd had no luck, but that could change. Larem needed to know how she was doing. Their last encounter had left too many things unspoken between them. After they'd found release in each other's arms, she'd calmly walked away without looking back.

And fool that he was, he'd let her go.

In the days since, he'd kept telling himself it had been the right thing to do, even with his soul screaming out that he was making the mistake of a lifetime. He'd already let one possible mate slip away. But that hadn't hurt nearly as badly as watching Sasha disappear down the hall and out of his life.

Later that night, after Hunter left and Lonzo turned in for the night, Larem had stood out on the patio and stared up at the stars, recalling each sensation as he'd taken Sasha up against that wall. Had he been too rough with her? He'd wanted to leave his mark on her soul, not on her creamy, soft skin.

He'd never experienced anything as sweet as the welcoming heat of her body when he'd come deep inside her while Sasha's own climax washed over them both. It was then that he realized they'd been so caught up in the moment that they hadn't used protection.

The thought hadn't been far from his mind ever since. Perhaps she was taking that pill humans used, but Sasha hadn't mentioned it. Even if that was the case, would it even be effective with his alien DNA?

So, yes, he needed to see her, needed to know. If he didn't run into her soon, he'd have to seek her out. For days his dreams had been filled with images of her, her belly round and ripe with their child—and mostly they'd been good dreams. Would she think him crazy for feeling that way? Would she cherish the child even if she rejected the father?

Too many questions with no answers.

Chance pulled at the leash, his tail a blur, yanking Larem back into the present. He whined in excitement and looked back at Larem with a big doggy grin.

There was only one explanation: the dog had spotted Sasha.

Evidently she'd just been heading into the coffee shop, but right now she stood frozen in the doorway. Larem signaled Chance to stop and sit. The dog did as ordered but clearly wasn't happy about it. Larem understood his feelings on the subject, but he didn't want to crowd Sasha.

Instead, the two males stayed right where they were and prayed their female would come to them.

Okay, at least the dog was happy to see her. Maybe Larem was, too, but right now it was hard to interpret his stoic expression.

"Excuse me."

Sasha jumped at the sound of the voice coming from behind and then realized she was blocking the doorway. "Sorry."

After pasting a bright smile on her face, she crossed the few feet to where Larem and Chance were standing. After all, she'd walked all the way to this particular coffee shop on the off chance she'd accidentally run into Larem. She had a decision to make and needed to see him before she made up her mind.

Perhaps a walk around the block with Larem and Chance was exactly what she needed to clear her head and let her think things through. Still procrastinating, she leaned down to let Chance give her a big lick before dealing with the other half of the pair. She found it interesting how everyone else passing by gave the two such a wide berth, as if sensing they were every bit as dangerous as they looked.

It was hard not to get lost in the intensity of Larem's gaze when their eyes finally met. Sometimes she wondered if his Kalith DNA gave him the ability to see far more about a person than she could. For sure, he seemed to look straight into the heart of her. Fearing what he might see there, she turned her attention back to Chance.

"Well, I see you and your buddy here are still wearing out the sidewalks."

"We have enjoyed our walks." The light in his eyes dimmed a bit.

She asked, "Mind some company? D.J. and Cullen managed to recoup an impressive amount of the money Kincade had stolen, and I've been holed up in my office dealing with it. Today I think I've earned some time out here in the sunshine before I go there."

"That is good news, but weren't you going to get some coffee?" He gave her the ghost of a smile. "We can wait for you."

"If you're sure." Before she'd gone two steps, Chance blocked her way. "It's okay, boy, I'll be right back."

When the dog wouldn't move, Larem held out the leash. "Why don't I get it for you. Do you want the same as last time?"

He remembered? Smiling, she nodded but then had second thoughts. "Better make it decaf this time."

"Afraid you won't be able to sleep?"

Once again she nodded. Better to let him assume that was the reason. She reached for her wallet.

He waved her off. "My treat."

While she waited for him to get through the line,

she tugged Chance over to a low concrete wall nearby where she could sit down and pet him. She hugged the dog close, taking comfort in his solid warmth. God, what was she going to do? She thought she could stay away from Larem; Lord knows she'd tried. But even without the latest complication, the temptation to seek him out, to make sure he was all right, had been unbearable.

The door of the shop opened again. He was back, carrying two coffees and a bottled water. Larem handed her the coffees and then pulled a shallow bowl out of his jacket pocket and filled it for Chance. She liked that about him, that he cared so much about his furry friend.

After the dog slurped his fill of water, the three of them moved on down the sidewalk. For the first couple of blocks, they concentrated on sipping their coffee and avoiding conversation.

The forced peace couldn't last. Nothing had changed. She was who she was—a woman with her future all planned out. There was so much she could accomplish here in Seattle given the time and opportunity. Ever since David's death, she'd hated everything connected to the Others and their secret reign of terror. It still made her sick to think about how many good men like her first love had burned out their lives trying to stanch the flow of crazies across the barrier.

With that idea never far from her thoughts, she'd worked long and hard with her goals in mind: to improve conditions for the Paladins, to make their lives better, to find a way to stop the mental deterioration that ended their lives far too soon. And yet, here she was with her heart aching for a man who should be her enemy.

Sasha had watched Larem talking to the barista inside the coffee shop with his usual quiet dignity. The woman had handed him his change with a smile that was a few degrees too warm to make Sasha happy, not that she could blame her. He was certainly handsome enough, but there was so much more to him than that.

The other problem was that Larem was a man without real ties to this world. Yes, he had friends, but it was obvious that he missed his home. Given the opportunity, she suspected he'd bolt back across the barrier. What had held him here this long? He'd yet to share his story with her.

Which left them where?

Now, walking along beside Larem, she was acutely aware of his every movement. It was as if something inside her was hardwired to respond to him differently than she had to any other man she'd ever met. He moved with a warrior's grace and wore the same easy self-assurance that Paladins did, as if he were the toughest thing on the block, ready and able to handle whatever life threw at him.

She hoped that was true. She really did.

Larem smiled at her. "You're thinking awfully hard about something, Sasha. Is everything all right? Devlin's not driving you crazy, is he?"

"No, Devlin and I've actually made real progress on a few things this week. I don't know where he got such a reputation for being uncooperative." She grinned. "Of course, it probably helps that I'm the one with the checkbook."

"That might be part of it, but maybe not. Devlin

swears he's always dealing with idiots and fools. I suspect you confuse him since you don't often fit in either of those categories."

"Thanks." She shot him a sideways look. "I think."

The corners of his eyes crinkled, confirming he was teasing her. Damn it, why did he have to be so perfect in so many ways? She'd really been hoping that seeing him again would prove to her that the heat they'd generated had been a fluke, or if not, at least that that's all it had been. Unfortunately, the attraction she felt for him was more than hormones.

So that settled one question but left so many others unanswered. As long as she was walking beside him, she'd never get her head on straight.

She stopped at the next corner. "Well, I'd better leave you here. All that work on my desk won't finish itself."

Rather than risk looking at Larem—fearing he'd see the confusion written in her expression—she knelt down to take her leave of Chance. "You take care, big fella. Next time maybe we'll go to a park and play fetch."

The big dog's tail instantly drooped, and he whined before licking her hand. Darn it, did she have to like the dog as much as she did his owner?

"There won't be a next time."

She tore her attention from Chance back up to his grim-looking companion, her pulse doing a fifty-yard sprint. "Why? What's going on? Where are you going?"

Please not back to Kalithia. Not yet. Maybe not ever.

"I'm not going anywhere, but Chance doesn't belong to me. He's from the shelter where I volunteer. Now that his injuries are healed, the vet has listed him for adoption. It's only a matter of time before Chance finds a new home."

There was no mistaking the pain in Larem's voice. She put her hand on his sleeve. "Can't you adopt him?"

"I would if I could, but I don't have my own place. I live with Lonzo, and the apartment is barely big enough for the two of us. Now that Chance's leg is getting stronger, he needs a big yard and a family."

The dog deserved a little happiness in his life, but what about Larem? It was clear he had developed a strong attachment to the dog. So had she, for that matter.

"Listen, I just moved into Laurel's condo, and I'm rattling around in all that space. Maybe I could keep Chance for you until you have a place of your own. I know it's not a perfect solution, but at least you'd still be able to see him whenever you wanted to."

And her, too. Though that could be a problem. Some secrets have a way of revealing themselves. She'd have to tell Larem the truth and soon, but not out here on the street.

Larem studied her for several seconds. "Are you sure? Adopting a dog is a big commitment, and my situation is unstable. Besides, I thought your stay here was only temporary."

"Not if I can help it. Besides, Chance would really be yours." She hesitated. "And I'll have to check with Laurel to make sure it's all right."

From the way Larem was looking at Chance, he was definitely wavering. "Let's do this. You check with Laurel and think about it overnight. I'll ask Dr. Isaac to take Chance off the list for the next couple of days. If you're still interested, call me and we'll make the necessary arrangements."

He still didn't look entirely happy, but she knew she really didn't need the extra time at all. If Laurel was okay with Chance moving in, this time tomorrow she'd have someone to share her new home with.

She patted Chance one more time. "Well, I've got calls to make and work to do. I hope to see you tomorrow. *Both* of you, that is."

"We'll look forward to it."

Larem nodded good-bye and tugged Chance's leash, pulling the dog in the opposite direction. Sasha allowed herself to watch Larem as he and Chance made their way back toward the shelter. When Larem stopped abruptly, she quickly turned away, not wanting to be caught staring.

Okay, it was time to get her head back in the game. She really did have more work waiting at the office. Later she'd think about all the implications of seeing Larem and Chance again tomorrow. At least, it had felt good to get out for a while.

Except she was suddenly being crowded. She inched forward, trying to put some room between her and whoever was hovering just over her shoulder. She was already standing on the edge of the sidewalk when someone jostled her, almost causing her to lose her balance. Before she could say something, everything went to hell.

One minute she was waiting for the light to change, her thoughts churning as she tried to make sense of her

life, and the next she was flying forward to the tune of
squealing tires and honking horns. The pavement came
up hard and fast as she instinctively wrapped her arms
around her abdomen, leaving her head unprotected.
The last thing she remembered was a dog barking and a
pair of strong arms muscling her up off the ground.

Larem ignored the crush of people gathering
around. Thanks to Chance, they were keeping a re-
spectful distance. Larem cradled Sasha against his chest
before setting her down. Yeah, a couple of helpful individuals mumbled something about not moving her, but
did they really think he'd leave her sprawled out in the
street, giving somebody a second try at killing her?

If he hadn't given in to looking back at her one last
time, he would've missed the whole thing. She'd been
waiting for the light to change when a man in a dark
sweatshirt with the hood cinched down over his face had
given her a shove out into traffic before taking off down
the street at a dead run.

Chance had led the charge back down the block,
barking and clearing the path for Larem. He didn't need
to tell the dog to stay close while he dropped the leash
to deal with Sasha's injuries. Chance gave him room to
work and glared at anyone who got too close. Larem left
it up to others to call the authorities. He had more important things to do.

He ran his hands up and down Sasha's arms, chanting softly under his breath. For once he was able to
focus his gift, pulling in the healing warmth of the early
afternoon sun and blending it with the magic of his an-

cestors. He found bruises and scrapes but no broken bones. Using the lightest of touches, he threaded his fingers through her hair, searching for the cause of her continued unconsciousness.

She jerked in pain when he came into contact with a large lump on the back of her head. His hand came away slick with blood. He paused to slow the bleeding and reverse the swelling, taking comfort that some of the tension eased in her facial expression. Next, he passed his palm over her chest and on toward her stomach. No bleeding. Her ribs weren't fractured but badly bruised. He sent another surge of energy to soothe them.

As he concentrated, hurrying to do what he could before the medics arrived and took over, he continued to pour everything he had into healing the damage. The sirens were growing louder. Knowing he had seconds left at best, he made one more pass over her, paying special attention for possible internal injuries.

And found something. His blood ran cold and his skin flushed hot. He checked one last time and then surrendered her care to the medics after pulling Chance back out of the way. At least the dog sensed that the uniformed man and woman were there to help his Sasha.

As the EMTs ran through their protocols, they kept up a steady stream of questions. A police officer had joined the party, jotting down the information Larem provided before moving on to take witness statements.

"Sir, we're going to transport her to the trauma center now. Is there anyone who should be notified?"

Larem, still reeling, nodded. "She has no family locally. Her father lives in St. Louis. I don't have his number with me, but I'll see that he and her personal physician are contacted."

That last was a stretch of the truth, but would give Laurel a chance to intervene if necessary.

"Does she have any allergies that you know of?"

There were so many things about her he didn't know, and that was one of them. "I have no idea, but there is one thing the doctors should know."

The EMT paused, waiting for Larem to finish.

"She's pregnant."

Chapter 16

Sasha's head felt as if someone were using it for bongos. Where was she? She focused her energy on listening for any clues she could pick out over the banging inside her skull.

Judging by the sounds and smells, she was at the hospital, most likely in the emergency room. It made sense considering her last coherent memory was fighting a losing battle against a very big car. Well, it had looked pretty darn big coming straight at her, but she'd been in no real position to judge for sure. How had it happened?

Yeah, she'd been a bit distracted over her encounter with Larem and Chance, but she knew for a fact she hadn't stepped out in front of that car.

As she tried to clear her mind, other worries rose up to demand attention—one in particular. Her eyes finally opened enough that she could look around to see who could answer her questions.

A familiar figure hovered at the edge of her vision, just inside the curtain that surrounded her bed in the chaotic world of the emergency room. She was hoping for a doctor or even a nurse, anyone other than the man standing there.

"Larem?" she whispered, trying not to jar her head.

He moved closer to the bed and enfolded her hand in his. As soon as their hands connected, the bongos faded to a more bearable level. She sighed in relief, briefly accepting the comfort of his touch.

But she couldn't relax, not until she knew. "Where's the doctor?"

"With another patient, but she said she'd stop back to check on you soon. The nurse was also called away, but I'm sure she's not far." His accent had grown stronger again; his emotions were running high.

"Who did this to me?"

"We don't know, but the police are investigating. Witnesses were able to give them a pretty detailed description of the guy who pushed you." His eyes closed, and he squeezed her hand tighter. "Sasha, I—"

"I'll be okay." Or would be once she could talk to the medical staff. "Can you ask the nurse to come back in? It's important."

He nodded and walked out. She heard the low rumble of his voice and then the sound of footsteps heading her way. She braced herself to ask some hard questions.

A woman wearing a lab coat walked in. "Ms. Willis, I'm Dr. Brand. I'm glad to see you're perking up. Give me a minute to check a few things and then we'll talk."

She poked and prodded and took readings, her touch gentle but firm. When she was finished, she pulled up a chair and sat down.

"You're one very lucky lady. According to the police, you took quite a hit. You have a few bruises and abrasions as well as an impressive bump on your head, but none of your injuries are life threatening.

"Your friend Mr. Jones told us about the pregnancy. We confirmed it with a blood test, but so far there are no signs of any problems in that quarter. Of course, you'll want to follow up with your OB/GYN about the accident as soon as possible."

Relief mixed with confusion. Thank God the baby was all right, but how in the world had Larem known? She certainly hadn't told anyone about any of the home pregnancy tests she'd taken over the past couple of days, least of all him. The man had a lot to answer for, but this wasn't the time or the place.

"When can I go home?"

Dr. Brand smiled. "I always figure it's a good sign when my patients start asking that question. However, I'd like to admit you overnight to keep an eye on that head wound, since you don't have any family in Seattle. Unless you have someone who can stay with you, concussions can be tricky. You don't want to take any unnecessary chances, especially with a pregnancy involved."

"I'll stay with her."

Larem had returned. No surprise there. She'd sensed that he'd remained close by, but then he did have a vested interest in the doctor's report. The last thing she wanted to do was spend a night in the hospital surrounded by strangers, especially since the accident hadn't been an accident at all.

"Thanks, Larem, that would be great." Sort of.

She told herself that she'd accepted Larem's offer simply because she didn't have any other close friends here she could ask. The real truth was much simpler: she trusted him to keep her safe.

The doctor may have sensed some of the tension between them, because she glanced at Larem before giving Sasha a considering look. "If you're sure . . ."

"I'm sure."

"All right then, I'll write your discharge orders, but I don't want you to go home until after all the test results are back. Also, the police are going to want to take your statement before you leave."

When the doctor disappeared, Larem ventured closer. "I've already spoken to the authorities. They were going to stop by soon to see if you were awake. Devlin and Laurel are on their way, as well."

Sasha leaned back against her pillow and felt the burn of tears. The last thing she wanted was to be grilled by either the police or Devlin Bane, but she supposed there was no avoiding it.

Larem's gentle touch melted the last of her self-control, unleashing a stream of tears. He immediately perched on the edge of her bed and slowly pulled her into the sanctuary of his arms.

"This really wasn't an accident, was it? Someone shoved me out in front of that car," she whispered, trusting Larem to give it to her straight.

He didn't even hesitate. "No, it wasn't an accident.

Devlin has D.J. monitoring the police investigation, and they're handling the case as an assault. There's no indication the driver was involved, but they're hunting for the guy who ran from the scene."

He stroked her hair, making her want to purr. The man certainly had a calming touch. No wonder an abused dog like Chance had taken to him. *Chance!*

"Where's Chance?"

Larem smiled at her concern. "Safe and sound back at the shelter. The two of us ran there and then the vet, my friend Dr. Isaac, drove me here to the hospital. I arrived shortly after the ambulance."

He wiped her tears away with a tissue and then held it to her nose. "Blow."

She did as ordered, as embarrassing as it was. "Will the vet hold on to Chance if I can't take him yet?"

"I told Dr. Isaac that you're hoping to adopt Chance. He'll keep him at the shelter until you're ready to bring him home. He said once a dog chose to adopt a human, there was no sense in arguing the point, especially when there was a beautiful woman involved."

Okay, that was sweet. "Thank him for me."

"I will."

Someone hesitated right outside the curtain. "Excuse me, Miss Willis, I'm Detective Lake, the investigating officer on your case. Are you up to answering a few questions?"

No, but that really wasn't an option. Larem immediately stood up and moved away from the bed. Sasha drew a deep breath and said, "Please come in."

If the detective was surprised to see Larem there, it

showed only in a slight widening of his eyes. "Mr. Jones, we meet again."

Larem nodded and remained silent as the police officer settled into the one chair in the cubicle. "I'm glad to see you're on the mend, Miss Willis. Judging by the witness statements at the scene, that was quite a hit you took."

Which sent a chill straight through her. "It sure feels like it. I should warn you that I don't actually remember much."

The detective smiled. "That's not surprising, but I'd still like to hear any details you can share. Why don't you start with how you happened to be at the intersection and go from there?"

Thank goodness, as an employee of the Regents, she had a cover story ready for just this kind of situation. "I recently transferred here from St. Louis to replace the administrator who resigned from the consulting firm I work for. I went on a walk from the office to a coffee shop, and as I was going in, I ran into my friend Larem out walking his dog. The accident happened just after we'd gone our separate ways."

Lake nodded, as if to say her explanation jibed with what he already knew. "Okay, slow down now and give me any details you can, even if they seem unimportant."

"I was waiting at the corner for the light to change. I distinctly remember the crosswalk light was still red. There were others waiting to cross on that corner, too, enough that I was feeling pretty crowded. Someone jostled me, but I didn't see who it was."

She closed her eyes, replaying the sights and sounds in her head. "I was still watching the light when someone shoved me hard from behind. The last thing I remember was the squeal of tires and then a loud thump. I guess that would've been me hitting the car or the ground."

The detective sat with his pencil hovering over his notepad. "Did you see the person who shoved you?"

She thought about it. "A vague impression of a guy, but I could be wrong. Maybe he ran into me by accident and then took off scared."

"Maybe," the detective conceded, but his tone clearly said otherwise.

He asked a few more questions until he was satisfied that he'd mined her scattered memories for any useful information. After tucking his notebook back into his pocket, he pulled out a couple of business cards.

"Here's my number. Call if you remember anything else, or even if you just need to talk. You seem to be handling all this pretty well, but trust me, it can blind-side you even days later."

Larem asked one last scary question. "What do you think the chances are of catching the guy before he tries again?"

"Without a better physical description, it will be hard but hopefully not impossible." His easygoing façade faltered a bit. "But rest assured, I'm going to do my best. Even if the guy ran into you by accident, I understand the first urge might be to run. However, any decent human being would turn himself in after the adrenaline burns off."

Sasha clutched his business card like a lifeline. "Thank you, Detective. I'll call if I think of anything."

"Sounds good. I hope you feel better soon." He smiled again and started to leave.

At the last second he turned back toward Larem. "Mr. Jones, the doctor says you'll be keeping an eye on Ms. Willis tonight. That true?"

"Yes, it is. I will make sure she is not left alone."

The two men exchanged a long look before the detective finally nodded. "Like I said, call if you need me. Bye, folks."

This time the detective finally left and with him, Sasha's last bit of energy. She tugged her blankets up higher and tried to find a position where her head didn't hurt quite so much.

Very aware of Larem still hovering nearby, she said, "Look, I'm going to sleep for a bit. I'm sure you've missed at least one meal. Why don't you go grab a bite to eat? I'll be fine."

Once again, he rested his hand on hers. "I'll stay here until Laurel arrives. You shouldn't be alone right now."

Stubborn man. "But I'm not alone. If I need anything, the nurses are right outside."

But then maybe he was talking not about her injuries but the fact that someone might be gunning for her. If so, she shouldn't be alone, and that idea scared her all over again.

She gave up and closed her eyes, determined not to cry. "All right, fine. Stay if you want to, but at least sit down. I don't like being hovered over."

He gently brushed her hair back from her face. "I'll try not to hover. Get some sleep."

Then he leaned down to press a feathery kiss on her forehead. That was the last thing she remembered.

Duke sat in his living room and shook. God, what the hell had he gotten himself into? His fingers traced the wound on his neck, a reminder that he'd already come within a hair's breadth of dying. It still weirded him how quickly the cut had healed, and now he had Devlin Bane riding his case. That wasn't going to change in the near future.

He supposed he was lucky he still had a job at all. Earlier, he'd been in Devlin's office when the Paladin had gotten a phone call. The man had started cussing a blue streak and immediately ordered Duke to go home and plant his ass there until further notice. On the way home, Duke had driven past a guy parked in an unfamiliar car down the street. Duke had just checked and he was still there.

Was his house being watched? If so, who was doing the watching? One of Devlin's boys? Or did Rusty have someone spying on Duke? It really didn't matter as long as he hunkered down on the couch watching TV and calming his nerves with a six-pack.

The mysterious watcher wasn't what had Duke all weirded out anyway. When he'd come home and turned on the computer, there'd been another anonymous e-mail with a video clip attached. When he played it, his blood ran cold. Someone had tried to kill Sasha Willis. Thank God he'd still been at headquarters with Devlin Bane himself when it happened. At least Duke's name wouldn't be tossed in the hat as a possible suspect.

The really creepy part was that someone had filmed the whole thing. He'd been debating whether or not to forward it to Bane for the past couple of hours and still hadn't reached a decision. It might help him start earning his way back into the organization's good graces. On the other hand, Rusty, most likely the bastard who'd sent it to him, was obviously willing to kill for the cause. Duke really didn't want to offer himself up as the next target.

Maybe it was time to think about asking for a transfer. Things here in Seattle were getting too damned weird. Yeah, sure, he'd insulted the new administrator, but what the hell did she expect when she took up with a freak instead of a human? That didn't mean he wanted her dead.

No doubt Larem q'Jones and his buddies were already on the prowl, looking for whoever was responsible. Once again, Duke traced the raised scar running across his throat, a permanent reminder of how Larem had slit him open. No way he wanted to give that Other an excuse to finish what he'd started.

The phone rang, causing him to jump about a foot in the air. He reached for his cell and checked the number. The ID was blocked; no surprise there.

"Hello?"

"Did you enjoy the video I sent you?" The male voice was altered, making it impossible for Duke to identify the caller.

"No, I didn't. Rusty, is that you? If so, quit fucking with me. You shouldn't have gone after Sasha Willis. I don't want anything to do with that."

"Aw, Duke, you disappoint me. And here I had such high hopes for you." Then he laughed, the distortion making it sound as if it came straight out of some cheesy horror film.

Duke hated cheesy horror flicks, but somehow his life had become one. "Don't call me again."

"You're in no position to be giving orders. You're part of us now. I'd suggest you do as you're told. When I need your services again, I'll call."

"And if I don't pick up?"

"Duke, you don't want to know the answer to that question. And by the way, for your sake, I'm really glad you didn't give in to the temptation to forward my e-mail to your friend Devlin. That would not have pleased us at all."

When the phone went dead, Duke reached for another beer. Maybe he should have bought two six-packs.

Larem studied Sasha's face, wishing he could risk performing another healing. His energy supply was running low, and he had to keep something in reserve in case he needed to act quickly.

The curtain stirred, warning him that someone was about to join them. He rose to his feet, prepared to defend Sasha if necessary. He relaxed when a familiar face appeared in the small gap at the edge of the curtain.

Laurel peeked in, taking in both him and Sasha in a

quick glance. She kept her voice to a soft whisper. "Okay if we come in?"

"Please do."

He backed into the corner near the head of the bed to make room for the Handler and her husband. Devlin followed her in, his broad shoulders taking up most of the extra room in the cubicle.

Laurel studied the readouts on the monitor on the wall. "How is she?"

"Tired, scared, sore," Larem answered, fisting his hands to resist touching Sasha, who stirred restlessly as if in pain.

She needed her rest, and he needed to bring the Paladin leader up to speed. "Laurel, will you stay with her while Devlin and I find a more private place to talk?"

"Of course." Laurel studied Larem for a second, those dark eyes seeing far too much. "Dev, take this man and get him some food. Judging by his appearance I suspect he's been practicing his mojo on Sasha, and he's running on empty."

"Will do. You two should be safe enough here." He jerked his head in the direction of the nurses' station. "There's plenty of medical staff around and security officers down the hall. We won't stay gone long."

"We'll be fine. Go before the man falls down." She gave Larem a gentle shove toward the exit. "When you get back, I'll hunt down the ER doc and get a full report as Sasha's primary caregiver."

Larem swallowed hard, knowing exactly what detail that report would contain. Sasha was going to hate having others find out about the pregnancy when she clearly hadn't yet come to terms with it herself. God, he was still reeling with the knowledge that they'd created a new life together.

He said, "That's good. The doctor was going to write her discharge orders but said Sasha had to stay here until the final reports are all in. I'll be staying at Sasha's place tonight because the doctor says she shouldn't be alone."

Laurel gave him one of those looks that very clearly said she knew there was more to that story, but at least she didn't press for details. He and Devlin made their way out of the chaos of the emergency room and followed the signs to the cafeteria.

Devlin handed Larem a tray. "Look, I know how much you guys like your veggies. However, if you're going to keep burning energy like you've obviously been doing, you need protein. Eat some meat or at least some eggs and cheese. Don't make me force the issue."

Larem appreciated the rough concern in Devlin's order, but he could take care of himself. He wasn't an idiot. Or maybe he was, everything considered. Rather than argue, he chose a salad with grated cheese and a bit of ham. After adding a couple of hard-boiled eggs to his tray, he picked up two cartons of yogurt and one of whole milk.

Noticing that Devlin was watching his every move, he sighed in disgust. "Satisfied?"

"It's a good start, although I'd rather you ate a big slab of the meat loaf and some of that chicken."

"We'll see how I feel after I eat this much."

"Fair enough." Devlin pulled out his wallet and told the cashier to ring up both trays.

"Thanks, Dev."

"Yeah, well, don't tell any of the guys I was so generous. D.J. would be hitting on me to pick up the tab all the time."

Larem smiled, partly because it was true, but mainly because he appreciated Devlin's efforts to lighten up the situation for a few minutes. They'd all had a big scare, and a little humor would go a long way toward helping them both find some balance.

For a few minutes, they ate in silence. Larem hadn't realized how hungry he was until he took that first bite. It wasn't long at all before his tray was filled with empty cartons and dishes. He waited until Devlin polished off the last of his sandwich and pushed his tray away before speaking.

He looked around the cafeteria. They'd deliberately chosen a table in a quiet corner, and the two closest tables were now empty. This was going to be their best shot at some privacy.

"Okay, here's what happened."

Devlin leaned back in his chair, balancing it on two legs as he listened. Larem started with meeting up with Sasha at the coffee shop and brought him up to speed on almost everything. He considered whether or not to tell Devlin the one thing he'd left out, but decided not to until he and Sasha had had a chance to talk.

Laurel would probably find out from the doctor overseeing Sasha's care, but he trusted her to keep that bit of information to herself.

Devlin rocked forward, bringing the front legs of his chair down with a thud. "You're holding something back, Larem, but I'll give you the benefit of the doubt. If I find out whatever it is puts Sasha at further risk, though, I'll kick your ass. Got it?"

"Got it, but I promise it has nothing to do with today." He fiddled with his napkin, tearing it into small shreds. It was time to lay the rest of his cards on the table.

"This was a deliberate attack on her, Devlin. The bastard shoved her out into heavy traffic, doing his best to kill her. It's only a matter of luck that she was knocked aside by the fender instead of getting hit head-on. Coupled with the fiasco in the tunnels, it would seem that someone is determined to see her hurt—or worse."

Larem bit his lip, fighting to control the renewed surge of murderous fury. "If I hadn't been there, that head wound could have been dangerous. I managed to contain the damage, but just barely."

Devlin's sympathetic expression almost proved Larem's undoing. The big man looked away, giving Larem a precious bit of time to collect himself before Devlin spoke again.

"So far, Duke's our only connection to whatever's going on. I'll sic Cullen and D.J. on his phone and computer to see if anyone's contacted him. I know for a fact that rat bastard wasn't involved today, but that doesn't mean he's completely innocent. I'll also call in Barak and Hunter to spell you on protection duty for Sasha. If Sasha is anything like their women and mine, she's going to insist on getting right back to work, and you can't be on guard twenty-four/seven."

"Thanks, Devlin. Promise me when we track down the monster who did this, I get first crack at him."

"You have my word. Now, let's go see if your woman is ready to get out of here. We'll drive by your place so you can grab a few things and then take you both to the condo. Just so you know, I had a top-of-the-line security system installed when Laurel was still living there. It won't stop someone who's really determined, but it should give you time to respond."

"That's good." Larem grimaced. "By the way, I'm not sure Sasha would be happy to hear herself referred to as mine."

Devlin's predatory nature showed in his grin. "Yeah, that doesn't make it any less true. I'm guessing you're both dealing with some pretty strong feelings for each other." Then his smile faded. "Seriously, Larem, you have to know you'll both be fighting an uphill battle if you try to make this thing work between the two of you."

Like he didn't know that already. "It wouldn't be the first human-Kalith pairing."

"True, but Sasha clearly wants to be the next Seattle Regent. And judging by what she's trying to accomplish here, I think she'd make a damn good one. I have to tell you that having someone like her after the shit we've put up with in the past is pretty incredible. I'd hate to see anything screw that up."

Larem got up to dump his tray, not wanting to hear another word on the subject. But Devlin wasn't the kind to take a hint, not when he had something on his mind.

"On the other hand, God knows I'm the last one who should be pointing fingers when it comes to this kind of thing. The Regents still aren't happy about me hooking up with my Handler. My advice? Do what you have to do, and we'll deal with it."

The knot in Larem's chest eased just enough to make him smile. "Thanks, Devlin. I know my presence in your world has caused more than a few problems for you, and I regret that."

"Compared to the grief I get from that bunch I ride herd on, you're hardly a blip on my radar when it comes to being a problem." He punched Larem on the arm. "Keep it that way. Now let's get a move on. I hate hospitals."

Chapter 17

Sasha counted the minutes until they reached the condo, where she could take a shower, crawl into bed, and pretend the world didn't exist.

It also didn't hurt that Larem had thought to ask Laurel about the possibility of Chance moving in with Sasha. Not only had the Handler agreed, she'd offered to stay with Sasha and help her get settled while the two men made a run to the pet store for the doggie necessities. Larem had also called Dr. Isaac, who agreed to wait until they got there to pick up the dog.

She couldn't wait. Right now she could use the comfort of her furry friend, because once Devlin and Laurel left, she'd be alone with Larem. Any kind of buffer would come in handy.

Devlin pulled the car into the garage and turned off the engine. Larem hurried around to help her out. Pride had her wanting to refuse, but the truth was she was so stiff and sore that she had to accept. Once he got her into the house, Laurel, bless her, took charge and shooed the men back out of the cono.

As soon as they left, Sasha stopped trying to maintain a brave front and sagged against the counter. "I'm sorry to be such a bother, Laurel."

"Don't worry about it. Besides, that's what friends are for. Now let's get you into the shower before the guys get back with your new roommate."

Sasha let Laurel help her down the hall. Funny, she hadn't realized they'd crossed the line into friendship, but she liked the idea.

The hospital had given her a pair of disposable scrubs to wear home. Her clothes had been torn and covered in blood, and the police wanted to check them for trace evidence from her attacker. Laurel stayed close by in case she needed help peeling the scrubs off, but she managed to do it on her own. A small victory, but a victory nonetheless.

The shower stung when it hit her scrapes, but the heat soothed away some of the stiffness. At first the water ran brownish red as it took two rounds of shampoo to get rid of all the blood in her hair. Washing away the last vestiges of the accident was well worth the price of a little pain.

Laurel was waiting to help Sasha dress in a clean pair of pajamas and her robe. "Why don't you sit on the edge of the bed and let me dry your hair? I'd like to take a look at your head, too."

Sasha eased herself down on the corner of the bed and let the Handler do her thing. She winced when Laurel's fingers pressed briefly on the bump.

"Sorry about that, but it's looking good. Not nearly as bad as I feared." She gently toweled Sasha's hair and then used the blow dryer to finish the job.

"Once we get you settled in the living room, I'll make us tea. I'm pretty sure I left some in the cabinet. One of the caffeine-free herbals will be safe for you to drink."

"Sounds good," Sasha agreed as she shuffled down the hallway to the living room.

The mention of herbal tea hinted that a question was coming. She'd hoped to have more time, but circumstances had made that impossible. When Laurel joined her with two steaming mugs, Sasha spoke first.

"So the doctor told you I'm pregnant."

Laurel nodded. "She did, and for what it's worth, I haven't told Devlin and won't without your permission. I take patient confidentiality seriously, but I do think he should be told. He can help you deal with any fallout."

"I'll think about it. I only found out for sure yesterday myself." She sipped her tea and blurted out the rest. "I guess you've also figured out Larem's the father. He knows, but I don't know how. I hadn't told anyone, not even him."

Laurel frowned. "Were you going to?"

"Soon, but not yet." She managed a smile and placed her hand on her still-flat stomach. "Of course, eventually the truth will reveal itself."

Laurel seemed to take it all in stride. "Have you had a physical yet, other than what they did at the ER?"

One more thing to add to her to-do list. "Not yet. I'm

so new here, I don't have a doctor of any kind, much less an OB/GYN. Never imagined I'd need one, at least not like this."

"I can make a couple of recommendations for you."

Okay, that took care of the basics. "Laurel, about Larem. I know this is going to sound crazy considering everything, but I'm worried about how he's going to feel about this. Before all this happened, the last time I saw him we didn't exactly part on good terms."

The Handler looked sympathetic. "From everything I know about him, Larem is one of the good guys. Devlin sure likes him, and he has made good friends among the Paladins."

Laurel stopped to sip her tea. Finally, she said, "If he hasn't told you his story, you should ask him. I can guess how he found out about the pregnancy, but you'll need to hear that from him."

The sound of the garage door warned them that their private conversation was about to end.

"Are you all right with Larem staying with you? If not, we can stay over."

Sasha couldn't avoid Larem forever, and the truth was that she felt safer when he was with her. "I'll be fine. Besides, Chance will keep both of us occupied."

When the kitchen door opened, Chance came bounding in, skidding to a halt in front of Sasha's chair. Then he approached her slowly as if he sensed that she needed a gentle touch. He laid his big head in her lap and sighed.

Laurel's eyes were huge as she took in the size of the beast.

"You said it was a dog, not a horse," she laughed.

Devlin spread out the cartons of Chinese food he'd brought on the coffee table. She could hear Larem rooting around in the kitchen, and a minute later he appeared with plates, serving spoons, and forks.

Sasha struggled to sit forward, trying to push the dog's head off her lap. "Come on, Chance, give me a break here," she said, giving his soft fur a stroke. "I promise to pet you all you want once I've eaten. Why don't you go check the place out?"

His ears immediately perked up and then he did exactly as she suggested. He made the rounds in the living room, accepting pets from all four people before taking off to investigate.

Devlin loaded up a plate for himself and one for his wife. "You got yourself a nice dog, Sasha. Larem told me his history. I've gotta tell you, it makes me want to hunt down his former owner and heap some serious abuse right back at him."

"Me, too, but he's really Larem's dog. I'm just Chance's roommate for now."

Although she had a feeling it would be really hard to hand him over when the time came. Rather than dwell on it, she concentrated on finishing her dinner before she gave in to sleep.

She set her plate back on the coffee table, content for the moment to listen to the murmur of the other three talking between bites. After a bit, their voices grew more distant, until they almost disappeared altogether. Right before sleep claimed her completely, though, a pair of strong arms lifted her off the couch. Bits and pieces of conversation floated past her.

"Can you turn down the sheets?"

"Here, let me help you with her robe."

The touch of cool cotton against her skin felt good as someone—Larem?—settled her on the bed. She thought maybe she smiled. Then there was nothing but silence and sleep.

"Call if you need us, and don't forget to set the alarm." Devlin jingled his keys in his hand. "Barak said he'd be glad to come over first thing in the morning if you need him to relieve you. I've also posted a couple of the young Paladins across the street to keep an eye on the place."

"Thanks, Devlin." Larem patted Chance on the head as he followed Devlin toward the kitchen door. "I know she appreciates both of you coming to help."

"Anytime."

Laurel joined the conversation. "Devlin, would you mind waiting in the car for me? I need to talk to Larem for a minute."

Her husband looked less than pleased as he started for the door. "You know, I really hate secrets."

"Yeah, I know. That doesn't change the fact that I need to talk to Larem in private." She frowned before adding, "And crank up the radio, so that super-duper Paladin hearing doesn't let you eavesdrop."

"Woman, you are way too suspicious." But Devlin was laughing as he disappeared into the garage.

Laurel waited until she heard the music turn on before speaking. "I wanted to remind you to wake Sasha up every couple of hours. Any sign that she's slow to respond or can't answer simple questions, call nine-one-one and then me."

"I will." But there was more—he could see it in the way her eyes kept bouncing between him and down the hall to where Sasha lay sleeping.

"Look, Larem, I know about the pregnancy and that you're the father. The ER doc saw no sign of any problems, but I'll be setting Sasha up with an obstetrician for a full workup as soon as possible. It would help if you made a list of anything you know about Kalith pregnancies that might be helpful. For example, the normal human gestation period is nine months. If it's different for your people, we'll have to keep that in mind."

Okay, he hadn't had time to think that far ahead. In fact, he hadn't let himself think beyond the next few minutes since the time of the accident.

"I'll do that. I'll also ask Hunter to contact Sworn Guardian Berk to obtain a medical book on the subject from my world."

"Good thinking." Laurel knelt down to pet Chance again. "And I think it's wonderful that you've been practicing your mojo on the animals at the vet's clinic. I assume you've also used it on Sasha."

Larem nodded. "I eased the bruising on her ribs, slowed the bleeding on a few cuts, and repaired some of the damage to her head. My gift wasn't strong enough to completely heal her, though."

Judging by the way Laurel hesitated, she was about to venture into awkward territory. "And I'm guessing that's how you discovered she was pregnant."

"Yes."

"Does she know about your gift?" Laurel stood and picked up her purse.

"Not yet. I was going to tell her, but it never seemed to be the right time. Now I guess I'll have to."

"You think?" Laurel said with a small smile. "And, Larem, sooner would be better than later. I don't know how things are in your world, but the women here tend to take it badly when they find out their men have been holding out on them."

"As I already pointed out to your mate, I doubt Sasha considers herself mine."

"Larem, I don't know what has happened between the two of you. Obviously you've got some serious stuff to work through, but stop and think for a minute. After almost being killed, Sasha has to be terrified, especially when she has no idea who's behind the attack. Right now, she's vulnerable, hurt, and barely able to take care of herself."

Laurel tilted her head to the side as she looked up at him. "So who is the one person she trusts enough to protect her tonight? You. Just you. And don't think we didn't offer to run you off and take your place if she wanted us to."

Then she gave him a quick hug. "Now, I'd better get out there before Dev decides to leave without me."

They both knew her warrior husband wouldn't do any such thing, but it was nice to part on a teasing note. He locked the door after Laurel and set the alarm.

"Well, boy, let's make the rounds."

The dog followed him from room to room as Larem

checked to see that the windows were locked. It seemed unlikely that anyone knew for sure where Sasha was living now, but on the other hand, someone had evidently been following her.

He saved Sasha's room for last, not wanting to disturb her. It was still another hour until the time Laurel said he should check on her. Chance quietly stalked into Sasha's room, acting like a perfect gentleman. He walked around the periphery of her bed, testing the air and whining softly. Obviously, Larem wasn't the only one who wished he could crawl under the covers and lay his head on the pillow beside hers.

After checking the window lock, Larem allowed himself the small privilege of watching Sasha sleep. The room was dark except for the light that poured through from the hallway. That didn't matter; his eyes functioned better in dim light than a normal human's, allowing him to drink in Sasha's beauty. He wanted nothing more than to gather her up in his arms and hold her tight.

The thought of how close he'd come to losing her made him physically ill.

Chance moved up next to him and rested his head on the foot of the bed. Larem smiled at the dog. Boy, talk about kindred spirits. Both of them had it bad for the same woman. That was okay—he was more than willing to share her with his four-footed friend.

Sasha might not appreciate waking up to the two males standing over her, although she probably wouldn't mind Chance sticking close by.

"Stay, boy. I'll check in on both of you soon."

•   •   •

The living room was a lonely place with both of the other occupants of the condo sleeping down the hall. Larem made the rounds again, more because he was restless than because he thought there was any immediate danger.

He stared across the street, trying to see where their Paladin guards were hiding. Even with his superior night vision it took him a while to spot them lurking in the shadows. It was doubtful that anyone passing by would see them at all.

Larem went back to trying to outdistance his demons.

Half an hour later, he finally admitted that no amount of pacing was going to help and stretched out on the couch. It was a few inches too short for comfort, but he needed to wake Sasha shortly anyway and didn't want to risk falling asleep.

Lying on his back, he laced his fingers behind his head and stared up at the ceiling. It was the first time since discovering Sasha carried his child that he'd had a chance to really think about things. It was almost impossible to sort out the tangle of emotions knotted up inside him.

Starting with the fact he was going to be a father. A child that he and Sasha had created in a moment of angry passion. He tried to picture an infant with his eyes and her hair or the other way around. The images made him smile even as they scared him.

True, he'd always imagined a day when he'd find the right mate and start a family, but that was before his life had been ripped out of Kalithia by the roots.

After that, he'd pretty much given up looking beyond the day at hand. Despite his efforts to find a place for himself in this world, somehow, someday, he'd always hoped to find a way to go back home and pick up the pieces of his life.

As unlikely as that possibility had been, it had kept him moving forward one day at a time, but now he'd been cut completely adrift. How could he return to Kalithia and leave his son or daughter behind? Here, half-Kalith children could blend in and live a normal life. In his world that wouldn't happen, and he'd never subject a child of his to the pain of prejudice.

He would've expected to be angry over having the decision made for him, but oddly enough, all he felt was relief and maybe a bit of excitement. It didn't really matter to him *where* he lived; the *why* was far more important. A child gave him a new sense of purpose, a new focus for his future.

But what if Sasha decided to return to her life back in Missouri to be closer to her father and friends? She might not want him to follow, but he would. Granted, the move would be hard. At least here in Seattle, the Paladins were willing to accept him as part of their inner circle. That was unlikely to happen anywhere else, but it was a risk he'd have to take to remain near his child— and the woman who held his heart.

From the beginning, he'd been fighting the attraction he felt for Sasha, but no longer. His feelings for her ran deep and true. There wasn't anything he wouldn't do to keep her and their child safe.

Anything, that is, but walk away.

•　　•　　•

Closing his eyes, Larem reached out with his senses to listen to the night. When he'd first arrived in Seattle, it had taken him weeks to grow accustomed to the noises that humans took for granted. Right now it was quiet except for the buzz of the city in the background. But for a second there, he could've sworn that something had jarred.

Sitting up, he waited to see if he heard it again. There. It was coming from down the hall. A soft moan and a whine. The first was Sasha, the second a worried Chance. Immediately, Larem was up and running.

He paused in the doorway. Chance stood beside the bed watching Sasha thrash around, twisted up in the sheets. The dog looked relieved to see Larem and backed away to give him space at the head of the bed.

"Sasha, wake up."

She stilled briefly but then started struggling again. Larem drew on his replenished pool of energy as he cupped her face with his hands and used a small trickle of healing warmth to soothe her. It didn't help.

He said her name louder this time. "Sasha, it's time to wake up."

No response.

"Please, honey, I just need to make sure you're all right." He shook her shoulder slightly, just enough to break the hold sleep had on her now.

Finally, she blinked up at him. "Larem? What's wrong?"

"Sorry to wake you, but you were having a nightmare."

"Yeah, I was." Her eyes looked haunted. "I keep hearing that car and then I jerk awake just before it hits me. Then I'm back down in the tunnels with someone following me. I keep running, but I end up going in circles. It's all mixed up together."

"I'm not surprised." He brushed her hair back from her face. "Are you hurting?"

She nodded, her hand straying up to where her head had hit the curb. "A little, but I don't want to take any more pain medicine. You know, because of the baby."

"That's probably wise." He wondered if he should risk giving her another dose of his energy. Maybe it would be better to wait until she was asleep again.

She petted Chance, who'd worked his big head under her hand as soon as Larem stepped back out of his way. Her eyes followed him to the door. "You've got to be exhausted, too."

"I'm all right. I was stretched out on the couch." He remained in the doorway. "If it helps ease your mind, Chance and I made sure everything was locked, and I set the alarm after Laurel and Devlin left."

"Thanks, I really appreciate all that you've done, Larem."

"I was happy to stay." He backed into the hall. "I won't be far. Don't hesitate to call if you need anything."

Clutching the covers with her hands, Sasha sat up. "I'd really sleep better if you stayed closer."

He blinked in surprise. "Okay, I'll go drag a chair in from the other room."

"That's not necessary." She flipped back the covers from the empty side of the bed. "I was thinking a lot closer. Besides, we need to talk."

Still he hesitated. His mind might know she was hurt and fragile right now, but he wasn't so sure his body understood. Before he could make up his mind, he noticed her smile was quickly fading. The last thing he wanted to do was hurt her feelings. He walked to the side of the bed and kicked off his shoes. When he started to sit down, she stopped him.

"Such a gentleman. Look, you might as well get comfortable."

In no mood to argue, he ditched his shirt and pants, conscious of her watching his every move.

"I promise to behave," he said as he slid in between the sheets.

"I know," she murmered.

Sasha slowly released the breath she'd been holding as Larem snuggled in close until her head was resting on his chest, his arm wrapped around her. Being near him soothed her in so many ways.

The two of them still had some major hurdles to face, no doubt about it, but for tonight, she needed his warmth and his strength to hold back the darkness. As they lay there in the quiet room, there was one thing she needed to know.

"Larem, how did you figure out that I'm pregnant? I only just knew for sure myself yesterday and hadn't told anyone."

"It's part of my Kalith nature, a gift that has been lost

to my people for generations because of the fading light in our world. But here, with your bright sun, I have become what you would call a healer."

She could feel the rumble of his words through his chest as his hand brushed lightly up and down her arm, leaving a warm tingle in its wake. Gradually the warmth spread, easing the aches that had kept her from really falling asleep. On the other hand, she could feel Larem tensing up.

"Tell me more."

"In my world, I could sometimes do small things— close up cuts, ease minor pain. But when Hunter was dying from a gunshot wound, I took a chance and tried to heal him. My efforts enabled him to come back faster than he would've on his own. By early the next morning, his injuries were all but gone."

He took a deep breath, relaxing a bit. "Other than that one time, I haven't used my gift on any humans or Kalith to heal major injuries until today."

He'd been staring up at the ceiling but now angled his head down to look at her. "My gift doesn't always work as it should, so I've been practicing on the abused animals at the shelter. Chance wouldn't have survived his injuries without my help, and it may be the reason he's learning to trust people again."

She smiled against his skin. "What a perfect use for your ability. I can see why you'd have some misgivings about using it to aid Paladins on a regular basis. Is it weird to have so many friends among those you always thought were your enemies?"

He briefly squeezed her tighter. "It is a problem that all of us who now live in the light must come to peace with."

"Do you think you'll ever go back?" God, she hoped not, although she wasn't sure she had the right to ask him to stay.

"I had hoped to someday, but now . . ."

She didn't need to ask what had changed his mind, not when his hand immediately settled over her stomach. A feeling of warmth and well-being spread through her, right up until it occurred to her that his magic was Kalith and she was human.

She caught his hand with hers. "Is doing that safe?"

"I would not harm you or the child—our child." But he withdrew his hand anyway. "But I understand why you would worry."

"Can you tell if it's a girl or a boy?"

"Not yet. Do you have a preference?"

She smiled again. "I haven't thought that far ahead yet, but I don't think so."

"But you'll keep our child?"

She turned to stare into his worried face. "Yes, I will."

"But the Regents—"

She cut him off. "I'll deal with them when the time comes, but the baby's more important. Push come to shove, there are other jobs."

His relief was obvious. "You'll be a great mother, so fierce and protective." He gently cupped her face, a small smile softening his somber expression. "Sasha, you know I want to be there for both of you."

She turned to nuzzle his hand, pressing a soft kiss to his palm. "I never doubted it."

When she yawned, he pulled her closer again. "Now,

you need to sleep. I have to wake you up again in two hours."

"All right."

She closed her eyes and relaxed. Maybe she should be worried about how good sharing this moment with him felt, but that was something she'd deal with tomorrow. Or maybe the next day. Right now, she needed this man beside her and that was enough.

Morning came slowly. Larem hovered somewhere between sound asleep and pleasantly aware of the warm female currently half-sprawled across his body, her head tucked under his chin. If this was a dream, he didn't want to wake up. If it was reality—well, he was in no hurry to let the outside world intrude.

Besides, neither of them had enjoyed a quiet night. Every couple of hours he'd had to make sure she woke up. Right now, it was enough to doze with Sasha in his arms.

"You're thinking way too hard." Sasha blinked up at him sleepily, her fiery hair surrounding her sweet face in a halo of unruly curls. "Got something on your mind?"

Yes, a couple of things, starting with how tempting it was to have her lush body so close to his. All that separated them was the thickness of his boxers and her pajamas. Even that kept them too far apart. Better to deal with one last issue.

"I was asked to befriend you deliberately."

He immediately felt a new thrum of tension in Sasha when she asked, "By whom?"

He stared up at the ceiling, not wanting to see her reaction. "The other Kalith and their mates. They thought if the new representative got to know me as a real person before finding out I was Kalith, it would change how all of us were dealt with."

"Why did they pick you instead of Lusahn or Barak?"

He didn't even try to sugar-coat it. "Because I was expendable. If it blew up in my face, I could disappear more easily than any of them."

Sasha was looking pretty darn fierce. "I understand why they did it, but that was mean of them."

"They meant no harm. They were trying to protect themselves." He trailed his fingers down her shoulder, trying to soothe away her anger.

"Yeah, I get that, but who was protecting *you*?"

Her question pleased him, sending another surge of desire for this woman burning through him. "I won't complain, Sasha, not if it led me here. Don't hold it against them. I wouldn't have said anything, but I wanted nothing but truth between us. Okay?"

He felt her nod.

"There is one other thing on my mind."

"Which is?"

When he didn't immediately answer, she raised herself up to look at him. Her eyes widened and her mouth curved in a seductive smile. "Never mind. I think I can guess what it might be."

Her playful mood had him smiling. "So now you're a mind reader?"

"Oh, I don't have to be when there's obvious proof readily at hand."

Her fingers traveled down his chest to stroke the hard evidence. He thought about claiming it meant nothing, that it was normal in the morning, but they both knew this time was different.

She caressed his cock slowly with the palm of her hand. Out of pure selfishness, he let her continue, wishing like crazy they could finish what she'd started. Finally, he gently grasped her hand, threading his fingers with hers.

She pouted. "Don't you like that?"

"You know I do, but you're testing my already shaky control." He kissed the top of her head.

"And if I want you out of control?"

She slowly slid her body up over his until her core was centered right over his erection. Dear gods, how was he supposed to think straight when she rocked against him like that?

"Sasha, I want you, but you were badly injured yesterday. I don't want to hurt you."

"Oddly enough, the pain is almost completely gone. Thanks to a certain healer I happen to know, I'm feeling positively frisky." She nibbled on his chin after each word.

He might be cautious, but he wasn't fool enough to dismiss her offer out of hand. Still, he had to ask, "Are we doing this because you were almost killed yesterday or because you really want *me*?"

She sat up and eased her hands under the hem of his undershirt and spread her fingers out over his chest. "A little of the first and a whole lot of the second."

He appreciated the honesty. "Perhaps, as your healer, I should reassess your injuries."

"Tell me what you want me to do."

He gently rolled her back onto her own side of the bed, and then lifted her head enough to tuck his pillow in on top of hers. "Now lie back and relax. I'll take care of everything."

He knelt beside Sasha and took her hand in his. Closing his eyes, he slowly traced the length of her arm, pausing over each bruise or scrape long enough to add a small jolt of healing. He repeated the same procedure with her other arm before moving over her shoulders and neck.

Her hair slid like silk over his fingers as he checked the bump on her head. "Any headache?"

Her eyes were closed, her face peaceful. "Not now."

"Good."

He leaned forward until his palms hovered a hair's breadth over her breasts. Sasha drew a deep breath and that small distance disappeared. When her eyes flew open at his touch, he started to pull back, but she stopped him by putting her hands on his.

"I like when you touch me."

So he did, gently kneading the soft curves until her nipples pebbled. As much as he wanted to linger there, he had more territory to cover. He continued down her sides to the curve of her hips and then checked each of her legs, top to bottom and back again. Sasha's breathing had sped up, as had his.

He held his palms over her stomach, smiling at the fierce bit of life that had taken hold there. Male, female, it didn't matter. The miracle was that he and Sasha had created the child together. He lowered his mouth down to press a kiss right above where his child rested, smiling when Sasha's legs stirred and her hips flexed.

The exam was quickly becoming a seduction. He eased the waistband of her PJ bottoms down and kissed the same spot again and then lower and lower still. Sasha lifted her hips in encouragement. He quickly peeled her pajamas off and then took his time driving his lover wild with his touch and his tongue.

Sasha shattered once and then a second time before she said, "Larem, I want you up here. Naked. Now."

She punctuated her demands by taking off her top and flinging it aside. He'd never seen a more beautiful sight than this woman staring at him with such powerful desire in her eyes. His boxers joined her pajamas on the floor.

Then they were skin to skin, his knee between hers, pressing against the damp heat at the juncture of her thighs. He kissed her, trying to go slow and losing the battle. Sasha's hands were everywhere, touching, teasing, stroking until she'd shredded what little sanity he had left.

"Sasha, I need to . . . no, *we* need to slow down."

But how could he when everything she did only drove them both crazy? Finally, he wrested control of the situation by pinning her hands over her head while he did his own little bit of tormenting. She arched back, demanding more, as he nuzzled and tongued her breasts into stiff peaks.

"Like that?"

Her expression turned solemn. "I like all of this, so much that it scares me."

She was right. What they shared was incredibly powerful. He wasn't sure where this exploration would take them, but right now it was simply too amazing to resist. He released her hands.

"I won't hurt you, Sasha."

She stroked the side of his face. "You can't promise that, Larem, but I believe you mean it."

He wanted to deny the truth of that but wouldn't lie to her, either. Instead, he set about stoking the fire again. Conscious of the vestiges of yesterday's injuries, he didn't want her to bear his weight. Instead, he turned her on her side facing away from him, her back against his chest. He lifted her leg back over his hips.

Slowly, he pressed forward, seating his cock deep within her welcoming heat. Sasha's head kicked back as he thrust in and out, her eyes half shut, her breath coming in shallow puffs, matching his rhythm. He memorized her satin smooth skin, the plump softness of her breasts, the way they fit perfectly in his hand. He loved the firm curve of her hips, flexing to absorb the power of his thrusts, and the throaty little moan she made when he moved in exactly the right way.

There was no longer a Larem and a Sasha. It was as if they had forged someone new, a combination of the two seeking the ultimate joining. He stroked her with his fingers as he accelerated the pace, no longer able to rein in his need to take her fast and hard. Sasha whimpered and called his name. Then she was shuddering in his arms, pressing back against him as he rode out his climax.

Then the tension melted away, both left gasping for

breath and basking in the aftermath. He gently kissed the back of her neck; there were no words for what had just happened between them.

Larem reluctantly withdrew from her body, once again stretching out beside her. "Are you all right? Was I too rough?"

"You were perfect. In fact—"

Before she could finish her sentence, Chance made his presence known, throwing a major fit in the other room. Larem could just make out the sound of the doorbell over the racket. There was a definite note of danger in Chance's bark that had Larem rolling out of bed, pausing only long enough to snag his pants and shirt on the way out.

The dog stopped barking as soon as Larem reached the living room. Even so, he growled deep in his chest, positioning himself firmly in front of the door.

Larem checked the time. Had Devlin said that Barak was coming this morning or that Larem was supposed to call him? Who else could it be? All he could tell through the frosty glass in the front door was that the unexpected guests were most likely male.

He hopped on one foot and then the other to pull on his jeans and then yanked his shirt on over his head. Palming the gun Devlin had left with him, he disconnected the security system and then threw the dead bolt. Opening the door a few inches, he peered out.

Two young Paladins stood flanking a disgruntled-looking human male, perhaps in his late fifties. The human had been glaring at his captors but immediately turned his bad mood in Larem's direction.

"Who is this guy?" Larem and the stranger asked at the same time.

The nearest Paladin ignored the human and responded to Larem instead. "This guy's ID says he's Charles Willis."

The glint of red in the older man's hair suddenly made Larem's question unnecessary. He had no doubt that he was facing Sasha's father. To once again quote Lonzo, *Holy hell, the shit was about to hit the fan.*

Chapter 18

*L*arem's first urge was to slam the door, but panic wasn't going to change anything. He opened the door the rest of the way and then grabbed Chance by the collar in case the dog took his same instant dislike to the man. Of course, that was probably a knee-jerk reaction typical of any male who'd just come from a woman's bed and was feeling a bit guilty about it.

"Thanks, gentlemen, I'll take it from here."

Turning to Sasha's father, he stood back to allow the man to enter. "Your daughter wasn't expecting you."

"No, she wasn't, but I'm here anyway. Deal with it." The man stalked through the door, careful to give both Larem and Chance a wide berth. "Where is she? Is she all right?"

"She's fine." Mostly anyway. Having her father show up on her doorstep would certainly complicate the situation.

"Have a seat and I'll tell her you're here. She was

just getting up when the doorbell rang. I'll make breakfast while she gets dressed."

"Fine, and when you get back, you can tell me who the hell you are and why you spent the night in my daughter's . . ." He hesitated briefly. "In my daughter's home."

Couldn't the man figure that out for himself? Perhaps not. Most humans lacked the enhanced senses that Paladins shared with the Kalith, so maybe Mr. Willis really couldn't detect the musky taint of sex in the air. If that was true, there was a small chance they could avoid a complete disaster.

Dragging Chance with him, Larem went back down the hall to the bedroom door and knocked. "Miss Willis, I hate to disturb you, but you have a guest."

The door opened and Sasha peered out. "Who's here?"

Larem glanced back toward the kitchen, hoping the man had stayed where he'd left him. "Your father."

"Oh God, why? And how did he find me?"

There was a definite note of panic in her voice. When Sasha started to charge out of the room, Larem blocked her way. The last thing she needed was to encounter her father looking as if she'd just gotten out of bed, especially one she'd shared with her lover. Larem shook his head, begging her without words to stop and think.

"Miss Willis, I'm sure your father won't mind waiting for a few minutes since he arrived unannounced. I'll tell him that you'll join us when you've had a chance to get dressed. As your bodyguard, I'll remain here only until my relief arrives."

He dropped his voice. "I'll call Devlin and suggest he send one of the Paladins instead of Barak. I'm not sure your father has recognized me as Kalith, and I'd like to keep it that way."

Then he leaned in and gave her a quick kiss. "Can you hand me my boxers and socks? I don't think your father would appreciate stumbling over them."

Her cheeks flamed red, but she actually giggled. "I like a man who thinks clearly in times of crisis. Wait here."

A second later she shoved the rest of his clothing through the door at him. "Give me fifteen minutes."

"Will do."

He stopped in the guest bathroom long enough to finish dressing. After washing his face and combing his hair, he studied his image in the mirror. The strain of the past twenty-four hours definitely showed in the dark circles under his eyes, but there wasn't much he could do about that. Hopefully Sasha's father would put it off to a night spent on guard duty rather than a bout of scorching hot sex with his daughter.

Before rejoining Mr. Willis, he texted Devlin about the situation, not wanting to risk a call that the Regent might overhear. Satisfied he'd done as much damage control as he could, he headed back to the kitchen.

Chaz parked his ass on a stool at the kitchen counter, even though he'd rather be pacing the floor. But from the way that damned dog kept staring at him, he'd play it safe and sit still. At least he could breathe again. Maybe the situation wasn't as out of control as he'd feared.

But as soon as that guy came back, he was going to demand answers. What the hell was going on? All he knew for sure was that he'd gotten an e-mail from Rusty about Sasha being hit by a car. It had taken him several phone calls to find out where she'd been taken, and then the hospital would tell him only that she was a patient there. After that, all he could think about was getting on the first plane heading west. He'd envisioned finding her safely ensconced in the hospital, craving the comforting presence of her father.

But upon arrival, he found out that she'd already been discharged. After digging through his backlog of e-mails, he'd located the address for her condo and grabbed another cab, hoping like hell that she'd made it through the night all right on her own.

But then she hadn't been alone after all, which raised a whole new bunch of questions. Like why were there Paladins posted outside? Not that he was complaining. But who the hell was that long-haired guy, and what was he doing in Sasha's home?

Even without knowing his name, it didn't take a genius to recognize a stone-cold killer on sight. Even without that gun in his hand, he had the same look that all Paladins did—like they were the toughest sons of bitches on the planet. Chaz had met enough of them over the years to know they might just be right about that.

But there was something different about this guy that Chaz couldn't quite put his finger on. The man's eyes were an unusual color, but it also could've been all that hair. Chaz hadn't really gotten a good look at him because he'd been too busy keeping a wary eye on that monster of a dog.

Which, he just noticed, was back again. The animal sat blocking the hallway that evidently led back to Sasha's bedroom. Even if Chaz were so inclined to go pound on her door and demand answers to his increasing number of questions, he wasn't about to challenge a dog that size.

A door opened somewhere behind the dog. Sometime between the time he'd gone back to tell Sasha of his arrival, the guy had straightened his clothes and combed his hair, which he now wore back in a ponytail. It looked better that way, but only marginally. Maybe Chaz should have a talk with Devlin Bane about enforcing a dress code. And that he was even worried about something so stupid was just a sign of how tired he was. It had been years since he'd pulled an all-nighter.

"Miss Willis will join us shortly. Would you like a cup of tea or would you prefer coffee?"

"Coffee, Mr.—I'm sorry, I didn't catch your name."

"Larem. Larem Jones."

"Well, Mr. Jones, would you care to explain what you're doing here? Forgive me for being a bit pushy on the subject, but fathers are always curious when they discover a man spent the night in their daughter's place."

And maybe in her bed. But surely not. This guy certainly had little in common with the men Sasha had dated in the past. Still, a father had to wonder.

Chaz drew some comfort from noticing the guy wasn't at home in Sasha's kitchen. He'd had to hunt for the coffee and then the sugar. Good. Finally, when the water was on to boil and the coffee pot was doing its thing, Larem slowed down long enough to talk.

"I'm assuming you're here because of the incident Sasha was involved in yesterday. Since Devlin Bane wasn't sure it was an accident, he asked me to stay over to keep an eye on things. He'll be sending someone to relieve me shortly."

Then he pulled a dozen eggs out of the fridge and began cracking them into a bowl. He dumped them into a skillet he'd had heating on the burner and started stirring.

A few seconds later, he pointed toward the other end of the counter. "You want to put bread in the toaster?"

Okay, so breakfast was going to be a team effort. Fine, he'd go along with the program for the moment. But when Chaz started to stand up, the dog took notice and didn't particularly like it.

Jones gave the dog the evil eye. "Chance, stop it. Mr. Willis has every right to be here."

The dog backed down but still followed his every move with a great deal of suspicion. Maybe Chaz would learn more if he asked a few questions, starting with the easy ones.

"Your dog is huge. What kind is he?"

Larem looked up from the skillet. "I don't know. Miss Willis adopted Chance from a rescue shelter. She brought him home yesterday evening."

A lump of disappointment settled in Chaz's stomach. If he'd had any doubts about Sasha wanting to make this move permanent, they were rapidly disappearing. The thought made him sick, especially if Devlin Bane thought she'd come under attack.

Short of the entire Board of Regents ordering her back to Missouri, there wasn't much Chaz could do. Besides, he wasn't sure she'd even listen to him, even if he told her it was unlikely the other Regents would ever invite her to join their ranks.

At the sound of a door opening down the hall, Chance lumbered to his feet, his tail wagging like crazy. From his reaction, the dog was already firmly attached to Sasha. When she appeared in the kitchen doorway, he made a beeline for her. At least the dog had the good manners to sit down and wait for Sasha to notice him.

In fact, this Larem guy acted much the same. Although he kept himself busy serving up eggs and buttering the toast, there was a new level of tension in the air. The bodyguard's reaction to Sasha's presence was definitely interesting—and pretty damned disturbing.

Sasha gave her dog a quick pat. "Good morning, big guy."

Then she walked over to kiss Chaz on the cheek. "Hi, Dad. What brings you here?"

He would've thought it was obvious. Her cavalier attitude infuriated him, but before he could sputter out an answer, she'd already moved on.

"Larem, that smells delicious. I'm usually not big on breakfast, but I woke up with quite an appetite this morning."

Jones shoved a mug of tea into her hands. "I'd think that was normal, considering everything you've been through since yesterday."

Sasha stared at the bodyguard over the rim of her

cup as she sipped her tea. "I'm not sure anything that's happened since yesterday could be classified as normal, at least not in my experience."

Why was she smiling at the man that way? Chaz studied the interplay between the two of them. He'd always been good at reading layers of meaning in any given situation, and what he was picking up right now really pissed him off. He was willing to accept that this Jones guy stood guard last night to keep an eye on Sasha. The real question was just how close he'd been to her while he carried out his duties.

Larem set out three plates of eggs and toast along with a glass of orange juice for each of them. "Do you take cream or sugar with your coffee, Mr. Willis?"

"Black is fine."

Why hadn't he noticed the guy's accent earlier? He was almost positive it was heavier now. Something niggled at the back of his mind. He'd give them all a chance to relax over their meal and then pounce.

Contrary to Sasha's earlier claim, she was merely toying with her food. When she thought Chaz wouldn't notice, she watched the grimly silent man seated at the far end of the counter.

As much as he respected the Paladins and the work they did, no father would want his daughter to get mixed up with one. There'd been no keeping Sasha from pursuing a career working for the Regents, but at least in St. Louis she'd had only minimal contact with the blood-and-guts part of the business. She had a tender heart, the kind that was ripe to fall for someone she saw as a real hero.

Chaz set his fork back down on the plate. "Thanks, that was good."

Jones grunted in response and started clearing things away. Sasha slipped a couple of bites to her dog and then pushed the rest of her breakfast away.

Her bodyguard shoved it right back toward her, adding another spoonful of scrambled eggs from the skillet. "Eat all of that. You need it."

Okay, so the guy didn't know her very well after all. Ordering Sasha to do something was a surefire way to get her to dig in her heels. But much to his dismay, she sighed heavily and then tugged the plate back and started eating again.

What was that all about? And why wasn't she reading him, her own father, the riot act for encroaching on her territory without calling first? There was something definitely off about her behavior.

"So tell me, Mr. Jones, where are you from? I don't recognize your accent."

The silence was deafening. A sick feeling settled in his chest, making it hard to draw a full breath. There was only one reason not to respond to such a simple question: the answer was damning in some way. He grew more sure of it when Sasha tried to distract him.

"Dad, so I'm guessing some helpful person took it upon himself to report back to you about what happened yesterday. I was going to call you myself this morning, but obviously someone saved me the trouble. Care to tell me who your spy is?"

"No, I don't. It was bad enough that I had to find out through the grapevine instead of hearing it straight from you." He took great pains to keep his voice calm. "And, Mr. Jones, you haven't answered my question, have you?"

"Dad, don't be rude." Sasha stood up. "Why don't the two of us go into the living room?"

He stayed right where he was. "Is there a reason you don't want him to answer me, Sasha?"

"Yes, because it's not your business. You're in my home, and I won't let you be rude to one of my friends."

He happened to be looking toward Larem at that moment. Judging by his reaction, he wasn't happy that she'd let that last part slip. The two of them had obviously conspired to act more like employer and employee in front of him. If they were reluctant to admit they were at least friends, it meant their relationship had gone way past that stage.

Chaz helped himself to another cup of coffee while he mulled over the situation. For now, he'd quit pressing for answers he really, really didn't want to hear.

Sasha buried her face in Chance's soft fur, taking comfort in the dog's undemanding acceptance. Could this be any more awkward? All she wanted to do was skulk back into her bedroom and pull the covers over her head—alone this time. Not that she regretted what she and Larem had shared, but right now life was throwing too much at her too quickly.

Footsteps stopped a short distance away. She knew without looking that it was her father who stood there. She had only one question for him. Was he there in his role as Regent or solely as her parent?

He sat down on the far end of the sofa and stared at Chance. "You know, if you wanted a pet, a goldfish would've been easier to take care of and a lot more portable."

She gave Chance one last hug before sitting up straight. "Yeah, but they're harder to take on long walks."

As if aware that he was the subject of their conversation, Chance wandered over to stare at her father for several seconds before laying his head on his knee, woofing softly as he did so. She had to laugh at the look of horror on her dad's face as he gave the dog an awkward pat on his head, sending up a small cloud of white fur.

Then he gave in with a rueful grin. "Are you sure this guy is really a dog? Did you check the news for any lost pony reports?"

She knew anything she and her father discussed would probably be overheard by the man in the next room, even over the racket he was making as he cleaned up the kitchen. Maybe Larem sensed she needed to talk to her father alone, because he appeared in the doorway with Chance's lead in his hand.

"I'm going to take the pony for a walk," he said, confirming that his Kalith hearing had picked up their discussion. "We won't go far, just up and down the block a few times. My relief will be here soon, but you should be safe with your father here and the guys across the street."

Then he pegged her dad with a hard look. "I left my spare gun on the counter. I assume you know how to use one. If not, be smart enough to admit it."

Her dad went into full Regent mode. "I do, and watch your tone with me."

"Dad, cut the man some slack. He's been up all night." Well, not all night, but an impressive amount of it. Not that she was about to share that little tidbit with her father.

"I'll be back, Miss Willis. Don't open the door for anyone you don't immediately recognize."

Then, while her father was looking at her, Larem winked at her and smiled. Then he was gone.

"He's more than just your bodyguard, Sasha, isn't he?"

Her father sipped his coffee, obviously prepared to wait her out if she didn't immediately answer. Fine, but she'd learned everything she knew about being stubborn from him.

"Frankly, what Larem is, Dad, isn't your concern. All you need to know is that he made sure I was safe last night."

She smiled sweetly. "Now, I get that you were worried, but why not just call? If you couldn't reach me, you could've called Devlin Bane or his wife for a status report before hopping a red-eye from St. Louis."

They both knew she'd inherited her temper from him. Her dad's eyes flashed hot before he visibly put a lid on it. "I'm here because you're my daughter. I have a right to be a little curious about this new life you're building for yourself here in Seattle. That coupled with the fact that you were almost killed seemed to warrant more than a phone call."

"Fine. I'm doing my job, Dad. The one the Regents sent me here to do. I spend most of my time knee-deep in reports and numbers and meetings. I'm making some real progress in reestablishing some trust between the

Paladins and the organization. That seems to have ruffled a few feathers in certain quarters."

She picked at a small thread that had come loose on the arm of the sofa. "I like the people I've met here, and the Paladins deserve better than the way they've been treated the past few years. Based on prior experience, they have no reason to believe that things are going to change for the better, but they've been willing to give me a chance."

She chose her next words carefully but let more than a hint of her anger show as well. "Kincade was a sadistic bastard who screwed with people's minds and lives for years. I can't believe no one listened when Devlin Bane and others tried to tell the Regents what was going on here."

He settled into the corner of the sofa, turning to face her more directly. "I'm listening now."

"Only if you promise none of this goes any further until *I'm* ready to make a formal presentation to the Board itself. I'd appreciate getting your opinion on some things."

Crossing his heart, he held his hand up. "I can keep a secret with the best of them. Let's hear it."

"Kincade was robbing the Regents blind. He funneled money out of every account he had access to, and then played with the numbers to cover his tracks. Over the years, it had to add up to hundreds of thousands of dollars. Not only that, but he stirred up animosity between all the departments out here to keep everyone on edge. What he did to torment the Paladins was nothing short of criminal. We're lucky there wasn't an out-and-out rebellion."

Then she narrowed her eyes. "He wasn't working alone either. As far as we can tell, he kept most of the money for himself, but the rest was sent to offshore accounts leading back to the Midwest Region."

Chaz erupted: "Like hell he did!" Then her father paused. "Wait a minute, surely you don't suspect me!"

"Of course I don't. But I can't speak for what Devlin Bane thinks. What I can tell you is that I've had two of Devlin's IT specialists working on breaking the encryption codes on Kincade's computer. I'm confident we'll be able to follow the money right back to Kincade's accomplices."

Her dad snorted. "IT specialists? Is that the new politically correct term for hackers? I'm guessing you've been working with D. J. Clayborne and Cullen Finley. God, Sasha, letting those two have free rein in a computer system is like turning a bunch of first-graders loose in a candy store."

She gave him her most innocent look. "I didn't mention any names, Dad. All I can say is that the gentlemen in question are doing a terrific job."

"Fine, but keep an eye on them. I can't tell you how many complaints I've heard over the years about their antics. Of course, I suppose there is some sense in that old adage about using a thief to catch one."

Sasha nodded. "My men have put in some long hours on the project, and that's on top of all their other duties. You know how Paladins are."

"Yeah, I do, which should explain why I worry." He softened the comment with a smile, although his gaze briefly strayed toward the door; clearly he was thinking about Larem. "I never wanted you to get entangled in their world."

"I know, but you've dedicated your life to serving the Regents and the Paladins. I'm following your lead. When do you think the Regents will make a decision about appointing a permanent Regent for this area?"

And did she really stand a chance? She couldn't bring herself to say that last part out loud.

"It will be discussed at the next general meeting, which will be a teleconference. If you're serious about applying for the position, put together some hard data on what you've accomplished and what's next on your agenda. Include any negatives, too, or they'll get suspicious. It would help if you listed possible solutions."

"That was my plan."

Her father sat up taller. "You have to know that with this possible attack on you, I'd feel a whole lot better if you finish up what you were sent to Seattle to do and come back home. Now that you've proven yourself here, the Board can find a position more commensurate with your abilities in St. Louis."

"So you'd vote against me." That hurt, but it was really no surprise either.

"Sasha, honey—"

"No, Dad, don't go there. We both know that as long as I stay in St. Louis, I'll be living in your shadow and under your thumb. I want more than that, and you should want it for me, too."

A knock at the door saved them both from going any farther down that road. She didn't want to fight with her father, but his heavy-handed protectiveness drove her crazy.

She got up and headed for the door.

"Sasha, wait." Her father was up and charging past her to grab the gun. "Stand back and let me open the door."

"All right, but at least let me see who it is."

He reluctantly stood back and let her look through the peephole. Great. What was Devlin doing back on her doorstep?

"It's okay, Dad. It's Devlin Bane, and I wouldn't be surprised if his wife is with him."

The Paladin leader walked in with Laurel right behind him. "Mr. Willis, what a pleasant surprise."

That was a lie, but at least her father let it pass. "I needed to see for myself that my daughter was all right. If I'd waited for a report from her or you, I suspect hell would be frozen over."

Laurel caught Sasha's attention and rolled her eyes. "Sasha, why don't I give you a quick checkup while these two finish their discussion?"

"Good idea. I don't know about you, but I truly hate the smell of testosterone in the morning."

Laurel laughed, although the two men didn't seem to get the joke. Too bad.

Feeling better now that the cavalry had arrived, Sasha led the way to her bedroom. She flipped on the radio next to the bed, hoping to give them some degree of privacy. When they'd closed the door, Laurel set her small medical case on the bed. Sasha dutifully let the doctor do her thing.

"Any problems?" Laurel asked as she wrapped a blood pressure cuff around Sasha's arm.

"You mean besides my father showing up unannounced? Or that I still have no idea who tried to kill me or why?"

"Well, let's start with the injuries from yesterday. Any headaches or dizziness?"

"Nope."

"Any cramping or bleeding?"

"Nope."

"Any problems having wild monkey sex with Larem last night?"

"Nope."

Oh, crap. As soon as the word slipped out, Sasha blushed furiously.

Meanwhile, Laurel finished pumping up the cuff and closed her eyes to listen as she let off the pressure. "Don't sweat it. Your dad couldn't possibly have heard us."

"Maybe not, but Devlin probably could."

Laurel put all her stuff back in her bag. "He's the one who bet me Larem wouldn't end up sleeping on the couch last night. By the way, we spoke to him before we came in."

"How is he?"

"Worried about you. Not sure what he should be doing right now, especially with your father here. He offered to let us bring Chance inside, so he could leave. Devlin told him to hang around a little longer until we knew what you wanted."

Sasha rested her elbows on her knees and buried her face in her hands. "I want more time alone with him, so we can really talk. That's not going to happen with my father here. Heck, Dad's already suspicious that Larem's more than just someone Devlin ordered to stand guard."

She prayed for patience. "Dad's asked Larem twice where he's from because he didn't recognize his accent. The man's not stupid. Sooner or later, he'll figure out that Larem is Kalith."

Laurel sat down beside her. "I know what you're going through. I love my parents dearly, but they've only recently come to understand that I'm never moving back home. It hurts them that I don't fit in there anymore, but they love me enough to let me go."

She laughed. "You should've been there when they met Devlin for the first time! Not exactly the son-in-law they had in mind. It was a dicey couple of days, I can tell you, but the bottom line was that they love me and so does he. They've managed to build on that."

All that was nice, except Laurel's situation wasn't exactly the same as hers. "At least Devlin's human."

Laurel's laugh had little to do with real humor. "Not exactly. He's also decades older than I am."

Sasha was pretty sure the front door had just opened and closed. "At least you and Devlin have each other. With Larem, I have no idea where we're headed."

"Where do you want to go?"

Sasha hesitated. "A month ago that would've been a simple question to answer. I wanted to be the first female Regent and make a difference in how Paladins are treated. Dad doesn't know this, but I dated a Paladin for a short time. He was a great guy, really special, but then they all are."

"What happened?" Laurel asked, although the shadows in the Handler's eyes said she already had a pretty good idea.

"He was killed and didn't make it all the way back. I didn't figure out that's what really happened until later, but the how didn't matter. Dead was dead."

Sasha grabbed a tissue from the nightstand. "I swore then that I'd do whatever I could to make sure we gave these amazing men the best of everything. And there has to be some way to stop losing them to the insanity, to save men like David. Like Trahern."

"Sounds like a worthy goal to me. What's changed?"

"That would seem obvious. Most of the Regents are a bunch of old-school traditionalists at heart. Not only am I going to be a single parent, but the father is someone they'd just as soon see dead or shoved back across the barrier. It could even affect my father's position if they want to get nasty about it."

Laurel stiffened. "Don't listen to them. No matter what they think, Larem's a good man."

"I know that, Laurel. I don't have wild monkey sex with just anyone. I care about him." Honesty forced her to add, "A lot. I've already told Larem that if the Regents won't accept me, I'll leave the organization and stay here anyway."

She wadded up her tissue and tossed it at the wastebasket, smiling briefly when she hit it dead center. "But I'm not the only one with decisions to make. I still don't know the story behind what brought Larem to our world. What if all he wants is to go home?"

"That's not happening," Laurel said, shaking her head. "No way, not now."

"But I don't want him to stay just because I'm pregnant." She wanted him for herself, too.

"No, you want him to stay for *you*," Laurel said, echoing Sasha's thoughts.

"Yeah, but—"

A soft knock at the door ended their chance for any more conversation. Sasha got up and opened the door.

Her heart fluttered in her chest. "Larem, we were just talking about . . . things."

His expression remained stoic, but there was a gleam in his eye that warned her that he'd heard at least the tail end of their conversation. "I wanted to let you know that Devlin is going to take your father to a hotel so he can get some sleep after traveling all night."

Then there was a spark of mischief in his eyes. "He wanted to stay here, of course. However, I pointed out that since your guest room is full of boxes, and your bodyguard will be sleeping on the sofa, there is no room for him. Devlin was kind enough to offer him a ride after I pointed out the problem."

"How considerate of both of you."

"Yes, we thought so." Then he looked past her to Laurel. "Devlin said he's ready to leave when you are."

Laurel replied, "Tell him I'll be right there."

Before he could leave, Sasha caught him by the arm. "So will you be staying?"

Larem's expression turned solemn. "It is my duty and my honor to protect you, unless you would prefer someone else."

They were both talking about more than just a few

hours of patrolling her condo, and she knew it. "I only want you."

He nodded and then stood back to let Laurel pass.

"I'd better go say good-bye to my father. Maybe we can take him out for a nice dinner tonight."

"If you're going to tell him about me, about us, about everything," he said, his gaze briefly dropping down to her stomach before returning to her face, "it would be better done in private."

What could she say to that? He was right, of course, but she couldn't find the words to respond. All trace of softness disappeared from his eyes. Once again, she'd hurt him without meaning to.

He stepped back. "Perhaps you should ask Devlin for a different guard."

"No, I was just thinking that you're right about talking to my father here instead. Once they all leave, we'll figure out what to say—together."

She rolled her shoulders to ease the knots of tension forming there. "God, this is going to be so much harder than when I was sixteen and had to tell him I'd wrecked his brand-new car. At least he can't ground me for a month like he did back then. He might try to take a swing at you, though."

He gave her a quick hug. "For the sake of family peace and since he's your father, I promise I won't hit back."

She laughed despite the lump in her throat. "Now that we've got that settled, let's go say good-bye."

Chapter 19

*C*haz Willis stood by the front door with barely disguised fury at being the one to leave. Larem trailed down the hall beside Sasha but positioned himself in front of her and slightly to the side to make sure that no one had a clear shot at her when the door opened. He suspected her father thought Larem was trying to protect her from him.

He wasn't wrong.

"So, Sasha, do I have to have your bodyguard's permission to hug my own daughter?"

"Dad, don't be a jerk." She stepped past Larem to give her father a quick embrace. "We'd like to have you back for dinner tonight. Say, six o'clock?"

Larem winced inwardly. Sasha probably didn't mean anything by her use of the word "we," but her father certainly picked up on it.

Chaz's hands balled up into fists. "I'll be here."

He might have answered his daughter, but the look

he shot in Larem's direction conveyed far more than a simple acceptance of a dinner invitation.

To make sure that they were both on the same page, Larem gave the older man a cold smile. "As will I, Mr. Willis. I look forward to seeing you again."

"Actually, Mr. Jones, no offense, but I'd prefer to have dinner alone with my daughter. She'll be safe enough with me, especially with the guards outside."

"No offense taken, but I'm afraid that's not possible. As her bodyguard, I plan to remain in very close proximity."

"Oh, brother." Sasha stepped between the two of them. "Larem, Dad—both of you—that's enough."

Devlin cleared his throat. "Look, we should be going. Larem, call if you need anything."

"Will do."

Larem stood back and held on to Chance's collar as they all filed out. The big dog had inexplicably taken a liking to Sasha's father, a feeling that wasn't at all mutual. The man had been trying to brush a layer of white hair off his pants as he walked out the door.

Now that everyone was gone, a strained silence settled over the room, but at least they were alone.

He and Sasha had a lot of ground to cover before her father returned. They certainly hadn't done much talking during the night, but they'd communicated in other ways. Never had he experienced something quite as sweet as holding Sasha Willis by his side. Making love to her had soothed his soul.

Larem watched Devlin's car disappear down the

street, with Chance at his side. Sasha had disappeared into the kitchen. If he had to guess, she was making a pot of tea. Maybe she needed a few minutes to gather her thoughts. If she didn't come out soon, he'd check on her.

A short time later, she returned carrying a tray with a teapot and two mugs. He crossed the room to take it from her, setting it down on the coffee table. Chance stretched out in front of the door and closed his eyes, leaving them to fill in the silence on their own.

She looked frustrated.

"Sasha, say what you need to say."

"You know, all of this is difficult enough without you deliberately provoking my father."

She poured herself a cup of tea and took a seat at the far end of the couch. He sat down on the opposite end.

"I'll try to do better, but there's not much about me that is going to make him happy. You know that."

"That might be true, at least at first, but there's no use making a bad situation worse."

"I said I'll try." He sipped his tea. "What else is on your mind?"

"I don't know why you're here. Not here in the condo, but here in this world." She angled her head to look him straight in the eye. "No one wanted to explain, saying it was your story to tell."

"All you had to do was ask."

As she listened, he poured out the whole tale. About serving as Lusahn's Blademate. About how Cullen Finley crossing into their world had changed everything. About the betrayals that would have ended with Larem's execution if he'd refused to follow Lusahn and her Paladin lover into this world.

"You loved her. Lusahn, I mean."

He considered the idea. "I thought I did, but now I don't think so. Not really, more that I liked the idea of being in love with her. For sure, Lusahn never felt anything beyond friendship for me. You only had to see her with Cullen once to know that he had claimed her heart."

"Still, it must have been hard for you to lose everything because of them. I'm surprised you're not bitter."

Hard didn't even come close to describing his rage over his life being shattered by the selfish actions of others. If Lonzo hadn't offered Larem both a home and his friendship, Larem didn't know how he would've survived those first few weeks. It wasn't until Hunter Fitzsimon had allowed Larem to serve at his side, hunting the traitors who had betrayed both their worlds, that he'd found a renewed sense of purpose.

"I'm not the same man I was then."

He thought he'd lost everything when he'd been dragged into this world. But now, with this woman and the child they'd created, he realized he'd been wrong. Nothing he'd left behind came close to what he stood to lose if something happened to Sasha.

"You're looking pretty fierce there, Larem. What are you thinking?"

"About what happened yesterday."

"There's nothing to be done about it now. The police will let us know when they find the guy."

Larem didn't want the authorities to get their hands

on her attacker—he didn't want the culprit behind bars. No, he wanted the bastard where he could watch him die slowly and painfully.

Sasha's eyes narrowed. "You're not thinking of going after him yourself."

He didn't bother to respond. Any warrior worthy of the title would insist on avenging his woman.

Sasha knew it, too. It was there in the frown lines bracketing her mouth. "I'm thinking maybe Dad's right. I should meet with him alone."

"Why?"

Although he suspected he knew. She wanted to make plans for her future, one that didn't necessarily involve him.

"Because he's going to be hurt and angry, and you don't need to be here for that."

"Why?" he repeated.

Sasha stared down at her cup. "Because you've already done enough, and it's not your problem."

He set his own cup down hard enough to slosh tea onto the table. He ignored the mess. "What is that supposed to mean?"

Slowly, her dark eyes came up to meet his. "It means I like you too much to tangle you up in my life any more than you already are. I may have to tell Dad that I'm pregnant, but that doesn't mean I have to tell him who the father is."

He couldn't believe what he was hearing. "And you think he won't be able to guess? And after everything we've been through . . . after last night and this morning . . ." It took all he had to ask the question. "Are you going to deny me my child?"

Before she could answer, Chance barked softly and then growled down low in his chest. He moved away from the door, dividing his attention between it and the windows. Larem stood up and reached for his gun.

"Sasha, get down behind the kitchen counter and stay there until I say otherwise."

As he spoke, he pulled out his cell and dialed the number Devlin had given him for the guards outside. No answer. He tried the Paladin leader's number next.

"Dev, something's going on. Chance is sensing danger, and the guards aren't answering their phones."

But any help Devlin might send was going to be too late. The front door took a heavy blow at the same time the window shattered. Two canisters of gas hit the living room floor and started spraying smoke into the air.

Larem shoved the phone back in his pocket and ran for the kitchen. The air in the living room was already growing hazy enough to make breathing hard.

Sasha was crouched down near the floor. "Larem, what's going on?"

"We've got to get out of here."

He quickly considered their options, which were damn few and none of them good. Whoever was after them had to be pretty desperate to attack in broad daylight.

"Where does the side door in the garage lead?"

"A sidewalk to the alley behind the building."

That was their best option. "Let's go. Crawl to the door. The air is safer down low."

He let Sasha go first as he called the dog.

"Chance, come!"

The dog backed toward Larem, never once taking his eyes off the front door, his hackles up and his teeth bared. The door gave way just as Sasha disappeared into the garage, and two men charged inside already shooting. A burning pain shot up Larem's left arm as he stood up and fired at the first guy, hitting him three times, while Chance leaped up to grab the second shooter's gun arm. The guy screamed as the dog savaged his wrist.

Larem's target dropped to the floor choking on his own blood while his companion tried without success to fight off Chance's attack. Larem stripped off the dying man's gas mask to cover his own face. The man no longer needed it.

Deciding the dog had done enough damage, Larem grabbed Chance by the collar and hauled him off the shooter. He kicked the injured man's gun out of reach and then dragged him into the kitchen where the air was slightly clearer. Stripping the guy's mask off, Larem pressed the barrel of his automatic against the guy's forehead.

"How many are out there?"

"Go to hell, Other," his prisoner choked out. "You and the other freaks are already dead. You just don't know it yet."

Larem leaned in close. "That may be, but I'm betting you'll be there before me."

Then he shot the floor right next to the cringing fool's head, sneering when the guy screamed as if he'd been hit. "Tell your friends that Kalith warriors defend their own."

Larem ran for the door with Chance hot on his heels. Sasha stood near the door, holding the handle of a rake like a ball bat, ready to defend herself. It wouldn't have done much against a bullet, but he loved her warrior spirit, loved her.

"Let's go."

She backed toward the door, keeping her eyes on the kitchen. "Are they dead?"

There was no point in lying to her. "One is. The other is chewed up but still breathing."

He unlocked the side door and peeked outside. If there was anyone waiting out there, he couldn't sense them. He could, however, hear sirens approaching.

"Someone called the police. We need to get out of here before they arrive."

"Why not wait for them?" she asked, but she followed him out anyway.

"Because right now we don't know who we can trust. I promised to protect you and our child, and I will."

He tossed the gas mask into a trash bin in the alley as they cut between a couple of buildings to the street on the far side. At the end of the alley, Larem stopped to think. His arm would be of little use if they ran into more attackers. At least he was wearing a dark shirt, so the blood wouldn't be immediately obvious to anyone who saw them.

For now, they were in the clear.

Sasha appreciated the chance to catch her breath, but why were they standing there so long? If Larem wanted to avoid the police, shouldn't they be putting a lot more distance between themselves and the condo?

"Larem, where are we going?"

When she looked at him, waiting for his answer, he was using the hem of his shirt to wipe away a trickle of blood running down his wrist.

"You've been shot!"

He winced in pain as he nodded. "It's just a graze. We'll go to the animal shelter. The vet will help us."

"You need a hospital. Or at least let me get you to Laurel's lab."

Larem was already shaking his head. "Can't risk a human hospital getting a look at my blood, and I don't trust the guards. We'd have to get past them to reach Laurel."

There was no time to argue. "All right, but let's get moving then."

He nodded as he tucked his gun in the back of his jeans. As they started down the street, she let him set the pace. As tempting as it was to run, walking would draw less attention even if it left her feeling exposed. Chance brought up the rear but stayed close.

Finally, Larem stopped outside a heavy door in an alley and rang the bell. A few seconds later a white-haired man in a lab coat opened the door.

"We're closed." Then he spotted Larem. "Oh, it's you. Did you forget your key?"

"Doc, I need your help." Larem held up his bloody hand.

The vet's bright blue eyes widened in surprise. He stepped back and motioned them inside. "Come in and let me take a look at it."

He managed a small smile for Sasha. "You must be Sasha. I'm Dr. Isaac."

"Nice to meet you." Although the circumstances seriously sucked.

Chance butted the vet's hand, startling a laugh out of him as he slipped the dog a treat. "And Chance, I certainly didn't expect to see you back so soon. Let's go see if your friend is a better patient than you were."

Larem was waiting in the closest examination room. Sasha hurried forward to help him remove his shirt. The fabric was slick with blood, and his white T-shirt underneath hadn't fared much better.

"There's a washer and dryer down the hall that you can use after we get him stitched up."

Then Dr. Isaac peered at her over the glasses perched low on his nose. "You're looking a bit shaky, so do me a favor and sit down. Were you hurt, too?"

"No, just Larem. That's bad enough."

"I'm sure," he said as he started gathering supplies.

Larem reached out to catch the vet by his arm. "Doc, I'm sorry to have brought troubles to your door, but I didn't know where else to go."

"Not a problem, son. What are friends for if not to help out in times of trouble?" He pulled on a pair of surgical gloves. "Now sit down and let me get this cleaned up."

When he started to fill a syringe, Larem stopped him. "Regular pain medicine doesn't work for me, Doc. Just stitch it up."

Dr. Isaac looked puzzled. "Why? Do you have allergies?"

Larem met Sasha's gaze with a small shrug. "No, it's because I'm not originally from this world and don't always react well to human medication."

The vet froze briefly and then nodded, a broad smile lighting up his face. "Well, that certainly explains a lot. Okay, so we'll do this the hard way. Brace yourself because this is going to hurt like hell."

Sasha couldn't stand to see Larem hurting and not try to do something. Maybe a distraction would help. She wheeled her chair over closer to his and took his other hand in hers.

"We haven't talked about names yet. What do you think of Ella for a girl?"

Dr. Isaac's bushy eyebrows shot up in surprise, but he continued working as Larem kept his eyes trained on Sasha's face. "That sounds almost like my mother's name, although in Kalithia we would put the emphasis on the last half of the word. Eh-*lah*."

She squeezed his hand. "Then that one goes to the top of the list. How about if we have a boy?"

Despite how much he was hurting, Larem shot her an impish grin. "If it would help your father accept me, perhaps we should name our son after him."

Perish the thought. "No way. One Chaz in the family is more than enough," she said, studying the vet's name tag.

Obviously the man and Larem were close friends, probably the only one Larem had outside of the Paladins. She liked the way the man had accepted Larem's explanation with such ease and offered his help without hesitation. Friendships like that were rare.

"Hey, how about Isaac? I've always liked that name."

Her lover didn't hesitate. "Isaac would be perfect."

In fact, Larem looked as pleased as his elderly friend did. The vet snipped one last thread and winked at Sasha as he applied a bandage to cover the wound. "You might want to hold off on that decision until you get my bill."

She tried to laugh—she really did—but instead, tears started streaming down her face as the combination of terror and fear for what might happen next broke through her last bit of control. Nothing like big gulping sobs to panic two grown men.

Larem jumped to his feet and pulled Sasha into his arms while Dr. Isaac pressed his handkerchief into her hand.

The vet then stammered, "Look, I'll leave you two alone and go see if Chance needs food or water or something."

Nodding to his friend, Larem rubbed his hand up and down Sasha's back in soothing strokes. "Let it all out, Sasha, but remember that I'm all right, you're all right, and Chance is out there happily pigging out."

The storm was intense but brief. Already the tears were slowing down. Still, he held her close as if needing the comfort as much as she did. Finally, she sighed and wiped her face dry.

"Sorry. I swear, I've never cried as much as I have in the past few days." She even mustered up a brave smile. "So what do we do next?"

"We call Devlin."

He fumbled for his cell phone, wincing a bit as he kept his good arm around Sasha and used his injured one. He punched in Devlin's number.

The Paladin answered on the first ring. "Where the hell are you?"

"Safe for now. Send Lonzo to pick us up where I do volunteer work. He'll know."

Thank the gods that the Paladin leader was the sort to remain calm, at least until the battle was over. There was more he should know.

"Devlin, the two who attacked the condo had to be guards. The one that I left alive said all my kind were dead even if we didn't know it yet. I want only men I can trust to protect Sasha and Mr. Willis while we deal with this. Warn Barak and Cullen. Get Lacey, Lusahn, and the kids someplace safe."

"What the fuck's this world coming to?" Devlin obviously didn't expect an answer because he kept right on talking. "I'll have the guys round up all the guards here at headquarters and throw the bastards in a locked room until we have time to sort them out."

Larem liked the way Devlin thought. "On our way in we'll stop and pick up Sasha's father. He should be in on what happens."

"Good idea. I'll call and give him a heads-up, but hurry. As long as you two are out there, you're both targets."

When Larem hung up, Sasha looked bewildered. "They were guards? Why would they attack you?"

"They obviously hate all Kalith, but that doesn't explain why they waited to come after me at your place.

They could've killed me anytime without drawing so much attention to themselves or risking injury to the daughter of a Regent."

"So you're thinking I'm the real target? Something I've done has set them off."

The explanation felt right. "I'd guess it's a combination of things. From what I've been told, once Kincade took over, there was always tension between the guards and the Paladins here in Seattle. It all started when one of them went rogue and tried to kill Laurel after Barak crossed over into this world. Then Cullen compounded the problem when he returned with Lusahn and her children."

"And you."

He nodded. "And me. Most likely the guards feel betrayed that the Paladins have accepted us as friends but not them."

Sasha sighed. "And then here I come, making it clear that my first priority is making things better for the Paladins, to correct the wrongs committed by Colonel Kincade. Despite how he treated the Paladins, he obviously still has loyal followers among the guards."

Dr. Isaac stuck his head back in. "Larem, come quick. Someone is at the back door."

Larem drew his gun. "It's probably my roommate, but just in case, you two stay here. I'll be right back."

Chance trailed along behind him, obviously thinking Larem needed backup. Rather than risk opening the door for the wrong person, Larem shouted, "Who is it?"

"It's the damned Tooth Fairy and his sidekick, the Easter Bunny. Now let us in."

Larem didn't know who the Tooth Fairy was, but he did know his roommate's voice and opened the door. Lonzo hadn't come alone, either. Hunter was right behind him, and both were heavily armed.

Larem stood back and motioned for them to come inside. "Thanks for coming."

"No problem."

As both men crossed the threshold, they came face-to-face with Chance. The dog eyed the two Paladins and woofed softly.

Larem patted the dog on the head. "They're okay, boy."

Chance immediately wagged his tail and sniffed the hand Lonzo held out. "Damn, Larem, he's huge."

"And a helluva guard dog. He not only gave us enough warning to stop those guys from killing us, but he took one out himself." He dropped his voice, not wanting Sasha to hear any more bad news. "How are the Paladins Devlin had watching the condo?"

"Drugged and a little roughed up. They'll be okay, so no problem there." Hunter looked around. "How's Sasha?"

"Shaken up. Scared."

"And able to answer for herself." The woman in question walked up beside him and held out a clean shirt. "Dr. Isaac said this probably won't fit, but it's the best he could come up with.

"Thanks for coming, guys," Sasha added as she matter-of-factly helped Larem ease the shirtsleeve up over his wound.

"No problem." Lonzo eyed the bandage. "Looks like you took one for the team. You okay?"

"I will be when we catch the bastards behind these attacks."

Larem rolled his shoulders and lifted his arm, testing its mobility. The pain was already starting to fade as his healing ability kicked in.

"Devlin has Cullen and D.J. tracking the guards through their e-mail accounts to see if we can pick out the culprits. Penn and Craig are manning the alley so we can get you and Sasha into the building safely."

"Good."

While they were talking, Sasha looped her arm through Larem's and rested her head against him. Lonzo's eyebrows shot up, but then he grinned.

She smiled back at him and then asked, "How about my father?"

"I told Devlin we'd pick him up on the way. Speaking of which, we'd better get a move on." Then Larem gave her a quick hug. "Sasha, can you tell Doc we're leaving?"

"Sure."

All three men watched until she'd disappeared into one of the exam rooms. Hunter punched Larem lightly on his good arm.

"So, you and the boss lady?"

"Yeah, me and her." Then softly he added, "And a baby."

"Holy shit!" Lonzo stumbled back a step. "Okay, I *so* didn't see that one coming. How in the world did that happen?" He slapped his forehead. "Wait, forget I asked that."

Hunter just grinned. "Congratulations!"

Then his eyes flicked past Larem in warning that

Sasha was on her way back. "I guess now's not the time to talk about this."

"No, but if anything happens to me . . ."

The good-humored Paladins disappeared, replaced by two of the deadliest warriors on the planet. Hunter's voice thickened with emotion, making it sound even rougher than normal. "You know we will. Now let's go get the bastards."

Chapter 20

*U*nder other circumstances, Sasha might have opted for more discretion when it came to the nature of her relationship with Larem, especially in front of his buddies. Things would've been too new, too unsettled for her to be completely comfortable with their openly acting like a couple in front of the rest of the Seattle contingent.

However, there was something about almost dying three times in the past few weeks that shattered all need for caution. She might not know how things would play out for the two of them, but not for one second did she want Larem to doubt that he was important to her.

She watched as he quickly checked his gun. Lonzo and Hunter did the same, the motions clearly second nature to all three of them. Just as they were about to leave the examination room, Larem's cell rang. Everyone froze and waited, the tension in the room immediately ratcheting up.

"Yeah, what's up?" He listened for several seconds without saying a word. "We'll check it out."

When he hung up, Sasha asked, "Larem, what's wrong?"

His expression was grim. "That was Devlin. He hasn't been able to reach your father. He's not answering his cell or the phone in his hotel room."

Sasha dug her nails into her palms, trying to stay calm. "Do you think they've taken him? And don't lie to me."

"Probably." Larem's answer was terrifying in its stark simplicity.

They started toward the door again, only to have their plans interrupted again with the sound of a phone ringing, this time Sasha's. She checked the number on the screen and should've been relieved. She wasn't.

"It's my father's number."

Larem caught her hand before she could answer. "Put it on speakerphone."

She nodded and did as he said. "Dad?"

"Sasha, run! Get the hell out of there!"

There were horrifying sounds of a struggle followed by a brief silence and then a different voice came on the line.

"Miss Willis, listen and listen carefully if you want to see your father again. Especially if you want to see him alive."

Fear and fury had her gripping the phone hard enough to break it. She forced her hand to relax, wishing she had the same control over her emotions.

"I don't know who you are, but if you hurt my father, you're dead. The Regents will authorize whatever it takes to hunt you down, along with anyone stupid enough to follow your orders. There isn't a place in this world or any other one where you'll be safe."

"Tsk, tsk, Miss Willis. Threats will get you nowhere. I want Kincade's account numbers, and I want the money you've stolen from him."

"That money wasn't his to begin with, and it definitely isn't yours."

Okay, that wasn't the smartest thing she could've said, but Lonzo was making circles in the air, telling her to keep talking. Was he having the call traced?

"You can't seriously think I give a rat's ass where he got the money. Kincade owes me for a couple of jobs I did for him and I have a rule about that. People who don't pay me end up dead, just like the targets they sent me after."

The cold pride in his voice was nauseating. "I get paid top dollar for what I do. I suspect you don't approve, but I'm really just a businessman with a specific skill set, one that happens to be in big demand lately. If it makes you feel better, I'm planning to retire as soon as I collect my pay, although I plan to do the world a favor before I disappear. Free of charge, too."

She hated encouraging the bastard, but keeping him on the line might help rescue her father. "And what favor would that be?"

"I plan to rid our world of that pale-eyed monstrosity who's probably standing right next to you. Just the thought of him walking the streets of Seattle as if he owns the place, passing for one of us and screwing human women, makes me sick. Who knows, if I get lucky, I might even take out a few of his mutant buddies, too—preferably while you watch."

Then he laughed. "Oops! Sorry, Miss Willis, I'm guessing from your father's reaction he just now realized your boyfriend is Kalith. I don't think he's happy to learn his daughter has been fucking an alien. Sorry if I let the cat out of the bag."

The humor in his voice disappeared. "You've got five minutes to get the account numbers for me."

Then the line went dead.

Hunter looked at Lonzo. "Tell me D.J. was able to track the bastard?"

Lonzo nodded and started cussing. "Damn it, he's right outside!"

Before she had time to absorb the implications, a ruckus broke out at both ends of the cavernous warehouse that housed the clinic. All three men immediately pointed their weapons at the examination room door.

Then the phone rang again. Larem took it from her hand. "I'm listening."

"Put the woman back on."

"You'll have to deal with me if you want those numbers."

There was another nasty laugh. "Fine. It's your funeral—literally. Come out unarmed or Willis and the vet die. You've got three minutes until I start shooting. Understand?"

"Yes."

Larem disconnected the call and then gently pushed Sasha back toward Hunter. "This guy doesn't know you and Lonzo are here. Keep her safe while I distract him. Tell Devlin to send backup."

Lonzo held up his phone. "Already did. ETA is ten minutes. They may not make it in time."

Sasha broke free from Hunter's grasp. "Larem, wait! Can't we hold them off that long?"

He backed away, shaking his head. "I'll try to buy enough time for reinforcements to arrive. They already have your father. I won't let them hurt him or Dr. Isaac because of me."

"I know, but—"

She gave up trying to explain and settled for throwing herself into his arms. Larem held her close and kissed her. Then she cupped his handsome face with her hands, memorizing the moment.

"Go, but be careful. I need you. We need you."

Before he could back away, she added, "I love you."

He brushed his lips across hers one last time. "Sasha Willis, you hold my heart. Make sure our child knows I loved—"

Sasha covered his mouth with her fingers. "I have faith in you. We're going to get through this, Larem q'Jones."

He nodded, but the regret in his eyes made it clear he had his doubts. He handed his gun to Lonzo and started for the door.

Lonzo and Hunter immediately moved to stop him. Hunter whispered low enough so that his words would've been inaudible to human ears.

"Slow down, partner. What's your plan?"

It was a warrior's question, so Larem gave his friends a warrior's answer. "I will free Chaz Willis and Dr.

Isaac and kill any of the bastards that get in the way."

The Paladins nodded in approval. "What's the layout of this place?"

"The room on the left is another examination room and has a door to the dog runs outside just like this one." He pulled his keys out of his pocket and handed them to Lonzo. "The big one will get you in that door. Maybe you can flank them."

"I'll give it my best shot."

Larem continued his description of the clinic. "Across on the right are the kennels, and beyond that is the surgical suite. The swinging doors at the far end lead to the lobby, which has the only other door out to the street. If this guy has any brains at all, he'll have someone covering it. He won't want to be trapped without a way out of here."

Chance bumped up against his leg. He patted the big dog on the head. "Stay with Sasha, boy." He looked toward Hunter. "If things turn ugly, get Sasha out of here even if you have to climb the fence of the dog run."

"Will do." Hunter held out his hand. "Watch your back."

Larem looked past the Paladin to where Sasha stood, her face pale with fear. "I will."

He waited until Lonzo was ready to slip outside into the dog run, hoping the enemy would be too focused on Larem to notice the sound of the second door opening and closing.

Out in the clinic, the scene was pretty much as he expected. He did a quick head count. There was at least one man stationed at each of the two exits. Chaz Willis was kneeling on the floor next to Dr. Isaac. Duke held a gun to Sasha's father's head. No surprise there. Another older man stood off to the side, looking awfully unhappy about being there even though he was also armed.

It wasn't difficult to pick the leader out. Although he didn't know the guard's name, he was all too familiar. He'd been the one who'd started yelling that Larem was an escaped Other, inciting one of the other guards to go on the attack that day by the elevator.

He acknowledged the bastard with a brief nod. "We meet again, although I never caught your name."

"Rusty." The guard smiled, looking pleased. "I wondered if you'd remember."

"I never forget my enemies." Larem returned the smile. "Not until I've buried them."

Rusty's smile faltered only briefly. After all, he had the advantage and knew it. He glanced toward his nameless companion. "So where's the bitch? I'm sure she'll be excited to know her beloved Uncle George has joined us."

The man in question flushed bright red. "Shut up, Rusty."

"She's going to find out anyway."

Rusty obviously enjoyed outing his partner in crime. "Seems George here has a bit of a gambling problem, which is how Kincade got his hooks into him in the first place. As a Regent, he's been feeding the colonel inside information for years, not to mention helping the man hide his tracks. But now that the money stream has dried up, he's hurting."

"Damn it, Rusty, I told you to shut up!"

"What's the matter? You didn't want her to find out that you ordered the hit on her? Sorry, my bad." Rusty turned his attention back to Larem. "But it's the truth. Seems he hasn't been at all happy about Sasha letting her hackers siphon money back out of his accounts."

Chaz flinched and then shot the other Regent a look that promised retribution. "You won't get away with this, George."

Rusty waved his gun in the direction of the exam room. "Tell her to get out here and join the family reunion. She'd better have the numbers I need. She can use my laptop to transfer the funds." He pointed toward the computer sitting on the exam table.

Yeah, like Larem was going to let that happen. "Here's our counteroffer: if you and your men leave now, she'll order the money you want transferred to your accounts."

Rusty fired a shot at the ceiling, causing everyone to flinch.

"Do you think I'm stupid? No way am I walking out of here without that money. Either she comes out now or I start shooting for real, starting with her father and then you. I figure that this old man only matters to you, so maybe I'll shoot him now just for grins."

Dr. Isaac straightened his shoulders. He might be about to die, but the man wasn't going to beg for his life. Larem met his friend's gaze and nodded, hoping he understood the unspoken message of how much he honored and cherished their friendship.

A movement caught Larem's eye. Hunter waved at him from the small window in the swinging doors at the far end of the room. The Paladin had regained control of the lobby. Good, but then where was Sasha?

Unfortunately she answered that question for him when the door to the exam room behind him opened. Her voice rang out across the room, sounding calm and collected.

"Lower your gun, Rusty. I'll get your money for you. But if you shoot anyone, the deal's off. My hacker buddies can make it disappear just as fast."

Larem wanted to throttle her for risking herself and their child, but he should've known she wouldn't cower in a corner if her loved ones were threatened. When she stood in front of him, he started to push her to the side when he realized that she'd tucked his gun into the back of her waistband.

He retrieved the gun, careful to keep it behind her back as he moved to stand beside her.

She whispered "Lonzo" under her breath before continuing her dialogue with Rusty. She held up a small piece of paper. "Here are the routing numbers you'll need to collect the money."

Then she looked around the room. "That doesn't seem like nearly enough to pay off all your men. After all, being on the run for the rest of your lives will be expensive, especially when there are five of you."

Clever woman! Now both Hunter and Lonzo knew exactly how many they were up against.

Rusty glared at her. "You don't need to worry about my men getting paid."

The reason for that was obvious: he had no intention of sharing the money. Larem didn't know about the other guards, but Duke was definitely looking suspicious.

"Give me the numbers and we'll finish this."

Sasha started forward holding the paper out, but then she deliberately stumbled and fell flat to the floor. At the same time, the door to the second exam room opened and Lonzo came flying out. He got off three shots, taking out the guard by the back door, Duke, and finally Sasha's godfather before Rusty returned fire. Sasha screamed when the Paladin flew back against the wall and landed in a crumpled heap as a blossom of blood spread across the front of his shirt.

"Sasha, stay down!" Larem shouted.

Meanwhile, Rusty looked behind him and realized his escape route was blocked. His eyes crazed, he grabbed Chaz by the hair and hauled him to his feet.

George managed to get back up on his feet and staggered toward Rusty. "Don't leave without me!"

Rusty's only answer was a bullet that hit the Regent high in the chest, sending him flailing backward to land broken and bloody on the floor.

The rogue guard kept moving toward the exit, dragging Chaz with him. "Shoot me and he's dead."

It was hard to hear him over Duke's moans as the man tried to stanch the blood pouring out of his arm. It didn't matter because there was no mistaking Rusty's intent. He shoved the barrel of his gun against the older man's temple and backed toward the alley door.

Larem kept his own gun aimed at Rusty's head but was afraid to take the shot. If Rusty moved at the wrong moment, the bullet could hit Chaz instead.

"Let him go and I'll come with you."

Rusty was already shaking his head. "No way I'm trading a Regent as a hostage for a worthless piece of shit like you, Other. Now get the hell out of my way."

Before he could drag the terrified Regent more than a handful of steps, Chance charged out of the exam room in a blur of white. The movement distracted Rusty long enough for Larem to make his move. The guard's gun went off just as the dog latched on to the back of his calf and bit down with all his might.

Larem's momentum combined with the dog's, slamming Rusty to the floor. Chaz managed to roll out of the way, leaving Larem and Chance struggling to subdue the guard before he could pull the trigger again. Larem clamped down on Rusty's throat with one hand and squeezed, but the bastard managed to get off one more shot before Larem could pin down his gun hand. Chance yelped and fell to the side, his white fur splashed with red. Larem bellowed in fury and cold-cocked the bastard with the butt of his gun.

Then he crawled over to the dog, calling on the gods to help him. *"Please, give me the strength!"*

He pressed his hands on Chance's shoulder and prayed as he'd never prayed before. The lights overhead faded and flickered as he drained every ounce of energy he could from them. As he stared at his bloody fingers, they took on a golden glow. Warmth and healing poured out of him and into his friend.

Almost immediately, Chance whined softly and his tail thumped the floor. The bleeding from the deep gash across the dog's shoulder gradually slowed and then stopped altogether. Already the wound was closing. Still Larem gave of himself, determined that his friend not suffer for his amazing act of bravery.

Finally, he had no more left to give. When he tried to look around for Sasha and his friends, he saw nothing but spots—and then darkness.

Damn, Larem hated waking up on cold steel. But then, that probably meant that the good guys had saved the day and he was back in Laurel's lab.

He pried open his eyes to find out if he was right. As soon as he turned his head, he was greeted by a wet tongue and a blast of doggie breath.

"Get down, dog."

Larem recognized Chaz Willis's voice and looked up.

"It's about time you resurfaced. Welcome back to the land of the living." Then the Regent smiled.

Surely not. Larem blinked to clear his vision, but Sasha's father really was standing over him.

"What happened?"

"Devlin and his men arrived about thirty seconds after you saved the dog and the day. Sasha's fine, although Laurel ordered her to lie down and rest until you woke up. Lonzo is across the room, already on the mend. Both me and your friend Dr. Isaac are safe and sound. We have you to thank for that."

"You're welcome."

Then Chaz's smile faded, to be replaced with the expression common to irate fathers everywhere.

"So about you and my daughter . . ."

Did they have to do this now?

Larem's head was pounding, and he seriously doubted he could mount any kind of defense if her father decided to go on the attack. Even so, he gathered enough strength to sit up. Chaz even gave him a hand. Chance stood up on his hind legs and laid his head in Larem's lap.

"What about Sasha and me?"

"Let me make it clear that I still believe allowing you and the others to live in our world might be a major mistake. Up until now, the Paladins' mission has always been clear. Having you here only muddies the water. However, short of inciting a rebellion, there's not much I can do about the situation. What's done is done, and that's the recommendation I'll be taking back to the Board of Regents."

Obviously Chaz clearly had more to get off his chest. Larem waited him out.

"Sasha has worked long and hard to get where she is. She has a real shot at being the first Regent of her generation, and I think she deserves the job. But with you in the picture, that may not happen. She's already made her choice clear, but I want you to understand what she may be giving up for you."

It was time to rejoin the conversation. "You aren't telling me anything that I don't already know. Sasha, too, for that matter. I might hate it, but that doesn't mean I'm going to slink off and hide."

"That's what I figured. And I'll do everything I can to make sure she gets the job. There's a lot to be done, not only here but in the organization as a whole."

His eyes filled with pain. "George didn't make it, and

his betrayal has sent shock waves throughout the organization. At least Rusty has been naming names, so Devlin has been able to start cleaning house. When the dust settles, Sasha will need to hire a bunch of new guards."

Chaz drew a deep breath and stared at Larem for several seconds as if choosing his next words carefully.

"Here's the bottom line. If you're the one who makes my daughter happy, there's not much I can do about it. If I were stupid enough to force her to choose, I'm pretty sure I know which one of us would be on the losing end of that argument. I've also spent my life working with Paladins. I've learned to trust their judgment when it comes to matters of honor and duty. From what I've been able to gather, the Seattle contingent claim you as one of their own. That's fine, but as far as the Regents are concerned, the jury is still out."

Even so, there was a strong hint of reluctant acceptance in Chaz's words.

Larem sat up straighter. "I plan to marry your daughter if she'll have me."

Chaz looked resigned. "Don't worry. She'll marry you all right."

What did he mean by that? "I won't have you trying to force her."

The Regent actually laughed. "Seriously, have you ever tried to force Sasha to do something she didn't want to do?"

"You mean like telling her to stay out of the line of fire at the vet clinic?" That was going to give Larem nightmares for years.

"Exactly. She'll marry you because that's what she's

made up her mind to do, even if you haven't asked her yet. By the way, I don't know how things are done in your world, but the men here like to do the proposing."

"It is the same in Kalithia."

"Then better ask her sooner rather than later, or she's likely to steal your thunder." Chaz looked toward the door. "And here's your opportunity. Before she runs me off, thank you again for my daughter's life, Larem."

Then he snagged Chance's collar. "Come on, dog. You've shed enough in here."

Sasha kissed her dad on the cheek and gave Chance a quick hug as they passed her on their way out. What had her dad been saying to Larem? She'd told her father everything that had happened. He'd taken it all pretty well, including the fact that Larem was Kalith and that Sasha loved him enough to give up her career with the Regents if necessary. He was still reeling from the news that he was going to be a grandfather.

She wasn't sure either of them would get over her godfather's betrayal anytime soon. He'd been such a huge part of her world, and his absence would leave a big hole in her life. That he'd been behind the attacks on her was almost unimaginable. An investigation had already been launched, and only time would tell how many more heads would roll.

But right now, she had more important things on her mind. Namely, the handsome man sitting on a cold stainless steel table. God, she loved him so much. Those beautiful pale gray eyes that spoke so eloquently even when his expression was so solemn. Right now, they looked at her with an intensity she could feel in her bones.

"Larem, please tell me my dad wasn't being a pain."

He reached out for her, spreading his knees wide so she could cuddle in close with her head against his chest and her arms around his waist.

"No, actually, he offered me some sound advice."

There was definitely a hint of laughter in her lover's voice. "And what's that?"

"That I should hurry up and ask you to marry me before you got it in your head to propose first."

Her face flamed hot, partially because her father was interfering and partially because he'd been right on the money. Before they crossed that line, though, she had questions of her own to ask.

"I still plan to apply for the job as Regent. Can you live with that?"

"Yes. The Paladins need what you can do for them. Can you live with the knowledge that there will always be people who hate me for what I am?"

"That's their problem, not ours. If we do this, you know you'll have to give up your world for good."

"No, actually I won't."

Larem crooked his finger and used it to tilt her chin up. He looked deep into her eyes and beyond. "Sasha Willis, don't you know that you and our child *are* my world? Marry me?"

The man sure knew all the right answers. But then, so did she. "You bet I will."

His mouth quirked up into a smile and she melted into him. Then she kissed him to seal the deal.

Turn the page
for a special look
at the next irresistible Paladins novel
from

Alexis Morgan

The Darkness Beyond

Coming soon from Pocket Star

$\mathcal{D}$.J. bent low and started forward, his gun in one hand, sword in the other. The blade would be his first choice of weapons, but he couldn't risk the Other getting the upper hand with Reggie depending on D.J. to rescue her.

The Other rose up to look around. Had the guy decided that he'd only been imagining someone dogging his footsteps? Maybe, because after ducking down briefly, the Other stood again to stare up the trail. After a few seconds, he started forward, his sword at the ready. D.J.'s prey moved slowly, his head sweeping from side to side, testing the night air and hunting using his sense of smell.

It was easy to know the instant the male picked up D.J.'s scent. The Other froze in midstep, slowly bringing his sword up into attack position. From where D.J. stood, he could take the Other out with a single shot. Tempting as it was, D.J. holstered his gun and followed the Kalith, Larem's sword in his hand.

He was able to get surprisingly close before the guy realized he was no longer alone. He'd started backing up, only to realize that his prey stood right behind him.

D.J.'s predatory nature had him smiling. "Looking for me?"

The Other didn't hesitate but spun and charged forward, swinging his sword in an arc designed to slash D.J.'s head from his shoulders. He blocked the blow with his own blade and shoved the bastard back a few steps.

D.J. taunted his opponent. "*Tsk, tsk*, is this how you usually greet guests in Kalithia? I didn't see any of us trying to kill you while you were in my world."

He went on the attack as he spoke. "Of course, I would've skewered both you and your buddy had I gotten the opportunity."

The tip of his blade sliced open the Other's cheek. Blood flowed in dark contrast to his pale skin, but the wound was more painful than serious.

"Did I mention that was my woman you kidnapped?" D.J. danced forward and marked the male's other cheek the same way. "Tell me who has her and why, and I promise to ease your passing."

The Other rejoined the battle, doing his own fair share of taunting in heavily accented English. "You will die screaming in my world, Paladin. I will celebrate your death by taking your woman to my pallet. I have already tasted her kiss and held her body against mine."

D.J. fought to control his burning fury, knowing cold hate served him better in a battle to the death. He studied his opponent's technique. The Other was good, but not great. No way this guy had the skills of a Sword Guardian. He might get lucky, but he'd never defeat D.J. on skill alone.

One thing was clear. The Other wouldn't offer any useful information, not unless D.J. subdued him long enough to use some creative interrogation techniques. There wasn't time for that, and it was doubtful the information would be reliable anyway.

But from the increasing panic in the guy's fighting style, the dance was about to turn lethal. So far D.J. had managed to stay out of striking distance, but it was going to come down to stamina or bad luck.

With a bellow loud enough to wake the dead, the Other charged one last time, nicking D.J.'s sword arm and then shoving him backward. D.J. ignored the stinging pain and pushed back, causing the Other to lose his footing right at the edge of the drop-off.

For a handful of slow-motion seconds the Other hovered there, his arms pinwheeling until he finally lost his balance and went flying backward over the edge. His scream echoed through the valley, only to be cut off in midnote when his body crashed onto the rocks below.

D.J. peered over the edge in a futile attempt to determine if the Other was still breathing. All he could tell was that the Kalith wasn't moving. Rather than wasting his time climbing down to make sure, D.J. opted for retrieving his pack and taking off down the trail after Reggie.

If the Other's dying scream had carried as far as the campfire, his partner might panic. At the very least, he'd be waiting for D.J. now, most likely armed and ready to use Reggie as a hostage.

This time, D.J. wouldn't hesitate to use the Glock. He ran full out, grateful for the boots that Barak had loaned him. They made little noise as he tore through the darkness. As he ran, he ignored the pain in his arm, his near exhaustion, and his lungs' struggle to filter enough oxygen from the thin air.

All that mattered was getting to Reggie.

$\mathcal{H}$er captor was practically twitching with nerves. So far, Jeban had been the calm one, but with Kolar gone so long, he paced restlessly, stopping every so often to listen to the night.

She knew the instant he sensed something because he turned in her direction, his pale eyes reflecting the flames of the campfire. His hand hovered over the pommel of his sword, as if unsure about drawing his weapon. What had he heard that had him so freaked out? Rather than sit there on the ground, she rose to her feet, not sure what she intended to do. But whatever was about to happen, she'd face it head-on.

"What's wrong, Jeban?" she asked, even though she doubted he'd actually answer. "Are your friends coming?"

He shook his head. "They aren't due until late tomorrow afternoon. Kolar went hunting. It appears he found something."

No, not something. Someone.

The two of them stood staring off into the darkness. She didn't know about Jeban, but she couldn't see much of anything beyond the circle of flickering light cast by the campfire. She tried closing her eyes, hoping that she'd be able to hear better that way.

After a few seconds of continued silence, a horrifying scream ripped through the night, only to be cut off abruptly unfinished. The night grew quiet again, but this time with a feeling of building tension. Jeban didn't hesitate. He drew his sword and then yanked Reggie close to his side, the blade at her throat.

"I would guess the hunt has ended," he whispered near her ear. "The question is, which hunter was successful?"

With chill of cold steel against her skin, Reggie could neither talk nor even swallow for fear the sword would draw blood. Her instincts told her that someone had died up there on the trail. There was nothing to do now but wait and pray that the footsteps running through the night belonged to D.J. and not Kolar.

Time came to a screeching halt. For an eternity, it was just her, Jeban, and the pounding of her heart. Her captor had turned to stone, his body stiff with anticipation. His gaze remained trained on some invisible point in the impenetrable darkness beyond. What was he sensing that she wasn't? Wave after wave of chills washed through her, fear quickly eroding her self-control.

Please, God, she didn't want to die alone in this alien world, but neither would she go down without fighting. Calling upon all her years of training, she yanked her focus away from the anxiety churning in her chest and on to the externals.

She could hear her sensei's gravelly voice in her head.

Breathe in and breathe out, slow and steady. Control your-self even if you cannot control the situation.

Good advice. As she gradually calmed down, she real-ized there was now a hair's breadth more room between her neck and Jeban's blade. If he so much as flinched, she'd go on the attack, using her bare hands if necessary.

Suddenly, she could make out the vague shape of some-one coming toward them. One minute the trail was empty, and the next, as if forming from the darkest of the shadows themselves, a man stepped into the farthest reaches of the firelight. He wore all black and a Kalith cloak, the hood pulled down close to his face.

Her heart sank as he calmly strode toward them, every-thing about him screaming that he didn't doubt his welcome. At first glance, she assumed it was Kolar. But then she looked again. After hours of trailing after the Kalith, she knew how Kolar moved. And this wasn't him. She was sure of it.

The weight of the silence pressed down on her, making it hard to breathe and even harder to hope. If something had happened to Kolar, it didn't necessarily translate to this guy being on her side.

Jeban shifted his weight, the first movement he'd made since he'd grabbed her. She leaned in the opposite direc-tion, but he only tightened his hold.

Then he rattled off something in his native language. Whatever he said, it clearly wasn't meant to be friendly. The newcomer showed no reaction at all, instead continuing his approach without a break in his step. If he was at all wor-ried, it sure didn't show.

Jeban spoke again, this time clearly in warning. He was growing more agitated by the newcomer's refusal to answer because he once again pressed the blade of his sword against Reggie's neck.

"I *will* kill her." This time he spoke in English.

The hooded figure paused a short distance away and tossed the edge of his cloak back over his shoulders as he drew his weapon. A Kalith sword. Then she saw the gun in his other hand.

For the first time the new arrival spoke. "If she dies, so will you, and it will be a death without honor. You will die screaming for mercy, just as your buddy did."

"Who are you?" Jeban demanded as he dragged Reggie back a few steps.

The stranger followed them, step for step. Then he tipped his head back and let the hood drop onto his shoulders. He was no stranger after all, at least not to her.

"Reggie, has this bastard or his dead partner hurt you?" D.J.'s dark eyes met hers, promising retribution if they had.

"I'll be all right now," she whispered around the pressure of the blade on her throat. "I knew you'd come."

Her captor didn't like that remark one bit. His hand dropped from her throat to her breast. "Tell me, human, is she really that good? That you risk dying for the chance to have her underneath you again?"

Did Jeban see his own death reflected in the Paladin's angry gaze? Reggie hoped so. She might not survive the night, but at least the two men who had dragged her into this hellish world would pay for their crimes.

Then she realized that Jeban was now pointing his sword toward D.J. rather than at her. This might be her one chance to break his hold on her. She slowly blinked three times right at D.J. and then slowly tilted her head to the side, trying to convey her intent. The corner of his mouth twitched up in a small smile.

"So, tell me, Other, do you prefer death by bullet or blade? This sword was loaned to me by a Kalith friend, if you're curious. Didn't want you to think I stole it off your dead friend."

As soon as Jeban started to respond, Reggie lunged to the side, dropping to roll out of his reach and leave him an open target for D.J. The Kalith charged after her, his sword raised and ready to slash down in a lethal arc. She had instinctively held up her arm to block the blow when a series of shots rang out. Jeban's murderous fury evolved into a look of stunned surprise as his life ended in a burst of blood and brains.

Pure panic took over as Reggie stared at the aftermath. Jeban lay sprawled on the ground, crumpled and broken. His unseeing eyes stared at her in dead bewilderment as someone screamed loud and long. Even when she realized that she was making all the noise, she couldn't seem to stop. It went on and on, ripping her throat raw.

Damn, D.J. hadn't meant for Reggie to catch the brunt of the Other's death. But if he'd delayed even a second longer to see if she could get out of range, the Other could've gutted her with his sword. Why the fucker had gone after her instead of D.J. was a mystery, unless he thought to hurt D.J. in the worst way possible by taking her life.

If Reggie had to end up covered in gore, at least it was the Other's. D.J. paused to cover the body with the guy's own cloak before kneeling down to wrap Reggie in his arms. She buried her face against his chest, still keening her pain and fear.

"Shhh, honey, it's over for now. I've got you. You're safe."

Slowly, her sobs slowed down and then stopped. But when she tried to wipe away the tears on her cheeks, her hands came away covered in blood.

She held out her bloody palms, her hysteria ramping up again. "Get it off! Please get it off!"

He'd love to accommodate her, but he had to prioritize what came next. He caught her hands in his as he looked around the Kaliths' camp.

"I will take care of this, but it will have to wait until I make sure there aren't any more of these bastards in the immediate vicinity. By the looks of things, this place was set up for more than just the two of them and you."

Reggie looked back toward the shrouded figure on the ground with a shudder.

"Jeban said the rest would be here late tomorrow." Her words came out in hiccups as she fought to control the sobs.

"Good. That's real good, Reggie. Okay, I'll go back and get some water. The creek I passed is some distance away, but I promise I'll haul ass. Will you be all right alone while I'm gone?"

"No, wait." She held out a shaky hand to point in the opposite direction. "Past the tents. There's water that way."

Better yet. "Good, we'll go wash all of that off you."

He picked her up and carried her over to the side of a quiet pool of water that fed into a narrow stream. After setting her back down, he rooted through his pack for something Reggie could use to clean up with. A spare shirt would have to do. He tore off a strip to use as a washcloth while keeping the rest for a makeshift towel.

Then he tested the temperature of the water with his hand.

"The water is clear but a little cold." He considered their options, none of them good. Best to just get on with it.

"Reggie, your clothes are covered in blood, so I need you to strip them off. Afterward, you can cover up with my cloak and sit by the fire while I wash out your clothes and hang them up to dry."

She nodded, but her hands were shaking too hard to manage by herself. D.J. reluctantly took over, starting with her shoes and then working his way up to her tunic and trousers. Yeah, he'd been wanting to get Reggie naked, but not like this.

For both their sakes, he left her bra and panties in place for her to deal with. He did his honorable best not to notice how her nipples pebbled up in the evening chill or the way her narrow waist gave way to the gentle flare of her hips. God, he was a bastard for even thinking about such things.

He held out the pieces of his shirt. "You're good to go. Use these to wash up."

Then he noticed a dark streak caught up in the curls of her hair. When he touched it, his hand came away bloody.

"Uh, looks like you need to wash your hair, too."

Her eyes widened in horror as the implication of what he was saying sank in. "How am I going to do that from the edge of the water?"

She was right. "Maybe a quick rinse won't get the job done. Maybe you should just go for broke and take a quick bath."

Reggie studied the dark sheen of the water suspiciously, but finally she nodded. "All right, if you think it's safe."

"It should be," he assured her, mentally crossing his fingers. "Give me a second so I can see what kind of supplies I have that you can use."

He dumped the pack out on the ground and studied the contents: shampoo, a toothbrush, a bar of soap, and even a spare tunic. Damn, Devlin and Barak had thought of everything.

He arranged the items on a flat rock next to the edge of the water. "Here you go, Reggie. I'll turn my back, but I'll stay close by in case you need me."

He did as promised, but listened to make sure she was doing all right. The rustle of fabric sliding down skin, the almost silent plop of something dropping down on the ground, and then the splash of water, followed by a blood-curdling squeal.

What the hell? He spun back around, gun in hand and ready to defend her against all comers. Except no one was there except a totally nude Reggie, standing thigh deep in the water and glaring back at him.

"I thought you said the water was just a little cold!"

He tried not to laugh, he really did. But she was so cute, standing there naked and absolutely furious. She had no idea how clearly he could see in the dark, so she wasn't trying to cover up. At least the little lost girl was gone, momentarily replaced by her usual feisty nature.

"Yeah, I may have exaggerated a bit on that point," he said, trying to sound apologetic and failing miserably.

"You think, you big jerk?"

She gave him a disgusted look and then gingerly waded out farther into the water. "Remind me to get even with you for this."

Fantasy.

Temptation.

Adventure.

Visit PocketAfterDark.com,
an all-new website just for Urban
Fantasy and Romance Readers!

- Exclusive access to the hottest
urban fantasy and romance titles!

- Read and share reviews on
the latest books!

- Live chats with your favorite
romance authors!

- Vote in online polls!

 www.PocketAfterDark.com

EXPLORE THE
DARK SIDE OF DESIRE
with bestselling Paranormal Romance from Pocket Books!

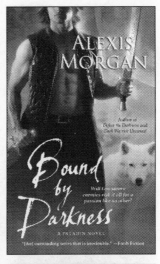

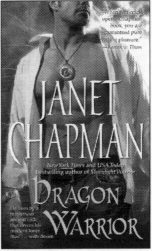

Desire a little something different?

Look for these thrilling series by today's hottest new paranormal writers!

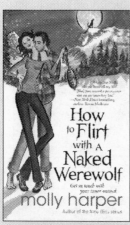

The Naked Werewolf series from Molly Harper

The Daughters of the Glen series from Melissa Mayhue

Printed in the United States
By Bookmasters